FALLEN 1

Born above a shoe shop in the 1960s, Neil spent most of his childhood in Wakefield, West Yorkshire as his father pursued a career in the shoe trade. This took Neil to Bridlington in his teens, where he failed all his exams and discovered that doing nothing soon turns into long-term unemployment. Re-inventing himself, Neil returned to education in his 20s, qualified as a solicitor when he was 30, and now spends his days in the courtroom and his evenings writing crime fiction.

To find out more about Neil go to www.neilwhite.net.

By the same author:

Lost Souls
Last Rites
Dead Silent
Cold Kill

NEIL WHITE

Fallen Idols

AVON

AVON
A division of HarperCollins*Publishers*
77–85 Fulham Palace Road,
London W6 8JB

www.harpercollins.co.uk

This paperback edition 2012

1

First published in Great Britain by
HarperCollins*Publishers* 2007

Copyright © Neil White 2007

Neil White asserts the moral right to
be identified as the author of this work

A catalogue record for this book is
available from the British Library

ISBN-13: 978-0-00748-448-5

Set in Minion by Palimpsest Book Production Ltd,
Falkirk, Stirlingshire

Printed and bound in Great Britain by
Clays Ltd, St Ives plc

MIX
Paper from
responsible sources
FSC
www.fsc.org
FSC™ C007454

I would like to express my heartfelt thanks to all those people who have offered advice and encouragement during the writing of *Fallen Idols*, and also all the family and friends who supported me in my earlier writing ventures. The staff at the Crown Prosecution Service in Burnley and at the Magistrates' Court in Blackburn deserve a particular mention, as do the members of the Colne Writers' Circle. Writing can be lonely, and sometimes a writer needs to hear the encouragement in order to keep going. Many people did just that. I know who you are, and I will always be grateful to you.

In particular, I would like to thank my agent, Sonia Land, for showing continued faith in me and providing sound advice whenever I sought it, and also my editor at HarperCollins, Maxine Hitchcock, for being so thorough and enthusiastic.

I am, of course, eternally grateful for the patience shown by my wife, who has had to share the disappointments as well as the celebrations.

To Thomas, Samuel and Joseph

ONE

Sunny afternoons in London shouldn't happen this way.

I was in Molly Moggs at the end of Old Compton Street, an intimate bar in theatreland, with rich burgundy walls and theatre bills on the ceiling. It was best when it was quiet, near enough to Soho for the buzz, far enough away from the noise.

But it wasn't quiet. Theatre-luvvies mixed with the gay parade of Old Compton Street, packed into a small room, blowing smoke to keep out the fumes from the buses on Charing Cross Road, the noise of the engines mixing with the soft mutter of street life. The people crammed themselves in to get out of the heat. They just made it hotter.

I rubbed at my eyes. I could go home. I lived just a few grubby doors away, in a small flat that cost the same as a suburban house. But I liked it, the movement, the colour, part porno, part gangland. I glanced outside and saw tourists slide by, young European kids with rucksacks hunting in packs. A homeless woman, big coat, too many layers, walked up and down, shouting at passers-by. She looked sixty, was probably thirty-five.

My name is Jack Garrett and I'm a freelance reporter. I work the crime beat, so I spend the small hours listening to police scanners and chasing tip-offs. I hang around police bars and pick up the gossip, the rumours. Sometimes I get enough to write something big, maybe bring down a name or two, backed up by leaked documents and unnamed police sources. Most nights, though, I chase drug raids and hit and runs. Dawn over the rooftops is my rush hour, blue and clean, as I condense a night of grime into short columns, each one sent to the big London dailies. Some of the stories might make the second edition, but most make the next day's paper, so I spend the mornings chasing updates. It's grunt work, but it pays the rent.

I didn't mind the night shift. I chased excitement, always one good tip from a front-page by-line. But the working week was like the city, fast and relentless, and it took the snap out of my skin and the shine from my eyes. I caught my reflection in a mirror and screwed up my nose. I could feel the night hanging around me like old smoke. My hair looked bad and my complexion was pale and drawn. My clothes looked how I felt, crumpled and worn.

I closed my eyes and let the sound of the bar wash over me. I needed a quiet day.

Sophie watched as Ben paced around the apartment. They were estate agents. It was all about sales and targets, and Ben seemed jittery. He was having a quiet month, but that just made him keener. Maybe the job wasn't for her. He had a focus she struggled to match.

'Ten minutes and we're leaving,' he said, snatching looks at his watch and then staring out of the window, down into Old Compton Street. 'We've got three more after this.' He looked round at Sophie, flashed a look up her body. She spotted it.

'What's the punter's name, anyway?' he asked.

Sophie glanced at her appointment checklist. 'Paxman, it says here.'

He looked back out of the window. 'Look at all this,' he said, shaking his head. 'Did you know it was named after a churchgoer?'

'What was?'

'This street. Look at it. Fucking queers, blacks, foreigners. It's just about sex, nothing more. Men looking for men.'

'Give it a rest, Ben.' God, she hated estate agents. Hated having to be one. She liked Ben even less.

She joined him at the window, tried to see his problem. The Three Greyhounds across the road was full of people. The black and white Tudor stripes looked too dark in the sunshine, but the tables were busy, the pavements full of movement, men laughing, smiling, flirting, all nations, all types. People drank coffee and were smoked out by delivery transits, cyclists weaving through. The apartment seemed quiet by comparison, empty of furniture, wooden blinds keeping out the sun.

'It's the only place in London where people seem like they're smiling,' she said, and turned away. 'Maybe it's a no-show.'

Ben turned round. 'Oh, there'll be a show. You know what it's like around here. They're all busting a gut to get a window over this. Fucking Queer Street.'

Sophie shook her head. He was a fool. Hated people. Maybe saw in them the things about himself he hated. But he could sell homes to people who didn't like them for prices they couldn't afford. Maybe it was the hate in him that helped him. And he would collect the pound, pink or not.

She was about to answer when the doorbell chimed.

Ben saluted. 'Time to earn some money,' he chirped, before skipping down the stairs to let the customer in.

When he returned, the buyer was on his shoulder, smartly dressed in a black suit, but nervous, twitchy, looking around, walking slowly. A large holdall clunked heavily as it was set down on the floor. The buyer took in the view from the window, the blinds clinking shut as Sophie exchanged shrugs with Ben. They had a weird one.

'Isn't it a great view?' Ben said, with saccharine sincerity. 'It makes this property a popular one. In fact, you're the third one today.'

The buyer turned around, smiling. Maybe guessed the lie. 'Yeah, I suppose so. I'm sorry.'

Ben flashed a look of disappointment as the buyer rummaged in the bag, looking for paper to make some notes, words coming out as a distracted mumble.

But then Sophie sensed something was wrong when she saw Ben's eyes grow wide. Then she heard him splutter, 'What the fuck?'

'Scream and I'll shoot.'

It was said polite and slow, as if the buyer were making conversation.

Sophie looked. She saw two handguns, one in each hand, long and mean charcoal steel, pointing straight at their heads.

Henri Dumas walked quickly through Soho, baseball cap on his head, hiding behind Gucci sunglasses, dodging between the tight T-shirts, admiring glances, men on the hunt.

As one of the biggest football stars in the Premiership, it was hard to walk around. Autographs, photographs, shaking hands. He preferred his car, with its tinted privacy. He liked Soho even less. Streets came at him from all sides, dog-legged twists of neon and movement; he was always scared of being photographed looking into the wrong shop, the wrong bar.

He sensed the mutter as he walked past pavement cafes, past busy pubs, alleys, sex shops, clubs. Men smiled at him, tilted and flirted as he passed them. If he just kept walking, he could get there. Get away from the glare, the seediness.

He thought about turning back, but he knew he had to get to the meet. He thought about his fiancée, the other half of a new celebrity brand, millions in the making. She sang in a band, he played football, and the press loved them, the new golden couple. They bought their contrived paparazzi snaps, so-called secret pictures set up by his agent and rehearsed until the look was just right, and filled the column inches with every new style or story. The press loved his Gallic verve, his brooding dark eyes, strong jaw, flowing dark hair. Their engagement was great business. On his own, he kicked a football. Together, they dominated the glossies, every word they spoke worth something.

He checked his watch. He was going to be early. He didn't like that, but he knew how the English liked to be on time. And if he didn't get there, his life as a tabloid hero would be over. At least, in the way he'd known it.

He stepped up the pace.

Back at the apartment, Ben was facedown on the floor, his hands behind his back, his nose pressed against the cherry wood. His eyes were wide, his breaths hot and heavy. Sophie was astride his legs, binding his wrists with silver duct tape, tight and strong, her tears falling onto his back, hot and wet. There was a gun pressed hard into the back of her neck, the other one aimed at the back of Ben's head.

Once she'd finished his bindings, Sophie looked round. She saw the muzzle of the gun and shrank back.

'Get on the floor, face down.'

'Why are you doing this?' wailed Sophie, tears streaming down her face. She was scared, the sounds coming in fast, her instincts running faster.

The gun was pressed harder into Ben's neck.

'Sophie!' he yelled, his voice quivering.

Sophie dropped her head, the tears now a stream.

The buyer put the other gun softly under Sophie's chin and lifted it, her streaked face coming back into view. Sophie opened her eyes slowly, the sparkle gone.

'Do as you are told or I'll kill him.'

It was said calmly, almost gently.

Sophie nodded, understanding, and she felt leaden inside. She lay down on her stomach, felt the buyer sit astride her, and then her wrists were strapped together by the duct tape. She was pulled onto her knees, then Ben as well, the buyer panting, straining.

Sophie watched as the buyer picked up the duct tape once more and walked over to them. She knew what was coming, and so she dipped her head to her chest, vainly trying to get her mouth out of the way.

She shot a look as she heard Ben gasp, coughing in pain. The gun was pushed into his throat, lifting up his head slowly. Ben was gulping back tears, the buyer over him.

Sophie closed her eyes as Ben closed his, and then she heard the rip of the duct tape, heard Ben's grunts as it was stretched over his face.

Sophie opened her eyes when she sensed the buyer standing over her. She glanced at Ben. He was red in the face, breathing hard, trying to get his lungs to catch up through his nose, his chest heaving, tears running over the silver tape. Sophie stared up at the buyer and then put her head back. The duct tape went over her mouth as well, but Sophie's eyes stared hard, trying to show she was strong.

Sophie watched as the buyer wandered over to the window and checked the time. The light breeze fluttered around the apartment for a while, before the buyer stepped back from the window and removed a tripod from the bag, opening the legs out on the floor before pulling out a collection of rags which clunked heavily. As the rags were unfolded, Sophie saw the pieces of a rifle.

She closed her eyes and prayed as she listened to the rifle being assembled, the soft clicks joined by Ben's deep breaths and the chatter and movement of Old Compton Street, the soundtrack to a glorious afternoon in Soho.

Henri Dumas looked around and checked his watch, a TAG Heuer. Five more minutes and then he was gone.

He saw people looking at him. He shuffled nervously. He knew he shouldn't be doing this. Some kids across the road were staring at him, pushing each other, egging on one of their number to speak to him.

He checked his watch again. The kids started walking over the road, one of them being pushed to the front, camera in hand.

Shit. Not what he needed. He pulled out his phone.

The crowds didn't hear the crack of the rifle. Neither did Dumas. He just felt the hot slice of the bullet and then went to his knees as it crashed through him. His breath caught, his hand went to his chest, the view of the street slammed into a blur, the neon and movement changed into rainbows, just streaks of colour as he turned. The crowd rushed back into his head, a loud murmur of concern as he bent over, trying to work out what the splash of red had been. It was by his feet, a tail of splashes that tracked his spin as he sank to his knees.

He took a breath but it didn't come. A waiter started to come towards him. The kids had stopped in the road. Dumas looked up, confused. Why was he gasping? Why was he burning inside?

The waiter didn't get there in time. The rumble of the crowd made way for the sound of the second shot, a loud crack, and then the people around him began to scream when his head shot back, away from the cafe, a spurt of blood spraying an arc in the air as he crumpled onto his back, coughing blood onto his cheeks.

Henri Dumas was dead before anyone reached him, his Penck phone tumbling from his hand, soiled silver against the grey of the pavement.

Sophie could hear feet banging on the floor, shuffling, scared, then she realised they were her own. She could hear the screams from outside, the sound of panic spreading, people trying to get off the street. She put her head back, began to moan. She glanced over at Ben. His eyes were wild, his breaths trying hard to keep up, the gag making his face go red. Her ears still rang from the shots. The first shot had bounced around the room until it seemed to come back at itself. Then the second shot had filled her head, and she knew from the way the buyer relaxed that what had needed doing was done.

Sophie began to sob, could feel herself shaking, her head back. All she could see now was the ceiling, brilliant white, flashes of blue getting brighter as the noise of sirens came in through the open window. She could hear footsteps, people running, some away from the shooting, some towards it.

Her breathing stopped as she felt the tip of the gun

under her chin, turning her face towards Ben. A tear ran down her face until it rested on the dark muzzle. Sophie looked at Ben and saw terror in his eyes.

Ben was shuffling backwards to the wall. His shoulders were shaking as he sobbed. The buyer stepped over to him, then lifted his chin with the gun so that it was in front of Ben's face.

'Tears for you, or tears for her?'

The buyer stared down at him and then pulled at the tape around his mouth. Ben's legs kicked in a silent scream of pain, the tape pulling hard on hairs, stretching his lips and taking soft flesh with it, flicking tiny drops of blood onto his chin. He looked down and grunted with pain, but it was cut short when the buyer thrust the gun into his mouth.

Ben didn't have chance to even look up before the buyer pulled the trigger, Ben's hair just blowing lightly where the bullet cut through on the way out of his head and into the wall behind. He slithered to the floor as blood began to gather around him.

Sophie tried to scream, tried to make the sound loud through the tape. It came out muffled, desperate. She felt the buyer grab at her shirt, her body jolted as the shirt was pulled open, the buttons scattered across the smooth wooden floor, spinning like dropped pennies. Her chest felt damp with sweat. She felt the muzzle run up and down her chest, cold and hard, and then nothing. When Sophie opened her eyes, she saw the gun, twitching in the buyer's hand, inches from her. She looked up, into the eyes of her captor, saw cold blue, and then looked back to the gun.

Sophie sniffed back a tear, looked at Ben on the floor, saw the pool of blood gathering around his head, and then slowly lowered her head to the muzzle of the gun.

The buyer stepped back, surprised. Sophie looked up and then sat back. She closed her eyes and began to sob. She thought of her parents, wondered what they would do when they found out.

Her thoughts were cut short when she felt something go tight around her neck. It felt soft, silky, but it was pulled taut.

She gasped, her eyes wet with tears. Her chest choked for air, tried to gulp it down, but the airway was blocked by the tape, cut off by the silk. Her arms pulled at the tape on her wrists, tried to get free, tried to get to her neck, her survival instinct engaged, but the tape held firm.

Panic set in, made her thrash, but there was no escape. Her chest strained, she could feel her face burning red. She fought against it, but the room started to speckle monochrome as she tried to force air into her body. Her chest tried to burst; sound amplified, distorted, and then it began to fade, the room turning white.

The last sound she heard was her feet scuffling on the floor, louder than the sirens, louder than the screams outside.

Then she felt peace.

TWO

I was just finishing a beer when I heard the sound of footsteps outside, running, the sound of crying.

I looked round to the barman. He hadn't seen anything, was too busy wiping glasses. I went to the door. People were running, looking shocked, hands over their mouths. I'd seen this once before, in 2005, on that awful July day, when Al Qaeda sent young men to the capital to blow themselves up and kill innocent people.

I grabbed someone's arm, a young woman, chain-store clothes, her eyes scared and upset.

'What's happened?'

She stopped, bent double, panting. 'Someone's firing into the street.'

I looked back up the road. 'Is anyone hurt?'

She nodded and wiped her eyes.

'I saw a man on the floor, blood on his face.'

I turned away. I had all I needed. I didn't wait to say goodbye, and when I looked back around, she had gone.

I thought I heard sirens. The Armed Response Team

was on permanent standby in London and I wasn't far from major terrorist targets. They would be here in no time and this would be as near as I would get. I saw it was getting busier ahead, the streets full of people getting away from the shooting. If there was anything in the story, the news agencies would get the official releases, the CCTV footage. I would have to feed on the scraps I could pick up here, something different. As I saw the crowd, the running, the panic, I knew I had the angle: the reaction of the people who had been there, the human story.

I pulled out my camera and set it to telephoto, squashing the spread of heads. As I took pictures, the tide kept on coming, some running, some walking. I saw a young family, a couple of children just under ten with an anxious young mother. She was panting, shaking, clutching her children tight. I got some pictures of the children. The first rule of journalism: always get the children.

All the time, their mother was talking. 'We were just shopping, you know, just walking around. People around us ducked, like out of instinct, then there was a second shot.' She waved her hand in the air, breaths short and panicky. 'Then people started running.' The woman straightened herself as if to emphasise her point. 'Someone was shooting into the street.'

I tried to concentrate on the children, but all the time I was making mental notes of what she was saying. She had tears in her eyes when she said, '. . . and what about my children? A daytrip to town isn't supposed to happen like that.'

I blinked. There was my line. I thanked her and set off again.

I didn't get far before I realised how close I was to it. I could see the bob of police helmets, silver glints reflecting sunlight. They were pushing people back, away from the scene. The crowd was getting thicker, but as I pushed I was able to get to the door of my apartment building, not much more than a door squeezed between two shops. I ducked inside and rushed upstairs.

As soon as I got in, I went to the window. I could see a crowd of police around a man on his back. There was a dark patch on the pavement next to him, spreading into the cracks. He had his arms by his side, a funeral pose. He was in front of the Cafe Boheme, green awnings keeping the inside in shade, but I could see frightened faces looking out. Soho had always been a brave place, always done its own thing. This was the outside coming in, and people looked scared.

I lined up the body in my viewfinder, ready to start clicking, when I paused. There was something about the face which was familiar. I zoomed in, and when I did, I felt my hands go slick. I had something big.

I zoomed in close on his shattered head, his face blood-red, his cheeks sinking, hollow. I pulled back to put it into context, the deserted pavement littered with a body, napkins blowing against his ankles. I saw the faces in the Cafe Boheme looking at me, half of them hating me, the rest looking for an answer. I didn't have one.

I heard a shout from the street below my window.

I recognised it straight away. It was the police. My dad was a policeman, up in the frozen north. One thing he always told me was that if a policeman shouts at you to stop, you make sure you stop, because he'll only ask once. And I knew I couldn't get busy with my hands. I didn't know if the armed unit had arrived yet, but they were only human. They would only get a pinprick of time to decide if the shine in my hands was a gun. If they decided wrong, I'd be dead.

I relaxed and looked down, nice and slow, my camera now slack in my hand.

'Jack Garrett,' I shouted. 'I'm a reporter, freelance. I live here.'

As I held out the camera, I saw the policeman relax.

'Okay,' he said. 'How long have you been taking pictures?'

'Not long enough to help. How is it over there?'

He didn't say much, and I could tell he was unsure. Was I the shooter? He didn't know. He was young, maybe younger than my own thirty-two. 'Quiet,' was all he said.

'Have you got the shooter hemmed in?'

He smiled warily. 'This is turning into an interview.'

I smiled back, wider, more teeth. 'Oh, come on, officer. It's all going to come out.'

He looked like he was going to start talking, like he was fighting an urge to help, to tell a story, but the conversation was broken up by the chop-chop of a news helicopter buzzing the scene for footage. We both looked up, but when I looked down again he had straightened himself, set his pose.

'Vultures, aren't they,' he said, flicking his eyes to the sky.

I shrugged. 'Freedom of speech,' I said, giving it one last try. 'It's a human right.'

'And so is the right to silence,' he replied, and then turned away.

I said nothing. I just wanted to keep my camera, not have it seized as evidence. I knew what was on there was valuable. The encounter with the policeman was already part of the story.

I looked at the pictures I had taken, I knew I was right. There it was, a small splash of colour on the back screen of my camera, the biggest story of the week. I zoomed in, just to make sure, but I knew. I had recognised the body as soon as I had seen it. Henri Dumas, the Premiership's top scorer, last seen wearing the big money blue.

I was stunned, too surprised to do anything at first. I took a deep breath and rubbed my eyes, weighing up the need for sleep against the need for the big story. I was freelance. I could go to bed, or have another beer. Let the big guys have their day.

I smiled to myself. Maybe it was my turn for the big time.

Turners Fold, Lancashire, is a small slate town on the edge of the Pennines, an industrial template, surrounded by scrap grass hills and the shadow of Pendle Hill, green at the base, bracken brown at the top, barren, always dark with cloud.

Turners Fold, 'the Fold' to the locals, is typically

northern: tough, proud, and hard-working. The colour is dark. The grass around it grows short and clings to the hills like stubble, broken only by grey stone walls. The towns and villages are all close by, but the hills intervene, and at night they sit like shadows, topped by the orange glow from the next town.

Like most mill towns, there was nothing before cotton. It breathed life into the town, built its buildings, shaped its people.

But it made the people tough, smothered the town in smoke and scarred the green hills in strips of terraced housing, lined up like computer memory, gutters zigzagging like saw-teeth, doors and windows right onto the streets, dots and bumps in the smooth lines. Cotton owned the town and owned the people, gave them a living, a bond.

The mills have gone now, the land left behind filled with prefab community centres and self-assembly superstores. Some tall chimneys are left, redbrick, out of keeping with the blackened millstone grit that makes up most of the town, reminders of what had once been. A canal runs through the centre, low metal bridges connecting the two sides of the town, weekend barges now the visitors. A hundred years ago the children went to work, their nimble hands good for the machines. Now, they hang around in packs, their faces hidden, living off cheap lager and stolen diazepam.

Just as cotton built the houses, the cotton kings sought a legacy in the civic buildings in the small triangular centre of town, large and impressive against the strips of Victorian shopfronts, dusty and dark, faded glory fighting against the superstores in the next town. Banks, pubs and estate agents cluster around the triangle, spilling onto nearby streets, spreading out like the points on a compass. In the middle of it all is the Horrocks clock, black and white face on a tall stone monument, hemmed in by the town hall and the old Post Office, just by the cobbled town triangle.

The Swan Inn was humming nicely nearby. The name didn't fit. It had neither grace nor beauty, it was just somewhere for the daytime crowd of never-worked and laid-off to swap stories and hide away. The whole place smelled of old smoke and spilled ale, the varnish on the small round tables cracked like veins and covered in white rings. A large screen hung from the ceiling at one end and there was a pool table at the other.

Two men were sitting on stools by the bar. They were just passing time, swapping tales over warm beer, watching the landlord prop up the bar in the other room, the snug, kept away from them by the wooden partition with stained-glass edges.

One of the men was Bob Garrett, the best policeman in Turners Fold never to be promoted. Middle-aged, his back not quite as straight as maybe it once was, the hair not quite as full either and scattered with grey. But there was a sharpness about him, like he could sense what was going on around him, a stern calm, the eyes brooding and mean. His jaw was set firm, no slack-jawed gum-chew.

He'd looked after the townspeople for twenty years, joined up after walking away from a lower-division football career to spend more time with his young wife and even younger son. He made new drinkers twitchy, drinking on the way home in his black trousers and white shirt, the creases and stiff collar marking him out, but when he was off-duty he was done with judging.

He looked up when he heard a shout.

'What is it?' he asked.

It was the landlord.

'Somebody's shot Dumas! Look, look! Henri Dumas, he's fucking dead.'

'What are you talking about?'

The landlord pointed excitedly at the television, permanently tuned to a sports channel, his stomach quivering with excitement, the sign of too long in the job. The drinkers in the bar shuffled towards the screen, the intermittent barks of conversation hushed into silence.

'Look at the news. Someone's shot Dumas.'

'What? Henri Dumas?' asked an old man, looking up from his copy of the *Valley Post*.

'Is there another? Someone has killed him.' The landlord reached for the remote to turn up the volume and then grabbed a glass without looking to pour himself a beer, the bitter all tumbling froth.

There was the sound of glasses being put down and then a respectful silence as the latest news from London echoed around the bar. Bob Garrett stared in disbelief.

The landlord walked away, his beer settling in the glass, shouting his opinion as he went. Foreign players. Bring nothing but trouble. Someone shouted that maybe he took a dive. The bulletin soon gave way for a Gillette commercial and everyone drifted back to their space. Bob Garrett watched them all go and then turned back to the television, wondering what sort of world lets people shrug off someone being killed in cold blood.

It didn't take him long to realise that he didn't have the answer, so he turned back to his drink. He looked around as he lifted the glass. The news had been a break in the day, nothing more.

THREE

It was quiet when Laura McGanity walked towards the corner of Old Compton Street and Greek Street. She could see the small huddle of people around a cafe table: a police photographer, the owner, a mini-flock of detectives, all looking at the floor. They were all grim-faced and quiet, and she knew what they were thinking: that they had met their idol, close enough to touch, but that it wasn't supposed to happen like this, stood in a flak jacket and protective helmet in a stone-cold empty street, blood at their feet.

There were a few detectives walking with her, the extra hands drafted in to help out. Laura was moving slowly, looking around her, trying to get a feel for where the shots might have come from.

'What do you think? Evidence collection or a vigil?'

Laura looked towards the voice. It was a young officer she had never met. She looked back to the scene ahead. She could see the photographer getting busy around the bloodstains, a compass on the floor, with a ruler setting the scene for scale. The long-range shots had

21

already been taken, the tourist snaps, a collection of views along a trendy London street. Now he was down to the money shots, the stained pavement under a green awning.

'I don't know,' she replied. 'Both, I suppose.'

They ducked under the crime-scene tape. The detectives exchanged smiles and nods, businesslike.

'Detective Constable McGanity. Glad you could join us.' It was one of the detectives, a young star on the rise. He glanced at his inspector as he spoke, looking for points.

Laura smiled. It wasn't how she felt, but the only defence she had was to look unbeaten. She knew what the other detectives thought of her. Token woman. Keep the politicos happy. A drain. Too wrapped up in childcare to do her job properly.

'Sorry, John, but I got held up finishing the jobs you couldn't manage.'

'Not today.' It was her inspector, Tom Clemens, a grizzly detective, known for his growls. He said it quietly, but everyone around him knew that he meant it. He was getting older, his stomach growing over his waistband, and what hair he had left was now grey and whisker-short. But every young detective wanted to end up like him.

Laura pulled at her shirt collar, throwing a warm breeze down the front of her flak jacket. Hot days in London just hang there, the heat swirled by traffic, disappearing only at night. She always thought that body armour must have been tested in December, because it wasn't made for days like this one.

She kept looking down as the detectives were briefed, and then they set off in their pairs, intent and thoughtful, leaving her behind.

She looked up when her inspector addressed her.

'What are they saying on the news?' he asked.

Laura shook her head. 'I don't know. We've maybe got a few hours of shock before we get grilled.' She looked around. 'So what have we got?'

'Not much,' he answered. 'We're going door-to-door, trying to find where the shots came from. But it's a slow job. If the shooter is still out there, he's going to be waiting a long time for the knock on the door.'

'He's gone,' said Laura simply. 'Joined the crowds, headed back into town.'

'I know that, but I'm not going to risk being wrong.' Tom looked down at the bloodstains, shaking his head. 'I don't know what Dumas did to deserve this, but he's upset someone.'

'Where do you think the shots came from?'

He nodded away from the Cafe Boheme, towards Charing Cross Road, past the bars and cafes, Ed's Diner, neon Americana squeezed into a corner plot. 'The guess is somewhere over there. The people sitting outside looked instinctively one way when they heard the first shot.' He looked back down at the floor. 'It gets him in the right side of his chest as he's standing. When he took the second shot, the one to the head, he had spun around, clenched up, looking into the cafe. His head snapped backwards like he'd taken the blow from the front, from inside the cafe. The people nearest to him ducked and looked that way, and that's when the scramble around the tables started. But I think that was just instinct, going from what they saw, and no one has reported seeing the gunman in the cafe. If he'd been nearby, somebody would have seen him, without any doubt.'

'No grassy knoll.'

He nodded. 'One gun, two shots.'

Laura smiled. She guessed there'd be a conspiracy website online within twenty-four hours, but Laura was aware that a bullet does strange things to a head. The bullet pushes the blood out, so it can force the blood and brains out of the exit wound like a jet spray. And Laura knew that a pressure hose kicked backwards, not forwards.

Tom raised his eyes upwards. 'We just need to know where they came from.'

Laura looked around, chewing her lip. There were five exit routes for the shooter and apartments above most of the shops and bars. Laura noticed For Sale signs, meaning empty properties. The best place to start.

'What theories are we working on?' she asked.

He sighed. 'Right now, we don't have one. Likely some crackpot did this, just for the attention. But we're going to look into Dumas, see if he has any secrets. We'll look at drugs, women, money, gambling, but I'm not convinced.'

'Why not? Drugs and gambling follow fame like a best friend. You get drugs and gambling, you get bad people chasing debts.'

Tom shook his head. 'Too much chance. This involved

planning. How did anyone know Dumas would be here? My guess is that it was a gay thing, you know, like targeting anyone down here. Just seems that Dumas was in the wrong place.'

Laura looked at her inspector. She could see his forehead glistening with sweat. It was a simple shooting but she detected a fear, like he knew that whatever happened from now on would be crawled over by every hack in the land, breakfast news for the masses.

'Maybe the gay thing was about Dumas,' she said.

'What do you mean?'

'I'm only guessing, but maybe it was some kind of violent outing. You read the papers. A few thousand men play football for money in this country, and maybe one, possibly two, have come out. There must be more gay footballers out there. Why not Dumas?'

'Have you seen his fiancée?' Tom said, knowing nearly everyone had seen virtually all of his fiancée, glamour shots and daily updates keeping the tabloids in business.

'Of course I've seen his fiancée,' she said. 'I'm just saying keep an open mind.'

'If you're going to kill a football star,' he said, 'you do it properly. He's got the money to get security, so you make it one hit, one shot, guaranteed no cock-ups.' He wiped his forehead. 'It will be some nutter. It always is.'

'I made some calls before I came out,' said Laura. 'To Drugs, Vice. No one's threatened Dumas and he isn't known to us.' When there was no answer, she asked,

'What next? Just try and work out where the shooter was first, to see what's there?'

'We've got people going round all the businesses, seizing any CCTV footage. Got any better ideas?'

Laura looked at the floor again. She guessed not.

'We need to catch this bastard,' he said.

Laura nodded sadly. 'Yeah, I know, and we will.'

As he turned away, Laura saw the other detectives glaring at her. She knew their problem: her inspector liked her, but she hadn't put in the hours crawling up his arse.

She smiled at them, wondering when they would ever work out the connection.

She was about to walk away, get some space to think, when she saw a uniform heading towards her. As he got up to her, he said, 'There's been a call from an estate agent. Two of their staff were meeting a client here, and they haven't been heard from since. They've missed two viewings.'

'What was the address?'

The uniform looked around and pointed. 'In that building there.'

As Laura followed his finger to the flats above the shops, she saw a window open just at the bottom. She turned around and followed the line of sight, saw how it looked straight down to where Dumas had been shot.

'At least we might have solved that part of it,' she said, and then shouted to her inspector.

I could see the media camp, kept back by crime-scene tape. They were further than I was from the scene, kept right back on Charing Cross Road, a tangle of cameras, tripods and boom microphones. With so much media around it was going to be a tough day for the freelancer. I could see the glare of spotlights as the television people filmed their updates, but there'd be little to report until the police were finished.

So, if there's nothing going on, report the press watching nothing happening. I framed the collection of cameras and frustrated reporters against the luminous jackets of the police manning the tape. I ran off ten shots and then looked towards the crime scene. I wondered about the shooting, as if the answer might be pasted on a hoarding somewhere. I wondered about a crazed fan. I remembered queuing for an age in a February snowstorm a couple of years earlier for a signed autobiography of some England player I had once admired. An age in the snow for a ghost-written collection of anecdotes, a shake of the hand, and a rushed scrawl on the inside cover. How far was it from that to this?

I shut my eyes for a second and let the sounds drift in. I could hear sirens and car horns, movement from the streets nearby, the cordon choking up traffic for a mile all around, but nearer to me I sensed just anticipation, a poised stillness. It seemed strange to have that calm enveloping me. It didn't seem like the city.

I needed a break. I looked around again. The tale of Henri Dumas would dominate the papers for the next week. There'd be no space for my hard-luck tales from the gutters of old London town.

I was about to sit down when I noticed that there

were more police officers than before. I zoomed in on a group of people around a table, their hands on their hips, talking intently. I zoomed in more, just to make sure. When I had confirmed it to myself, I smiled. I didn't need to stay up to get the story. It had just come to me.

FOUR

David Watts walked into his flat and paused to look in the mirror. He felt tired, still torn up by the Henri Dumas shooting. His eyes looked red.

He turned away and walked into the kitchen, going to the fridge to pull out a beer. The cap snapped off with a pop. At least he was alive.

He looked out of his window, his apartment on the top floor of a complex overlooking Chelsea Bridge, a glass and cedar block sandwiched between two bridges, with wooden boards lining a chrome balcony and sunshine streaming inside through large glass panels. The lucky ones get the Thames, the light. The others get Battersea Power Station.

David Watts, midfielder, the biggest football star in England. He had been on the other side of the city, at the training ground, when the news broke about Henri Dumas. The changing room was in shock when he left, queuing for the television cameras to make their feelings public. David hadn't done that. He couldn't find words for himself, so he wasn't going to try for the cameras.

As he looked away from the river, he saw billboards, his own face gleaming back at him, the face of a new razor campaign. His trademark stubble was shaved on one half of his face, pink and clean, the other side dark and rough. On the hoarding next to him was Dumas, advertising sportswear with moody looks into the camera. He felt his stomach turn. He had met Dumas countless times, at award ceremonies, photo shoots, charity events. They had even gone drinking together after a game. Henri Dumas had been a good man.

He turned on the television, flicking through to Sky News, to footage of an armed police unit storming a building, shot from the news helicopter. Things were happening.

David turned round when he heard footsteps. He saw Emma standing there, dressed in one of his shirts, running a towel over her long hair.

'I didn't know you were around today,' he said. He should have been pleased to see her, but the news about Dumas had left him feeling empty.

Emma smiled, her eyes full of regret. She walked over to him and put her arms around his chest. Her wet hair made a dark patch on his clothes. 'I thought I had some time off and I didn't think you'd mind.'

'I don't.'

She sighed. 'One of the girls has called in sick, so I can't stay.'

'Where are you going?'

'I'm on the overnight to JFK, so I need to be back at Heathrow for six. I should get a quick turnaround though, so maybe I'll only be gone for a couple of days.'

He kissed the top of her head. 'Too long.'

She squeezed him and then pulled away.

David turned back round to the window, looking out over the river. Everything looked so perfect. He could see the trees of Battersea Park. The Thames slid past, moving slowly, catching sparkles of sunshine as it went.

Emma, the air stewardess. They'd met a few months earlier. She'd walked into a bar in her uniform, pulling a small black case behind her, cool and distant, that airline arrogance, smart and made-up, with a long, athletic body and trailing blonde hair. Most of all, she seemed unimpressed by his fame. That had been the attraction. He was young, good-looking and famous, and so he had done the easy sex circuit. But Emma had reminded him of how much he enjoyed the chase. He was a winner, and to win there has to be a contest.

'I suppose you heard,' said David.

Emma stopped drying her hair and put down her towel. 'I heard.'

He exhaled and roughed-up his hair. 'He was a decent bloke, you know, a good player.' He bent down to put his beer on a table and then leant against the window.

'What happens now?' asked Emma.

He shrugged. 'I don't know. Maybe a minute's silence on Saturday. They can't cancel games; the season's just started.'

'Do you think you should play?'

'No reason why not.'

'Is it worth getting shot over?'

David bristled at that. He knew what the 'it' was. It

31

was football. Just a game. David is paid for playing a game. He had heard that before, too many times.

'It's not about what's worth getting shot over,' David responded, his irritation showing. 'It's about me doing my job well. And that job gets me all of this.' He waved his hand around the apartment, every room filled with designer furniture, every window looking out on one of the most expensive views in the city.

'Okay, okay. I'm sorry.'

'You got that right.' He sighed, not wanting to argue. 'Look, Emma, it's a business, not a game.'

'Should it be?'

David turned back to the window and picked up his beer, looking back down to the river. 'No, maybe not.'

He sounded rueful. He remembered his childhood, when football wasn't about money. It was about muddy shirts and the feel of the grass beneath your boots. Messing around with your friends, Saturday morning kickabouts, swapping cards.

'If they cancel the games, come to my parents. They would love to meet you. My dad's got a new boat and he'll want to show it off.'

David nodded. 'Maybe it's time to say hello.'

He stayed by the window for a while, and then he turned around as Emma began to get ready, watching her shrug off his shirt so that she was naked. He turned back to the window. That's what he'd miss when she was gone for a couple of days.

But then she'd be back and he'd get on a bus to the next away game, maybe a plane to Europe. That was their life. He played football. Emma flew around the world. When they connected, they made sparks, but most of the time it felt like they'd hardly met.

Most of all, he liked her because she was so unlike all the other players' wives and girlfriends, who were greedy and predatory, all with a hunger in their eyes that frightened him. And it used to be just about money. Now it was a route to their own fame.

He looked out of the window and drank his beer. Emma was different. She avoided publicity. Didn't ask for money. Hadn't done a magazine shoot.

Maybe that's why he liked her.

Laura was one of the first into the flat, Tom just behind her. When she saw the bodies, she stopped. She didn't need to get any nearer to know that they were dead.

She stepped back out of the flat and blocked the way in. 'We're too late. Save it for crime scenes.'

Tom sighed and turned around, pushing police officers away, asking for someone to get the photographer. When he turned back into the flat, he said, 'We can presume this is the place, can't we?'

Laura nodded. 'If we can't, it's been a busy day in Soho.'

There were two people, a male and a female, both smart in suits. Except that one had a pool of blood around his head, gravity doing the job that the heart had stopped doing, and the other hadn't moved for some time, despite the open eyes.

'Is it some kind of suicide thing?' he said, looking back into the room. 'He shoots Dumas, strangles the girl, and then turns the gun on himself?'

Laura peered into the gloom, tried to see the detail of the scene at the other end of the room. 'Unless he could do it with his hands tied behind his back, I doubt it.'

Tom looked back into the room and then looked down.

'Shit. Three murders in one afternoon. Looks like we better cancel everyone's leave for a few weeks.'

Laura sighed to herself. Her parents' goodwill was stretched already by her childcare needs, her ex-husband regarding that as her job to arrange. 'Have we spoken to the estate agency yet?' she asked.

Tom looked up. 'Someone's on the way there now. Appointment made in the name of Paxman, but nothing else. Done over the phone. That's why there were two here, just in case.'

'Do you get a bad feeling about today?'

He nodded. 'Very.'

Laura was about to say something else when she felt her phone vibrate in her pocket. It was a text, a simple message, two words: 'call me'. It was from Jack Garrett. She stopped the smile which started when she saw his name. She hadn't heard from him in months. He would have to wait.

She checked her watch and realised how late the day was going to get. She caught Tom looking and she cursed to herself.

'Kids?' he asked.

She shrugged. 'Police life. They understand.'

He nodded. 'If you need to go, Laura, you need to go. Maybe you're the one who's got it right.'

Laura said nothing; just cursed some more and then snapped open her phone. She knew straight away what he was getting at. This will be a long haul. If you don't have the time, step aside.

But then she thought of something.

'There is one body of people who might know all about Dumas,' she said.

Tom nodded. 'Go on.'

'The press. They'll have all his secrets,' and as Tom began to smile, she pressed the call button.

I smiled when my phone rang. I knew Laura would call. She always did.

I tried hard to hide the skip in my voice.

'Hello, detective. Fancy hearing from you today.'

'Jack, you know I'm busy.'

'Detective McGanity, why on earth do you think I'm calling?'

'Look, Jack, I can't talk right now. There's too much going on.'

'When?'

I heard her sigh.

'Where are you?'

'In my apartment, a few doors down from where you are.' I lowered my voice. 'What's in that building? Quite a crowd went in there a few minutes ago.'

'I can't disclose any secrets, Jack, you know that.' There was a pause, and then, 'We could meet up. I haven't seen you for a while. It'll be good to catch up.'

I was suspicious. It looked hectic out there, and Laura wanted to pass the time.

But then I thought about Laura, and I remembered how I felt whenever we met up, and I knew I would go. And what could I have that she needed?

I had a quick look round my flat. There were dishes to be washed on the drainer and too many magazines to pick up if she came to me.

'Do you know The Pearlie Queen?' It was a cockney theme pub, almost like satire, with a piano in the corner and a dark wooden snug. More importantly, it would be just behind the media lines. 'I can meet you there. How soon?'

'Ten minutes. I'm due for a break.'

I felt myself grin. 'Okay, ten minutes. I look forward to seeing you.'

And then I hung up.

I was surprised she had agreed to meet me so quickly, but I found myself unable to say no. I felt that creeping flutter in my stomach whenever I thought of her.

I checked my hair. I needed to get there first.

FIVE

I had been at the bar for nearly an hour before Laura walked in, tucked into an alcove, trying to write the story I hoped would squeeze in somewhere between the shock and the tributes.

I had been struggling, though. I hadn't slept in nearly twenty-four hours, not recovered from the night shift, so the words just floated around in front of me, not getting onto the screen. I had to close my eyes for a few minutes and let the bar fade away. The breeze blowing in through the open door kept the scene drifting in, until all I could sense were the images and sounds from nearby Soho. Then I had remembered the young family, shaking with shock. I remembered something the mother had said. It was a good starting quote. I began to type.

'"A daytrip to town isn't supposed to happen like that."

'That was the voice of a frightened mother, her two young children resting against her leg.'

It was high-school prose, but it was a start.

As I tapped away, the words began to tumble out,

and by the time Laura arrived I had written a first draft.

I was the only person who looked up when Laura came in. I saw her look around. The smoking ban had taken away some of the atmosphere, but the flock wallpaper and etched windows kept it dark inside. It drew in the tourists, sold the spirit of the blitz back to German students, who didn't realise that it used to be a disco bar before a renovation turned the clock back. Retro-style televisions were tuned to the news channel, the subtitles bringing the updates over the noise of the bar, the talk all about the shooting.

She looked fabulous, she always did. I felt myself take a breath. She was tall and slim, with deep green eyes that sparkled when she blinked and a smile that spread slowly, so that her face lit up like a slow yawn until dimples flickered in both cheeks. Her hair fell down over her face, a sunset brunette, that reddish darkness the Irish have.

As she came in, she said, 'I don't get to hear much country music in London.'

I looked over at the jukebox. It was Johnny Cash playing, Orange Blossom Special, that railroad rhythm.

'It's my dirty secret,' I said. I looked around the bar. 'Sorry about this place, but they've got music I understand. Is beer okay on duty?'

'One won't matter, in the circumstances,' she said.

Once she had a drink, I nodded towards the speakers. 'He always takes me home.'

'Johnny Cash?'

'My father spent nearly every spare minute he had

listening to Johnny. I'm not sure I got it then, as a child, but now I just seem to have him playing all the time.'

'Where is home? You've never said.'

'Turners Fold, in Lancashire.'

'That explains the accent,' she said. 'Don't know it.'

'Not many people do.'

'Ever think about going back?'

'Why do you think I live in Soho?' I said. 'It's just about as far from home as I can get.'

'That bad?'

I tugged at my lip.

I'd started as a journalist back home, but it had been all small-town news, lost-dog stories and job gloom. I'd come to London to get away from all that, taking a job as a staff writer with the *London Star*.

It had been fun at first, chasing around the city, my days filled with new sights and sounds, but it was hard work. The paper owned me. That was the deal, twenty-four hours a day, seven days a week. If the paper wanted me to do something, I did it. And the paper wanted a lot, so I felt like I was always running, always trying to increase my by-lines, doing what I could to keep my stories elbowing themselves into the paper.

I lasted two years, but six months ago I'd given it up and turned freelance. The money was less certain, but it was *my* money, earned by *my* work, *my* sweat.

I shook my head. 'No, it's okay up there. But I like the city too much.'

'A lonely place sometimes.'

'Very lonely,' I agreed. 'You know, it seemed like when I stood still in Lancashire, people stopped to talk, asked me how I was. In London, they just push me out of the way.'

'And steal your wallet at the same time.'

I laughed. 'And what about you?'

'Grew up in Pinner. So this is all I've known.'

'You ever been up north?'

'A week in the Lakes once, and a hen night in Blackpool.'

'The best and the worst in two visits. You've done well.'

She laughed, her eyes twinkling. 'How about you? You seem to have settled okay.'

'No one settles in London. It moves too fast.'

'So you started bugging off-duty police officers?'

I smiled at that, just about stopped a blush.

That's how I had met Laura, trying to build up police sources, drinking in the pubs where the police hung out. I'd spotted Laura on the edge of a group of detectives. When it was her turn to buy the drinks, I got talking.

I'd tried the flirt at first, we were around the same age, but I got nowhere. She had a husband and a child, and she wasn't going to risk any of that. So I gave it to her straight. If she wanted her cases to make the news, if she wanted to have some control over how they were told, she ought to use me.

And she did. I snapped her arrests, got the inside track on her cases. She told me that she used me to get her cases in the headlines. I told her that I was doing the same thing.

Laura looked around and I watched her eyes dance.

I felt that spark of interest again. I watched her fingers wipe at the condensation on her glass, a gentle stroke. But then I felt a jolt when I looked down at her hand. Her wedding ring had gone.

When she looked back towards me, she pointed towards my laptop. 'How's the story?'

'Slow. I might not file it,' I said, but I was distracted, wondering what had happened to her marriage.

'Can I read it?'

I shrugged. 'Why not?'

Laura looked at the screen for a while and then turned back to me. 'You write well. Why do you just work the crime stories?'

'It's a good life. No one owns me.'

'Don't you fancy the salary, nice and regular?'

I shook my head. 'I've been there.' I lifted my bottle towards her. 'You're looking good. Family life looking after you?'

Laura's toughness, that cop façade, was swept away by a blush.

'Same as always,' she replied. 'Too much time at work, and then too much time hating my ex-husband.'

'How long has he been an ex?' I tried to sound innocent, a friendly enquiry, but it stumbled out all clumsy. I felt my pulse quicken as I asked.

'Since I caught him with a probationer, except that she wasn't wearing much of the uniform.' She looked sad for a moment. 'Never marry a copper.'

I didn't reply at first, but then we both started to say something and then stopped, grinning, like new lovers banging noses.

'No, go on,' I said.

She looked bashful for a few seconds, and then said, 'I need your help, Jack, with information.'

That surprised me. Our relationship had a pattern. I reported crime. Laura told me about crime. It didn't go the other way.

I nodded, curious. 'Go on.'

'We need to know about Dumas. We want to know about his lifestyle, his secrets, anything that could lead to a blackmail, or a murder.'

'We all know everything there is to know about Dumas,' I said. 'You can't open a paper without seeing him or his fiancée doing something newsworthy, like walking or talking.'

'I don't mean that rubbish. I mean the real stories, the ones that don't get into the paper.'

I knew what Laura meant. The papers often held on to scandals when they got them, on the promise from worried agents that they'd get the best access to whichever celebrity it was. If a rival got hold of it, the story was run just to strike a blow at the competition.

'I can make some calls, try and find something out, but this is quid pro quo.'

She held out her hands. 'Name it.'

'What did you find at the house?'

Laura stalled at that.

'C'mon, Laura, the television had police swarming into a house just a few doors from mine.'

She looked at me guardedly. 'This is off the record?'

I shrugged.

She sighed. 'Estate agents, there for an appointment,

both dead, with a sniper's view of where Dumas queued for his last latte.'

I exhaled. 'So you found where the shots came from?'

She nodded. 'Looks that way.'

'So you can trace who had the appointment?'

'That's the theory.'

'How did they die?'

'He died from a gunshot, point blank. The woman was strangled.'

I raised my eyebrows. 'Unusual?'

It was Laura's turn to shrug. In her career, she'd seen things I couldn't even imagine.

'So the shooter's killing off the witnesses?' I asked. 'Why are you keeping it quiet?'

'We're not. We're going public soon, but we wanted to do the forensic sweep first.'

I sat back. It sounded interesting, but I wasn't sure it fitted my story.

'What was Dumas doing there?'

'That', she replied, 'is what we are trying to find out.'

'Do you think it might have been just chance? You know, Dumas in the wrong place?'

'Not sure. The bodies in the flat made it seem professional, planned, which is a lot of trouble for a random shooting. The shooter would just shoot, if it was random.'

'So if it was a set-up, you should be able to find that out.'

Laura smiled. 'Hey, you're sharp!'

My eyes twinkled at her. I was just thinking about what else to ask, really just to keep her there, when she asked, 'How quickly can you find anything out?'

When I looked uncertain, she said, 'This is the golden hour, the time when any evidence has to be captured. We might get a lead in a few days, but any forensic evidence from the scene will be long gone by then.'

'No pressure then.'

She smiled, and any resistance I had melted.

'I'll see what I can do.'

And as I picked up my phone, she slid out of her seat. I was about to start dialling when she leant forward and I felt a soft peck on my cheek.

'Thanks, Jack. It's good to see you again. Call me as soon as you find something.'

I smiled, had to stop myself from putting my hand where the kiss had been.

'You've got my number,' I said. 'Not just for work. Anything.'

It was her turn to blush, but I saw a glimmer of a smile as I watched her walk out.

David Watts was at the front of his apartment building, facing cameras and reporters. They had been outside there for a few hours, hungry for a quote.

'I just want to say that I knew Henri Dumas. He was a good player. No, a great player – but above all of that, he was a good man, and football will miss him. I'll miss him. I would like to express my condolences to his family, and I'm sure the footballing world is in deep mourning right now.'

And at that, he went back into his building. He didn't feel good. His words sounded irrelevant when he thought about Dumas; just a token footnote. Dumas was dead. Who cared about his condolences?

When he got back to his apartment, he saw the parental look of his agent. She watched the press disappear from the window, and then turned back to the room.

'That will get you good billing on the news, remind everyone that you're the statesman of English football.'

He shook his head at her. Karen Klavan. She was a good agent, but she was one cold-hearted bitch. She looked like a pin-up, blonde hair and breasts like weapons, but he guessed that when she fucked, she did it with a motive, not a passion.

'Someone died today, Karen. Doesn't that mean anything?'

'It means you get a chance to raise your profile.' When she saw the look of disgust, she said, 'You worry about Dumas, and I'll worry about making you money.'

He would have smiled normally. Her directness gave her an edge in negotiations, but he wasn't in the mood. And as he looked over to the billboards again, as he thought about the gossip magazines for sale in the shop just down the road, as he imagined all the children wandering around the country with his name on the back of their shirts, he reckoned his profile was pretty high already. He didn't want to use Dumas's death to raise it higher. The thought of it sickened him.

'I think we should look respectful, take some time out,' he said, his anger snapping the words out.

'Yeah, yeah, that too, but look, I've got you a slot on breakfast television, to talk about Dumas. Is that okay? It won't clash with your training.'

He shook his head. She made him money, but she made him mad as well.

'I'll end up tired at training.'

'The country will forgive you if you're jaded. In fact, they might be furious with you if you look bright and bubbly when you play.'

'I take it Dumas wasn't one of your clients.'

'Can you hear me sobbing? No, he was with that prick Newcombe.'

And then she laughed.

Laughs didn't come naturally to her, so when they came, they came loud and shrill.

'He'll be crying into his vodka tonight,' she said, ignoring David's look. When he didn't respond, she said, 'You'll be picked up at five. Be up and ready, dressed soberly.'

'Where will you be?'

'Oh, out and about. I've some new clients to see, so I'll be away for a couple of days. I'll keep in touch.'

'If you leave it a bit longer, you'll be able to dance on Dumas's grave.'

She winked at him and then picked up her bag, not bothering with goodbye. She could tell he was angry. Worse than that, though, was the thought that she didn't care. He was just an asset, and she had him tied into an agency agreement. He was twenty-eight, so he didn't have too long left at the top. In a few years' time, when some younger star started to grab the headlines and his hamstrings were ripped to hell, she'd shunt him off her books as quick as one of his crosses.

When the door clicked shut David turned back to the window, hoping that the view would make him forget about Karen Klavan. He knew she didn't care about him. He wasn't sure she cared about anybody.

SIX

Any warmth Laura had when she left the bar disappeared as she went through the swinging double doors of the autopsy room. Thirty-eight degrees Fahrenheit. Warm enough to work, cool enough to stop bad things from multiplying. The room was a purpose-built unit, a step above the dusty hospital wings used by most police forces, with specially designed ventilation and plumbing, designed to keep the smells inside while letting the carcinogenics and acids out.

The room was already full. She saw Tom near the autopsy table, down by the feet, two green-faced detectives behind him, trying not to give in. The task force had been assembled quickly, and it was mainly those who were available rather than those who were the best for it. The two detectives on Tom's shoulder were young and ambitious, one dressed like a fashion victim, with big collars and bleached tips, his face pink from a bad shave, all except for the little triangle he left deliberately, just under his lip. The other was old-style bully boy, dressed in a black leather coat, his hands thrust

48

in pockets, his stance aggressive. His hair was crew-cut short and his stare hostile. They were trying to crack jokes to distract themselves, but nothing they said was particularly funny. She nodded at Tom and he gave her a small smile back.

Laura stayed near the head. It was closer to the action, but those at the feet got the smell, that mix of warm meat and chemicals, carried there by the ventilation. Tom had been in the job too long to be bothered by the smell, but the other detectives had been too keen to stand by him.

Tom lifted a small bottle of wintergreen oil, used by many to mask the smell of the dead. She shook her head. Laura wanted to smell the dead, just so that she could feel the pain. It would make her work all the harder.

Laura didn't say anything, just let the pathologists wander round the body, speaking notes into the overhead microphone. There were two there, checking that nothing was missed, knowing that this would be a high-profile case. The one looking closely at the body was fifty and dignified, with a gentle face looking from behind half-moon glasses. The other was younger, a bookish-looking woman, with pulled-back dark hair and a pointed nose.

Laura looked over to the wall and saw evidence bags stacked up. She could see the woman's clothes along with her body bag, bagged and tagged, part of the continuity. Important pieces of evidence can come off the body in transportation, nestling in the bottom of the body bag.

The woman was naked on the aluminium table, young and pale. Laura checked that the men weren't looking too hard. She noticed a half-finished tattoo on the woman's shoulder blade. The outline was done, two lovebirds intertwined, but the colours had yet to be added. It was details like that which always made Laura sad. They were part of a life in transit, so many things still to do, but something went wrong which left her naked on that table.

Laura saw the male detectives look away with a grimace when the pathologist picked up a syringe. They knew what was coming next. So did Laura, but she steeled herself.

The needle was plunged into the girl's right eye and a sample of fluid was drawn out. Laura knew why it was being done, to test the potassium levels in the eye to get a more accurate time of death, and she had a strong stomach, but it always made her shudder.

The cause of death was easy to determine. She could see the brown mark around the neck where something had been pulled tight. She knew what the eyes would show: burst blood vessels, tiny red pin-pricks, the tell-tale signs of strangulation.

Tom indicated with his head that they should talk outside. As he stepped away, Laura saw the two detectives nearby instinctively step with him, but they were told to stay put and keep an eye on the proceedings.

Outside the swing doors, Tom asked, 'How did you get on with your reporter friend?'

Laura felt herself blush slightly.

'He didn't know anything about Dumas, but he says he will make some discreet enquiries.'

'Can he be trusted?'

Laura nodded. 'Yeah, he's okay.'

They both turned around quickly when the doors burst open. It was Fashion Victim.

'Sir, he's found something.' He looked breathless, excited.

Laura and Tom exchanged glances, and then headed for the doors. Tom got to them first, and as Laura passed the detective he whispered to her, 'It's past your bedtime, McGanity. Shouldn't you be tucking in your little boy?'

Laura felt her chest heave, a burst of emotion, felt her eyes fill up, more from anger than anything else. She knew she attracted jealousy. She was young for a detective, still in her late twenties, a university degree her background rather than years in the force, and she expected some comments. But that had hit a weak spot.

Didn't he think that she thought that every time she left the house, every time her little boy waved her goodbye when she left him with her mother? But she had fought hard to be a detective, against every jibe she had suffered about being a university girl, against every macho man who thought it was man's work, the sort who watch reruns of *The Sweeney* and spend their spare time wondering why their wife has just left.

She pushed past him, her cheeks flushed, and went back into the autopsy room. Fashion Victim was still smiling.

When she got alongside Tom, she saw him looking at something the pathologist was holding up. It twirled and twinkled under the spotlight over the table.

It was a gold chain with thick links, with some kind

of a medallion hanging from it, maybe an inch across. Laura peered closer, trying to refocus on the investigation. As she looked, she thought there was something familiar about it. The chain was thick, but it was a Celtic weave, not gangsta links. Then she realised why she recognised the medallion. She'd had one very similar as a child.

The medallion was a Celtic symbol, three curls meeting in the centre, embossed deeply into a disc.

'It's called a triskele,' said Laura. She was addressing Tom, but she was looking at Fashion Victim. His mouth twitched. 'The benefit of being Irish,' she said, and shrugged.

'What does it mean?' asked Tom. The other two detectives glared at her.

'A whole host of things. The three elements of the planet: earth, water and sky. Some say it's to do with the sun, afterlife and reincarnation, or the three symbols of the Mother Goddess: maiden, mother and crone.'

'So it basically means fuck all.' It was Bully Boy.

'You know more now than you did thirty seconds ago,' she snapped back, making Tom smirk.

'I would prefer it if you chaps played with your cocks elsewhere.' It was the pathologist, looking at Fashion Victim and Bully Boy with disdain. 'This might mean something.'

He was still holding the chain over the naked body.

'There's an inscription on the back,' he continued. He peered closer, trying to make out the words. 'Looks like, hang on, they're not words I recognise. And then he spelled them out. '*Rath Dé Ort EW*.'

'What the hell does that mean?' asked Tom.

The pathologist shrugged. 'I found it, that's all.'

'It means one thing,' said Laura. 'Messages only ever come from people who want to be caught.'

'How do you know it's a message?' Tom looked confused.

Laura gestured towards the body. 'She's been naked for as long as I've been here, and I suppose there are only so many places a girl can hide a chain. That tells me that she wasn't wearing it when she left home this morning.'

Tom flashed a look at the pathologist. 'Where did you find it?'

'In her throat, right at the back.'

'Pushed in, rather than swallowed?'

He nodded. 'There are some grazes on the roof of the mouth.'

Laura and Tom exchanged glances. At least they now had a lead.

SEVEN

The answer machine was blinking at me when I walked in. Two messages.

The first one was from Laura. I had stayed at the bar longer than I intended, just one more drink turning into three.

'Hi Jack, it's just me. Just ringing to let you know that you can ring me any time about this. We need all the help we can get.' Then there was a pause. *'And I just thought,'* and then another pause, before, *'Oh, no, forget it, it doesn't matter. Sorry. We'll talk again. Bye.'*

As I heard her voice, I felt flutters, like dances in my stomach. I remembered how I felt the first time I met her, and then the same feeling every time after that. It was like a need, a tightness in the chest.

But she had been married, and I don't go out with married women. They bring trouble I don't need.

Now she wasn't married any more, and I could feel all those yearnings coming back. And I had felt her get close earlier. Just a brush, warm lips, maybe just friendly, but it reopened whatever I felt when our paths crossed.

I sighed and laughed to myself. It must be the beer talking, all this teenage mush.

I reached into the fridge for another beer, popped off the cap, but stopped when the next message started.

'Hello Jack, it's Dad. I heard about Henri Dumas, and it looked like it happened near you. I just thought I would ring to see how you're doing. I haven't spoken to you for a while. Give me a ring.'

And then it clicked off.

I sighed. I felt the skip I'd had before fade. I glanced at the picture I had of him on the wall, from when he was still a footballer, trying to dribble past a sliding tackle. He looked young, full of promise. I looked away. He wasn't that man any more. I see a man a little lost, and maybe a lot lonely.

I thought about calling, but, as always, I didn't act on it. I tried to ignore the nagging guilt, and instead began to think about the article I hadn't quite finished, and about the calls I still had to make for Laura.

But my thoughts turned back to my father. It had always been the same with him. He calls to say hello, but we don't get much beyond that. He doesn't know much about my life, and there's not too much to talk about with his. He goes to work, sometimes goes to the pub. Any time he has left, he spends it messing around with his car, a 1973 Triumph Stag. He bought it when he was still a footballer, it was the car he had when he met my mother, and he had kept hold of it, some kind of nostalgia thing. He has other cars, routine runarounds, but it is the Stag that sees him with a rag in his hand, cleaning and mending and waxing.

It had been like that with my father since my mother died a few years earlier. She was where I got my darkness from, with her long brunette curls and chocolate eyes. She had been funny and vivacious and loving. She had provided the emotion, my dad the steel. A cancer had killed her, sneaked up on her and then danced all over her body, reduced her to bones, pain-killed to a stupor.

It was a relief for me when she died. I couldn't watch her suffer any more, and I saw what it was doing to my dad. He'd stopped talking, stopped smiling. I was able to move on when she died, still with my own life ahead, but I think my dad thought that the best bits of his life were behind him, and he didn't seem keen on facing the rest on his own. By the time he came around, we'd become strangers in the same house. He didn't know my friends, didn't know where I went. We still talked, like if we needed milk, or the rubbish needed putting out, the routine stuff, but not much else. I moved to London and he stayed in Turners Fold.

I turned away from the answer machine, ignoring the knot of guilt I had in my stomach. He was all the family I had left. But we could talk another time.

The only sound Bob Garrett could hear was the sound of his tyres humming over the cobbles as he went through the town triangle.

Turners Fold seemed quiet. He saw the lights flick off in Jake's, the end of another endless day for him, competing with the all-night garage and the new late

56

shop at the end of the street. He would return once Jake had locked up. Jake was having problems with youths using the side of his shop to meet and get drunk.

It wasn't just the noise that bothered Jake. It was the sheer waste of it all. All hooded up in black, indistinguishable, tracksuit bottoms tucked into their socks, they sat around the town at night, drinking cheap cider. Mostly, they'd just get noisy, but when it got warm they'd look for trouble.

Bob knew their parents. They were decent people. The kids would be, given the chance. Bob just didn't see many chances coming their way.

Bob looked back at Jake's and waved. He didn't know if Jake could see him, but the gesture felt good.

He looked down the road, towards where the town drifted into darkness, the lights of houses the only spots of life. He saw the house where James Radley used to live, his old police friend, until the house burnt down, James and his wife choked by the smoke, burnt to death by the flames. It was all new now, the black grit-blasted away.

He sighed at the thought of the night ahead. He had some bail checks to do, making sure people were obeying their curfew, and a couple of statements to take.

He cocked his ear at the radio. A drunken husband was banging on his door, making threats. Same again. She'd had him back three times in the last month, despite the beatings. She needed the police when they argued, but wouldn't take the help when he was prosecuted, always attending court to beg for his return.

Time to go. He didn't want her murder to take place on his tour.

I had filed the article before I called Laura. She sounded sleepy when I called, and I tried to be brief when I realised she had her young son asleep with her.

'I didn't wake him, did I?'

I heard the smile in her voice, wrapped up in a yawn.

'No, just me. Have you got anything?'

'Not much, but I've called a few contacts. Seems like the celebrity engagement isn't what it seems. There are rumours that neither party to the couple treasured their fidelity too highly, although nothing the papers would dare to print. Rumours of one-night stands for him, secret liaisons with a dancer for her, but nothing else.'

'Can you get any details?'

'I'm going to see someone in the morning for you. He might open up to me.'

'Thanks, Jack.' There was a pause, Laura thinking how far she could go, and then, 'What do you want to know?'

'Just what's happening? Anything unusual about the post mortems.'

She sighed, and I sensed her waking up. 'Just one thing, but this is still off the record. Don't write it up unless you have our approval.'

'That's understood.'

I sensed the pause, the uncertainty, and I knew something was coming. And I sensed the trust. If I used what she was to tell me without approval, I could forget about any help from the police.

'In the woman's throat, we found a Celtic medallion with some engraving on the back.'

I was surprised. None of that had come out in the news conference.

'What did it say?'

'Is this truly between us?'

'Trust me, Laura. But why are you keeping it quiet?'

'We can use it to filter out the crank calls.'

That seemed reasonable.

'So if it was in her throat,' I said, 'you're thinking it's some kind of message?'

'Can it be anything else?'

And then she told me what the medallion had engraved on it. '*Rath Dé Ort EW.*' She said it like 'rah-jay-urt'.

'It means "the grace of God be with you" in Irish Gaelic,' she said. 'Not sure about the EW though. It doesn't match her name, or his.'

'It could belong to the shooter. You know, bitten off in the struggle.'

'No, we don't think so.'

There was a pause then, each of us unsure how to fill it.

'Knowing how the press work,' I said, trying to plug the silence, 'you'll get about five days before they publish anything on his private life. They won't touch it before his funeral. Then they'll get the weekend tributes out of the way, those before the games. But one of the Sunday red-tops might run something, so I might get something before it goes public.'

'Thanks, Jack. I owe you one. Give me a call when you get something.'

And then we said our goodbyes. I was left looking out of my window, my flat feeling a little emptier than it had done before.

EIGHT

Laura rushed into the dawn meeting late. A few looked over when she clattered through the doors, but most acted like they hadn't noticed her.

She was breathing heavily, angry, another bad start to what would be a long day.

She hadn't had long at home, just a brief sleep, and then it was up at five to take her son to her ex-husband's new bachelor pad, a rented new-build just a few hundred yards from the matrimonial home, little Bobby wrapped up in a duvet, still dozing.

It was her ex-husband's rest day, but still he didn't look pleased when he found out he had his son for the day. Laura knew plenty of divorced fathers, and most of them loved their children, hated being separated from them. It seemed like her ex was the other type, the type who love their kids, but only every other weekend, and provided that they don't have to pay too much for them. Laura's ex preferred the alternate Saturday treat day, when Bobby could have six hours of fun and treats before he was returned, the duty done.

She was the one who was up in the middle of the night when the sickness bugs kicked in.

There had been another car on his drive, a Nissan Micra, with a pine air-freshener hanging from the mirror and a felt pig on the parcel shelf.

She didn't suppose it mattered any more, but that didn't stop her stomach from taking a kick when she saw it.

She tried to shake the memory away and concentrated instead on the room. She could smell the coffee and bacon sandwiches, everyone's favourite kick-start.

It seemed like the murder squad had grown. There weren't many faces she recognised, and she guessed that detectives had been drafted in from further afield than yesterday. She sensed some satisfaction when she saw Bully Boy and Fashion Victim towards the back of the room.

It was a mix she might have expected. There was the genuine talent in there, the shrewd, the sharp, and they were padded out by the grafters and the keen. There were a few of the old school, and too many of the climbers, but it looked a good mix.

Tom Clemens was at the front, leading the parade. The two detectives flanking him looked organised and efficient, one a middle-aged bottle-brunette and the other a shaven-headed blue suit. Behind them were pictures of the three victims. Dumas was the main picture, but the estate agents were given a good billing as well. The deaths weren't just about Dumas.

Laura listened as those in the room gave their updates.

Crank calls had been the biggest problem. Most of those had come after closing time, but they would all be chased. Laura knew that football would go into mourning, and Saturday would see men crying for someone they'd soon forget, their scarves hoisted over their heads, but it didn't stop rival fans from gloating when the beer took hold.

Tom told everyone that Dumas's fiancée would have to be investigated, but he didn't think there was much progress that way. She was on the first part of a European tour and would be flying back later that day. Laura guessed not before she had carefully chosen her mourning clothes. Then Tom warned everyone that the press would be all over this story, and all over Dumas's private life. Any leak could harm the investigation, and if anyone was caught giving unauthorised leaks, they would be disciplined. Any information from 'inside sources' was to be carefully managed.

Laura looked down quickly when Tom mentioned leaks, but then she became aware that Tom was addressing her, asking for a media update.

'Nothing yet, sir,' she said, her voice quiet in the room. 'There's talk of both of them sleeping around, but I'll be calling my contact soon. He's promised to ask around.'

She became aware of the rest of the squad turning away. She had arrived late and added little. She had expected some surprise about Dumas's private life, even though little had been said. Tom looked like he already knew.

Then she saw Tom take a deep breath. He looked

nervous, pensive, gazing around the room. He seemed to be weighing up his audience before making his announcement. After a few seconds of him flexing his jaw, his lips twitching, he said, 'There's one thing no one knows yet, and I only received confirmation of it shortly before I came in.'

He had an edge to his voice, and Laura sensed the squad take notice.

'The two estate agents were bound with silver duct tape,' he continued. 'We all know that. The male had dark hair. The female had mousy hair.' He looked around again. 'Stuck in the duct tape which bound the girl's wrists were three blonde hairs.'

Laura sensed the meeting tense up. And she knew why. If the hairs had been snagged in the adhesive, they would have been yanked out. And if they had been yanked out, some skin would have been attached to the hair root. And if there was skin, there was something else. DNA. As far as evidence that can be used in court, it's the pot of gold at the end of the rainbow.

Tom raised his eyebrows, waiting for the muttering in the room to subside. 'As you might have guessed, we think they are from the shooter.' He began to pace. 'We didn't find any other hairs, and we didn't find any other fingerprints or anything else linking another person to the murder of those two estate agents.' He stopped pacing. 'As far as we can tell, there were only ever three people in that room. And two of them are dead.'

The muttering in the group rose to a chatter, cops in clusters whispering asides.

Tom held up his hand.

'That isn't the news, though,' he said. 'At least not all of it.'

The room fell silent again. Everyone was waiting for the next instalment. Laura sensed it was important, from a look she had never seen in Tom's eyes before. It was excitement, surprise, uncertainty, a mix of all that, along with some emotions Laura couldn't decipher.

'The lab coats have been looking at the hairs,' he continued, his voice deliberate. 'It's too early for a DNA analysis, although they have promised to prioritise it. However, they have had the chance to examine the hairs, and they have made some findings.'

The rest of the squad looked expectant.

Tom looked around, almost as if going for the drama, before he continued.

'The analysis carried out suggests one thing.' He paused, sighed, and then raised his eyebrows.

He said it simply, but it made it no less surprising. He looked around the room, into the eyes of everyone, and then said, 'The shooter is a woman.'

When David Watts stepped away from the lurid sofas of breakfast television, away from the glare of the lights and into the grubby darkness behind the line of cameras, he felt his phone vibrate in his pocket. He winced when he saw the caller ID.

He thought about not answering, but then just like he always did, he clicked the answer button.

'Morning, Karen.'

'David, you were wonderful. Just the right amount

65

of remorse. Not too gushy. You don't want to be embarrassed by this in a year's time.'

'Thanks for the compliment,' he answered, although he didn't sound grateful.

'Exposure, exposure. You can never get enough.'

He took the phone away from his ear, not wanting to hear her obsession with his earning power. She had told him too often that she wanted to earn enough so that she could retire at thirty. She was only a year away from that, but David couldn't see her retiring. She loved the power games too much. And from what he had heard, she loved the footballer parties too much as well.

When he was far enough from the studio microphones, he put the phone back to his ear and said, 'Someone died, Karen. You're coming across like a vulture. And if you do, I might come across the same.'

'Bullshit. You're the face of football for the next few days. I've spoken to the major news networks, and I've promised them you'll be interviewed whenever they request, just to give the players' perspective.'

'Why me, for Christ's sake?'

'Because you're one of the few footballers who can string a proper sentence together. And because you're the most senior English footballer living in the capital. They can have a camera round at your apartment in no time, and you can make it into the studio.'

He sighed. He felt like he was being dragged under by the current.

'You've got some sponsorships coming up for renewal at the end of this season. You'll be twenty-nine by then, maybe only a couple of seasons left in an

England shirt, and companies will shy away from a long investment. It'll do you no harm if you're an English saint by the end of the season.'

'I thought you were going away for a few days,' he said, sounding irritated.

She laughed. He pulled the phone away from his ear, grimacing. Then he heard her say, 'I am, but I'll stay in touch. And by the time I return, you'll be a fucking hero.'

And you'll be getting richer, he thought, but he said nothing. Instead, he turned off his phone and wondered whether this was what he had dreamed about when he was a child, when he was sticking his Panini stickers in the albums or shouting at the hand of God as it sent England out of the World Cup. It was supposed to be about football, that's all.

Laura was as surprised as anyone. A woman? Women don't kill like that. If women kill violently, they do it out of passion, like a woman who catches her partner in bed with someone else. Laura remembered that sickening rage herself. If women kill cold-bloodedly, they do it quietly, non-violently. Women kill out of passion or greed. Like nurses who overdose their patients, or the scheming old widows who poison every new rich man they meet. Passion or greed, but not a cold-blooded assassination.

'Are they sure?' Laura heard herself ask, and felt the eyes of the room on her.

Tom looked at her. Thankfully, he smiled.

'The answer is no, they cannot be sure, not yet. The

lab should know by tomorrow, but the early indicators are that it is a woman. It is long, blonde, but treated. It's been straightened recently. It has all the characteristics of a female hair, but they have still got some more tests to run on it.'

Laura thought she knew what they would be. The DNA would confirm it, but they would also do a sex chromatin test, as the results would be cheaper to obtain, and quicker.

'Woman scorned?' someone shouted from the side of the room. Some people laughed, but Laura noticed that Tom didn't.

'We might have to consider that.'

'But what about the gay angle?' came another shout. The meeting was turning into what Tom wanted, an exchange of ideas. 'Dumas was in a pretty gay part of town. Is that something to do with it?'

Tom considered how to answer that, and he did it by walking over to a television and turning it on.

'We've got the evidence from Dumas's phone,' he said. 'There are some texts.' He went back to where he had left his papers. He shuffled through them until he found what he was looking for. 'They make interesting reading, and for now we want the press off them.'

He looked down at the piece of paper he was holding, and then began to read from them. There were some giggles, some chuckles. They were intimate, sexual. And it was immediately apparent that Dumas was having affairs with a number of women around the country.

The worst part was the names given by Dumas in his phone address book. It wasn't by name, but by location, as if he had ready company wherever he played. Liverpool. Manchester. Newcastle. And the texts these women sent made it clear that he had slept with them. Sometimes they weren't alone. Laura felt that she was learning more than she needed to know about the sex life of a footballer.

'How do we know these people are women?' said a voice. As Laura looked, she saw it was the same person as before, pursuing the gay angle.

Tom gave a small smile. 'My eyes are getting old, but there's no mistaking some of these.'

And then he pressed play on a machine below the television.

'These are all the pictures and video files from his phone.'

The room went silent as the screen lit up with images. Then Laura could hear nervous shuffling as Tom scrolled through them.

'This is Manchester.' And onto the screen came a young brunette, shapely and naked. She was smiling, and it would have looked almost innocent had she not been naked and with her legs open for the camera.

'And this is Newcastle,' and it was much more of the same, except that there were pictures of her with a man, presumably Dumas. 'There's some moving footage of her,' and then Tom flicked onto some grainy footage of a blonde rolling around on a bed, giggling and laughing, enjoying the party.

Then Tom grew serious. 'We have pictures and some movies for every contact in his address book, and we can see the face of every one, and we have a number for every one.' Tom flicked forward to a picture of a naked girl. 'Except for this girl.'

As everyone looked at the image, Laura could sense the tension in the room.

The image was of a naked woman, explicit and sexual, the image just from the shoulders down, her legs open, a sex toy in her hand. Laura guessed she was older than a teenager; her body was well-formed, with good shoulders and strong legs, but she didn't have the spread of a woman in her thirties. The skin was still young and taut; it was obvious that she looked after herself.

'We think these are more of the same woman,' and more images flashed onto the screen. They were all similar, except that sometimes the sex toy was being used, sometimes it wasn't.

Laura thought there was something mechanical about the pictures, compared to the others. The other pictures were of young women having a good time, either posing for the camera or taking part with Dumas. It was a little black book, in digital, and it seemed that Dumas never went lonely. But the headless girl stopped anyone from telling whether she was enjoying it or not, and her poses looked stiff, formal.

'There's some video footage as well,' and Tom forwarded to some more grainy footage.

There were three sets, and it was obvious that this woman did not know she was being filmed. Laura guessed that she wouldn't have said yes to it if Dumas had asked, and that made her different from the rest on the phone.

The first was footage looking down Dumas's body,

at the top of a blonde head, and it was obvious what she was doing, her head moving backwards and forwards in rhythm. It looked like Dumas had grabbed the chance for a memento while her eyes were engaged elsewhere.

The second was another shot down Dumas's body, except this time the woman was facing away from him, on all fours, the rock of her body making it plain to everyone that they were having sex.

The third was less sexual, and it lasted the longest.

It was a shot into a bathroom, and Tom said that it was Dumas's bathroom. It showed a shower cubicle, steam misting up the glass, and inside the shower was a woman. There was just over a minute of a woman standing under the showerhead, washing her hair or rinsing Dumas away.

The steam probably stopped her seeing Dumas with his phone in his hand, but it also stopped everyone else from seeing what she looked like. All Laura could tell was that she was tall, with long hair, light in colour.

Tom switched off the television.

'We think that woman has something to do with Dumas's murder.' He started to pace, sensing how quiet the room had become. 'The posed photographs were sent from a withheld number, the only ones on the phone that were. The movie files taken by Dumas have been given the file names *London 1*, *London 2*, and *London 3*, so we know she's local, but it seems like she has tried to keep her identity secret.'

'Maybe she was shy?' someone said, and everyone laughed, breaking the tension. She didn't seem that shy.

71

Tom shook his head. 'There's something else.' He picked up his piece of paper again. 'We don't know if they're from the same person, but Dumas received a number of texts in the last few days, all from a with-held number.' Tom looked around the room, making sure he had everyone's attention. 'And one of them, sent four days ago, told him to meet her yesterday outside Cafe Boheme on Old Compton Street.'

A murmur spread around the room.

'Does it say why?' asked Laura.

'The nearest hint we get is when he says no at first, and she answers back that either he goes public or she does.'

'With what?'

Tom shrugged. 'If we knew that, we'd be knocking on doors right now. But she says that if he meets her, they might be able to sort it out.'

Laura sighed. Blackmail, she thought. All of this for something as grubby as that.

Tom flicked the television back on. The picture of the naked woman flashed back onto the screen. 'We need to find this woman urgently,' and then he sighed, scratching his head. 'Releasing her picture to the press is going to be tricky, though.'

Laughter rippled around the room.

Tom looked at Laura. 'Your press contact could be crucial. Keep on him, find out what you can.' He looked around. 'Everyone else knows what they have to do.' He raised his eyebrows. 'And as for me, I've got a fiancée to visit.'

NINE

I headed for Canary Wharf. The Docklands Light Railway twisted between the flyovers like a fairground ride, but I was able to avoid it, knowing that what I wanted wouldn't be there.

I'd had a bad night's sleep. My father's phone call kept on waking me up.

No, that wasn't true. It was the thought that I was avoiding him that had kept me awake; keeping a distance left me feeling empty. I remembered how long it had been. In the cold light of morning I wanted to see him. He was all the family I had left. And I thought I had found a way of doing it.

I walked along the Poplar High Street, bright and deserted. There were green spaces, tree-lined pavements, small parks, and quaint English pubs with window boxes and murky interiors.

But it didn't feel quaint. It felt inner-city, with the street filled with local teenagers heading for the Tower Hamlets College, bouncing down an empty street. They were mainly black and Asian, all working hard for a better life. But it was the England flags I saw, hanging over balconies of crumbling flats like a last stand, scared, defiant, seeing a threat that wasn't there, fighting the wrong fight. As I walked along, all the time I could see the towers of Canary Wharf, a glass island, the real threat, the real fight, swamping the skyline.

I was looking for Harry English, newsdesk editor of my old paper, the *London Star*. Even though his paper was based in Canary Wharf, I knew Harry hated it, from the shopping malls underneath the towers to the buzz of suits and smugness. Harry hated seeing neighbourhoods replaced by workplaces, saw it as a modernist scam, Metropolis with added latté.

I knew what he meant. It didn't peter out, like most centres of commerce. It stopped abruptly as soon as it crossed into West India Quay, like it was scared of going into the real East End.

I turned quickly into a small back street just off the Poplar High Street and went into the Poplar Diner, a formica cafe serving full English all day, grease and fat at no extra cost. Dirty windows and a faded sign kept tourists away, although not many ventured into Tower Hamlets anyway.

As soon as I walked in, I saw Harry English. He was hard to miss. Six feet tall and twenty stone, the cafe slipped into darkness for a second whenever he came in through the door. He had been in London all his life, and I could see the pace and the fumes etched into his sallow skin. He ate in the Poplar Diner to avoid the chrome tables near his office. The Poplar Diner kept him in touch, or so he thought, and to edit the *London Star* he had to stay in touch.

I sat down next to him. There were newspapers spread all over the table, Harry checking how the previous day had gone. Every paper led with the Dumas shooting. Before I could say anything, he said, 'We've got a full paper this week, so it will have to be good.'

I ordered a coffee to let him know I was there for a while. I only got one choice: milk or no milk.

'How are you, Harry?' I looked at his plate. Full English. I could guess the answer. 'Didn't fancy a croissant and Americano?'

He looked at me. His eyes were yellow, nicotine and dark clubs reflected back. 'You're not here for my health.'

I thought I heard a cough. I looked around Harry and groaned. It was Dan Jones, a small man with a big attitude from the sports desk. I hoped he heard the groan. I smiled at him, but it wasn't meant to reach the eyes.

'Still writing nil–nil every Saturday, Dan?'

Dan looked shocked so Harry stepped into the pause.

'What do you want, Jack?' he said tersely. I knew what it meant: he liked me but don't annoy his staff.

'I fancy a slow down for a few days,' I said, nonplussed, 'and so I wondered whether you'd want a feature from me.'

Harry wiped his mouth on a napkin. 'What have you got?'

'An angle on the Dumas shooting.'

Harry coughed. 'Everyone's got an angle. Have you seen today's paper? There isn't a page left for regular news. One shooting, and the people want it, bullet by bullet.'

'And you give it to them, Harry. C'mon, it's a big story, the biggest human drama since Jill Dando.'

'Don't I know it. I've had all the C-listers on the phone, trying to get their remorse onto the pages.'

'Yeah, but it's not just another shooting.' It was Dan, his voice back. 'I knew Henri Dumas. He was a good man.'

'Yeah, you knew him,' I interrupted, 'but I'll put ten quid on the table now that you won't get a funeral invite.'

Harry tried not to smile, the corners of his mouth taking a small flick upwards. 'What's the feature, Jack?' he asked.

I turned to Harry and said, 'I just got to thinking last night how this shooting might be playing on a few players' minds, you know, like it could have been them. It has made them vulnerable. Fame is an exposed and lonely place.'

Harry nodded. 'Go on.'

'Which sports star in England sells the most magazines?'

'You know who it is: David Watts.'

I nodded. 'Just like I thought. And a feature in your Sunday magazine about David Watts and the shooting will shift some units. The private effect on a public man. It will humanise the shooting and the footballers, make it more of a personal tragedy than a shock story.'

I heard Dan laugh. 'What makes you think you can get under David's skin?' he said. 'I've met him a few times. You've got to get to know him first.'

'So the feature is worth a shot?'

Dan stopped laughing.

Harry lit a cigarette and then said, 'Dan's got a point. You don't know him.'

'I know him better than you might think,' I said. 'David Watts, the private man, I mean.'

'How so?'

I took a breath. This was it. The final pitch.

'We're from the same small town in Lancashire,' I said, and then shrugged. 'I don't know David Watts, but I know people who knew him really well. And these are real people, not football groupies.' My eyes glanced at Dan when I said it.

'What, Turners Fold?' said Dan dismissively. 'A dead-end mill town full of cousin-fuckers.'

'Turners Fold, Lancashire,' I continued, ignoring Dan. 'He was the local football star who went to a World Cup. He's a local hero. Anything he does makes the local front pages. I don't know David Watts, I'll admit that. We're no blood brothers or secret cousins or anything. But his family are well-known around town, and he's only a few years younger than me. We learnt to smoke in the same places, rode across the same fields, went to school discos in the same school hall. Even played football in the same school strip. If you want the real David Watts, you'll need to go to Turners Fold.'

Harry let smoke trickle over his lip. 'Do you think you can get enough on him in the next couple of days to go into an interview with him?'

I nodded, trying not to smile.

'Exclusive?'

I nodded again. 'If you'll run it, it's all yours.'

Harry smoked some more. 'Okay, Jack. Get under his skin. Let's have the hometown David Watts. Let him know where you're coming from and see if he'll open up.' He turned to Dan. 'And you lend Jack your biographies and contact numbers.'

I looked at Dan. I thought he was going to hit me. His kiss-ass breakfast was blown away. He wiped his mouth, threw his napkin onto the counter, and headed off to the toilet. I wrote my email address on it.

I watched him go, and as soon as the door closed, I leant into Harry.

'There's something else, Harry, now that your monkey's gone.'

He looked at me, his curiosity piqued, his fork going down for the first time.

'I've got a good contact in the murder squad for Dumas,' I said. 'She's willing to feed me with information provided that I do the same for her.'

'What have you got for her?'

'That depends on you.'

'Go on.'

'The police need to know about Dumas's private life, and not the shit you print. The real private life. Does he have any dark secrets?'

Harry laughed. 'They all have dark secrets. Most are just thick kids with good feet when they first start out. We would have won the World Cup five times over if they could learn to stay in a bit more.'

'But what about Dumas?'

78

'What's in it for the *Star*?'

'I'll feed you what I get, if you can find things out for me. Just don't tell little Dan, because he'll worry about Dumas's memory being tainted.'

'Leave that little prick to me.' He paused, and then thought about the little things he had heard. 'There was one thing. He was a randy little bastard, and she was about the same. It just seemed like it was never with each other. And that's the trouble with these footballers. Have you ever met a footballer's wife or girlfriend?'

I shook my head.

'The most ruthless set of bitches you'll ever meet. They target their man, and they get him, and then every pound that goes with him. They talk dirty, act dirty, promise dirty, and they look as good as any young man could want.' He shook his head. 'The poor bastards never stand a chance.'

'But it was different for Dumas,' I said. 'His fiancée was already famous when they got engaged.'

'And a hell of a lot more famous afterwards. I reckon she locked onto his career value, and he couldn't find a way out of it.'

'Anything else about him? Any darker secrets?'

Harry shook his head. 'I'll ask around and let you know if I hear anything.'

I thanked him and stood up to go. I had what I'd gone there for.

Harry's voice stopped me. 'One more thing, Jack.'

I turned around and I saw Harry had a slight smile just creasing his cheeks.

'Yeah?'

'You speak to whoever you think will give you the best story, but keep in mind that we want it quick. We'll be back to tits and bingo after the weekend.'

I nodded gravely, thanking Harry, and then left the Poplar Diner, stepping back into London. Yesterday, the city had lost one of its sons. Now I was going back to Lancashire. More than that, I was going home.

Then I remembered Laura, and I remembered the thrill of her from the night before. It seemed flatter now, a good sleep and then the morning casting a different light over how I felt. My father had taken the shine out of that. And I realised now how little I could help her. I had made contact with the people I could trust to help me, but all I could do was wait. I looked at my phone. Three missed calls.

I would give her a call when I got home, just to let her know that I would get in touch if I heard anything. I would keep plugging, just for her, but I wondered whether my moment had slipped by. There wasn't much to tell her, and now I was writing a different story.

TEN

She was strumming her fingers on the steering wheel as she entered Manchester, drumrolling to the thoughts racing through her head, the images of Dumas as he died, of the two people in the flat. She had stayed in a motel, some chain place just off the motorway, but her sleep had been broken, angry, woken by jolts whenever she fell asleep. She had asked to view the flat alone. They had insisted.

She closed her eyes for a moment, tried to focus, muttered to herself, took some deep breaths and tried to calm herself down. She talked to herself some more, and when she spoke, she felt the panic retreat.

She leant back in the car seat, stuck at a red light by the Manchester Arena, the railway bridge coming out of Victoria the shadow on her horizon, red and gold, the Victorian north. She could see the shadows of Deansgate gathering in front of her, cars bunching, getting busier, with the new steel and glass of Manchester ahead, the rebuilding after the bomb, modern and dynamic, sharp angles shining light behind the dark stone of the cathedral. In her mirror, she could see Strangeways, the Manchester prison.

She moved on when she got the green and then the sun disappeared as she drove between the tight buildings of Deansgate. It went out altogether as she pulled into a car park below an apartment building. The wind was no longer in her ears, no more of the city sounds. Now it was dark and full of echoes, with the sound of her warm tyres screeching on the dry concrete.

She pulled into a parking bay, her stomach taking a roll when she saw the Porsche, his mid-life crisis. She thought she heard someone laugh. She gritted her teeth, knew not to look behind.

She did a slow count to ten, then stepped out of the car, her bag swinging, playing the part, and took the lift into the lobby.

As she stepped out, the security guard gave her a nod, a look of recognition.

She made it to the lift that led to the apartments, not wanting to talk, the silence almost crushing her, her breaths bouncing around the walls. Ten floors up, almost as high as she could go, she stepped out and paused outside his door. She took another deep breath and screwed up her eyes to keep the voices away.

She went into the apartment slowly, using the spare key she'd coaxed out of him, peering round, working out where he was. She could hear the shower running.

She saw *The Times* on a chair. She turned away. She'd read all she could about the shooting. No one had mentioned the chain yet. Not even on the television.

Maybe she had pushed it too far in? Maybe they didn't understand it? She would have to do something about that.

She walked quietly into the bedroom. She could hear singing coming out of the bathroom just off to its right, out-of-tune opera, and through the steam she could see him, a middle-aged divorced accountant happy to believe that she was interested in him.

She tried to slow down her breathing. She had been waiting for this moment, ever since that first time, when she had met him in a bar near the courts, when he had bragged to her where he lived, in the plush new high-rise with a central location and a view right into the city bustle. She had been trying to find a location for part of her plan when she realised that the answer was in front of her, bragging to her, chatting her up. She had smiled back, her eyes full of promise, and when she had seen the view out of the window, she had known it was perfect. Since then, it had just been a matter of keeping him interested.

She pulled back the shower curtain quickly.

He jumped back, gasping in shock, covering himself with his hands. When he saw who it was, he laughed, splashing water at her.

'Hey sweetness, you're early.'

She raised a smile. 'I like surprises.' She turned away. 'I'm going to get a drink. You joining me?'

She left the bathroom and went to the living room. Modern and minimalist. Cream carpets, black chairs, big windows, and a view to die for. The irony almost made her laugh.

She went to the drinks cabinet and poured two vodkas. She would need hers.

She walked to the window. The apartment was on the corner of the building, all modern steel, the signs of Manchester coming up, balconies all around. The site of the IRA bomb was just at the end of the street, and what it had blown away had been replaced by optimism, by a new start. What had survived had been the old buildings, the grand Victorian buildings, solid in stone, the people below scurrying between them, all busy and small, St Ann's Square as thriving as ever. The city was growing in front of her, a different place to the Manchester she had visited as a child.

She was looking down, thinking about the city, when she felt him approach her from behind, in a dressing gown, his passion pressing into her. He murmured in her ear, nibbling at her, pushing against her.

'It's good to see you again,' he whispered, his breaths short and hot.

She stared down at the sunlight as it glanced off the roofs below. His hands made their way up her stomach. 'Hey, slow down. We've got all day.' She felt cold inside.

He began to fumble with her shirt buttons. 'I can't wait all day.'

He pulled her close, breathing hard into her neck.

Not long now, she told herself. Keep calm. Not long.

Bob Garrett was in the Sunshine Cafe, a quiet breakfast place on the edge of the town triangle, in the shadow of the town hall and the Horrocks clock. Bright vinyl seats gave the colour, red and dated, either bolted to the floor against the counter or in rows against sparkling white tables. The counter ran in front of the large windows, so it attracted the biker crowd, summer afternoons a parade of leather and chrome. During the week it was labourers and workmen looking for a good start to the day, or the retired and out-of-work looking to waste an hour with cheap coffee. Art deco pink tiles made it stand out, giving it the feel of the sixties. It served up honest food while the rest of the country marched under golden arches.

Bob was just coming off his night shift, making his way through sausage and fried bread, eggs and bacon, draining his tea. He looked up and smiled at the waitress as she sauntered over to wipe a table. She was pretty and young, but her face was getting hard, council-house blonde, too many rings on her fingers.

As she reached him, she smiled, nodding back towards the television in the background. 'I saw that last night,' she said. 'Sounds pretty bad?'

He nodded thoughtfully, chewing. 'It is.'

'Do you think they'll catch him?'

He smiled at that, infectious innocence.

'I hope so, but it's a big city down there.'

She wandered back to the counter. 'I went to London once. Bloody crazy place. Why would anyone want to spend all day rushing around? No one speaks, no one smiles. Not much please, thank you, goodbye.' She wandered back. 'Glad I stayed in the Fold.'

'The best breakfast this side of Pendle Hill.'

At that, she sighed. 'I'd always hoped for more.'

He turned back to his breakfast. He couldn't provide an answer for that.

He was halfway through his next mouthful when he felt someone's hand on his shoulder. He looked round and saw Jim Smith, one of his drinking partners from the Swan.

'You're out early.'

'Peggy's in one of her tidying moods. One of the problems with retirement. You spend all day with the person you went to work to avoid.' He looked at the counter. 'Same as Bob, flower.'

The order was shouted towards the kitchen, where the cook's hands could be seen through a serving hatch, breaking eggs and flipping bacon.

'No food at home, Bob?'

He shook his head, his mouth full of food, and then dabbed a napkin to his mouth. 'If I feel like a treat, I eat out.'

'Busy night?'

He sighed. 'Couple of drink drivers and some kids growing up on White Lightning. Apart from that, nothing.'

Jim puffed as he shuffled his large frame along the vinyl bench opposite Bob, and then pointed at the television. 'Makes me mad the more I think about that. He must have been up to something. Too much money on an empty head, and this is what you get. Football has turned to shite.'

Bob didn't say anything. It had been a few years since he had cared about football. It had been his life once, but things had happened to change that.

'Anything new yet?' Jim continued.

Bob shook his head. 'They just keep on talking until they catch somebody.'

Jim rearranged his trousers, and then asked, 'Nothing on the police grapevine? No rumours from London?'

Bob laughed. 'I keep off the police grapevine; it's usually full of shit. But they'll get somebody. They always do, with crimes like that.' He looked at Jim. 'It's going to happen again.'

Jim was about to answer, but he was cut short when a plate of fried food landed on the table in front of him, so Bob slid off his seat, tossed his napkin onto his plate, and smiled at the waitress. He patted Jim on the shoulder and went to leave. 'See you around, big man. I need to sleep.'

'Yeah, get some beauty sleep,' came the reply, mumbled through a mouthful of food.

The bell over the door tinkled as he went back outside. The sun was sharp but the streets were virtually empty. He saw a couple of tracksuits heading for the Fold's only solicitor's office, he guessed for a lift to court. A couple of old chaps, brown trousers, were heading for the greengrocer's, hoping for the best of the early fruit. The butcher's shop rolled out its red awning. The charity shop moved a rail of old clothes onto the pavement.

Another ordinary day in Turners Fold.

ELEVEN

In an apartment high above the streets of Manchester, she was at work.

They were in the bedroom, naked, white curtains keeping the room in a softer version of daylight. She was kissing his shoulder as she straddled him, her hand gripping his neck slightly, her urgency mistaken for passion. His arms were stretched out, his wrists tied to the steel bedstead with two of his own silk ties. His short breaths were loud in her ear, his forehead glistening with sweat.

She turned her head to whisper, 'I've got something for you.'

He slowed down and opened his eyes.. 'You're doing pretty well.'

Her hand stroked his hair. 'No, something else.'

He smiled dreamily. 'Will I like it?'

She smiled back, still rocking gently. 'I think so.'

He closed his eyes. 'It feels like a yes.'

She smiled again and pulled herself off him. 'Keep your eyes closed.'

He nodded and lay back. The bedstead clanged against the wall.

She walked over to the corner of the room and knelt down to her bag. She looked round and saw him looking over. His legs were pale and blotchy, his paunch like a basketball in his lap.

'Eyes closed,' she scolded, schoolteacher style.

He grinned and did as he was told.

She rummaged in the bag, her eyes on him all the time. When her hands locked onto the silk scarf, she smiled. She could hear deep breaths, expectant, waiting. She didn't know if they were his or hers.

She stood up and turned round, her hand behind her back. He looked at her, up and down. She knew she was framed against the window, the light outside shadowing her eyes. There was just an outline of her body, long and slender. He settled back, his eyes closed again, smiling.

She walked over slowly, feeling the carpet give way under her feet. He was grinning now. The voices in her head got faster, louder. She stood naked next to the bed, the scarf held behind her back, her chin trembling with tears. He had his tongue on his lip, expectant.

She straddled him again, felt a tear run down her face as they joined together. She stretched herself out, buried her face in his neck, her arms behind his head, rocking gently. She could feel the rise and fall of his hips, could hear his pleasure, light gasps in her ear.

She sat back up again and held out the scarf, one end in each hand. She watched his face, his pleasure, and then she leant forward to wrap the scarf gently around his neck.

He opened his eyes, stopped moving for a moment.

She pulled the scarf tight, just so that it made the skin pinch. The voices in her head were screaming, 'Now, now, now.' She tried out a smile and rocked faster. He understood.

His breaths got shorter as he rocked with her. She closed her eyes, screwed them tight. He pushed harder, so she pulled harder on the scarf. He was gasping, half-pain, half-pleasure. She began to cry, soft sobs, felt his legs go taut, his breaths coming fast. She pulled tighter. His chest puffed out, his eyes open, his teeth bared, his face red, searching for the air as he pushed. She put her head up and wailed. He put his head back, moaned, smiled.

She pulled tight on the scarf, felt him rise beneath her, then again. She leant forward, kept her hands on the scarf, gritted her teeth, pulled it hard. He gasped. There was nothing there. She started to cry out loud, rocking faster, pulling tighter. His eyes were wide open now, his face blood-red. He gagged. His chest puffed out, wouldn't go back in. The bed started to crash against the wall as his arms pulled at the ties. Confusion mixed with passion mixed with fear, they all ran across his eyes, his body pushed out to meet hers. She kept on rocking, backwards, forwards, screaming at the noise in her head.

He started to struggle but he had no air left for the fight. Her hands were red, her fingers white as she pulled, and then he started to shake. He bucked hard beneath her but she still held on tight, her tears running onto his shoulder. She held him tight until he stopped shaking, the voices getting quieter now.

As the room fell still, she was aware of the silence.

The security guard nodded and smiled as he listened, and then he put the phone down. He shook his head. People can't even have a noisy fuck these days without someone complaining.

He came out from behind his desk. He'd just make sure everyone was okay, and then he could get back to his newspaper.

She didn't hear the door buzzer at first.

She was in the shower, her head in her hands, the water pounding her legs. Then the buzzer went again and she pulled her head up, startled.

She pulled the curtain back and saw him there, lying back on the bed, dead. The scarf was still around his neck, a gold neck-chain across his chest. She could see the medallion, the words 'Rath Dé Ort EW' etched across it. She took a heavy breath. Stay focused, stay sharp, think of the end.

The buzzer went again, this time for longer. She moved her head to the sound and stepped out onto the floor. She crept out of the bathroom, through the bedroom, and went towards the door. As she got nearer, she heard a cough, nervous, embarrassed. She pressed her eye to the peephole and saw a fisheye view of the security guard. She pulled her eye away, worried, thinking back to the noise of the bed. Had one of the neighbours called the police? She put her head to the door. She saw him looking around, bored.

She pulled away from the door. She looked down at herself, wet and naked.

'Who is it?' she shouted, trying to calm her nerves, not knowing what she would do if things went wrong. This hadn't been in the plan.

There was a pause, and then, 'It's Carl, miss, from downstairs. Someone called me, saying they were worried about the noises.'

'Why? What's the problem?'

'Are you both okay, miss? I just need to check you're all right. Would you open the door please?'

'Hang on.'

She looked around for her bag. She saw it by the window. She ran over and found a handgun. It felt cold, like it had no memory of what it had done the day before. She went back to the door. As she looked through the peephole, Carl was pacing around.

She put the gun flat against the door, and with her other hand she put on the chain and opened the door slowly. She put wet hair and a bare shoulder into view.

She saw him step back slightly. He looked apologetic. 'I'm sorry, but someone said they heard someone choking and gasping, like they were having a heart attack or something.'

She blinked, and then caught herself. She put more of her body into the open door, felt her hand tighten around the gun. Her left leg was showing and most of her shoulders and breast. He stared down, taking in the view, couldn't stop himself.

'It's okay. We were, well, you know, it's been a while.' Her eyes were all mischief, her face mock-innocent.

He looked back up and blushed. 'Okay, thanks. I'm sorry.'

She grinned. 'Everything's fine. Thanks for your concern.'

He held up his hand in apology and turned away. Her grin turned off like a light.

She watched him go and then closed the door quietly. She leant back on the door and heaved a big sigh, her heart beating hard. She looked at her hand. The gun was trembling. That wouldn't help.

She stayed like that for a few minutes, the water running down her body and gathering around her feet. Once she'd recomposed herself, she looked over to the window. Her rifle was in the bag. All she had to do was set it up and get the sights trained. And then wait.

The billow of the curtains as the wind blew through made her twitch. A laugh came from somewhere. She spun around. She told herself to stay calm. She knew she had to get this done right. The element of surprise would be lost this time. She had to fire the shot and get out within three minutes. That would give her enough time to get to the lift and get off at the second floor, then take the service stairs to the garage in the basement. She'd done the run many times, practice runs when she'd had the apartment to herself. No need to rush, just fire the shot, dismantle the rifle, and get out. Walk down the hall like she was going out for milk and leave.

She peeled herself off the door and walked back to the bedroom, her wet feet making footprints on the light carpet, lighting up her trail back to the bedroom.

She had work to do.

Johnny Nixon, tough defender, pride of the Manchester blues.

He wasn't feeling good about himself. He looked around, twitchy, nervous.

He was on the corner of St Ann's Square. The street was busy around him. There were people streaming in and out of Marks and Spencer just across the road, and in the square behind him bank workers and lawyers strolled around, peacock struts, enjoying the rush, the vibe, summer in the city.

His chest felt tight. He knew it was his own fault, but it was always his fault. He had a beautiful wife and three beautiful children. So why did he always stray when he got away from home? He knew he had a self-destruct button. It had plagued him throughout his career, from the over-the-top tackles – and there had been too many – to the fights in bars. He had always seemed like he was trying to wreck his career.

And now this. A one-night stand turned into an affair. It was sporadic, igniting itself every few weeks, but it had grown into a habit. He had tried to break it, but she had said it was her or the media. His wife would find out anyway, so why not get some happiness out of it?

He looked around, pretending to talk into his phone. It was what all footballers did. Talked into a phone, just to stop people from talking to them. But the phone was where his trouble had begun. Meet him or she goes public; text messages telling him what to do.

He'd had no choice. At least this way he might be able to talk her out of it.

He spun around, looking for her, hoping no one else had seen him. This wasn't a time for photographs.

He heard a crack, and then it hit him in the head like a hammer blow.

As he went to the floor he saw faces. People on the street, twitching from the noise, eyes wide. Then he saw his children, smiling at him, laughing with him. His wife. The warm smell of her body. They rushed through his head as he saw the pavement get nearer, all the time getting darker.

The world had already turned black by the time his head hit the floor.

TWELVE

It was late afternoon before I arrived in Turners Fold.

I was surprised at how nothing had changed, like it had a different time-frame, existing in a bubble; like driving around a photograph album, sepia print, reminders of why I'd had to leave.

I entered the Fold the usual way. There were just two ways in, from the north and from the south. All the roads that headed for the hills either turned into tracks or turned back on themselves. Pre-war bay fronts were at the entrance to the town, and then came the terraces. But these weren't the narrow two-storey strips found nearer to the centre of town, the old mill-workers terraces with doors right onto the street. These were much grander, three storeys high, with neat gardens at the front protected by low stone walls. They gave way eventually to shops, but they were tiny affairs, crammed into Victorian fronts with stone-edged door frames, the insides dark and uninviting.

There was grey as far as I could see, lines and lines of it, the severe stripes brightened only by the fake red of suburbia as new developments filled the gaps left behind by derelict industry. I dodged slow drivers and bolting dogs for half a mile and then passed my old high school. I gave a look left. I always did when I passed it, the sign by the entrance announcing what it was, the view over the town reminding me why I had to get away.

I saw a flash of the sports fields just behind. There was a football field, goals warped and irregular, and beyond that there was a cricket pitch, really just a rectangle of short grass protected by a rope, surrounded by benches framed against the rising hills. That would be a good place to get a picture, and so I made a mental note to call back early in the morning, when the light would be sharp blue. It was where the career of David Watts had started, where he had dominated the school league and ended up signing for Burnley before making the trip to the south. From then on it had been millionaire and superstar.

I shrugged off my school memories when I drove into the town triangle. I pulled over at Jake's and stepped out of the car, feeling the Pennine breeze on my face for the first time since Christmas. The air felt clean, like it was coming in straight off the craggy tops, packed full with chill. It didn't have that urban warmth of London, where the air was sodden with smoke and fumes. I'd forgotten what it was like, this clarity, this purity.

I looked up at Jake's Store and smiled.

Jake's had been there as long as there'd been Turners Fold, or at least that's how it seemed. It had an old wooden frame around the front, painted blue, casting shadows over the windows, making it impossible to see in. The front had been painted many times, the wood now bending with age and the effects of the sun, when it came, so the paint had chipped and flaked and pointed jagged fingers.

As I walked towards it, I could hear the sound of a brush on the old tiled floor drifting out to the street, like it always did when trade slackened off.

I turned as I heard a car rumble over the cobbles running alongside the town hall. It was an old Mondeo, windows down, someone from my old school at the wheel. His arm rested lazily out of the window as he drove slowly along, tapping lightly to the beat of his radio. Robbie Williams swirled around the square and washed over me like cleanser, the simple pop anthem a change from the usual club-land thump that seemed to bang out of every bar in London. The music matched the slow crunch of the tyres as I watched them roll away.

I walked into Jake's. The shop was dark and shaded, so it took my eyes a couple of seconds to adjust, and when they did I saw Jake by his broom, nodding his head and smiling.

'Well, look who it is,' he chuckled. 'Jack Garrett. You tired of old London town?'

I grinned and held out my hand. Jake took it and gave it a gentle shake. His fingers felt old and brittle in mine. His skin was soft and cold, and I could feel the thinness of the skin. He looked bonier than I remembered, and he seemed to be stooping more than he used to. His skin just didn't fit as tight these days.

'I think London's tired of me,' I replied, laughing. 'How are you, Jake?'

He skimmed the brush across the floor absent-mindedly. 'I'm fine, Jack. The winters get colder and the summers make me want to sleep, but I feel fine.'

'How's Martha? Is she still working?'

'Oh, she's still with the police. They tried to retire her a couple of years ago, when she got to sixty, but the inspector talked the big shirts around. She mans the front desk now, checking for forged car insurance.'

'And looking out for my father?'

He cocked his head. 'And some of that.'

Martha, Jake's wife, had worked for the police for as long as my father had been in the service. Her title was now a Civilian Support Officer, but in a small place like Turners Fold, it had always seemed like she was the station mother. She used to man the radio, draw up the shift roster, kept the station running properly. She did it so well that no one noticed, but when it was all centralised and taken out of the Fold, things never went as smoothly again. Ask any police officer who they treasured most at the station, and they would all reply Martha, because she looked after everyone. When she was in charge of things, if a young officer had a baby he didn't get a night shift for the first year. Martha made sure of that. Things had changed now, but people remember.

'You here to see your dad?' asked Jake.

I shook my head. 'He doesn't know I'm here. I'm here for work.'

He gave a small laugh. 'You won't find much around here.'

'No, no, I'm here for a story, connected with the Henri Dumas shooting, the footballer.'

He looked surprised for a moment, and then glanced out of the window. 'The world is going crazy. And now Nixon as well.'

I felt my stomach turn. 'What do you mean, "Nixon"?' I asked, my head already telling me the answer.

Jake looked surprised. 'Haven't you heard the news?'

I gave a thin smile and shook my head. I'd had the radio on for the first part of the journey, the stop–start crawl out of London, but once I got onto the motorway, flying through grey and green emptiness, I needed more lift, so I did the last hundred miles with the CD player on.

Jake stood up straight and flicked his brush across the floor again. 'Same as Dumas. Johnny Nixon, stood on the corner of a street in Manchester.'

I leant against the counter. If this was just some nutcase, it was a well-organised nutcase. Two cities a couple of hundred miles apart.

Jake snapped me from my thoughts by asking what I wanted. I looked around the shop at a loss. I couldn't remember. Maybe I had just wanted to say hello. He smiled at that and told me that was free. Everything else in the shop had a label on it.

Then I thought of something.

'I'm going home next. Does he still have a sweet tooth?'

Jake smiled and nodded to a shelf at the back of the shop. 'Army and navy.'

'Okay. I'll take some of those. Is it ounces or grams in here?'

He tapped his nose like it was a secret. 'For you it can be ounces, but don't tell everyone.'

He walked to the back of the shop, slow and deliberate, and then said over his shoulder, 'He'll miss you when you go back.'

Jake's comment halted me for a second, made my throat catch. 'Oh, he'll survive,' I said glibly. I paused then, realising that I didn't know what my father did with his time. What did he do when he went home to that empty house?

Jake sensed my thoughts. 'He spends most nights in the Swan.'

I felt a kick of guilt, thinking of my father with just a pub and his job to keep him company. Then I thought of how he could have called me. I would have come up, if he'd asked. He never had.

I paid Jake for the sweets and went outside, leaving him with a promise that I'd call back before I returned to London. Then I went for a walk round the triangle.

I knew where I was headed: the *Valley Post*, the start of my career.

Laura looked out of the window of Dumas's home.

It was a tall Georgian house with pillars, bright white, part of a sweeping crescent, overlooking a small patch of green. This would normally be a quiet street, apart from the purr of Ferraris. It wasn't quiet today, she thought, the street outside packed with reporters and cameras. They were kept back by two policemen, the line broken periodically by the delivery of flowers, the pavement outside now bright with colour and cards.

Tom was upstairs with two other detectives, going through drawers and cupboards, looking for any hint of a secret life. Laura had been left downstairs with the grieving fiancée.

There weren't too many signs of grief. Anger was the first emotion Laura had detected, as if a major business deal had been lost. She had dressed all in black for the flight back, but it was designer T-shirt and jeans, a Mets cap and shades shielding her face. For the last thirty minutes she had been on the other side of a glass door talking into a phone. Laura guessed that she was working out how to use all the angles.

Maybe when she was on her own, she would begin to think about the man she had lost, but Laura wasn't sure about that. It seemed like their life together had been more about what they were rather than who they were.

Laura sighed. She was being too harsh on her, she knew that. Laura didn't know what it was like to live with the press writing up her every move. And let's not forget the obsessives, those fans who want more than a smile or an autograph. Being good-looking and famous had a pretty high death rate.

Then Laura noticed activity in the press camp. They were talking into phones, getting their cameras ready. She went out of the room and looked up the stairs. She could hear Tom on the phone, talking quietly.

When he started to come down the stairs towards her, she couldn't tell if the look in his eyes was anger or relief.

'There's been another shooting,' he said. 'In Manchester. Johnny Nixon.'

Laura was shocked. 'Definitely connected?'

'Shot in the street from a distance.'

They would lose it now, Laura knew. It would go to a much bigger task force.

Then she realised why Tom looked relieved.

As she went back into the room, she saw Dumas's fiancée still on the phone. She would have to share the limelight now. Laura sensed that would be the biggest blow of all.

THIRTEEN

I kept on walking, away from the triangle to the buildings just behind, to the *Valley Post* premises. It had been stone-built for the Wesleyan Society but then taken over by the Weavers Union, with church windows and steps that ran to the first floor, so that the ground floor seemed more like a basement. Wooden beams ran along the ceiling, and the ground floor still had the original York stone flags, thick and grey. It used to be in most of the houses, but if it wasn't ripped out to modernise in the sixties, it was stolen by thieves whenever a house stood empty. The windows had their blinds down on one side. I remembered how the sun caused reflections on the computer screens as it came over to the west in late afternoon.

As I walked into the building, a buzzer went off, set to alert them that someone wanted to place an advert or buy a photograph. After a few seconds, a woman in her early thirties came to the small hatch, and it took a couple of seconds for my face to register.

'Hey, Jack Garrett,' she said eventually, 'what you

doing here? Come to pinch our big stories?'

She was joking, but I sensed it held barbed traces, maybe that I thought I was too big for the Fold. Maybe I did.

'Hi Traci.' She spelled it with an 'i'. 'How's life treating you?'

She tilted her head in a flirt. 'Oh, you know, same as ever. Come to work. Pay for childcare.' She leant forward. 'There's been nothing nice to look at since you left.'

'Maybe you scared them off. Is Tony around?'

She smiled and lifted up the gate on the corner. 'Yeah, where he always is. Come through.'

I went through into the office and had another look at where my career had started. It was open plan, with clusters of desks splitting a big team into lots of smaller ones, the space broken only by large black iron pillars. I glanced over towards my old desk. It didn't look like it had changed much. A few photographs had appeared on the desk, a young child and a dog, but other than that it was as if I had never left. I looked at the desk behind it, and I saw my old mentor, Tony Davies, tapping away on his keyboard. I recognised his head, huddled as it always was in front of the screen, the light from the monitor reflecting back off his baldness.

I nodded Traci away and then walked over to him. He was intent on finishing whatever he was doing, not looking up. It was only when I began to say hello to people as I went, and someone shouted, 'Hey, big shot,' that he looked up. As soon as he saw me, he grinned, that strange lopsided grin, a rugby match costing him his two front teeth many years ago, replaced with false ones, but his smile always looked like he still felt the impact.

He stood up and walked around his desk. I thought he was going to hug me, but he didn't. He just stuck his hand out towards me, and when I shook he squeezed hard until my knuckles crackled.

'Jack Garrett, good to see you.' His deep voice sounded rich in the newsroom, as warm as ever.

I grinned back. 'How you doing, Tony?' I looked down at his jumper. Reindeers in spring. 'Your dress sense hasn't improved.'

He let go of my hand and tugged at his jumper. Maybe he was too old now to care, but he had worn bad jumpers for as long as I'd known him. 'Hey, I like it. And how the hell are you? Sit down.' He gestured towards my old desk.

I sat down in the old swivel chair, the smell and feel all too familiar, taking away my time in London as if I'd never left.

'What are you doing here?' he asked.

'Working. I'm doing a feature on David Watts, because of these football shootings, trying to get the hometown angle. You know, simple northern lad in the big bad city.'

Tony nodded, whistling. 'I can see the angle, but a feature. You must be doing something right.'

I shook my head. 'I just liked the idea of coming home.'

'Well, forget about coming back here because your job's gone.'

'It's been over two years. Even I know that broken hearts mend. Who have they got?'

Tony looked past me and towards the other side of the room.

I looked round and saw someone coming towards me carrying two cups of coffee, a woman, I would guess in her early twenties, eyes concentrating downwards, making sure the coffee didn't spill. Her hair was long and dark, falling in straight lines like a waterfall, running over her shoulders and down her back. Her skin was tanned, and even from a few feet away I could see eyelashes that curled upwards in long black flicks. When she got near the desk, she looked up and saw me, and I saw deep brown eyes twinkle with surprise.

'Sorry, I'm in your seat,' I said, getting up to give her the seat back.

'Alice, this is Jack Garrett. He worked here before you started.'

Alice placed the cups down and smiled. 'I know.'

That made me curious. I moved out of the way to let her take her seat, and I noticed how tall she was. I'm six feet tall, but Alice wasn't much underneath that.

She must have seen me looking quizzical, so she said, 'You went out with my sister.'

I shrugged. 'That narrows it down, but not enough.'

'I'm Alice McDermid.'

My eyes flashed wide and surprised. 'You're Megan's sister?'

Alice grinned now, nodding. I looked her up and down, disbelieving. The last time I'd seen Alice, she was a gangly, clumsy girl not yet in her teens, and I was going out with her older sister.

'It's the Funfest again next month,' she said quietly, her eyes dancing with mischief.

I blushed. I could feel it, my cheeks getting hot.

My first time was with Megan. We'd spent weeks talking about how special it was going to be, but in the end it had happened as an uncomfortable rush in the long grass at the Funfest, the annual Turners Fold fair. The day always ended with a folk festival, and while the town was dancing nearby, we slipped away into the grass at the edge, just where the lights from the stalls and rides wilted into darkness.

'Fiddles and waltzers aren't my thing any more,' I stammered, trying to dismiss her. 'How is Megan?'

'She's got two kids,' she said, nodding at the photograph on the desk, 'and a husband who works in insurance. Other than that, she hasn't changed.' She looked amused again. 'And neither have you.'

I laughed. 'You have. You were all, well . . .'

'All legs and hair?' Alice finished off.

'Yeah, kind of. You've blossomed.'

At that, it was Alice's turn to blush.

I heard Tony cough. It was intentional, an attempt to stop the conversation. I looked round and saw Tony's eyebrows arched, amusement lighting his eyes.

'Anything else I can do for you, Jack? Once you've put Alice down, that is.'

I looked back at Alice, then back at Tony. Then I remembered why I was back in Turners Fold.

'There is something else.'

Tony raised his eyebrows.

'I need to plunder the archives. I haven't got long to submit this, so I just need the quick stuff, you know, the school football results, any articles from around that time, that kind of thing.'

Tony watched me for a while, and then asked, 'How long are you in town for?'

'A couple of days. Deadline is Friday at noon as it's a feature. I'll be trying for an interview with David on Thursday.'

'So who else are you going to speak to?'

I scratched my nose and thought about it, realising that I wasn't really sure. 'I thought I'd start with his football coach, and then go on from there.'

Tony shook his head. 'He died last year. Heart attack. David came back for the funeral.'

I exhaled.

'If you want the stats, get on the internet,' he continued. 'Most of the high school stuff ends up on the web these days, and it will save you some time.'

'And if I want more of the man than the player?' I asked.

'Get round the pubs,' Tony suggested. 'It's the best place to interview people because they're already loosened up. Fame is a seductive drug, so everyone will have some story that's personal to them about David Watts.'

'But what about your archives?'

Tony smiled. 'You can for me, but you know how funny the boss is about the archives. We know where most of his stories are, because other papers call us from time to time wanting an old picture or article.'

I held my hands up in surrender. I remembered my old boss. He was good to work for, but he was very protective of the archived newspapers. They were a history of the town, and he wasn't going to let just anyone spoil them.

I saw Tony snatch a glance at his watch. I spotted the time and I realised that the *Post*'s deadline was approaching. I knew Tony wasn't being rude. The paper had to get out, and that was all that mattered.

'I'll move on,' I said, giving a wave to Tony, nodding and smiling at Alice. 'I'll see you in the morning, to go through some back issues.'

Tony smiled. 'Work late and put yourself about tonight. You might come in tomorrow knowing what you want.'

And with that, I left the *Post* building.

I made it around the triangle and back to my car. I knew I had to go to the old house. At least if I got it out of the way, I could get on with writing my article.

I got in the car and started it up, easing out into the street, no traffic to avoid, and slowly pointed it home.

David Watts was still at home when Johnny Nixon was shot, tuned into BBC News 24, waiting for the latest from the Dumas shooting. The apartment seemed quiet with Emma on the other side of the Atlantic some- where. The traffic from Chelsea Bridge crept in through the open balcony door, mixed in with the sounds of the river cruises, but it didn't disturb the calm.

He'd been for a run earlier in the day, but it had been a different kind of run. He usually ran in a cap,

110

the visor pulled down, just enough to keep the recognition at bay until after he had passed. There had been no need today. He had noticed people staring, maybe wondering what he was thinking, but there had been no shouts or catcalls.

He had returned to the apartment, hoping it would be a respite, but he had become fidgety. The newsflash about Johnny Nixon stopped the fidgeting with a slam. Now he was sitting bolt upright on the sofa, the apartment shielded from the rest of the world by drawn blinds, watching the television news for updates.

Not much was coming through. He'd sat through repeated shots of the scene, now just crime-scene tape and litter.

David got up to pace around the room.

He knew there was no connection between Henri Dumas and Johnny Nixon. Dumas had been a clean-cut guy from Paris, urban and sophisticated. Nixon had been from Leeds, and even the transfer to Manchester hadn't knocked the inner city out of him. He had played like he had spent all his life, fighting, and David had left games with him bruised and blue more than once. Nixon and Dumas hadn't played together as far as he knew, and were unlikely friends. That made David nervous, because it could only mean one thing: that there was no connection. And that put him at risk. Any footballer who went out in public was at risk of getting his head shot at. And then there could be copycat shootings.

He turned round when he heard a sense of urgency in the broadcaster's voice.

'. . . *and it does seem a breakthrough in the case.*'

He stepped away from the window and sat down.

'Thank you, John. And there you have it: the surprising news that the murderer of Henri Dumas might not be a madman after all, but a madwoman.'

David whistled.

'In the sniper's nest where two bodies were found, both bound, one shot at point-blank range through the head, the other strangled, hairs have been recovered from the tape that bound them. Those hairs are female hairs.'

David took a drink of beer. There were two men on the television. One was tanned and dark, the hair too dark to be natural for a man in his forties, looking warm in a grey suit, whereas the other one was much younger, blonde and relaxed in just a shirt, standing at the scene of the Dumas shooting, mostly back to normal, full of shoppers and ghouls, the cafe the only business still closed, the grey shutters bright with flowers from people Dumas had never met.

'Well, this is turning into quite a story.'

David snapped off the television and walked towards the window. Is that what it was: just a story?

He tried to call his agent but all he got was the answering service. Where was she?

He watched the city beneath him for a few minutes and then turned back into the room. For the first time in his life, he felt powerless. He had always won, no matter what the contest. High-school hero to Premiership superstar. However, all he could do with this one was sit it out, and he hated the sidelines.

FOURTEEN

I sat in the car for a few minutes outside my father's house.

It used to be the family home, when the sash bay-windows were painted pastel-clean and the lawn borders overflowed with colour. The house looked colder now, darker, the paintwork old and listless, flaking in places, the windows dusty and full of shadows.

I hadn't spoken much with my father since I'd been back at Christmas and for a week last summer. He was working mostly, so I just slowed down for a while and then headed back south.

As I sat there, my childhood came rushing back at me. I could sense that freshness of early-morning spring mists that I never got in the city, or the bite of a November wind when it blew into the valley from the north. I saw myself cycling down here, a skinny kid with legs whirring over the pedals, or running and skipping along, kicking autumn leaves. Teenage screams and screeching tyres, the clunk of car doors on a Sunday morning as people went to church, a catholic town. I'd grown from boy to man along this road, and as I sat there it was as if nothing had changed.

But it was changing. People weren't moving in any more. The young families wanted either the bright new boxes or original features. Those who had made their old house move with the times got lost as trends turned back full circle. The neighbours were still the same as before, but were wearing out like the houses. I had passed Bob Coleman outside his front door, watering plants. I remembered him as a large solid man, strong and powerful, callused and blackened hands from hard work. Now he was starting to bend a little, some of his bulk gone, and he moved with more shuffle than before.

I climbed out of my car and felt nervous, like I was expecting a fight. I don't know why. My father and I hadn't parted on bad terms. We'd just parted on no terms, and as I stood there, looking up at the house, I wondered whether he blamed me.

I didn't go to the door. I went to the garage instead. I pulled up the door and smiled as I saw the sunlight blink back off the Calypso Red bonnet of the Triumph Stag, my dad's pride and joy. When I was younger, I would polish it once a month for extra pocket money, and if the weather was good we would go for a drive, the windows down, the radio playing.

But that was a long time ago.

I looked up when I heard a door open into the garage. I saw my father standing there. He didn't say anything at first, just looked at me like I was a stranger. Then he nodded.

'Jack.' That's all he said, but his accent sounded strong, blunt, flat.

'Dad.'

'You all right?'

I nodded. 'Not bad.'

He turned to go into the house. I took that as a sign to follow.

As I walked in, I crinkled my nose at the musty smell. It was like all the bad habits of a man living alone were hanging in the air. I wandered through into the living room, a light and spacious area at the front of the house, south facing, so that the incoming shards of light caught the dust as I moved around the room. I sat down and looked around. Nothing had moved. It was as if I'd only ever gone into town, a short car trip or something, not moved to London. It was tidier than I remembered, but it lacked feminine warmth, those fragrant touches here and there. Johnny Cash album covers were strewn around the corner of the room, my father's special place.

'Do you want a beer?'

I looked round and saw him heading for the fridge. 'Always.'

As he handed me mine, I pointed the bottle towards his clothes. He was in his dressing gown, just shorts and a vest underneath.

'Working nights?'

He looked down. 'You could have been a detective.'

I laughed, couldn't help myself.

We both took a drink, smiled at each other for a while, and then he asked, 'What brings you back here?'

'I've got a deal for a feature on David Watts,' I said.

His eyes flickered, so quick it was hard to see, but just as quick his look turned thoughtful and then he said, 'Is this because of the Dumas shooting?'

'It's Johnny Nixon as well now.'

He looked surprised and went to sit down.

'There's been another one, in Manchester.'

He reached for the remote and I watched him as he flicked around the channels, looking for the news.

'What are they saying?' I asked, even though I could hear.

He watched for a while and then said, 'They're filling. Nothing to say, so they say it over and over, hoping it might turn into something.'

I went and stood behind him. He smelt familiar, like warm sleep. I couldn't place it at first, but then I realised it was the smell of Sunday mornings, when I'd creep into my parents' bed and watch television with my mother until my dad brought her breakfast.

My eyes flicked to the screen and I thought about Johnny Nixon. Thinking aloud, I asked, 'What have they got in common?' When my dad looked round, I pointed at the television. 'Dumas and Nixon? What's the connection?'

He scratched his head. 'Does there have to be one?'

I shrugged. 'You'd expect one. Must be a reason why they both got shot.'

He pointed at the television. 'These things take planning, and two days running, that's a quest for attention. But what if Nixon had stayed at home today? My guess is that he knew they had a routine, somewhere they would always be. Maybe that's the connection.'

I nodded. It was a possible. 'Maybe, but why go all the way to Manchester?'

'Why not? He couldn't stay in London. Too much heat.'

'Okay, that's fine, but why risk making a trail?'

He smiled. 'A ransom.'

I looked at him curiously. 'Ransom? What's the demand?'

He looked back at me shrewdly. 'Whoever he is, however little he thinks his life is worth, he'll shut down football. That's a lot of money. He could just about name his price right now.' He raised his eyebrows. 'And this is a spree. So it will keep going until either he is caught or he kills himself.'

'Does it have to be that way?'

He nodded. 'With a spree, it's always that way.'

Then we heard something that took us both by surprise. They suspected the perpetrator was a woman.

'He's a she,' I said, my eyes wide. 'Shit.'

My dad shook his head, ruffling his hair. 'This is one weird dream. Firstly, you're here, and now this. A woman doing all of this.'

I smiled. 'No, you're awake.'

He tugged on his lip, and then said, 'Changes nothing, though.'

Then something occurred to me. 'She's still making a trail,' I said. 'She started in the south but came up north. Surprise might work at first, but it will be harder the more this thing goes on, so she will want somewhere she knows, so she can get away quickly if it goes wrong. So maybe she's from the north?'

My dad smiled. 'If she wanted a two-day shooting streak, she had to come up north once she'd been through London. A northern player would see it as a London problem and carry on as normal. In London, footballers' routines will have changed immediately.'

That made me quiet. As did the thought that we'd spoken more in the last five minutes than we had in the preceding six months. It had been comfortable, and I found myself wanting to hear more from him, just so I could hear him think.

'Where are you staying?'

I smiled at that. I'd assumed I'd be staying at the house, hadn't considered anywhere else.

He guessed from my smile what I was thinking, and he nodded towards the stairs. 'I haven't moved anything.'

Just then the doorbell rang. My dad didn't look up.

I was about to go to the door when he asked, 'What kind of article are you writing?'

'Just a biography. You know, the hometown boy turned into England's biggest hero.'

'Just that?'

'What else could there be?'

He looked down, and I thought I saw something cross his eyes, just a subtle mood change, but I put it down to tiredness. I knew he hated working nights.

The bell went again, so I turned away from him and went to open the door.

I was surprised to see Alice. She blushed when she saw my dad there, but she turned straight to me.

'Tony thinks it will be good experience for me if I

shadow you. We don't get many big-city feature writers passing through. Is that okay?'

She said it like she thought I might object, as if she had to get the whole request out before I had chance to turn her down. She looked past me. 'Hello, Mr Garrett.'

He nodded. 'Hi, Alice,' and then sensing that I was stalling because he was there, he stood up. 'I'll leave you both to it.'

I watched him go, and then I turned back to Alice. 'Whatever you hear, it's my story,' I said. 'You understand that?'

Alice agreed but looked hurt. 'I'm not doing it to get a by-line. I want to do it so I can get away, like you did.'

'Turners Fold no good for you?'

'Was it for you?'

I didn't have an answer to that.

I sighed. 'I'll go get my file. We'll split the numbers and start making calls. Is that okay?'

'Nothing better.'

She sat in her car on the edge of the town, at a red light by the old Clifton Mill, a scene distant to the buzz of Manchester which she had left not long before. This was quiet, derelict. The mill looked cold and dark, a brick block lined on all sides by windows, five floors of glass a hundred yards long, light for the cotton workers, only now they were either broken or bricked up. She could see strips of housing climbing away from her, blackened millstone, chimneypots, no gardens. A bus, single-decker, went through the lights across her path, all empty seats. The town seemed as quiet as she remembered. But she knew that was deceptive. The road into town stretched in front of her, a slow crawl along the valley floor.

The journey was a haze now. She'd rushed out of Manchester, the flash of speed cameras as she headed for the M60 circular making her paranoid. But she knew it wouldn't matter soon. The radio had been off at the start; she didn't want to hear about the shootings. She'd seen through the sights of the gun what had happened. She had tried to focus on the road, but it had been like a dream sequence, like she hadn't been there. But then her mind would snap back to the scene in the apartment and she would find herself fighting the wheel, the tyres dancing with the tarmac.

The voices had made it harder, like flutters of laughter whenever she was alone, whispered taunts she couldn't really hear. They'd been with her for a long time, but they were getting louder now, more frequent, like the hiss of escaping gas, hard to pin down. She remembered driving past the Lancashire sign, and then it was all blurred images until she saw Turners Fold ahead of her.

When her lights changed to green, she paused for a while, and then she began her crawl into town.

The road took her to the town triangle. As she drove, she passed the old library, some shops in decline, lines of houses with low bay fronts and gardens just a step wide. Some youths walked in a pack, faces hidden by hoods.

In the town triangle, the town hall was lit by flood-lights, the afternoon beginning to fade, the sandstone cleaned up and bright, built with cotton money, Greek pillars shouting a grandness it never had. Most of the shops and businesses around it were closed, so she drove along before stopping at another red light. As she sat there, the warmth of the late sun crept in, but she went cold when she noticed the police station. It was a long grey rectangle with a flat roof, with the white and orange of patrol cars just visible down the side of the building. Some lights were on inside, but it looked quiet.

It was the jolt she had been waiting for, but when it came, it took her by surprise. Her light changed to green but she still sat there, rooted. Just as the lights were about to change again, she slammed her foot hard onto the accelerator and then turned around to drive back through town.

She didn't know where she was headed at first, so she just drove through tight streets, some cobbled, some not, with wedge-end corners and sash windows. It was when she found herself passing the high school that she realised where she was going. Just at the edge of town, before streets became fields, it sat big and brown, sixties in style, dated modernism, flat-roofed prefab, the windows now all in darkness. She stopped the car for a while, let the silence and all those memories drift back in through the open window. She felt the prickle of tears.

She put the car back into gear and turned down a lane running along the side of an old church, the route made narrow by walls covered in moss, the green bright against the grey stones. When she came out of the lane, she saw Pendle Hill in front of her, standing as a dark, giant shadow, the threat over the bright green of the playing fields before it.

She came to a stop, her tyres crunching, the occasional rumble of a distant car the only thing she could hear when she stepped out. Although the voices rushed back in, they were cheering her on, willing her to keep going.

She was by a park. It seemed pathetically small now. Flowerbeds ran up the grass slopes, with a tarmac path running around the top in a crescent. She looked up the hill and felt her stomach tumble. It was there, right at the top, the edges picked out by shadow. The aviary, or so the locals called it. It hadn't housed birds for a long time, the local kids too cruel now, but the name had stuck. It was a local landmark but it was really nothing more than a brick shelter on a concrete base. There was a cenotaph at the bottom of the park, with the names of war dead chiselled into the base, somewhere to sit and reflect. The kids used the aviary at the top of the park to smoke and take girlfriends, making sleazy memories there.

It looked like so much of nothing, but she knew what it meant, what it stood for. She could feel midges dance around her face, felt the season, sensed the dreams of perfect summers.

She stepped onto the grass, felt it sink beneath her feet. She turned in a circle as she walked, letting the surroundings swirl around her, allowing Turners Fold to fade into streaks as the earth began to rise. She slowed down, felt nervous, sick, wanted to turn around and run away, but she had to keep going. This was why she had come, to remind herself.

She stepped onto the path, the edge of the park, and the sudden noise of her footfall was like an electric shock. She looked ahead and saw the aviary, dark, still in shadow. Her breath shortened, a sudden rush of nausea made her sway. She turned around and looked over the town. She could see it all from here: the mill chimneys, the strips of housing, the double-glazed tangle of a new estate eating into fields.

Then she saw someone there, just a shape, standing by the railings, watching her. Her breath caught. She recognised the face, like a distant memory, an old photo, a sunshine smile. A voice whispered at her, a light hiss.

She smiled at the figure and the voice faded. She felt the darkness surround her, the air suddenly cold.

The path was about to run out in front of her so she stopped. She looked down at her shoes, saw the concrete base by her toes. She knew where she was but she felt like she was on the edge of a crevasse, her feet stuck but her body lurching forward. Her head was light, her mouth dry. She looked back to the stars. They were bright and far away.

She took a deep breath, steadied herself, and then stepped forward.

The path gave way to concrete, cold hardness under her feet, and when she refocused she was inside the aviary. She could smell drink and old cigarettes. She looked down. She thought she could see a stain, or were they scuffs in the stone? She looked back and tried again to make out the figure by the railings, but she couldn't focus. She thought she could hear screams, echoes from ten years ago, and they made her clamp her hands over her ears, made the stone shift and move. Shadows fell over the park, blocking out the moon, crushing the sound, until all that was left was the sound of her heartbeat.

She didn't know how long she stayed there. She looked around, realised she could see through the shadows, remembered where she was. She put a hand to her cheeks. They were wet. She looked back to the railing and tried to see who was there. She couldn't see anyone, but she thought she could hear whispers.

She stepped back, stumbling. She looked over to the railings again, her pace quickening. There was no one there.

She wiped her cheeks and ran to her car. She could hear someone laughing, loud and insistent. She jumped in and sped off, her tyres spewing dust, her lights coming on as she approached the top of the lane. Her engine broke the silence until her lights disappeared into the distance as she headed out of town, leaving the park in a growing dusk, the dust from her departure settling again.

FIFTEEN

The next day started like many others, with a cold sun, but I still remember it like it was today.

It started for me in the Sunshine Cafe, looking for my father. He'd eaten there for years, soaking up cholesterol like it was a delicacy. He was by the window, the empty breakfast plate in front of him, a cup of coffee flicking steam into the air. I patted him on the shoulder and sat down. When he looked round he smiled. I was looking for an edge, something not right. I couldn't see anything.

'Hi, Jack. Bit early for you, isn't it?'

'I've got myself some good habits since I went to London,' I said, and waved an order for coffee at the waitress and then turned back to him. 'Did you have a good night?'

I didn't get the answer I expected. When it's warm like this, the true smile of summer, the hoods get artistic or horny, and both mean trouble.

He shook his head, the tiredness showing around his eyes. 'Nothing much going on. I've spent the night driving around.' He drank some coffee. 'What about you? Did you get much done?' He looked down as he asked the question.

'Yeah, not so bad. I have a few contacts for interviews, and I'm going to speak with David's agent later. I'll fill it with tales from the Fold, make it sound like a great place, and then just try and get a good interview with him.'

He looked relieved somehow, although I didn't know why.

'How was Alice?' he asked.

I found myself smiling. Alice had flirted and teased out Watts's titbits and ridden her brush with big-time journalism as hard as she could. I'd tried to tell her that the big city wasn't like that, how every day was a catfight, a nonstop hustle for the best story, but she hadn't cared.

I caught my smile quickly, replaced it with a quiet nod and concentrated on my coffee. 'She did okay.'

'She's a pretty girl.'

That surprised me. I felt caught out, but when I looked at my dad I saw a mischievous twinkle behind the lines around his eyes.

Then he smiled, the twinkle replaced by something I couldn't fathom. Maybe sadness. He drained his coffee. 'Time for me to go. Are you staying out? You look like you've got some reading to do.'

I looked down to the newspapers I had in my hand, all of the national dailies. I wanted to see what they were saying about the shootings. The television had done most of that already – Dumas and Nixon weren't friends, had no connections together, had never played on the same team – but I was a newspaper man, so I wanted to read words, not hear them. I had skimmed the papers on the walk over and they seemed to be saying the same thing. There was talk of Far Eastern gambling syndicates, but that was just rumour. Nixon was old-style, too blood and thunder to throw a game, and Dumas won too many to be a candidate for that.

'I'm checking out the *Post* archive once I've read these, and then I've got a couple of interviews. Do you want me to stay away?'

'No, but I need to sleep. Do what you need to do, but keep the volume down.'

I agreed to that, and then watched as he stepped off his stool, moving slower than I thought he might, just showing the traces of the old man that was waiting for him a few years along. When he went, waving his goodbye to the waitress, I felt alone in there.

She felt the dew rise through her toes as she walked on the grass in front of her house, a glass of juice in her hand. Summer mornings that started like this always turned out to be the best of days. This was the day after Manchester and she hadn't expected it to feel like this, so free, so right. Her hand brushed the damp strands of a willow tree, and she closed her eyes as the leaves trickled over her fingers. The breeze tickled her hair, light and fresh.

She felt herself relax, just for a moment, but then just as fast, like a reminder, her eyes opened, quick and darting. The sounds around her were like soft bliss, but she felt like someone balancing feathers, one quick movement and the calm would all be gone.

She took another drink. She noticed the faint scars on her forearm, like old memories she would rather forget. But she couldn't forget. She remembered well the nights when she was on her own, wrapped up in memories and hurt, dancing the knife across her skin.

She put her glass down and flexed her fingers once more. She had a memory of leaving Manchester, but it was scrambled, like staccato bursts of light and noise, driven by pure adrenalin. It was only when she'd got back home that things became clear again. But she knew the peace in her head wouldn't last.

The grass ran out and she walked up the steps to the house, to the front porch, dark stone framed by trailing roses. She turned and looked down the fields in front of her. They stretched out long and sloped, meadow grass dotted by buttercups, running down to the river a quarter of a mile away. Beyond that lay trees, a buffer between herself and the rest of the county, green as far as she could see. The road through her land snaked up from a stream, a potholed dust-trap running over a metal cattle-grid, her own personal alarm. She always knew when she had visitors because the rumble of tyres over the grid carried along the currents.

She drained her drink and looked down to the old wooden seat, painted soft blue. She saw her phone and her nerves crept back in. That's why she was outside: trying to stay calm for the next part of the plan, the crucial part.

Her eyes caught a movement, a dark shadow moving

across the porch. She looked over quickly, but whoever was there was gone. She turned round at a voice, just a light whisper, but there was no one there.

She took a deep breath and turned back into the shade of the porch. Now was the time. She'd planned it this way. Now was the time.

She reached down and picked up the phone. She felt suddenly nauseous, the phone hot and heavy in her hand. She held it against her chest, heavy breaths, trying to stop her hands from shaking. She looked around. There was still no one there, but she thought she heard movement, saw petals move, a soft brush like a whisper.

She took one last deep breath, looked down at the handset, and then pressed a key to activate a stored number. As she put the phone to her ear, she heard the steady ring. She imagined it ringing in London. It rang four times before the answer machine kicked in.

'Hello, you're through to David Watts. Please leave your message and I'll get back to you. Thank you.'

She clicked the phone off quickly, almost dropping it. Her breaths came fast again and she sat down hard on the floor.

She sat like that for a while, her chest tight, her hands clammy, looking at the floor. She tried to listen to the countryside, to drown out his voice. She opened her eyes to check the sky. She saw birds just circling over the river.

Eventually, calmness returned. And with it came fresh determination.

She pressed redial.

Same as before. Four rings. Answer machine. The tone. She let the silence fill the earpiece, and then put a small electronic box over the mouthpiece. It was a microphone that distorted her voice, picked up from a gadget shop. After a few seconds, she spoke.

'Hi, David.' She said it cold, like it would freeze him the second he heard it. The microphone took the rest of any emotion out, her voice coming out as electronic distortion. 'It's me.'

David was in his apartment, trying to relax after his breakfast. The shooting of Johnny Nixon was still playing with his thoughts: who was doing this?

The telephone rang. He looked over and then decided to ignore it. He had dealt with enough press queries the previous day and he had nothing else to add.

He lay back on the sofa, a cushion over his face. The darkness felt good, silent, the only clear noise his breathing, steady and warm.

The answer machine clicked off and he relaxed. Perhaps if he stayed like that it would all go away?

The telephone rang again. He ignored it again until the answer machine clicked on.

'Hi, David. It's me.'

He paused, the voice strange, electronic distortion.

'Do you recognise my voice?'

He sat up.

'C'mon, David, you must recognise it.'

He was bemused. A new silk to her voice distracted him, soft seduction despite the electronics.

'Think back to your last night in Turners Fold, the last night before you left to be a star.'

His face froze. His mind hurtled back through the

last ten years, back to a balmy night in Lancashire, a mosaic of sad goodbyes, prolonged best wishes.

'*Do you, David? Do you remember me?*'

His face went pale, his mouth went dry. The room around him shrank away. The only thing he could hear was the machine, which came at him clear and crisp, cutting through the sound of a thousand bad dreams rushing at him.

'*Perhaps if I sobbed, David, you'd remember.*' The words were beginning to snap out. '*Do you want me to scream? Would that work? Beg for my life?*'

He felt his stomach turn over. A cold sweat prickled his lips. His chest became tight. He stood over the machine, wanting to pick up the receiver.

The voice continued, softer now.

'*Do you still go down to the old school, throw a few memories around? Do you think about how you hurt me? Do you remember how I looked when you left me, my scarf pulled tight around my neck?*'

He could hear his mind screaming at him to turn it off, but he couldn't. All he could do was stand and listen, his jaw clenched firm, his mouth set hard so that his lips turned pale.

'*Do you ever, David, when you're alone in the dark, just you and your conscience? Have you ever thought about me?*'

He felt powerless, transfixed.

'*No, you haven't, David. I know that, because you didn't even look back.*'

He looked at the ceiling, and it seemed to swirl at him.

'Enough reminiscing, David, it's time to come clean.'

The snap of anger was back. David looked down at the answer machine.

'Get on the TV, David. Tell them what you did. Tell them everything you did.'

His hand was over his mouth, shocked, confused.

'If you do it right, I stop shooting.'

He went pale and sat down hard, felt himself go dizzy.

'That's right, David, it's me. I'm the one doing it, and I'm doing it all for you.'

There was a laugh, but it sounded cold.

'Oh, Christ,' he gasped. 'Jesus fucking Christ.' His eyes were wide and his face was drawn and grey.

'But this is the rub, David. You get on the TV and tell everybody what you did. The truth, the whole truth, and nothing but the truth. You do it right and no more footballers die. But, if you don't do it right, if you try to get yourself out of this jam, I keep on shooting, until the only person left to shoot in football is you.'

David looked back at the machine, numb now, unable to speak.

He put his hand over his face and slumped backwards. The sound of the voice was the only thing in the room now, filling the spaces between the walls so that it felt like they were all coming in on themselves.

'You could tell the police, David. That would stop it. But if they catch me, I'll tell them everything. Would you want that?'

His fingers clenched around his hair.

'This call is being recorded, David, so everyone will

know you had a chance to stop it. Any which way, you're finished. So just do it, David, and you might get lucky.'

The message ended. The silence in the room felt like it was loaded, a barrier, not a gap.

He looked at the machine, and then down at his hands. He was shaking.

When she clicked off the phone she felt the swish of the willow tree replace the dead air of London. She looked back to the house and saw a figure leaning against the wall.

She dropped the phone and clenched her fists, her palms damp, trembling. She felt the sky spin, the earth turn beneath her feet. Her breaths were coming fast and her hands covered her face, her cheeks wet with tears. She thought she felt raindrops on the back of her neck, but when she looked up it was still a bright day. She raised her hand to her eyes to shield the sun, but when the glare was gone, so was the figure, blown away like dust.

She fell to her knees and began to sob, her face buried in the grass, the sounds of summer gone.

SIXTEEN

The *Post* didn't seem quite as welcoming as it had the day before. I had been a novelty then. Now I was just a distraction, most people barely raising their heads over their monitors.

Tony had stuck me in the old smokers' room, now empty after they were relegated to the canal towpath that ran behind the building, but the smell of stale tobacco still clung to the walls.

The *Post*'s back issues were kept in a windowless room a few doors down from where I was, the metal shelves stacked to the ceiling, filled with large brown binders, one for each month, organised in years.

I wasn't being allowed into that room. Instead, Tony had brought me some computer disks containing scanned images of old stories about David Watts.

'We get a few enquiries,' he said, 'so the paper put everything onto disk. You can take them, provided you don't reproduce them without permission.'

I indicated I understood, and Tony went to leave the room.

'Are all your jumpers about Christmas now?' I asked.

Tony laughed, looking down at his chest, woollen outlines of holly creeping across his chest. 'Oh, it's just Eileen's little way of keeping other women off me.' And then I saw him look out of the door. 'Speaking of women in pursuit, your number-one fan is heading this way.'

I followed his gaze as he went back to his desk, and saw Alice coming towards me. She was smiling at me, but her head was dipped coyly, Diana-style. She was almost laughing by the time she came into the room.

'Hi, Jack. Are we going anywhere today?'

I watched her eyes, saw the pupils grow large, black dots under long, curling eyelashes.

I held up the disks. 'I just want to look through these, and then I'm heading up to St Mary's to speak to the old guy who used to run the youth club. David Watts spent a lot of time there.'

'Yeah, that's right. I think he donated some money to it a couple of years ago. They built some new changing rooms with it.'

As Alice sat there, I flicked through the images on the disk, copying the ones that might be useful into a separate folder. There wasn't that much there: mainly junior-league game reports, and then updates on his progress in London and all the way to his first England cap. The town was proud of him, I had always known that. As I went through the disk, I could feel Alice watching me all the time, leaning forward, playing with her hair.

I was enjoying the attention, any man would. Alice was a pretty woman, with a smile that brightened a room, half sassy, half cute. I had a problem, though. I still saw her as a young girl, the gawky adolescent getting in the way of the quiet moments I had tried to enjoy with her older sister.

When I realised I would have enough information to pad out the feature, I reached for my phone.

'I'm about to ring a superstar,' I whispered, flicking my eyebrows.

Alice grinned even more and leant forward as if she might get to hear.

I listened to his phone ringing, and then felt disappointed when his answer machine kicked in.

'Hello Mr Watts, my name is Jack Garrett and I'm a freelance reporter. I'm writing a story about you based upon your past in Turners Fold, because of the murders that have taken place this week. It would help me if you could ring me,' and I left my number, 'so that we can arrange a time for an interview. I'm in Turners Fold now, doing some digging, but I'll be back in London soon. Look forward to your call. Thanks. Bye.'

When I hung up, I said to Alice, 'That should be okay.'

David Watts looked out of his window, unsure what to do. His palms were wet, his chest tight and heavy.

Then he heard the phone ring again. He swallowed, nervous, his eyes focused on the answer machine.

The message made his head drop, made his day seem worse. He didn't think that was possible, but he could feel his life unravelling quickly. Now there was a reporter.

The sound of the message echoed in the room. And

the more he thought about it, he realised that there was one person who might know what to do.

He pulled out his phone and called Karen Klavan.

She sounded distant. 'Are you all right, David?'

'I've just received a telephone call,' was all he could say at first. His chest was heaving in and out quickly, his heart beating fast. 'It's saved on my answer machine.' He took a deep breath. 'I don't know what to do.'

'What does it say?'

'Just listen to it,' he said, and then he played the message to the mouthpiece, let the threat travel all the way to wherever she was. He closed his eyes as it played, tried to tune out from it.

When it finished, he put the phone back to his ear. He could sense the tension even before she spoke, and when she did, she sounded quiet.

'What the fuck is all that about, David?'

He said nothing for a few seconds, the voice from the answer machine still ringing around his head, and then he put his face in his hands and sat backwards. He stayed like that for a moment, and then his hands came away from his face. He looked up at the ceiling, and then said, 'This sounds like trouble.'

'I never had you as one for understatement,' was her reply. When David stayed quiet, she asked, 'Who is she?'

'I don't know.'

'Don't fuck me about, David. I've just listened to someone who claims that she is shooting footballers, and somehow my biggest asset is dragged into it.' He could hear her heavy breaths, could sense her anger. 'If we're going to deal with it, I've got to know.'

He gave a small laugh. 'It's nothing.'

'Bullshit.' She was shouting down the phone. 'This is a whole lot more than nothing. I can hear it in your voice. Tell me.'

He didn't answer for a while, maybe as long as a minute, and every second of it crawled by as he stared at the floor.

'It's all about me,' he said eventually. 'This whole damn fucking mess is all about me.' He shook his head. 'What do we do?'

'I don't know until you tell me about it. What is she talking about? Who is she?'

'She', David said, his eyes wide, 'is dead.'

He could hear the confusion in Karen's voice. 'No, I'm lost now?'

David took a deep breath. His ready-made speech had deserted him. 'This isn't easy to say.'

'Say it.'

He sighed. 'A girl died, just before I came down to London, and some people think it was my fault.'

Before Karen could say anything, he said, 'It wasn't my fault. It was a long time ago, and I was just the last person to be with her before she was killed.' He felt his voice grow calm. 'I didn't kill her. I didn't get arrested.'

'Why haven't you mentioned this before?' She sounded quiet, suspicious.

He gave a little laugh. 'It's not the sort of thing you mention. "Hi, I'm David Watts, footballer and murder suspect."' He sat back. 'I didn't mention it because there was nothing to mention. A girl was found dead, and I had been with her not long before. There was no evidence against me. I had half the town as an alibi. The police did their job well. They investigated it, they found the killer, and that was the end of it all. He's still in prison, the killer, as far as I know. Case closed.'

Karen didn't respond straight away.

'Why should I mention it?' he continued. 'It was nothing to do with me, and the smell of it would linger around my career like old boots. It would ruin me. The words "alleged rapist and murderer" would always be the subtitle to my headlines, like silent words in brackets after my name.'

'Rape as well?'

David nodded and looked at the floor. 'Yes, rape as well. They said the girl was raped before she was killed.' He sat up, feeling more in control again. 'Don't you understand why I kept it quiet?'

'But what is that call about?' she asked. 'If the girl is dead, who was that on the phone? And why would anyone blame you?'

David didn't respond. Instead, he walked over to the window. He could see the pleasure cruisers on the Thames and he thought how simple it looked out there.

After a few moments of reflection, he heard Karen say, 'Tell me about it now.'

'Karen, it's dead and buried. Leave it.'

'So why the fuck did you call me?' She sounded angry again.

'I don't know.' He said it quietly, his voice unsure. 'I just want to know what to do.'

When she spoke, she sounded calmer, more supportive. 'David, sit down and tell me about it. You have called me, so you want to tell me. So just do it.'

He looked around the room. It looked the same as ever, but it seemed different, as if the sound of the voice, distorted and electronic, had tainted it somehow.

'It was my last night before I left Turners Fold,' he began. 'You know the story. I was spotted and signed, and so I left home to play football down here. Anyway, one of the kids in my class lived on a farm on the edge of town, surrounded by fields. We thought it would be cool to have a party in one of the barns. We could make some noise and get no complaints.'

'Was it a party for you?'

'It started off that way, like a good luck and goodbye party, but we were all splitting up really, either going to college or staying in town, so it became a party for everyone. We invited the whole school year, and a lot of them turned up. We rigged out the barn with lights and a sound system.'

'Sounds like *Animal House.*'

'Not really. Most of the parents came. Their lives were going to change too. I had to stay in control because I had to do the shaking hands part, getting the good advice from all the old heads. A few of the kids got drunk, but there were a lot of hugs and goodbyes.'

'Who died?'

'Annie Paxman,' he said. 'She'd been a school nobody for most of the time, studied hard, kept herself quiet. Her dad was a chef at a restaurant somewhere, but it was pub food, so they didn't have much money. Not many people did, but to Annie it was like she wasn't bothered. Even the kids from the estate had the latest

140

phones and clothes, but to Annie it was as if friends or fitting in didn't matter, so she grew up and got good-looking without anyone really noticing. Suddenly, there was this pretty girl in school and most of the lads started to notice her.'

'Tell me about the night.'

'Not much to tell. Annie was there. It looked like she'd made an effort. She had some new clothes on and her hair looked great. And her eyes. She had the nicest eyes, like her smile would come spilling out of them. I watched her all night, and then towards the end, I thought, What the hell, and started talking to her. When she said she had to go, I said I would walk with her.'

Despite himself, David smiled at the memory.

'We didn't walk far. There was a shortcut into town, and it was a warm night with a bright moon. We only got as far as the edge of the farm. I had taken hold of her hand before we got out of the party, and before we left the farm I kissed her.'

David stopped smiling.

'There was a door open in the last barn. I tried to get her to go inside.'

'You wanted to fuck her in a dirty old barn like a farm dog.' Karen sounded angry.

'That's not fair,' he snarled. 'It wasn't like that.' Then he sighed. 'I was eighteen years old, for Christ's sake. I'd have fucked her on the town-hall steps if she'd asked nicely.'

'So what went wrong?'

He shrugged. 'She said no, so I wanted to go back

to the party. I should have walked her home, or at least got someone to drive her, but I didn't.'

'And why didn't you?'

He took a deep breath and shook his head. 'Because I just didn't. Because it was my party, and so I couldn't just leave it. Because she said she didn't mind. Because it was a light night, with the sounds of the party carrying her all the way back into town. Because this was Turners Fold, and nothing bad ever happens in Turners Fold. Because, because, because.'

'Why did she die?' The question came out bluntly.

David ran his hands through his hair again.

'Someone got her on the way home,' he said.

He looked down, watched his feet shuffle on the floor, his hand around the phone wet with perspiration.

'I should have stayed with her. I know that now, I've wished over and over that I did, but I didn't. She was a mile from home, it was late, it was dark. I should have taken her home. But I didn't, and I can't change that.'

His voice softened.

'A policeman found her. There's an old pavilion in a park at the top of the town, the aviary. Kids and tramps hang out there. She never got further than that. Someone must have seen her, maybe even followed us. She was raped and strangled, left naked, just her scarf around her throat to keep her warm.'

He felt a tear run down his cheek.

'I was due to leave early the next day, so I only found out about Annie a couple of days later, when the police called to find out what time I had left her.' The tears started to come now. 'The man who did this was drunk and crazy, and he's still in prison. Some local retard.'

Karen didn't say anything for a while, trying to take it all in, then asked, unsure, 'Is that the whole story?'

He nodded. 'Everything. Sordid and juvenile, but not a crime.'

'Did the police ever suspect you?'

'No reason why they should. I suppose they asked around at the party and realised it couldn't have been me. They caught him the same night. And now some bastard is trying to blackmail me.' He wiped his eyes. 'So what do we do now?'

'We manage it when it gets out, that's what.' She sounded quiet, as if she was trying to work out how many ways it could go wrong.

'It might already be out,' he said.

'What do you mean?'

He bit his lip, knowing that what he had to say was going to make it worse. Then he realised that not saying it wouldn't make it better.

'There's a reporter up in Turners Fold,' he said. 'On the phone, he said he is looking into my past, and he is connecting it to the shootings.'

Karen went quiet, and then David was surprised to hear her sound brighter.

'It sounds like a cheap blackmail stunt,' she said. 'Someone calls you making demands, and then a reporter calls you afterwards saying he's looking into you.' She snorted a laugh. 'Relax, David. Ignore it, and if he rings back, call the police. At that point we'll go public. It's another Wearside Jack, and he got eight

143

years. The thought of that will make them back off.'

'But what if it gets out?'

'As you said, the real killer is in prison. Which paper is going to accuse you of anything if the real killer is in prison? I can tell you now that the answer is none will.'

David began to relax, even started to smile. He could see the logic of what Karen was saying. At that moment he even felt he might like her.

'Karen?'

'Yeah?'

'Thanks, that's all.'

'Yeah, right,' and then David heard the phone go dead. She'd gone.

He exhaled loudly. Why had the day turned so complicated?

He sat on the sofa for a few minutes, just watching the light from the Thames shimmer on the ceiling, feeling like he had just won his freedom back.

Then he felt the phone ring in his hand. His mouth went dry, his stomach lurched. He pressed the answer button.

'Hello?'

There was a pause and he took a deep breath. All he could hear was a clamour, the noise of people and movement. Then he let out a sigh when he heard Emma's voice.

'David?'

'Where are you?'

'Sorry, David, I can't really hear you. It's not a good line. I'm in New York. Just thought I'd give you a call. How are things?'

He thought about her, wondered what she would think if he told her. Then he listened to the echoes behind her, voices and footsteps, a tannoy announcement. It sounded ordinary, everyday. He didn't want to spoil that for her.

'I'm okay,' he shouted. 'Isn't it the middle of the night over there?'

'Yeah, but it's best to leave the body clock where it is on short stays. Anyway, the city is more beautiful at this time of the morning. I'm going for breakfast soon, and then I'm going shopping.'

'When are you back?'

'That's why I'm calling. They're putting me on this evening's flight, so I'll be back in the morning, your time. I just thought I'd let you know.'

He paused, and then, 'I miss you, Emma.'

She faltered, as if she hadn't expected it, and then said, 'I miss you too. Look, I have to go. I just wanted to hear your voice, that's all. I'll see you tomorrow.'

He put his head back when the phone went silent. His apartment seemed suddenly empty. Then he remembered the reporter saying he was in Turners Fold.

He needed to make one more call.

SEVENTEEN

David tapped his fingers on the arm of the sofa, a thick leather tap. A woman answered, sounding bored. It was a central communications centre. When she asked him why he needed to speak with Detective Inspector Glen Ross, he said quietly, 'Just tell him it's about Annie Paxman.'

The phone went quiet as he was put on hold, and then after a couple of minutes he heard a voice he hadn't heard for a long time. It was easy to remember. DI Glen Ross was a small man, strong and stocky, his hair dyed dark brown to cover his grey, his voice strong and booming.

'David?'

He paused, imagining the detective in his office, surrounded by honours and photos of dignitaries and celebrities, a reminder of his occasional snatches of fame.

'DI Ross, long time no see. Is it still Detective Inspector? I thought you might have retired by now.'

There was an audible sigh of relief. 'You don't have

to say her name to get me to answer. What can I do for you, David?'

'Don't you go relaxing. I'm calling about her.' David put it as simply as he could. 'She's come back,' he said.

There was a pause before Ross responded, 'What do you mean, "come back"?'

'What I mean is,' said David, slow and deliberate, 'is that I've had a call.' He wiped his forehead, damp with sweat. 'Is it safe to talk?'

'Yes.'

David exhaled and said, 'She wants me to come forward, hold a press conference and tell everyone I killed her.'

'Are you feeling all right, David?' Ross said, sounding concerned. A small pause, then, 'Annie Paxman is dead.'

'I know that,' David hissed. 'It's someone pretending to be Annie Paxman.'

Glen Ross spluttered a half-laugh, and then went quiet. The silence lingered for a while, and then he said, quieter than before, 'She's crazy.' There was a pause, and then, 'You're not going to, are you?'

'Of course I'm not.'

'But what happens if you don't?'

David took a deep breath and held the phone against his chest, the implications of what he was about to say rushing at him like a fast wind. He stayed like that for a few seconds, heard the plaintive squeaks of 'David? David?' come from the telephone, and then put it back to his mouth. He said it slow and clear.

'She says if I don't do as she says, she'll keep on shooting footballers, until the only one left to shoot is me.'

'What?' was the response, confused and quiet.

David didn't answer. He let Glen Ross do the connections in his head. He thought he could hear the blood draining from the detective's face. He imagined him, pale and insipid, his career flashing before his eyes. He could hear mutterings, attempts to start sentences that drifted into nothing, then a resigned voice saying wearily, 'What proof has she got that she's the shooter?'

David wondered for a moment what the policeman had been doing two minutes earlier. What mundane thought had occupied his time before his sense of order turned on its head?

'None,' David answered, 'but the police are looking for a woman. I saw it on the news. My agent thinks this is a blackmail shot.'

'Why blackmail?'

'Because I received another call straight afterwards from a reporter. He said he was freelancing and was in Turners Fold, looking through my past.'

Glen Ross sounded like his mouth had gone dry.

'We get reporters all the time,' he said.

'This one said it was in connection with the football murders.'

'Shit.' A pause again, and then Glen Ross added, 'Did he have a name, this reporter?'

David thought back to the voice on the tape and the name he'd said. 'Jack Garrett, I think it was.'

Glen Ross didn't answer. David noticed the silence.

'Are you okay?' he asked.

There was another pause, and then, 'Jack Garrett is the son of the cop who found Annie Paxman.' He gave a small laugh. 'Bob Garrett is his father.'

David didn't listen to anything else the inspector said. He clicked the phone off and sat down in a slump.

'Fuck,' he muttered, and then put his head in his hands. The day was not getting any better.

He closed his eyes for a moment. He felt the sunlight paint his face, but also felt the faintest of breezes just lick his cheeks from the open window. He sat like that for a while, his eyes closed, the rest of the world shut away, but then he opened his eyes again. He was still in London, and the nightmare was still happening. Then he wondered if she was outside, watching him.

He got to his feet and shut the apartment into semi-darkness.

I called Laura, just to find out how things were going. I'd made some calls, but it didn't seem like the press knew much about Dumas's private life. There were the same rumours about playing around, but no names, no specifics.

'Hi, Jack, how's life in the north?'

'Quiet. How's the investigation?'

'I wouldn't know,' she said. 'I'm off it.'

'How come?'

'They've set up a task force, a dedicated unit. There are two forces involved now, so I've been put back on my normal duties.'

'Relieved or angry?'

I could sense her thinking, but then I heard her give out a small laugh. 'Relieved, I suppose. At least I'll see more of Bobby.'

'Does everyone think like that?'

'It depends on how quickly it's over. If they get someone quick, then yeah, they could have taken the quick credit. But if this drags on, the decent cops know it would have taken over everything. The ones who would have messed it up are pretty pissed off about it.'

'I bet they spent last night shopping for press-conference suits.'

I felt myself smile when she laughed.

'Thanks for calling,' she said. Then she paused. 'Keep in touch, Jack.' She said it softly, a step away from professional courtesies.

'I will,' I said, and then when I hung up, I felt like my head was lighter, with a smile on my face that I couldn't shift.

Detective Inspector Ross put the receiver down, his hand trembling. His mouth was dry, his chest felt tight, and he could feel the prickle of sweat on his upper lip.

He made a quick phone call, and a woman in her early sixties came into the office. She wore a grey suit, neutral and unassuming, and her brunette bob just reached the collar. She was polite, as always, smiling courteously rather than warmly.

'What can I get you?'

'Would you get me a file, Martha?'

'Which one?'

'It's from around ten years ago. Is that a problem?'

'Closed or open?'

He paused for a moment, and then said, 'Closed.'

She smiled. 'Yes, sir, I'll have a good look for it. Later on today okay?'

He nodded, distracted. 'Fine,' and he gave her the details.

He didn't hear the door close. And he hadn't noticed her pen falter as she had taken the name of the file down.

David Watts spent an hour staring into the semi-gloom of his apartment. It felt like he had stopped breathing he was so still.

He thought about Bob Garrett. He knew what Bob Garrett thought of him. He made it plain every time he saw him, staring at him, his eyes cold with hate, his anger just simmering in the background somewhere.

But he was the only one who thought like that. Everyone else in the town knew about Colin Wood, trapped by DNA, convicted by a jury. It was only Bob Garrett who thought differently.

There was a problem. If the reporter was Bob Garrett's son, he'd only get one version.

David could taste his nerves in the back of his throat. He had to find whoever made those phone calls. He needed to know if they were true. If it was the woman shooting footballers, he would decide what to do then. If it was a cheap blackmail scam, he would frighten them off.

But who could he trust to find her? That would be one more person who knew about it.

Then he remembered how he had lived his life when he first arrived in the capital, his hand always round a bottle, his nose always near a line.

Karen had saved him. She had told him that if he got clean, she would get him a contract twice as big as the one he had. If he didn't, his footballing days were over. The tabloids had been sniffing around him, waiting for a slip, but he saw the harm he was causing before anyone found out.

If he didn't want anyone to find out about this, he needed to put himself in the company of people who didn't want to be investigated.

And that meant visiting the life he thought he had left behind.

EIGHTEEN

David parked his car around the corner from the Club Sorrento, a dance bar loved by the rich and famous deep in the heart of Soho. Black wooden panelling, low-key signs, steps downwards. The sight of the club made his stomach roll. It was all of his bad memories.

He thought about Emma. She didn't know everything about him. This was his reminder of what she didn't know. Three seasons of powder-fuelled late nights and in the palm of the London gangster set. He'd got away, but the help he wanted was back there, with people who wouldn't talk to the authorities.

He paused for a moment, wondering whether he was doing the right thing. But then he thought of what he stood to lose if he chose the alternative.

He walked quickly into the club, hiding away behind sunglasses and a baseball cap. Although the club wasn't open, he knew the door would be. The owner did his best business when the club was closed. The club was a cellar bar of red velvet alcoves around a raised dance floor, the ceiling a tangle of lights and speakers. It was nothing special, but all those who wanted to be on the up could meet people who were already there. For those at the top, it was a place to flaunt fame in front of the hungry. When he went in through the doors, familiar faces from his past turned around, all sitting by the bar, and when they recognised him, they grinned.

'Hey, look who it is. Gold Dust Watts.'

It was the barman, a fat Londoner, all slicked hair and gold, an open-necked white shirt and bulging fore-arms marking him out as more than a student treading time. The rest of the people at the bar laughed along. In their world, they were kings. David was just a jester.

David nodded, gritting out a smile. 'Is Marky in?'

The barman laughed aloud. 'What's wrong, super-star? The new leaf turned back over?'

David didn't respond, knowing from bitter experi-ence that these people weren't the laugh-along types. 'I'm looking for Marky? Is he here?'

The barman looked around. They were the only people in there. 'I don't see him,' he said, shaking his head with fake regret.

Four big faces laughed among themselves, cackling like a pack of fat hyenas.

'Cut the crap,' David snapped. 'Is Marky in or not?'

The barman put his hand on the shoulder of one of the apes by the bar. He had started to get off his stool, a gap-toothed hulk, his shirt too tight for his neck. 'Cool it, superstar. Why do you want him?'

'That's between me and Marky.'

The barman shook his head. 'Wrong. You're the big man around town, but in here you're shit, so you either state your business or you get out.' He nodded towards the four people by the bar, all watching with quiet interest. 'You can have an escort, if you want, but maybe you won't get to play on Saturday.'

David stared back at him and considered the odds. His fame was an irrelevance. Marky arranged the supply of high-grade cocaine to some of the top movers and shakers in town, and David was just another happy customer. No, he was less than that. He was an ex-customer, unlikely to return.

'I want to find someone,' said David, 'and I thought Marky might be able to help me.'

The barman stepped closer until David could smell the warmth of his breath.

'You think Marky is in the missing person game now?'

David shook his head, defiant. 'I really need to find this person, and I reckon Marky might know someone.' Then a pause. 'So get him.'

The apes by the bar shrieked and covered their mouths, acting up like they were frightened, and then burst into laughter. The barman nodded, stroked his chin, and held his hand up to quieten the others in the bar. He looked David in the eye and saw that he was serious. 'Wait there.'

David was left in the bar, looking at the scuffs on the toes of his three-hundred-pound moccasins, and wondering how long he would be there. He could hear the men talking by the bar, back to small-talk to let David know that they no longer cared about him. David looked up when he heard a door open on the other side of the bar. It wasn't Marky. It was the barman, and he was holding a small cellophane wrap of white powder.

David looked confused. He didn't do coke any more. Not since before Emma. That was an old life, not the one he had now.

'Marky sees you as a lost opportunity,' the barman said. 'He wants you to be sociable when you meet.'

David looked at the bag, knowing what it contained. 'What if I say no?' he asked, already knowing the answer.

The barman grinned. 'Then so does Marky.'

David's heart dipped. He had hoped past custom might have counted for more. He heard someone making chicken noises by the bar.

He grabbed at the powder and walked to the bar. He barged into the middle of the apes and made a space on the bar top. He poured a couple of lines, used a drinks stirrer to tidy them up, glanced into the eyes watching him, and then rolled a ten-pound note into a straw. He gave a silent prayer, then lowered the note to the powder and snorted the lines hard, one for each nostril. He put his head up and back, sniffing hard, trying to get the full sensation out of his nose, the insides of his nostrils hot.

The cocaine kicked in quickly. The leers and laughs of the voices around him receded to an echo as he felt his own inner fires take over, like a steady roar, a hot wind driving him forward. He turned to the barman. 'My turn now. Take me to Marky.'

The barman laughed and turned away. 'Follow me, arsehole. Oh yeah, before we go,' and he pointed towards a blinking red light just above the row of spirits, 'if you fuck us about, the *News of the World* gets the tape.'

David said nothing. He just felt his grip loosen on events as the laughs of the apes by the bar faded to nothing. He walked towards Marky's office, a room at the back of the club. He felt a hand stuff a bag of white powder into his pocket. Maybe later.

David had been told to wait at a bar in Covent Garden.

It was a balcony bar, overlooking the cobbled piazza between the old market hall and St Paul's Church. He was inside, sitting at a table behind panelled French windows, watching the stairs for whoever he was to meet. He'd had to sign a couple of autographs, pose for a photograph on someone's phone. He had bought an apartment at Chelsea Bridge so that he could be in the city. As he sat there, just a face in the crowd, he wondered whether he lived in the city at all. Didn't he just shut himself away, to avoid the waves and smiles and autographs and handshakes?

He sat back, twitchy and edgy, his adrenalin making him flick looks around the bar. He couldn't see anyone likely to be Marky's contact. He rubbed his eyes and then his nose. He felt tired. He sniffed and exhaled loudly. He couldn't meet anyone like this. He had to be clear and focused, and right then he was anything but that.

Then he saw him.

David knew he was the contact as soon as he saw him. It was the poise, the menace, like contained fury.

And his clothes made him stand out. Black shirt,

black denim, black cowboy boots. David almost laughed. Marco had sent him John Wayne. His head was gleaming pink, shaved to a shine, with a dark moustache and silver rings on his fingers.

David caught his eye, but the man kept on walking. As he passed the table, he said, 'Outside.'

David got up to follow him, and ended up on the balcony, overlooking the piazza. The balcony was busy, a good place to rest and have a drink and watch the tourists go by. A street entertainer was plying his trade, a man in red dungarees juggling chainsaws, surrounded by a circle of onlookers under the Roman portico of St Paul's Church.

The contact was in a corner, by the metal struts of the market roof, a couple of scruffy pigeons behind him, just resting, heads twitching.

As David reached him, he said, 'Tell me what you want.'

David leant against the stone balcony rail and considered the man in front of him. He noticed the American accent but couldn't place its origins. His gaze was impenetrable, tough and fierce.

David began to talk. The man's expression never changed, whereas David's face was animated, and his hands flailed around as he told the story he had told to his agent. When David told him about the phone call and the links with the football shootings, the man smiled.

'And you want me to find this person?'

David nodded, looking nervous.

'Do you want her bringing to you?'

David's cheek twitched. His reply was whispered, nervous and twitchy. 'If she's the shooter, I just want her to stop shooting.'

'You're no salesman, are you, Mr Watts.'

'What do you mean?'

'You just doubled the price.'

'How come?'

'How come, Mr Watts, is because I know how much you want her. I could go to the police and tell them what you just told me. I could sell this story and make a six-figure sum with no risk.'

David went to walk away. 'I've had enough of this. I'm going.'

The man smiled and took a cigarette packet out of his shirt pocket. He lit a cigarette, the smoke clouding his face.

'You've no choice now, Mr Watts. If you get someone else to do it, hell, I'll go to the police and tell them you offered it to me, and then they'll be on your doorstep.'

'You wouldn't go to the police. That's not what people like you do.'

He smiled back at David. 'No, because people like me are uncaring bastards, who will squash anyone for a small price. And, Mr Watts, I could squash you.' He raised his eyebrows. 'Easy money.'

'Fuck off. Look where we are. Everyone in here knows me, and if I get arrested for anything, you're in the same shit.'

The American pointed his cigarette at him. 'Maybe that's why I picked it. Because I'm going to do what you ask, and then when I'm done, I'll get my money.

159

And if the police catch me, you go down with me. I'll shout conspiracy, and everyone will remember you and me enjoying a drink.' He sat back. 'And I accept the job. Whether I do it or not, the price is the same.'

'So what's the price?'

The American smiled. 'You got it now.' He drew on his cigarette, eyeing David carefully. 'One million pounds.'

David laughed aloud. He carried on laughing for a few moments, the absurdity of it all coming crashing in on him.

'One million pounds,' he laughed. 'Are you fucking daft?'

The man shook his head, and then leant forward. David felt the point of a blade just above his kneecap. He swallowed.

'If you fuck me about,' the man continued, 'I will put this knife so far into your kneecap that you'll never straighten your leg again.'

David felt his mouth go dry.

'You promise me one million pounds and your problem is solved, every angle gone forever.' He smiled in David's face and stared hard into his eyes. 'If you don't, you won't stop her and you'll never play again.'

The American then sat back and drew on his cigarette.

David went pale. He could think of nothing to say. The afternoon had drifted away from him, he knew that.

'And what if I say no?'

The American smiled. 'Look at the crowd down

there,' and he pointed at the crowd of people around the juggler.

David looked. 'Yeah, what is it?'

Then David carried on looking as the American smiled. And then he saw the barman from the club. He was in the crowd, but his camera wasn't pointed at the juggler. It was pointing up at the balcony bar, clicking away as he took pictures of them both talking, stopping just to give a smile and a wave at David.

David whirled round in fury. 'You bastard.'

The American nodded. 'You got it. So add those pictures to the video from the club, and we've got a half-million-pound story. You double it to a full million and I'll do the job. Say no, and I sell the story.' He raised his eyebrows. 'Your choice, Mr Watts.'

David Watts said nothing. He just stood there, his jaw clenched, his face pale with emotion.

The American smiled. 'Good. I've enjoyed it, Mr Watts. Have a good day.'

He held out his hand to shake. When David snapped 'Fuck you' at him, he put his hand in his pocket and pulled out a small mobile phone, still wrapped in cellophane. 'Take the phone, Mr Watts, and give me back the wrapper.'

David did as he was told.

'I'll contact you on this. Pay-as-you-go, with plenty of credit. My number is keyed into it. I'll call you on this phone, and this phone alone. You need this doing quickly, so I'll go pack now. I'll be in Turners Fold this evening. I'll keep you updated. If you get any more calls that give you clues as to where she might be, call me straight away.'

David nodded, staring at the phone. He began to wonder what he had started. He could have gone to the police and handed over the answer machine. This would be harder if it went wrong. He had a sick feeling in his stomach; the surge of confidence brought on by the coke was slipping. He couldn't afford to lose that.

He looked up when he heard the man get to his feet. He was turning to walk away, so David asked him, 'If you do this, how do I get the money to you?'

The man stopped, his cowboy boots scuffing on the wooden floor. He turned around. 'You've given me your word. When the job is done, I'll come and collect.' There was a glint in his eye. 'And I will collect.'

David felt a flicker of panic. 'What do I call you?'

The man thought for a moment. 'Mr Christ,' he said eventually, 'Mr Jesus Christ.' He smiled. 'I'm your saviour,' he said, then laughed to himself and walked away.

When he was gone, David felt alone. As he looked around the bar it seemed like everyone had stopped talking and was turning to look at him, pointing, eyes wide.

David got up quickly and ran out of the bar.

NINETEEN

Bob Garrett woke with a groan, the hammering on the door downstairs interrupting his sleep. Great! He'd been up all night.

He scrambled out of bed, went downstairs, and flung open the door. It was Detective Inspector Glen Ross.

Bob was surprised, alert now, helped by the sunshine glaring bright outside. Glen Ross had only visited him at home once before, over ten years ago. Back then they had both been going places. Only Glen had got there.

Bob nodded politely. 'Sir?' He didn't move away from the door.

Glen Ross looked past him and into the house. 'Can we talk, Bob?'

Bob paused, then turned and went back into the house, Ross following him. Bob stopped and folded his arms, gestured towards the chairs and offered a seat. 'Can I get you a drink?'

Ross shook his head. 'It's not a social call.'

Bob was intrigued. 'What can I do for you, sir?' As always, Bob emphasised the word 'sir'. He watched Glen

Ross carefully, sensing that he was being weighed up, as if Ross was unsure what to say. His opening gambit surprised him.

'Do you remember Annie Paxman?' he asked.

Bob's eyes widened. He'd thought about her now and again over the last ten years, but initially less and less, as if it had stopped mattering as much. In the last couple of years, as everyone else had got older, she'd come back into his thoughts. 'Clear as day,' he responded. He eyed Ross suspiciously. 'Do you?' he added, the question flecked with sarcasm.

Ross licked his lips nervously and jammed his hands into his pockets. 'Annie Paxman has come back.'

Bob blinked.

Ross waited for a reaction, but he got nothing. The silence of the house became something neither of them wanted to break, until Bob said, smiling slowly, 'That's quite a trick.'

Ross glared at him. 'Don't be an arsehole, Bob.' He paused to calm down, and then continued, 'Someone is blackmailing David Watts.'

Bob raised his eyebrows and whistled. 'Truth has a way of haunting people. Doesn't it, Inspector?'

Ross stepped away and tried to stay calm. He needed Bob, maybe more than Bob needed him. 'She wants David Watts to go on television,' he said, 'and confess to Annie Paxman's murder.'

Bob laughed aloud.

'This is not funny.'

'No,' said Bob, nodding, 'it isn't. It never was.' He narrowed his eyes. 'How much will it cost him?'

Ross shook his head and licked his lips again. 'He doesn't know yet.' Ross knew there was a strange truth to that answer.

'He'll never confess.'

'No, he won't, but if this starts to pick up some speed, people might want to look closer at it. And if they do, they might look at you.'

Bob scowled. 'Don't threaten me, Glen. If you've come here to tell me to keep quiet, not to cause problems, I did just that ten years ago. It will be hard to do anything new now. And it is just me, now that James Radley has gone. That was one convenient fire for you.'

Ross said nothing.

'Yeah, keep quiet,' Bob continued, 'it's your right. But remember that what happened wasn't right. That girl was killed by David Watts, and you covered it up.'

'That's crap,' snapped Ross. 'David Watts had nothing to do with it. There was no proof then. There's no proof now. For fuck's sake, Colin Wood is in prison for this. His DNA was inside her. What else do you want?'

Bob laughed. 'You're even starting to believe it now.'

'Yes, I do, because it's the way it is. It was a long time ago. It's gone, forgotten. I just want you to know in case it all blows up again.'

'That's all you want, is it?'

Ross nodded.

Bob stepped closer to him. 'I don't believe you. If he's so innocent, why doesn't he just ignore her? Why do you come here, waking me up, running scared? It was over ten years ago, and suddenly Annie Paxman rises from the dead? Something isn't right here. Are you sure there's nothing else here I don't know?'

Ross flinched when Bob said it. He felt like he was sinking, like things were sliding away from him. 'No, Bob, there's nothing. I thought you ought to know, that's all.'

'Okay.' Bob stepped back, calming down. 'If I find out you're bullshitting me, Annie Paxman's memory might get itself an ally.'

'You wouldn't dare.'

Bob tilted his head. 'Try me.'

'I can see you're angry about this. All I'm asking is that when this is all sorted, Annie Paxman returns to the grave and rests in peace. Let David Watts sort it out.'

'Yeah, like last time.' The answer was thick with contempt.

Ross looked at Bob and nodded. 'Yeah, just like last time.'

Glen Ross knew he was in front now. He had Bob where he wanted him; the reason for the visit had paid off. He could tell by Bob's anger that he would keep quiet. That's why he was angry. And once Bob knew of the connection between the shootings and Annie Paxman, he would *have* to keep quiet. He would have known about the blackmail for too long, and no one would believe he hadn't known all along. Let Bob swim in his own conscience for a while, and then one day he'd know that he'd drown if he tried to struggle out of it.

Then the front door opened.

There was a car on the drive I didn't recognise when I went back to the house with Alice. When I went in through the door, I was surprised to see Glen Ross stood there. There was little love lost between him and my dad and this certainly couldn't be a social visit.

'Good afternoon, Mr Ross,' I said, trying to ignore Alice's elbows knocking into me. Her arms were full of notes and clippings, and I heard her giggle quietly, the effect of going over our morning's work in a pub. I hushed her quiet, but it was hard not to smile. She was pushing into my back; I could feel her elbows wishing me on, the faint aroma of beer drifting over my shoulder.

Ross turned and nodded at me, not at all cordial. Then I noticed that my father didn't look too happy to see me. He was dressed in his pyjamas, glaring at me. I guessed it wasn't me he was angry about, but whatever had upset him, I didn't want to hang around.

'Are you okay, Dad?'

His glare softened, and I thought I saw him loosen up. 'Yes, Jack. DI Ross just came round to ask me how last night's shift went, but he's going now.'

The comment was loaded enough for me to know that it wasn't about last night. I shrugged. Not my sleep ruined. Not my battle. 'Okay. We're just going to my room to throw this feature together. Are you staying up now?'

He looked at me, not really listening to what I was saying. 'Uh, yeah, I suppose so.'

Once we got into my room, I put my laptop on the desk by the window, the desk I'd used when I was at school. It seemed ridiculously small now and I could still see the doodles I'd scratched into the wood: some rock bands and a football team I used to support. I saw Megan's name on there, Alice's sister, etched into a love heart. I smiled to myself and slid my laptop over it.

I sat down on the bed. 'What do you make of Glen Ross being here?'

Alice looked towards the stairs. 'It means something is happening.'

'Why do you say that?'

'Because the only time I ever see him is when he wants to be in the paper. He briefs us so that we have his quotes ready for when things happen.' She shook her head. 'He's just a big sleaze.'

We were silent for a while when we heard the front door slam, and then a car started. I guessed Glen Ross had just left.

Then I heard my father come upstairs. He sounded like he was rummaging in drawers. When I heard him go back downstairs, his footfalls sounded different, as if he had put shoes on. There was a short pause, and then the front door slammed again. I looked at Alice.

'Maybe he's run out of beer,' she said, hinting that I should ignore it.

I nodded, smiling, and then tried to think about my feature. I could see Alice watching me, her eyes glinting, biting her lip.

'Let's work,' I said, grinning now.

Bob Garrett crunched along the shale path running along the school field.

As the football pitch came into view, he saw a game

168

taking place. He walked round the edge and sat down to watch.

It was a high-school game, young kids, early teens, all legs and eagerness, playing for nothing more than school pride and for fun.

Bob found himself smiling as he watched. It took him back to his own teenage years, spent kicking footballs in a suburb of Liverpool, full of dreams of pulling on the Everton blue. He had been the best player in his team by a long way, but his talent had still only taken him as far as the lower divisions. He had just been good. When he had first seen David Watts play on this field, he'd known he was looking at someone great.

He had loved football then. His playing days hadn't ended long before, so he would come down to the high-school field just because it was the nearest place to hear the sound of a boot on a ball. And then he saw David Watts, tall and majestic, grace and power, all wrapped up in a skinny teenager. He watched David a lot, so that by the time David was leaving town to join up with his club, Bob knew everything about him – from the way he jogged off the field to the way he punched his leg forward when he let one fly, the final flick of his body as the energy rippled up from the base of his spine and into his shoulders.

He shook his head. Being something big somewhere so small can be a bad thing sometimes, because you can end up feeling like you own the town, because the town wants to own a bit of you.

Bob made himself comfortable as he watched. He

liked the way they mimicked their heroes most of all. It gave it a playground quality. He could see the images of glory in their heads, could sense the imaginary crowd. He smiled. It was the innocence of the game. The game wasn't about players, it never had been. It was about the game itself.

He settled back to enjoy the match. He wanted to wash away some of the dead air that had been hanging around him all afternoon.

TWENTY

She was in the lobby of the Atlantic Tower, looking out of the front doors onto a narrow Liverpool street, the grey spread of the Mersey not far away, trying not to give anyone chance to memorise her face. Her hair was coloured with a reddish tinge. It made her look younger, too young to be doing what she was doing. A picture had been released from Manchester, from the security camera in the apartment building, and she was worried she might be recognised. She was ready to be caught, but not yet.

She got through check-in okay. A business conference had booked in while she waited, so the reception staff paid her little attention when she approached the desk on her own. She'd booked her room some time ago, using someone else's credit-card details as security. When she arrived, she paid in cash. There were no suspicious looks when her room number came up on the computer. The request to be looking towards the river didn't seem unusual when she'd booked it. It was one of the hotel's selling features, with the building shaped like the bow of a ship, and her request had passed into history. Tomorrow, it would attract suspicion.

She went to her room and looked out. It was perfect. She was looking down towards the river, the mythical Mersey, with the Liver Building to her left, a northern beauty, a concrete masterpiece. She could see the Liver birds topping the two small towers, cast in copper, strapped down to stop them flying away. Liverpool would be no more if they flew away, so the legend had it. She thought she knew how they felt.

Her gaze moved right. She wasn't there for the Liver Building. She was there for the Crowne Plaza, a five-star hotel just across the road from the Atlantic Tower, where the Tottenham players were staying that night, ready for the game at Everton the following day. There was speculation on the news that the weekend's games might be cancelled, but for now they were still on.

She moved away from the window. She thought she heard her door open. She whirled round in fright. There was no one there. She felt a cold breeze wrap around her and she shivered. The room darkened and she felt alone.

She grabbed the remote control and turned on the television, filling the room with noise and dancing colours. She found the news channel and then rushed to the bathroom, locking the door. She would stay in there until it was time. No one could get her in there. The television boomed through the door, so she ran a bath to drown it out with noise. Another hour, she said to herself, another hour and she could start again.

TWENTY-ONE

I was downstairs with Alice when my father returned.

It was nearly seven o'clock and we were winding up the day. I'd tried calling David Watts again but got the answer machine. His agent wasn't answering her phone either. I was moulding the feature without his input, and it had a form, but it needed bulking up, needed more source work. Most of all, it needed some style. When I looked at my dad, he seemed breathless, eager, excited, as if he'd rushed back with some news. He stalled when he saw Alice, as if he'd forgotten that she might be there.

'Things okay, Dad?'

He looked at me and nodded, then glanced towards Alice and I felt he had just wished her out of the house.

Alice must have seen it too, because she glanced at her watch and said, 'I really should be going now.' She walked towards the door, and then turned back to me and said, 'I'll call you, Jack, if that's okay. We'll go out for a drink.'

I waved and nodded, confused. 'Yeah, fine. Give me a couple of hours.'

Then she was gone and I felt the house go quiet again.

I watched my father. He had an itchiness, like he couldn't sit down but didn't know what else to do. He didn't say anything for a few minutes, just chewed on his bottom lip and stared at me. I stayed with him because I could sense he had something to say. I raised my eyebrows at him. He was normally calmer than this, and so I knew it was important.

He stared for a bit longer, and then eventually he spoke.

'You journalists protect your sources, right?'

I nodded. 'First rule of writing. If you don't protect your sources, you stop getting them. Why?'

'I've been thinking about this article you're writing. About David Watts. Hometown feature.'

I nodded and folded my arms. Time to let him speak.

'I've been down at the school fields since Glen Ross left,' he said.

'Why?'

He exhaled. 'Just to remind myself of something.' He looked at me. 'Answer me this, Jack: What do you think I miss most about not playing football any more?'

My mind went blank. That wasn't the question I'd been expecting, and he didn't talk about his football days too much. I had my own memories of him, as a lower-division hatchet man, sliding across boggy pitches with long hair and a moustache. He hadn't been the quickest of defenders, but he had made wingers nervous, his studs always high.

'The travel?' I answered glibly. 'The glamour? The girls?'

He laughed. 'Spend a few hours on a bus with pissed-up footballers and you'll know why I don't miss that. And as for the girls? Forget it. There weren't that many groupies around in the lower divisions.'

He stopped laughing and looked more distant. I didn't see him get nostalgic much. He normally thought forwards, not back. As he sat there, taking himself back to his playing days, some of the years fell away that had been hanging around his face since my mother died.

'It's the sense of tradition I miss,' he continued, not really looking at me. 'I was playing our game, England's pastime, and I was getting paid for it. I felt special. Every time I stepped onto that field, I found it hard to believe that I was being allowed to do it. Every kick of the ball. Every shout of the crowd. It was only the bottom rung, but I loved it.'

'Why did you stop? You've never really said.'

He regained some of his age and smiled, the lines around his eyes creasing back into life.

'I wasn't good enough. Simple as that. Enjoying it wasn't enough for the clubs. I didn't mind that. They weren't there for my fun. They were there to build winning teams and mould young talent into football stars, ready to sell on to keep the cash drawer full. I thought I might have improved, but I stayed average and just got slower. I had dreamt of playing in the top flight, walking out at Old Trafford, looking into the shadows of the stands and seeing the ghosts of the greats, but passion isn't enough.' He smiled at me. 'And then I met your mother and got tired of being away. I didn't try as hard, wanted other things than a football career. You came along and I got to hate being away.' He smiled, almost embarrassed. 'I wanted to watch you grow up, so when my contract ended, I didn't try to renew it.' He gave a small laugh. 'I don't think I was going to get an offer anyway. I came to Turners Fold and joined the police.'

I blinked away an itch in my eye. 'Any regrets?' I asked.

He looked wistful. 'Maybe that I'd been born with a better right foot, but I'm happy with the way things have turned out.'

He came out of the reverie and looked at me direct. Some fire had returned to his eyes. 'Why are you writing this feature on David Watts?' he asked.

My eyes narrowed. 'I've told you. It's because of the shootings. There aren't many Premiership stars with British passports these days, so the paper wants the home-grown boy angle. I worked out an exclusive.'

'Is that what you see when you look at David Watts? A Lancashire lad made good?'

I nodded. 'Sometimes. It's nice to know that we're the same, deep down. He's just a better footballer than me, that's all.' I shrugged. 'The paper wants to humanise him, thinks it will be a good angle on the shootings, make it even more tragic.'

'And because his face will sell the paper, especially with the shootings.' My dad looked scornful when he said it.

I didn't respond. My job was to write stories so that papers would sell. No point in trying to hide from it.

My dad sat back, looking up at the ceiling. 'Do you want the real story about David Watts? None of this anecdotal crap you've been collecting?'

I cocked my head, surprised. 'Depends on what you've got. If it doesn't fit into the story, it won't go in.'

He waved his hand dismissively. 'Forget the paper. What I have is real news, a story that has never been told. And someone *needs* to tell it.'

I regarded him closely. He looked passionate, bursting with something to say. I had nothing to lose by listening.

'Okay, go on.'

He sat forward. 'If you want to write a story about David Watts, if you want a real story, go back over ten years ago, to the night before he left town. That's where you'll find the real David Watts.'

'Why?' I asked cautiously.

'You won't name me as your source?'

'No way.'

He stared at me hard in the eye. His look became angry, contemptuous, but he was contained, as if he was considering his words. He had one last wrestle with his conscience, and then said, slowly, deliberately, 'David Watts is a murderer. A murderer and a rapist.'

She was at the window, her room in darkness, looking out over Liverpool. The lights from the street below seemed to brighten up the hotel, but the area was quiet, the office workers long gone home.

She looked down and saw the rifle propped against the wall. She knew she would have to be quick this time. Everyone was jumpy about the shootings. This would be the most difficult one so far. The shot would echo around her room and around her floor in the hotel. She reckoned on having two minutes before people worked out where the shot had come from. If she wasn't out of her room by then, she would be in trouble.

The fire escape was only a couple of doors down. She was going to ignore that. If security got in a rush and headed to her room, she'd see them on the way down. She was going to wait for the lift. Once in there, she was okay. She didn't think they'd be able to react fast enough to be waiting there, not expecting a calm exit that way, so she'd just rush out of the front door with her bag over her shoulder. Her car was parked away from the hotel, further along the waterfront, so she was going to cross the street and head for the river. She would sink into the shadows, and once in her car she would head out of town fast. She had done dummy runs, and she thought she could take the shot, dismantle the gun, and get to the lift in a minute. If she got unlucky with the lift, she got unlucky, but in every practice run she'd never waited more than forty-five seconds. It would be tight, but she thought she could do it.

But now it was time to call David Watts.

I didn't respond at first. I was sure I must have misheard him.

He kept his stare. 'You heard it right.'

I laughed nervously and then let the silence grow. I thought he was joking, but I knew my father, and glib comments weren't his style.

A few more seconds passed, and then I said, 'You need hard evidence before you say things like that.'

'Get a recording machine. I know you've got one. I'll give you the evidence, my evidence, right now.'

I paused for a moment. Whatever story there was, I didn't want my father to be the source. But rapist and murderer? I dismissed it. You can't keep things like that quiet. But then I thought about how serious he looked. And I liked the fire in his eyes, an excitement I hadn't seen in years.

I did as he said and went upstairs to get my voice recorder. Before I came down again, I paused, wondering if this was really happening. I had a quiet sense of excitement, wondering what was going to come out. I looked down at my hands and saw a slight tremble.

When I came down again, he was pacing in front of the fireplace. I put the recorder on the table, clicked it on.

'Tell me what you know.'

He stopped pacing and put his hands on his hips. He took a deep breath and then started to tell me the tale.

'I was on nights, as ever, just driving around, checking that everything was all right. We didn't always go down by the high school, but school had just finished for the summer, and the place is a magnet when it's closed down. I drove down the side of the football fields and ended up at the bottom of Victoria Park. There was nothing happening, so I was just turning the car around when I caught her in the headlight beam.'

'Who?'

'A girl called Annie Paxman.' He looked sad. 'Really sweet girl, if you ask the people who knew her. Same school year as David.' He shook his head at the memory. 'She was on the floor in front of the aviary. Her dress was pulled up around her waist and ripped across her chest, with a scarf around her neck. She was dead. Hadn't been dead long, but she was past the point of being saved.'

'What had happened?'

I'd guessed the answer from what he'd said before, but I had to ask.

'David Watts,' he said, his voice rich with contempt. 'Your hometown hero had raped her, on a stone floor overlooking the town, like he was collecting his last trophy. Once he'd done with her, he killed her, strangled her to keep her quiet.'

I exhaled loudly. The story bounced around my head, somehow unreal. It took me a few moments to regain my thoughts.

'Why haven't I heard of this?' I asked. 'I'd remember a dead girl at the aviary.'

'You were away at university. I don't think I saw much of you then.'

'Tell me more,' I said. 'I'm here now.'

My dad sat back down in the chair and sighed, and I watched him roll back the years.

'There'd been a party at a farm,' he started. 'Bailey's farm.'

I nodded that I knew it.

'The party was for David Watts because he was leaving town the next day, off to start his football career, but it seemed like half the high school was there.' He shrugged. 'Just kids and a few parents. Everyone behaved themselves, but David was drinking like he was trying to flush out the town before he left.'

'So who was Annie Paxman?'

He sat back and put his hands behind his head. 'I suppose the prettiest girl in the school, if that matters for anything. Her problem was that she was the only person in town who didn't see that. She wasn't from a wealthy family, and she didn't hang around with the in-crowd. She was one of the few black kids in school, but I don't suppose that mattered too much either. She went to school, worked hard, and made her parents proud. Had an offer of a place at Leeds University studying law. She was dark and skinny and bright and shy, eyes like frantic fireflies. But she didn't sleep around. She was a good girl.'

'She was a challenge.'

'That's right,' Dad said, pointing. 'A challenge for the high-school hero. And David Watts wins at everything, that's the rule.' He paused for breath, and then, 'So Annie's at this party, and she has to go. She hadn't planned on staying out late, and was about to call her dad to pick her up, according to witnesses, when David offered to walk her home.' My dad looked like he had a bad taste in his mouth. 'David always got the girl. Another rule. He was good-looking, he was the local football star, and whatever David wanted, he got. He wanted Annie Paxman. And he wanted her because no one else had had her. As soon as she agreed to let him walk her home, he had the green light.'

He shook his head and took a drink.

'No one saw them leave. But he wouldn't have needed long, just enough time to walk her half the way home, try it on, get refused, and then lose his temper. Next thing anyone knows is that David doesn't look good, he's got his head in his hands and is looking all emotional. People put it down to the beer and the fact that he was leaving town and someone took him home. No one knew that Annie Paxman was dead on the park floor.'

'How do you know David Watts did it?'

He looked at me. I saw certainty in his eyes, a resolve.

'Because I saw him, running away across the fields,' he said. 'He was a hundred yards away. I couldn't have caught him, but I knew it was him.'

'At night, from that far away?'

He nodded. 'I know what a defence lawyer would make of that, and I suppose the prosecution would agree, but that kid was going to be the next big thing. I'm an ex-player. I had watched him, studied his every movement, the way he ran, the way he kicked a ball, the way he held himself. So when I saw him running, I knew damn well who it was.

'It was brutal. When I found her, her clothes had been ripped apart and her heels were raw as she'd thrashed against the floor. The scarf had come loose, but I could see the mark around her neck where it had been pulled tight. There were fingernail gouges in her skin where she'd tried to get her fingers underneath. There were deep fingernail gouges on her legs, on the inside of her thighs, where he'd forced her.'

I didn't know what to say. No one in London knew about this, not even as a whisper.

'Had you missed him by much?' I asked, coughing lightly.

He shook his head. 'I don't think so. He must have seen me coming down the track by the fields.'

'What's your theory?'

He grimaced. 'It's a timeless tale, but I suppose he thought she would do whatever he asked, and because he was drunk, he didn't listen to what she wanted. She struggled, so he fought harder, and then when it had all finished, with Annie screaming rape, crying and upset, he sees his football career disappearing like sand running through his fingers. He panics and grapples with her. She struggles, fights back, but he's too strong. Before he has time to think straight, she's dead.' He shrugged. 'That's pretty much it. The prisons are full of that kind of story. David Watts wasn't the first. He won't be the last.'

I stood up and walked to the window. I felt the need to see some daylight. I saw dusk was settling in, the sky turning lilac as the sun disappeared somewhere towards Blackpool.

No sound came from my father now. But that couldn't have been the end of the story. I turned around.

'What happened to her family?' I asked. 'Are they still in Turners Fold?'

My dad shook his head. 'No, they left.' He looked

down. 'I went to the Paxman house after a month, just to see how they were doing. I spoke to Annie's dad. He looked tired, like he hadn't slept in days. His eyes were red and heavy, and his skin looked drawn. I didn't see her mum. He thanked me for everything the police had done, but said they were leaving town.'

'Did he say why?'

He shook his head. 'Not really, but he didn't need to. He just couldn't stand to be in the same town any more.'

'Did they know about David Watts?'

My father gave out a joyless laugh. 'This is the part I find hardest to take.'

'He was arrested, though, wasn't he? I mean, his knees would be scratched and scuffed, right, maybe scratches on his face?'

Dad looked at the floor. 'We let him go.'

'What?'

He nodded. 'That's a whole different story.'

I got the feeling I was getting to the worst part.

TWENTY-TWO

He ignored the telephone. He tried to sit it out. It would only be the press, or Karen. He could do without her bending his ear right now. He'd turned off the answer machine when there had been another message from the reporter, so it just rang out, each ring cranking his mood upwards. He clamped his hands over his ears and growled.

He felt hollow, his eyes heavy. He needed some coke, needed something to lift him.

He gritted his teeth and tried to last out the rings. But whoever was at the other end wasn't letting up. He got up and marched over to the phone, stepping over a couple of empty beer cans on the floor. He snapped up the receiver and barked, 'Yeah?'

'David, I thought you'd never pick up.'

It was her. It had gone round in his head, that same metallic distortion, the disguised tones emotionless, but soft and seductive at the same time, mocking him, unpicking his seams all day like soft flicks with a knife. He went to sit down, his legs suddenly weak. His stomach turned over and he fought back an urge to scream.

'What do you want?' he answered, his voice quiet and creaky.

'Liverpool tonight. Tottenham are staying at the Crowne Plaza. When they arrive, I shoot. It's your choice, David.'

He swallowed, his mouth dry.

'What do you want me to do?'

'Call Radio Five and confess. If you do it, I'll fade away.' There was a small laugh. *'If you're feeling brave, call the police in Liverpool. Tell them I'm looking at the hotel now. If I hear the sirens, I'll know. But give your name. If they ever catch me, they'll know all about you, so you might as well get your version in first.'*

David started to get angry and his grip on the receiver tightened.

'Look, you bitch, do you know who you are fucking with?'

There was a click, and then a hollow silence.

His hand dropped away. He felt helpless, sick. He looked around the room, but it was like looking through water. He was out of focus, off-kilter. Then he began to feel a seething rage. It welled up inside him, moving through his body, until his grip on the telephone turned his knuckles white and he bared his teeth in an angry snarl. His eyes went wide, his nose screwed up and red.

He screamed and smashed the telephone hard against the coffee table. It didn't break, so he did it again, and again, until his knuckles were torn and bloody, the receiver a tangle of plastic and wires. He stood up and kicked the table, and then hurled the telephone against the opposite wall. It smashed on impact.

He stood there panting, his rage subsiding. As it left him, he began to shake. He felt his insides churn and cold sweat crackled over his forehead. He sat down with a heavy thump and put his head back. The room seemed to spin so he gripped the chair and concentrated hard on getting calm.

He felt himself even out, the room slow down. Then he remembered the phone he had in his pocket, the one given to him by the American.

He turned it on. He scrolled through to the address book and pressed dial on the only number programmed into it, his fingers shaking as he did so. It rang only once before he heard the cold, clear voice of the American say hello.

'It's David.'

There was silence.

'It's David. Are you there?'

A small laugh. 'Yes, I'm here, Mr Watts. Have you got something to tell me?'

'No, well, yes.' He was breathing heavily. 'I've just had a call from that crazy bitch. She says she's going to shoot some more players tonight.'

'Don't worry, Mr Watts. I'll start work tonight.'

'Where are you?'

'I'm on my way to Turners Fold.' A pause. David could almost hear the smile. 'Sounds like a nice part of the world.'

'But she's not in Turners Fold. She's in Liverpool.' He sounded desperate, his voice high and frantic.

'But the trail starts there, Mr Watts. Don't worry. I'll find her. It's my job.'

And then the line went dead.

He looked at his phone in disbelief. He'd been cut off twice now. He wasn't used to this. If he went somewhere, people jumped for him. It was how he lived. In charge. At the top.

He put his head in his hands. Why had everything gone so wrong so quickly? He rocked lightly and gripped his hair in his hands. He tried hard to stay rational and consider his options.

He could do as she said. Call the police in Liverpool and tell them to stop the coach.

He shook his head. That was no good. All roads would then lead to him and she might still be bullshitting, riding pillion to the real psycho out there.

He took his head out of hands, wincing into the light. Patience. That was all he had left. If he could just sit out the night and nothing happened in Liverpool, he'd know it was bullshit and he could forget about her. He could call off the American, make a goodwill payment, and then just forget about it all.

He turned up the volume on the television and put his head back in his hands. If he just waited it out, he'd find out.

TWENTY-THREE

'Why did you let him go?'

I was confused.

My father's expression was blank, like he had gone through the reasons so often he'd run out of feelings about it.

'We never had him,' was all he said.

'I don't understand.'

He ran his hands across his forehead, a rueful smile making his eyes sad. 'David Watts was never arrested.'

I was astounded. 'At the moment, the police don't make good copy,' I snapped.

He gave me a thin smile. 'We come out of it smelling of shit.'

I held out my hands. 'Go on then. Let's hear it.' I'd never spoken to him like this before, as if I was in charge. But I was on my patch now.

He stood up and walked to the window. He looked out for a while, and then said, 'It went fine at first.' He leant on the glass pane with his arm. 'I called the ambulance and then got some more officers up there. All the

189

crime-scene routines went by the book. The photographs were taken; the swabs were done. There was only one suspect in my mind: David Watts. There was just one problem.'

'What was that?'

'Glen Ross.' Dad sighed, then said, 'He was the first on the scene. I told him what I'd seen, and he just went quiet. When I tried to explain, he just rubbished me, said that I had been too far away to tell.'

'So what did you do?'

Dad looked me in the eye, but when he saw my glare, he looked away again, thinking back to a time over ten years ago. I let him think, watching the red light on the tape machine shining bright as dusk kicked in. I was aware of the room slowly slipping into darkness.

'I did nothing,' he said quietly.

'Why?'

My dad smiled, but there was no pleasure in it.

'Glen Ross is a politician in a police uniform. Even back then, he used to talk about going places, about running the town, making it great. Thought he could clean up crime and make it a better place.'

'Didn't want too many black faces fouling the air?'

My dad shook his head. 'I don't know if that was the reason. Glen Ross hadn't planned this. It just sort of landed in his lap.'

'If it had been the mayor's daughter on that cold ground, would he have done the same?'

Dad shook his head. 'Probably not.' He looked away, uncomfortable.

'So you went along with it for the good of Turners Fold, to help Glen Ross clean up the town?' I was incredulous. Was this collection of forgotten streets worth a dead teenager? A dead black teenager?

He then said something that knocked my outrage off its rails.

'I went along with it for you.'

I paused, unsure what he meant. Then I asked, 'Why me?'

'We're not from Turners Fold. We just found ourselves here, trying to make a living and bringing you up to be a good man. Glen Ross is Turners Fold to his core. His dad was a policeman, and his dad before him. His family know everyone in the town, they have all the secret handshakes they need, can play golf at all the right courses. And so do the Watts family. I'm new, I always will be in the eyes of people like Ross and the Watts family. You were getting to the end of university and you had that job at the *Post* all lined up, and your mother was happy here. If I went out on a limb, the two people I cared about the most would suffer, because there was no chance of Glen Ross backing me up.' He sighed. 'So I stayed quiet to keep the peace, for you and for your mother.'

I sat down and ran my fingers through my hair. I had never imagined my dad as helpless, but right then he seemed it, controlled by a small town to forget the murder of an innocent young girl.

'Is that it?'

He said nothing, so I carried on, 'You could have come forward.'

'They had someone else's DNA inside of her. All I would have done is messed up a murder trial. Can you imagine how that would have gone down?'

'It would have freed an innocent man,' I said. When he didn't answer, I said, 'Tell me about him.'

My father shrugged. 'Nothing much to say. Just some local unfortunate, found drunk on a seat in the middle of town. Back then he was well-known, one of the local strange ones. You know what it's like round here, how the gene pool gets a bit thin sometimes. He was at the pub most nights, and most nights he drank too much. But he was okay. He was harmless. If we ever found him, we just took him home. He lived with his mother in a small bungalow, and she would stay up worrying every night until he came home.' Dad gave out a heavy sigh. 'Glen saw him in town, sleeping off the beer on a bench. He lifted him, processed him, and then let him go. A couple of days later, when we got the DNA results, he was arrested for rape and murder. The town got a murderer, moved on, and my career ground to a halt.'

'How come?'

'Because I turned down promotions. Glen Ross thought he could buy people. He thought he'd bought Watts, and he thought he could buy me. He was wrong again. He tried to get me to sit my sergeant's exams, or get me into CID, just trying to give me too much to lose. Make me high enough so that I couldn't stand the fall. He was right in a way. I had you. I had your mother. I needed the job. But at that moment my job stopped being a vocation. If that's what lies higher up the pole, people like Glen Ross, I don't want it. I'll sit out my career in uniform. Just take the money, and when the uniform comes off, I stop being a copper.'

'But how can you be so sure about David Watts if someone else's DNA was inside her? What makes you so right and everyone else so wrong?'

He took a deep breath and raised his eyebrows at me, trying to remind me who was the father and who was the son. I ignored it. I was being a journalist now, not a son.

'I saw him, Jack, running away from the scene. That's all I can say.' He shook his head. 'I've hardly followed football since. I used to love it, and I mean really love it, but a footballer's career should never be worth more than a girl's life.'

I looked at him and I felt disheartened.

'I can't do anything with this, Dad. All I can report is that a girl was killed walking back from David's farewell party. My paper won't print that. It's a sidebar to the feature, but that's all.'

'So you're saying you don't believe me?'

I sighed. I wanted to believe him, I really did, because he was my dad, and because I was getting a sense of why my father hated Ross so much, but journalists spend half their time spiking dead stories. But I knew that I didn't care about the truth most times. Journalists don't. It's the story that matters.

'It's not that, Dad, but you can imagine the power David Watts has in the media. If I try to run this, his lawyers will be all over me, and I'm just freelance. I've no paper to back me up. No one will ever use me again and I'll be back here, skint.'

My father clasped his fingers together and put them against his nose. I got the feeling he was trying to decide how much more to say.

'Stop looking at me like that then.'

'What do you mean?'

'Like it was me that left Annie Paxman dead on that ground. I stayed quiet to keep my job in my town. You're doing just the same thing.'

'That's a cheap shot. You could have done something. I can't. It's too late.' I was angry now.

'There was something else,' he said. He sounded uncertain.

'Go on.'

'A gold chain.'

He put his head back and let out a deep breath. He stayed like that for a few moments, and then smiled. 'A chain,' he said. 'As simple as that. I saw it in her hand, clasped in her fingers.'

'What was it like?' I was starting to feel uneasy.

'Some kind of Celtic design on a thick chain. Like three curls. It looked like it had been ripped off in the struggle. It had some engraving on the back, just a few words. Some kind of a Gaelic phrase.'

I leant forward. 'What Gaelic words?'

He looked at me, curious, and then said, '*Rath Dé Ort EW.*'

It felt like a door had slammed shut in my head. My father's voice retreated to a whisper, my head filled with adrenalin, the rush, the words from Laura bursting back. *Rath Dé Ort EW*. Twice in two days. I could hear my heart beating, my pulse racing fast.

'It means . . .' he started.

'*By the grace of God*. I know.'

He looked at me in surprise.

I tried not to smile. It didn't matter now whether David had killed Annie Paxman or not. It linked in with the football shootings, and I had the story.

I watched the red light blinking on the voice recorder. I thought about telling my father about the link with the football shootings, but I guessed he would find out soon anyway. And then I thought about Laura. I had a reason to call her.

But then something occurred to me.

'EW?' I asked. 'What does it mean?'

At that, Dad grimaced.

'Eugene David Watts,' he said. 'But he prefers David.'

She had the players in the crosshairs. Her finger was squeezed tight on the trigger, a whisper's width from firing.

They were milling about at the back of the coach, waiting for their bags. One of the players was speaking on a phone, standing still. She scanned the other players with the scope, but they were all moving around, either laughing and joking or just disappearing out of sight behind the coach. She didn't recognise him, but that didn't matter. He would be enough to make David Watts take notice, and that was all that mattered.

She took a deep breath and calmed herself, took another look down the scope, set herself. He hadn't moved, was still on the phone. She would go for his back. He might get lucky and the bullets would miss some vital organs. It was the message that counted, not the outcome.

The body of the gun was out of the window, a sheet wrapped around the stock in the hope it might muffle some noise. She had a mattress against her back to keep the noise out of the room. The more the ring of the shot stayed out of the hotel, the more time she would have to get out.

Her breathing stopped, time seemed to slow, and then she started to squeeze the trigger.

I didn't know what to say. It was a lot to take in. If he was right, David Watts was a rapist and a killer. Was that the last time? Were there any more victims out there like Annie Paxman? Then I thought about proof, and wondered whether I only believed it because my dad was telling me.

But then I thought about what my father had always told me when I was growing up, that truth is always the most important thing.

I tugged on my lip and looked at my father. Was he just obsessed? There was someone else locked up for this, caught by his DNA, found guilty beyond any reasonable doubt by twelve of his peers.

But I had always wondered why Dad had stayed a constable. I had known he was better than that. Now I knew why.

Then something occurred to me.

'Why are you telling me this now?' I asked. 'It was over ten years ago. Is it because of the feature I'm doing?'

He smiled. 'Yes, I'm telling you because you're doing a feature on him. If you weren't, I wouldn't have told you.' He paused, again looking like he was thinking about how much he should tell me. 'But secondly,' he continued after a few moments, 'I'm telling you now because Annie Paxman has come back to haunt him.' He looked at me, scrutinising me. 'David Watts is being blackmailed.'

'Because of Annie Paxman?'

He nodded.

I whistled. That changed things, gave a direct link to David Watts, and the neck-chain was maybe the missing piece. 'What's the demand?'

'A full confession.'

I paused, waiting for more. 'No money?'

He shook his head. 'Seems not.'

'Who told you?'

'Glen Ross.'

'Do you believe him?'

He shrugged. 'No, but I've no proof.'

'And that's why he was here,' I said slowly, everything slipping into place.

'Yeah, that's right. He was telling me to keep quiet, to remember the script.'

'And you changed your mind?'

He smiled, broader now. 'If Annie Paxman's story has to be told, I'll help. That bastard has been sitting pretty for too long now.'

'Watts or Ross?'

'Both.'

I stood up, my turn to pace. I walked to the window and turned round. I realised I had to write the story now. My father had told me that David Watts was being blackmailed. Dad hadn't done anything about Annie Paxman and it had haunted him for a decade. If he did nothing about the football shootings, it would kill him.

But then I realised that my father hadn't mentioned the football shootings through any of this. It had only ever been about Annie Paxman. I looked at him and wondered whether I should tell him about the neck-chain being found at the scene of the shootings. Then I thought about Laura and my promise to her. And the police decision to hold that information back. He didn't need to know. Not yet anyway.

'Are you doing this for Annie Paxman, or for you?' I asked.

He stayed silent for a while.

'Maybe both,' came his answer. 'Annie Paxman was a victim, but she wasn't the only one. What about that poor sod stuck in prison for the last ten years? Did I let him go there too easily, because I could see some-thing of myself in Watts? A young man about to start a football career, about to have all the things I had dreamt about? England caps. Success. I just don't know. What I do know, though, is that justice wasn't done, and if justice needs a hand, then I'll give it.'

I smiled at him, pleased to see something of the angry old man I remembered from my adolescence.

Then he turned to me again and almost pleaded, 'Are you going to write the story?'

My smile faded. 'I don't know, Dad. It's not the story I've been asked to write. And the evidence isn't there to print. You can see that.'

He nodded, looking resigned.

'Was there anyone else there who knew?' I asked.

He looked down, a shadow skimming across his face. 'I wasn't on my own in the car. James Radley was with me.' He looked up at me. 'Do you remember James?'

I remembered him as one of the local coppers. I also remembered when he'd died in a house fire, along with his wife, trapped in their beds by the thick, acrid smoke.

'So you're the only living witness?'

Dad nodded again. 'If I get evidence, will you write about it?' he asked.

I thought about it for a moment, worried about where it might lead. People were dying and my father was the final link with what had happened ten years earlier.

But I gave a journalist's answer.

'If you can get me evidence, someone will print it. It's the scoop of the year, if I can get it.'

Dad stood up and stretched, and then he rubbed his eyes. He looked tired, and I remembered his disturbed sleep.

I leant forward and clicked off the machine. 'Get some rest, Dad, and let me think about this.'

He patted me on the shoulder and left the room.

I became aware of how quiet it was. The last strains of daylight were coming in through the window, the clouds in the distance turning red. I thought about the story I'd written that afternoon and realised how empty it now seemed. I had a feature, an exclusive. That was in the bag. But now I had a huge story, one that would make the red-top editors shake with excitement, knowing it would be the talk of every bar in Britain, and it was one that would make my name.

But then I remembered my deadline, and my personal promise to myself to never get personally involved in a story. I smiled. Aren't promises there to be broken?

TWENTY-FOUR

The player stayed still as she squeezed the trigger that last small measure.

The gun kicked and the noise of the shot blasted around her ears. Through the scope she saw the player sink to his knees, his hand shooting forward to his chest, the other players turning towards him.

She pulled the gun back into the room, her hands already unpacking the rifle, running on adrenalin, each section coming apart neatly and going into her overnight bag. She put the bag over her shoulder and headed for the door, trying to stay calm as she heard the shouts from the street coming in through the window.

She took some deep breaths and then reached into her pocket, pulling out a gold chain. She let it twirl in her fingers for a moment before turning to toss it onto the bed, ready to be found. The papers hadn't reported the chains yet, but David Watts would have to take notice now.

Her hand paused on the door handle as she tried to

compose herself. She closed her eyes, exhaled, and then opened the door.

She almost shouted out loud when she saw that there was someone standing right outside.

I sat on the concrete base of the aviary, looking out over Turners Fold.

The aviary had ceased to be anything special a long time ago. Birds were kept there once, a summer attraction, budgies, parrots, cockatiels. Time had turned it into a dirty brick cube with a mesh front and seats under its roof, painted black, the slats scratched by graffiti.

But I wasn't there to wonder why the birds were no longer there. I was looking for something else. I was looking for a feel of whatever had happened here all those years ago.

I looked around. I could see green fields and clusters of trees rolling away, until they rose up to Pendle Hill in the distance. Across from the park was a playing field, a burnt-out cricket pavilion at one end. The road around it curved and faded away, lined with pebble-dashed semis, blues and creams and browns mismatched until they got lost by a curve in the road.

It all seemed so separate from the scene I had left behind in London, sitting here on a concrete base to a derelict brick cube.

But I knew there was a link between the football shootings and whatever had happened here years earlier. It was the neck-chain that confirmed it. Those words, so simple in Gaelic: *Rath Dé Ort EW*. Etched onto the back of neck-chains in London and Manchester. Found clasped in Annie Paxman's hand as she lay where I was standing, the life squeezed out of her.

I knew I had to act. I had information that could be used, but I owed it to my father to speak with him first, because I was about to bring London's finest detectives onto his patch.

She came face-to-face with a woman. She was old, late sixties, dressed tourist-style in white slacks and a flowered T-shirt.

She caught her breath and stopped, almost turned back, but she made herself carry on. They exchanged glances, the older woman curious, uncertain.

'What was that noise?' The accent was American, probably in town for The Beatles experience.

She looked back into the room, her mouth dry. She gritted out a smile. 'There are some fireworks down by the river. Some kind of concert. They were starting around now.'

The old lady nodded and shrugged, unconcerned, and turned to walk away.

'I was wondering if you could help me,' she said.

The old lady turned back. 'What's the problem, honey?'

She stood there, swallowing hard, trying to think what to say. There was now a witness, someone who had heard the shots. Her mind flew back to Manchester. She knew the security guard could identify her, describe her, but she wouldn't be going back there. The police would be at the hotel soon, looking for where the shot came from, and if the American woman tried to help them, pointed out where she was heading, they would catch her nearby with a rifle in her bag. It was too early for that.

'Could you show me where the lifts are please? Once you turn a corner all these corridors look the same.' She cursed to herself, but it would get her away from the room.

The old lady smiled. 'Sure I will. I'm going that way myself.'

She let out a deep breath and rushed back into the room, collecting the gold chain. It might make it too hard to identify it as the crime scene if the chain wasn't there.

And they walked off together, the old lady making small talk about the restaurant and the view.

They arrived eventually, in between the two sets of lift doors. She pressed for one to go down, and when the old lady wasn't looking, she pressed the button for the one opposite.

She stood and smiled as the old lady talked, willing one of the lifts to her floor as she listened to tales of trips around the Beatles sites, visits to Aunt Mimi's house and a walk down Penny Lane. She put her hand into her pocket and felt the silk scarf. Underneath that there was the gold neck-chain. She was improvising, and she cursed herself. She had planned this for too long to have to change.

She thought she could hear sirens outside, shouting downstairs. Then she heard machinery slow down, and with a light ping the doors opened. The lift was empty.

She gave a small glance upwards and smiled a thank you.

She stood aside to let the old lady go first. As soon as the old lady was in there, she pulled the scarf out of her pocket. The lady started to turn at the movement. Too late. Her head was snapped backwards by the scarf as it went around her throat.

She pulled hard and back, bringing the old woman to the floor, her frail shoulders blocking the doors. They tried to close, banging forwards and then back. The old lady was kicking, her hands reaching backwards, so she pulled harder, her teeth gritted, perspiration flickering across her head. The old lady was heavy, cumbersome, hard to hold on to as she kicked at the ground, but the grip on the scarf stayed firm until the old lady slowed down and her chest puffed out one last time. The struggle ended with a gargle and the movement stopped.

She thought she could hear something.

She got into the lift and pulled in the old lady's body, limp and heavy. She reached into her pocket and pulled out the gold neck-chain. She put it in the old lady's hand, the links swaying gently, and then pressed the button for the lobby. The door started to close, so she stuck her foot in it to make it pull back and then stepped out. She stood in front of the lift as the doors closed again, and then she heard the pulley wheels turn into life as it descended.

Her breathing evened out but still she knew she had to move quickly. She wasn't sure how long she had before security burst onto the floor. She jabbed at the call button and then waited for another lift to arrive. She listened for the sound of movement but it seemed like the hotel had become still. Too much so.

The other lift arrived. She entered it, every step bringing some relief. As the doors closed, she felt the end get nearer, began to imagine the effect of the news in London. Just as the lift began to gain speed, she thought she could hear screaming from below. She guessed the old lady had been found.

The lift stopped and the doors opened. She was looking at the backs of people, all shocked and jabbering, crowded around the lift opposite hers. She saw a security guard to her left, the only way out, listening intently to a walkie-talkie. He looked shocked, part-confusion, part-horror. He glanced over and noticed her bag, and then he looked back to where the old lady lay and forgot about her.

She headed away from the lift and towards the lobby. The doors were only a few seconds away, and as they got nearer she could hear the clamour from behind the reception area as the manager started to bark out instructions. The police must have called. She was nearly there when she heard sirens from the street and she faltered for a moment. There were lights outside flashing blue and red and moving fast. She stared at the doors, transfixed. Then she saw the reception staff come out from behind the desk, heading towards the lifts. It was now or never.

She went out through the doors and walked quickly across the street, into the Old Church Yard, using the shortcut as a shield. She ended up in Tower Gardens, a dark narrow street where ship merchants had once lived, until the commerce of Water Street guided her down to the waterfront. The wail of sirens converging on the hotel got louder. She tensed, waiting for the shout, the grab from behind, the shot.

None of that came. She made it to the Liver Building, ran across the wide lanes in front of it, the traffic gone, the daylight yellow, and headed straight for the river. The noise began to recede as she got near the water, and the dark spread of the Mersey came at her like relief. She paused for a moment by the river to get her breath back, sucking in deep lungfuls of air, and then carried on.

As she rushed along, she felt a kind of peace return, every step taking her away from the hotel. She thought she could hear someone cheering her on, running alongside her, but the sound was coming out of the shadows, out of the old warehouses of the Albert Dock, so she walked faster, her heart beating in time with her steps.

She burst back into streetlighting and found her car. She looked back along the river and saw the red and blue flashes bouncing off the buildings. It was quiet and still where she was. She threw her bag onto the passenger seat and climbed in. She was sweating, breathless.

She didn't wait around. Within ten minutes of the shooting, just when the area around the hotel had been cordoned off, the streets being searched for signs of the shooter, she was pointing her car away from the river. It had all gone to plan.

She thought she heard a laugh from the seat next to her and she jumped, gave out a small scream. She looked but there was no one there.

She focused her mind back on the road and headed out of town.

David Watts still had his head in his hands when the newsflash came on the television.

'Reports are coming in of another shooting.'

David looked up and went white. He saw the newscaster looking at sheets of paper and then staring at the camera as messages came through his earpiece.

'Reports are coming in that there has been a shooting in Liverpool,' he continued. There was a pause as the announcer received more information. He looked surprised and said, *'We have this report from the scene.'*

The picture moved away from the studio to a man standing by a police barrier in front of the Liver Building.

'Good evening. Yes, that's right, Gordon. I'm by the Mersey in Liverpool, the scene of another footballer shooting. The police aren't saying much at the moment, but the news coming from a nearby hotel is that someone has fired a shot at the Tottenham players as they were getting off their coach. Someone has been hit, but we don't know who and whether anyone has been killed.'

David wrapped his arms around his stomach and rocked gently.

The pictures from Liverpool faded. *'We'll return to Liverpool when we get more news.'*

A pause again. David just looked at the floor. He

moaned and then ran to the bathroom. He retched over the toilet bowl and then collapsed backwards, panting and hot.

He had to get out. He'd known about the shooting in Liverpool and done nothing. More blood on his hands. He had to get out, go somewhere, decide what he was going to do.

He retched again and then sat back with his head in his hands, clammy and hot.

Then he thought about his agent. He needed to speak to her, she would advise him.

He rushed back into the room and jabbed her number into his mobile. He listened as her phone rang out. No answer. Shit. He ran his hands through his hair. He tried her number again. Still no reply. Where was she?

He rummaged through his pockets and found the cocaine. He needed something to help him focus.

He shook his head. He couldn't do this.

He went back into the bathroom and his hand hovered over the bowl. But then, as he gripped the bag, he knew that he would do better with it than without it.

He opened the bag and poured out a small pile of powder onto the cistern, and then pulled out a credit card. This would help, he thought, just to get him through.

TWENTY-FIVE

The American smiled as he drove into Turners Fold. Small towns made his job so much easier. Everyone knew everyone else, so it made people easy to find.

He stopped at a red light, and as he wound his window down, warm air assaulted him. He watched as a handful of people walked slowly from a shop, looking drab, unhappy. It was nothing like London. There was no rushing in Turners Fold, none of the excitement. It seemed like everyone was waiting for bad news. He watched the faces: the sullen teenagers sitting on benches; the big-bellied men walking to the pubs, faces scarred by broken veins; the grim-faced women marching down the street, T-shirts flapping in the breeze, cigarettes clenched between their fingers. There was a challenge in their eyes, like they wanted to meet his gaze, not avoid it.

He knew he had to be careful. He sensed the anger, the grit, but he also intuited a togetherness, even as he drove. Do the job, get out.

He had the tools. There was a semi-automatic

handgun in a holster, hooked onto the back of his belt. A long knife, jagged blade, was strapped to his leg, and there was a small can of pepper spray in the glove compartment, ready for his pocket, good for disabling a target quickly, giving him time to get his other weapons ready. And into his jacket pocket would go an old handgun that he'd bought a few months before, with the serial numbers scrubbed off, stored away especially for occasions like this.

He checked himself in the rear-view mirror, saw certainty in his eyes. He put his head back and breathed deeply, flexed his fingers, stretched his muscles, and then relaxed back down again, breathing out, his head coming down slowly, so that when he saw the reflection of his eyes, he knew he was ready.

He wanted to see the town, hear its heartbeat. He parked his car in front of the town hall and walked around the triangle, sat on a seat for a while, watched the cars go by. Then he noticed the Swan.

Time to check out the local nightlife.

I found it hard to think properly.

I had come back to Turners Fold to write a biography of the town's local star, prompted by the football shootings. Now I'd found out that the town's star wasn't as pure as I'd thought.

But murder? And rape?

I would have heard about it. *Someone* would have heard about it. And there was a man in prison, serving out a life sentence.

But if it wasn't true, then my father was lying, or

making such a mistake that he was right to keep it covered up. No one else believed him. Was I too close to him to see what other people could see in him?

But in both cases there were the words on the back of the chain: *Rath Dé Ort EW*. That couldn't be a coincidence. For some reason, David Watts was being blackmailed. He was being told to confess to the murder of Annie Paxman. And football players were being shot.

But I couldn't find a why. It felt like I had the what, but not the why.

I needed to call Laura. She needed to know what I knew. But something stopped me. Maybe it was because none of it made any sense. Or maybe I was just trying to protect my father. He had just admitted to me that he had told lies. He would go to prison for that.

Then I realised that Alice was talking, but I'd heard little of it.

We were in the Bridge Inn. It was a modern pub made to look like an old one. The wooden sign swinging outside was like battered driftwood, and inside, its tables and dim intimacy made for a relaxing place to spend an evening. No pool tables, no fruit machines, no television. It was less real than the Swan, but it had a bar full of beer and my father's friends didn't go there. Sometimes, that's enough.

Alice was bubbly, happy, trying to kick-start conversations, pleased to have someone from out of town to talk with.

She asked me if I ever thought about Megan, her sister.

I didn't reply. I was swirling my bottle absent-mindedly, thinking about what my father had told me. The story I had been sent to write was almost written, but I had a real one to write now, one that would dominate every headline for days to come. But now I was worried. What would happen to my father if he went public after all and told his story? He could go into print and say how he saw David Watts leaving the scene, but his bosses wouldn't back him up, and there'd be no other evidence to help him out.

I sat back and glanced at Alice. She had an expectant look on her face. I felt my heart sink when I realised she was still waiting for an answer to her question.

I reached out and put my hand over hers. She blushed.

'I'm sorry, Alice. I was thinking about the feature, just something I should have put in there and didn't. It's bugging me.'

'That's okay. I was trying not to talk about the job.' She eyed me carefully. 'I was asking if you ever thought about Megan.'

I smiled. 'Yeah, sometimes. Even men remember their first time.'

She laughed at that, her eyes shining with mischief. She looked down at her drink and then back to me, now coy.

'Did you know that I'm a journalist because of you?' she asked.

I laughed, taken aback. 'No, I didn't.'

'Because you used to talk about it with Megan, about your dreams, your hopes, and make it sound like the most exciting thing in the world. I thought that if I became a journalist, I would meet exciting people, or travel the world, have celebrity interviews, exclusives, maybe even uncover Watergates.'

I nodded, smiling, understanding what she meant. I had felt the same, expecting to break big news, my name at the top of the front page. 'And now you write up council meetings and car crashes.'

'That's right.' She laughed. 'You've got a lot to answer for, Jack Garrett.' She watched me carefully over the top of her beer bottle, and then asked, 'What have you forgotten?'

I looked back at her blankly.

'The feature,' she said. 'What have you forgotten to put in?'

'Oh yeah,' I replied hurriedly. 'Just some anecdotal stuff my dad told me.' And then I cursed myself for mentioning him.

'And you want to get it down?'

'I'm sorry, Alice.' I squeezed her fingers. 'I'll be bad company until I do this.'

Alice nodded, but she looked like she didn't agree.

I smiled at her. I could tell what she was thinking, that there was an attraction, maybe a rekindling of something she thought she had forgotten. I knew it was one way, though. I was flattered, she was young and beautiful, fun to be with, but ever since I had sensed a change in Laura, that maybe we had begun to connect, I had thought just about her. And I wished I was with her right then.

Alice nodded and smiled ruefully. 'Okay, Jack. I know you've come back to work, not for a holiday. Promise me we'll finish this drink.'

'I promise.'

And with that, we both left the Bridge, walking along the canal so I could take her home, and then go back to whatever thoughts were buzzing round my head.

Bob Garrett headed down to the Swan.

It was quiet. The evening crowd were still making their way back from work, so it was just him, the land-lord, and a couple of drunks.

He wasn't making good conversation.

'Everything okay, Bob?' said the landlord.

Bob smiled, but looked distracted. 'Everything's fine. Just tired, still trying to get back into the nights routine.'

The landlord didn't pursue it. His pub was a refuge for the local men, he knew that, and if they wanted to unburden themselves over a pint, that was fine. If they didn't, that was okay too.

Bob looked into his beer. The inn was quiet. The television was on, as ever, a large white screen pulled down at one end of the bar, but its echo emphasised the lack of life.

Bob was only half-watching the television. He was thinking about what he would say to Glen Ross. He felt good about it at last, knowing that he was trying to do what was right. It was ten years too late, but at least it was something. Now he had to get something good enough to make the papers run it.

But there was something else troubling him. The whole story had lain as dead as Annie Paxman for more than ten years, and then suddenly it comes rushing back again. None of it made sense. Where was the sudden proof to make David Watts panic and send Glen Ross round to fight his battles? And why had Glen Ross agreed to it? What was making him nervous now, after all these years?

The door creaked open and into the bar walked a stranger. His head was razored bald, and his black shirt was tight against his muscles. He was tall and walked slowly, with a purpose, as if he expected the room to divide for him, as if all eyes were on him. They weren't. The drunks glanced over, but when they saw it wasn't a regular they returned to their beers and glances at the television. Bob Garrett didn't look up at all.

The stranger asked for beer. 'This place seems a nice little town.'

The barman looked up. 'Fuck me, it's Clint Eastwood.'

The drunks sniggered.

'What are you doing in Turners Fold?' asked the landlord. 'We don't get many tourists around here.'

The American gave half a smile. 'No, I'm sure you don't.' He took a drink, the creamy bitter tinting his moustache. 'I'm just passing through. Seemed like a quaint place to stop.'

'So what brings you to Lancashire?'

That half-smile again. 'Like I say, I'm just passing through.'

Bob glanced along the bar as the television broadcast news of the shooting in Liverpool, his attention grabbed by a gasp and a shout of 'fuck me' from the landlord. He didn't see the American stealing glances at him.

The landlord turned to the American and asked, 'What do you think of the football shootings? I thought your country had all the psychos.'

The American took a slug of beer and then shook his head. 'You've had a few.' He looked over at the television, taking another gulp. 'This is soccer, right?'

'No, it's football. Played with your feet.'

The American shrugged. 'Yeah, sorry, I forgot how good you English are with games. Cricket? That's the game you play with a paddle, right?'

The American ignored the landlord's glare and turned to look again at Bob. He saw the black trousers, the stiff white shirt, the black boots. The tie was off, but he still recognised the uniform.

Bob wasn't listening. He was looking at the television screen. It was showing a picture, coloured but grainy. It was of a blonde woman, mid-twenties, tall and trim, but the features were vague, indistinct. It was from the security camera in the Manchester apartment building. The video continued, and then suddenly Bob sat upright, jolted. He thought he knew her, but where from? Why would he know her? He was just from some small deadbeat town in the Pennines, famous only for . . .

And then his mouth went dry. He felt himself shoot back ten years. The drunks' chatter faded to nothing, his head filled with memories racing back at him. David Watts. A female blackmailer. A female shooter.

He dropped his glass.

The landlord turned round to look at him, but Bob didn't see him. The thoughts streamed in too fast to catch, a prickle of realisation. It was like he was running through dense woods, clawing at branches, knowing the way out was close and that he was about to burst into sunlight. But everything had tilted off-balance.

He turned and walked out of the bar, leaving just a broken glass and the intense stare of the American.

TWENTY-SIX

Glen Ross looked up when the visitor was ushered into the room.

The first thing he noticed was his height. Six feet four, maybe more. He stood up to greet him, just to match him, stare him down. He puffed up, couldn't help himself, and held out his hand to shake. The handshake was firm, strong, and Glen Ross was met with a look he couldn't hold.

'I'm Detective Inspector Ross,' he said, meeker than he intended. He dropped his hand and gestured towards a chair. 'Take a seat . . . uhm?' he asked, waiting for a name.

The visitor nodded and sat down. He stayed silent.

Glen Ross put his hands together and rested them on his desk. He smiled, the genial host, and asked, 'What can I do for you?'

'I'm here on behalf of David Watts.'

Glen Ross nodded. 'I know. I called him while you were waiting. Do you have a name? I've got to call you something.'

The stranger shook his head. 'No you don't.'

Glen Ross started to speak, then stopped. He took stock of his visitor: not a young man, maybe forty, but he had a fitness, a physical presence, that most people lose in their thirties. He could see a wide strong chest, no hint of a stomach. Ex-army, he thought. Then he realised there was an accent.

'American?'

The stranger nodded.

Glen Ross sat back and arched his fingers, putting space between them both. 'I've always wanted to go to the States,' he said, trying to draw something out. 'Which part are you from?'

The American shook his head slowly, smiling tightly. 'No details. That's the deal.'

'I haven't got a deal with you. I'm just helping out an old friend.'

The American smiled again. 'I think the phrase you guys have stolen from us is "the loop".'

Glen Ross's grin faltered. 'What do you mean?'

The American leant forward in his chair. 'If you're not in the loop at the start, you're never in it.'

'I don't understand.'

'Just think about this: it isn't the fault of David Watts that this shooter hasn't been caught. He did his civic duty and told you the shooter had called him. Have you passed the information on?' The American paused for an answer, but when he didn't get one, he smiled. 'Didn't think so.' He sat back and looked around. 'There's been another shooting, in Liverpool this time. How will you explain that?'

Glen Ross was silent, the simple truth of what the American was saying creeping up on him. That you are either in the game, or you're not, and it was his choice. 'You bastard,' he said quietly.

The American nodded in agreement. 'You got it.'

Glen Ross sat and thought for a minute or so, trying to avoid the stranger's gaze, which was too direct, too hard, too focused. He had to regain control, so he softened his tone and got his head nearer to the desk as if conspiring. 'Okay. If you're working for David, you can work for me, if that's the way you want it.'

The American smiled at that, but it was as if he was enjoying something else. He shook his head. 'I work for David Watts. You can do what you want.'

Glen Ross felt a chill and began to shift about in his seat. He was wondering what to say when the American asked, 'Who knows about David and the girl?'

Ross straightened his tie. 'Hardly anyone. Most people realised pretty quickly that there was nothing in it. A couple of officers didn't believe that, but they didn't say anything. Not publicly, anyway.'

'Who were they?'

'There's only one left. Bob Garrett. The other officer died a few years ago.'

'Bob Garrett?'

'One of my officers. He's got it in his head that David did it.'

'And you know different?' The American had spotted the 'my'.

'Of course I know different. I was there.'

The American smiled and crossed his legs. 'Does

221

anyone know about the link with the football shootings?'

Glen Ross exhaled and wiped his hand across his forehead. 'No one knows, don't worry.'

'I never worry.'

Glen Ross began to fidget in his seat.

'What about this Bob Garrett? Does he know?'

Glen Ross shook his head. 'No, not yet, and when he does, he'll have known for too long to do anything about it.'

'Like you.'

Glen Ross faltered again.

The American smirked. 'I went for a drink in a bar on the way here,' he said. 'Dark and smoky place, but the beer was okay.' He paused. 'There was a cop in there.'

Glen Ross shrugged, feigning nonchalance. 'Go to a pub, you'll always find a policeman in it.'

'This one ran out when the television started talking about the shootings.'

Glen Ross chewed his lip. He could feel his chest tighten, his breaths coming faster. 'What did he look like?' he asked.

'Tall, strong, fifty-odd. Crew cut, thinning on top, fair complexion.' He grinned and examined his finger-nails. 'Bob Garrett, I presume.'

Glen Ross looked down at the desk and took a deep breath. He stayed that way for a few moments, and then asked quietly, 'What do you need to know?'

The American smiled. 'That's better.' He looked around and spotted the photographs dotting the walls behind the desk. 'You're an important guy.'

Glen Ross started to smile, relax slightly, but then

he realised he was being mocked. He felt his shirt collar dampen.

The American pointed at a framed photograph on the desk. 'Wife and children?'

Glen Ross nodded, felt his stomach lurch.

'They must be proud,' the American said with menace, and then waved it away, looking back at Glen Ross. 'Tell me about her. The girl who died. About the same age as your daughter?'

Glen Ross paused for a few seconds, trying to gather his recollections, and then began to recount the events of that night over ten years earlier.

He got as far as saying how David Watts was nowhere near when she died, when the American put up his hand to intervene.

'I don't want your version of what happened. I don't care what happened. I just want to know about her. Where she lived. Her family. Her friends.'

'I was starting to tell you.'

He shook his head. 'No you weren't. You were trying to convince me that you did the right thing.' He stared. 'I don't care about that.'

Glen Ross nodded nervously. He knew he'd lost control of the conversation.

'She was called Annie Paxman,' he said flatly.

'Are her family still around?'

He swallowed. 'They moved.'

'When?'

'Right after her death. Probably couldn't live with it.'

'And you can?'

Glen Ross didn't answer.

'Okay, where did they move to?'

'Somewhere in the Ribble Valley.'

'Is that it? Is that all you know?'

Glen Ross nodded again, more slowly this time.

'Has she got any relatives in the town?'

'No, I don't think so.'

'There are a lot of negatives in your story, chief.'

'I had no need to know.'

'Well, you do now.'

Glen Ross reached down and undid the top button on his shirt, loosened his tie. 'Do you think it might be one of her family?'

He shrugged. 'The girl doing the shootings is a white woman. Annie Paxman was black, right?'

Glen Ross nodded.

'But whoever did it made Bob Garrett drop his drink, like he'd seen a ghost.'

Glen Ross rubbed his forehead.

'No one has ever asked for the murder investigation to be reopened?'

'No.'

'There's never been any local pressure about it?'

'No. We got the murderer, some local drunk called Colin Wood He's still in prison. The last thing people in Turners Fold want to do is reopen it all. It's a quiet place, a safe place.' His tone was unconvincing.

'A drunk?' The American looked amused and sceptical. 'Does he have relatives in town?'

Glen Ross nodded. 'His mother, but she's been quiet since Colin was convicted.'

'Too ashamed, or too bitter?'

Ross looked down.

The American was about to ask another question when he saw Glen Ross look up quickly, his eyes wide, a shocked look on his face. There was a bang on the door and it burst open, carrying Bob Garrett into the room. He looked angry, his face flushed and red, his eyes wild. He pointed at Glen Ross. 'You knew, you bastard.'

Glen Ross stayed silent. He didn't know what to say. He looked at the American, and then back at Bob Garrett. His mouth went dry.

The American intervened.

'PC Garrett, I believe,' he said, and stood up. He held out his hand to shake.

Bob Garrett whirled round. He stopped when he saw the visitor.

'You were in the pub?'

He nodded. 'It was on the way here. I'd had a long drive.'

'And what are you doing here?'

The American smiled. 'I think you know.'

'Bollocks. Enlighten me.'

The American looked at Glen Ross, then back at Bob Garrett, and then reached into his jacket pocket. He pulled out a wallet and flashed a warrant card. Police.

'We got a call from David Watts,' he said. 'Someone's called him claiming to be the shooter. I've come up here to check it out.'

'Just you?'

He smiled. 'This is a major investigation, and this is one lead of many.' He gave a conspiratorial smile. 'You can imagine we're a bit stretched at this time.' He paused for effect, glancing at Glen Ross. 'And above all else, he claims that the person who called him has been dead for ten years.'

Bob's gears were slipping into place, the haze clearing. 'Annie Paxman?'

The American smiled in response. 'You can guess that it's not our strongest lead.'

Bob started to calm down, his hands on his hips, his breathing heavy. He began pacing, his fingers scratching his chin as he thought. 'What's this person saying?' he asked eventually.

'That if David Watts admits he killed Annie Paxman, she'll stop shooting football players.'

'Fucking hell!' Bob exclaimed. He stopped pacing and turned to Glen Ross. 'Why didn't you tell me all this before?'

'I asked him not to,' the American intervened, stepping in before Glen Ross could utter some crass remark. 'We're trying to keep all our leads quiet, so the press don't get wind of it. You remember the Beltway Sniper, John Muhammad, back in my country? They were giving things away so fast that he would have escaped if he had been watching television.'

Bob nodded and held a hand up in apology. He began to pace, starting to accept what he was being told, his temper dissipating. Then something occurred to him. He whirled round and pointed. 'But I saw the shooter on the television.' He looked at a loss of what to say, his face pained, then blurted out, 'I knew her. I fucking knew her.'

Glen Ross and the American exchanged glances.

'Who was she?' asked Ross, nervous, looking down. He wished Garrett would shut up, but if Garrett knew who it was, he needed to know.

Bob exhaled and then shook his head. 'I don't know. I felt like I could almost put a name to her, but I can't quite get there. The pictures are too blurred.'

'I mean, we know that it isn't Annie Paxman. She's dead,' Ross continued.

'I know. I found her.' Bob flashed a bitter glare at Glen Ross and then ran his hands over his hair, a perplexed look on his face. He went to a chair in the corner and sat down. 'So is David Watts going to do this?'

'That doesn't concern me. I'm only concerned about stopping the shootings.'

Bob shot Glen Ross a look which said that David could stop it all in an instant if he told the truth, but the American intervened, asking, 'Could you show me where Annie was found?'

'Okay. I'll take you there now.'

The American shook his head. 'No, better not. We'll go down separately. I'm trying to keep my stay in Turners Fold quiet. Keep the press out.'

Bob shrugged. 'As you want. Ready to go now? I don't start for a couple of hours, but this is important.'

He nodded. 'Just give me a minute with the inspector. I'll see you down there in a half-hour. The inspector will tell me where to go.'

Bob nodded, glanced at Glen Ross, and then left the room.

As the door closed, Glen Ross looked at his visitor. 'What are you planning?'

'Research.'

'Where did you get the police warrant card?'

He smiled. 'You don't want to know.'

Glen Ross slumped into his seat.

'I want a full family history in a couple of hours. And I want to know where the family is now. Every damn branch. Can you do that?'

'But the shooter was blonde. Annie Paxman was black. They can't be related.'

'Just do it.'

Glen Ross nodded again.

'I'll call you in the morning to arrange a meet.'

Glen Ross looked up but said nothing.

The American smiled. 'It's been a pleasure, Inspector.' Then he left the room, closing the door softly behind him.

As the door closed, Glen Ross looked at the family photograph on his desk and closed his eyes.

TWENTY-SEVEN

I walked through Turners Fold, heading for Tony's house.

I'd acquired the walking habit in London. In Turners Fold, it seemed like everything worth seeing was in a different town, so I'd always driven. In London, I strolled, the traffic all stutter and snarl. It felt good to be walking to Tony's house, the soft pat of my feet on the pavement the only sound.

I turned onto Tony's street and saw the lights on in his house.

He lived just a few streets from the town square. It was one of the oldest houses in town, a double-fronted Victorian charmer, Accrington brick, with ivy on the corners and a small sheltered doorway at the front. It was framed against swirls of deep purple and grey, the build-up of heat from the previous few days brewing up a storm. The sky matched my thoughts, as the story around Annie Paxman's death clattered about my head. A glitter of stars shone through the occasional gap in the clouds, a sight I realised I'd missed in the light pollution of London. I needed to speak to Tony to find my own gap in the clouds, some confirmation that my gut feeling was right about what I should do. I was enough of a journalist to know that it was a good story, but was I prepared to risk my father to write it? Tony had been a journalist longer than I'd been alive, so he knew his way around. I guessed what his advice would be, but I needed to hear him say it.

I saw Tony through the window. He was in a chair, reading by a red-fringed standard lamp in a room awash with books, walls covered in paintings, Victorian land-scapes, and photographs of his children, all grown up now and living elsewhere. Eileen, his combatant of thirty years, was sitting at a table reading a newspaper. They looked like they fitted each other, one right foot, one left. They made me think of how happy my parents had been when my mother was still alive. Did my father feel angry, somehow cheated? Or did he just miss her? It made me think of Laura, hundreds of miles away, and I wondered whether she was thinking of me.

I walked up to the front door and stood under the light. The heat was getting oppressive. I sensed the rain before I felt it. As I rang the bell, a coin-sized raindrop splattered onto my shoulder.

It was a while before anyone came, perhaps thinking it was too late for visitors. By the time the door opened, with Tony looking wary, the rain had increased to a steady tap-dance. When he saw it was me, he relaxed and flung open the door to beckon me inside.

We exchanged our greetings, smiles and handshakes, and I followed him in. As we walked down the hall, he barked towards the room he'd just been in, 'Eileen, it's Jack Garrett. You want to say hello, you're going to have to make it quick, because we're going outside.' He rolled his eyes at me and started walking towards the other end of the hall. 'I'll get us some beers,' he whispered.

I turned round when I heard Eileen come into the hall. I hadn't seen her for a few years, and I was surprised at how she looked. Age had crept up and dragged her neck and pulled at her face, so that it was kept in place by the criss-cross of lines around the eyes.

'Jack,' she said softly, hugging me. 'Tony told me you were back. How are you?'

'I'm fine, Eileen,' I said, smiling warmly. 'How are you? You look well.'

She smiled and wrinkled her eyes at me. 'Don't lie. That fool over there has made me old.'

I laughed, while at the other end of the hall, a voice said, 'Don't you listen to her.'

They'd been that way for as long as I'd known them. Like mirrors, bouncing each other back.

Tony opened the door to the back garden. He had a covered deck, and the rain on the roof had increased to a drum-roll, the noise disturbing the hush of the hallway. Tony stepped outside with two bottles of beer in his hand, their beads of coldness disappearing into the evening heat like smoke-trails.

Eileen looked over and then patted my arm, winked and gave a hint that she knew she wasn't wanted. 'I'll see you before you go back to London,' she whispered.

I smiled and watched her go, and then headed down the hall to join Tony.

When I got outside, he passed me a beer and sat down on an old chair. I leant against the wall of the house, looking into the darkness of Tony's garden. The rain was coming down hard and water began to run off the roof, dropping in streams just inches from my shoulder.

'What's the matter, Jack?' Tony asked.

I looked back. 'How do you know anything's the matter?'

Tony laughed. 'Because you've come here at night, when you could have just called into the office tomorrow. It's nearly nine o'clock.' He smiled and took a gulp of beer. 'Call it a hack's hunch.'

'I've a dilemma, Tony, and I don't know what to do.'

'That's the thing with dilemmas,' he replied, chuckling. 'What's your problem?'

I stepped away from the wall and began to pace, scuffing my feet on the decking.

'What do you do, Tony, when a story lands in your lap that is good, potentially *very* good, but writing it might hurt someone close?'

Tony looked at me, watched my face, and then I wasn't sure that he was seeing me at all, like he was casting back through some old memories.

Tony put his beer on the floor. 'Is this about David Watts?' he asked.

I looked at him but didn't answer.

'What have you got?' he asked quietly.

I stood still for a moment. I thought about telling him, but then I shook my head.

'I can't say,' I replied. 'It's such a good piece, I'm sure of it, but the more I think about it, the more I know it will hurt people, and I can't get anything from anyone else to use.'

Tony sighed.

'That's your answer,' he said. 'Like it or not, you don't have free will. You have a promise of a feature. Grab it. You can hunt for exclusives or go on crusades if you want, but you're paid to write commuter fodder. You're being paid to write a sentimental biography of David Watts. If you do that and nothing else, you'll have done your job.'

I looked back out into the garden.

'Should it just be about doing my job?' I asked. 'I always thought there might be more to writing than paying the rent.'

Tony smiled. He didn't need to say it. I knew he was thinking back to his greener, more naïve days.

'Ask yourself this question,' he said. 'What if you write your new story and forget about your feature?'

I turned round. He was leaning forward, his eyebrows arched.

'That's the only other choice you've got,' he continued. 'The *London Star* has got a space for a feature. It's getting bigger everyday. You've heard about Liverpool, haven't you?'

I shook my head. I had been drinking with Alice instead of watching the news, but I guessed the story.

'Another shooting,' he said, 'so if you don't write the feature, someone else will get the slot, and they'll never commission you again.' He shook his head. 'No editor is going to forgive you just because you thought you had stumbled upon a goldmine. He's going to want to know why his feature hasn't been written.'

I sighed, understanding the truth of what I was being told.

'If you want to change the world, or break exclusives,' Tony said, 'get off the crime beat. Write a book. But for as long as you get your money from sidebars and fillers, you'll write what the papers want.'

'You're right, Tony, I know that. Maybe I just needed someone to point it out.'

Tony smiled and took another drink of beer. He watched me swirl the amber liquid around, trying to read what I was thinking.

'Back to work?'

I nodded, and then went to walk past him. I patted him on the shoulder and was walking back into the house to make small talk with Eileen when he asked, 'Is it about Annie Paxman?'

I stopped dead. It was as if he'd just thrown a sucker punch as I was walking back to my corner. I looked down at him, stunned, wondering why I felt like I'd been slapped.

'You knew?'

He nodded slowly, uncertain.

'For how long?'

Tony sat back and sighed. He ran his hand across his forehead as he tried to think of a way of sanitising the answer. There wasn't one.

'All along, I suppose,' he said eventually, looking ashamed.

'How do you know?'

'You know what it's like, Jack. You hear rumours, drunk talk.'

'What did you do?'

'What do you think? I pitched the story.'

'What did the paper say?'

'I was told to bury it. The police had no proof, so neither did we, and anyway, they'd got someone for it. DNA evidence. Foolproof, so they said.'

'But that's inhuman.'

Tony shook his head. 'No, Jack, you're confusing rumour with fact. What was there to report? We weren't concealing a murderer. He was in a cell, waiting for his trial, and if we had printed it before the trial, it would have wrecked it. The killer would have got away with it because of a quick glimpse in the darkness. That wasn't enough to get Watts, and it would just let the other guy off the hook.'

'But what about you, Tony? Weren't you tempted to run it?'

He looked at me hard and direct. 'I hadn't been around for long. I'd just moved back to Turners Fold and I needed the job. I did what I was told.' He pointed at me. 'I had the same dilemma you did, and I reached the same decision you are going to reach.'

'How do you know I'll come to the same decision?' I snarled.

He sat back now. 'Are you going to go out on a limb on this one? David Watts has influence in this town, as does his family. You know that his father is in line to be mayor next year? And that his two brothers run the David Watts Trust?'

I shook my head. I didn't know.

'They do a lot for this town. The Trust takes a lot of

the poorer kids away on adventure holidays, and helps pay for a few of the local youth football teams. If you get it wrong, you'd upset a lot of people, and it would make it very hard for anyone close to you left behind here. And what about his spending power? He can afford the best lawyers in town. Do you really want to take them on? Put that good life in London in jeopardy?'

I shook my head slowly, resigned to the inevitable.

'There you have it,' he said, and then he looked at me. 'Remember, Jack, that however much this might hurt, your father could be wrong. It was dark; it was from a long way away.'

'He seemed pretty sure,' I replied.

'That doesn't make him right.' Tony put his hand on my shoulder. 'Your father is a good man, but no one is perfect.'

I turned away, feeling hurt. I had looked up to Tony when I was first starting out, always thought that he was different to the rest, prepared to say what had to be said. But I felt angry as well, because I knew Tony was right.

'What if I could prove that David Watts was guilty?' I said.

Tony widened his eyes. 'If you can do that, we'll both go freelance.'

That made me laugh. I held my hands up in defeat. 'Okay, okay, back to work. I'll write my feature.'

Tony stood up and patted me on the back. 'See me before you go. But remember, Jack, he just might be innocent.'

*

236

Bob Garrett was sitting in his patrol car by Victoria Park. The rain was deafening, a constant rattle on the roof. He was smoking, but it made the windows steam up, so he had to keep wiping the side windows to see out.

He had been there for around ten minutes, but already he was getting edgy. It was an isolated spot on any night, not overlooked, up on a hill, the last thing between Turners Fold and the rolling countryside. In the driving rain it seemed utterly desolate.

But it wasn't just the location that made him nervous. Something about the meeting made him uneasy.

He checked his watch. He thought he might have time to call Jack. He had told him all about David Watts, but if it was connected with the footballer shootings, he had to stop Jack from writing the story. It could get him into trouble if he revealed the investigation.

Bob took a long pull on his cigarette and made more mist on the windscreen as he exhaled. He smiled to himself. It was good to see Jack again, to hear his voice around the house. Whatever distance had grown between them over the last few years, Jack was still Jack, his precious son. He reached into his pocket for his phone. He needed to speak to him, to tell him to lay off the David Watts story, at least for now. Afterwards, he'd take him fishing, just the two of them, a quiet riverbank, and a cool-bag full of beer.

He was about to dial Jack's number when he saw a shadow through the windscreen. Once he had cleared it with his hands, he saw the American walking along the path behind the church.

He was difficult to make out at first. He was in dark

clothes and visibility was bad, but he kept on stepping into shards of light still making it through from the street on the other side of the church. He had an umbrella, which had the effect of shielding his face, but Bob recognised him instantly. It was that air of nonchalance, like a relaxed menace. Even from this distance, even from that earlier brief encounter, his casual manner was easily recognisable.

Bob's unease deepened. He wasn't sure what it was. Something just wasn't right. After many years of policing, Bob knew to beware the quiet man. You never knew when or what was coming from him.

Bob stepped out of his car and pulled up his collar. His hat kept out most of the rain, but his neck soon got wet. As the American got closer, Bob could feel water beginning to seep down the back of his shirt. He grimaced. There was a long night ahead, and he didn't want to spend it in wet clothes.

As he got closer, Bob held up his hand. 'Hello again?'

The American nodded and smiled in response. 'How you doing?' he asked. Then he looked up. 'Wet, I guess,' he continued, and then nodded up the hill. 'So this is where it happened.'

Bob looked over and sighed. 'I was just about here,' he said. 'I was looking out for vandals. There was nothing happening, and as I swung round to leave, I caught her in my headlights.'

'Grim sight.'

Bob shivered. 'Yes, it was.' He looked up at the sky and pulled his jacket together. 'What do you need to know? It's a pretty shitty night.'

The American looked up towards the aviary. 'Just a flavour really.' He began to walk away, heading across the park, leather soles squeaking on the wet grass. 'Why do you think David Watts was involved?' he shouted over his shoulder.

Bob sighed, and then stepped onto the wet grass to follow him. He trotted to catch up, and, once there, answered, 'Because I saw him running that way,' and he pointed over towards the field sloping upwards and away from town.

'That's quite a distance in the dark.'

Bob shrugged. 'It's what I saw. It was Watts. I'd watched him play for a couple of years. He was big news around town. I knew how he walked, how he ran. It was David Watts. No doubt. I knew it was him even before I knew that he was the last person to be with her.'

The American stopped by a flowerbed and looked away, out over the fields. He seemed focused, so Bob let him concentrate, and took another pull on his cigarette, the end shining bright as he sheltered it from the rain with his hand.

He was just finishing his cigarette, stopping to flick the glowing filter into the grass, when the American spoke up again.

'If you're so sure, why have you kept it quiet?' he asked, still looking away. 'It's been over ten years.'

Bob thrust his hands into his pockets and looked at the ground, his shoulders hunched to keep out the rain.

'Because I was a lone voice. What could I do?'

'Go to the press?'

Bob sighed. 'That would have cost me my job. I had

239

a young family. I hadn't been a police officer that long so I went with the flow. And let's face it, my suspicions counted for nothing.'

The American turned round and nodded, seeming to understand. He carried on walking, Bob trying to keep up, until they ended up on the stone floor of the pavilion.

'What about the girl's family?'

Bob shook his head. 'I haven't seen or heard from them since they left town not long after.'

'Do you know where they were headed?'

Bob shook his head but said nothing.

The American stepped forward, getting close to Bob. He smiled. 'If you know, say so. This is a major investigation. If this turns out to be relevant and you've held it back, you'll be in shit up to your knees.'

Bob glared at him. 'I do not know where they went. I didn't need to know, so I didn't bother to find out.' He snorted. 'Maybe I just had a little trouble looking them in the eye. So pack it in with the threats, arsehole.'

The American leant forward so that their noses were almost touching. 'Who was she?'

Bob swallowed. Even in the darkness, he could sense the menace. 'She?'

'The girl on the television, the one who made you run out of the bar.'

'I told you before. I thought I knew her, but now I'm not so sure.'

The American stayed close to him for a few seconds, wondering if anything else was going to be said, and then he stepped away. He smiled.

240

'DI Ross tells me your son is in town.'

Bob stiffened. 'What about him?'

'I'm told he's a reporter. What's he writing about?'

Bob's jaw set firm. 'Maybe he just came back to see his old man,' he hissed.

'So he is back?'

'Yeah, he's back. So what?'

'So what is he writing about?'

Bob didn't answer straight away, but he could feel himself getting angry. The American was asking about his son, and as far as Bob was concerned, that was off-limits.

The American let Bob's anger fizzle in the rain, and then asked, 'Is he writing about David Watts?'

'You ask him,' Bob snarled, his finger pointing. 'And then see how far you get, hotshot. If you expect me to talk about my son, you can go fuck yourself.'

And with that, Bob turned round to walk away.

'PC Garrett. You are obstructing a murder investigation.'

Bob stopped and turned around slowly.

'No, I'm not,' he answered softly, trading menaces. 'I've told you all I know.'

The American stepped over to him.

'Not everything.'

Bob said nothing. He stared the American in the eyes. His stare was met coldly.

'Have you spoken to him about it?' the American asked quietly. 'Yes or no?'

'About Annie Paxman?' Bob asked, a sneer making it through, but then he shifted his gaze at the last

241

moment, one quick blink, and scuffed at the stone floor with his foot. Not much, just a press with his toes, almost invisible, but it was spotted.

'Course not,' said Bob. 'It's confidential, right.'

The American nodded.

'Thank you, officer,' he replied.

Bob stepped away and pulled another cigarette out of his packet and lit it, cupping it in his hand to keep out the rain. The smoke drifted away, quickly broken up by the strips of water still coming down hard. He was waiting for the next question.

The American put down his umbrella, checking it as if there was a problem with it. Bob looked at the ground and took another drag on his cigarette.

Bob didn't hear him pull the gun. He was looking out over the town, at the lines of orange streetlights. He just heard a rustle as the umbrella dropped, and then looked over to see it on the floor, rocking lightly. He didn't know what was happening at first, but his eyes carried on moving, everything slowing down to fractions of time.

Bob saw the American's hand sweep through the air. He was holding a gun, and it seemed to go so slow that he could hear the wind brush against the barrel. Bob tried to move, but he couldn't react, couldn't do anything. His eyes tracked the slow arc, but his body slowed down as well, so his legs felt leaden as he tried to step away. His arms felt strapped together as he thought about his baton, his instincts slowly kicking in.

The cold metal pressed against his forehead. His eyes widened. His legs started to react, his body starting to turn so he could get away. His hand started to come up to knock the gun away.

There wasn't time. It was all too quick. There was an explosion. It echoed, his ears bursting with noise. His forehead felt on fire. Then a hammer blow, hard and heavy, knocked his head back, no chance to scream or cry for help. There was no time for that. No last goodbyes.

He began to fall backwards, his eyes rolling, the stars coming into view, burnt by an image of the American with his arm out, smiling, pulling the gun back in recoil. The stars blurred as he fell, the dots of light rushing together, making a bright sunshine, a spotlight, a beam that began to pull away from him fast, crowded out by darkness.

The last thing he felt was the rain on his face as he arched backwards.

He was dead before he reached the ground.

The American looked down, the gun in his hand. He was still smiling as he watched the rain drip onto the cigarette. The red ember slowly sizzled to black ash, and, once gone, Bob Garrett lay as still as Annie Paxman had done ten years earlier.

The American wiped the gun and put it down next to Bob Garrett's hand. He stepped back, turned around, and then walked away.

TWENTY-EIGHT

I got the knock in the middle of the night.

I didn't know the time, but the solid darkness told me that it was still a long way from morning. I knew what the knock meant as soon as I heard it. It's born from a fear that stalks everyone close to a police officer. It's a fear of that cracked-out burglar, or that gone-wrong domestic, or those wrong-place wrong-time crazed psychos. As soon as I heard the knock, I knew it was my turn.

I ran down the stairs still dressed in my boxer shorts, my mind jerked awake, skipping steps, my mouth dry. I tried to compose myself as I got to the door, hoping to put off the moment long enough so that it would never arrive, but as soon as I flung open the door and saw two policemen there, I took a deep breath and steadied myself against the doorframe.

They didn't say anything. They didn't need to. There were two of them, one male, one female. He was there to break the news. She was there to break the fall.

I looked away and pushed myself off the doorframe

before walking back into the house. I left the door swinging and I heard them follow me in. My knees didn't feel strong so I sat down.

I don't remember much else, apart from snatches of emotion. I remember the female officer putting her hand on my shoulder. There were no tears then. It was too soon. I felt many things rush at me, assaulting me so hard that I lost all sense of my surroundings: the nausea, shock, disbelief. But there were no tears. Not yet.

I think the female officer might have been crying. I can remember her mumbling words of comfort, but she wiped her eyes and sounded embarrassed. She was there for me, although maybe she didn't realise that it helped me to know that I wasn't alone, that other people felt a loss. I realised that they were my father's friends and colleagues, and that their loss might mirror mine. I'd lost a man I loved, my father, but he was a man I didn't really know. They had lost Bob Garrett, fellow officer, friend, someone much like them, facing the same risks as them. Maybe they saw themselves lying there.

I asked them what had happened, and I was told that he had been shot, but nothing more. But what more did I need to know? He was gone, dead. I felt deserted, desolate, nothing left, the last real connection with my childhood had disappeared.

The guilt set in next. It came at me in unforgiving waves. I felt guilt for leaving him and going to London. Guilt for not seeing his side of things enough, like I might have let him down too often. Guilt for not trusting him as a father, for not believing that he might have loved me whatever my faults were. Wasn't that what parenthood was all about? Unconditional love. Why can't a son's love be unconditional? Why had I fought him so much, as if I had always wanted him to be different?

Guilt was eventually submerged by an overwhelming sadness and time became a blur.

The police were gone before daybreak. There was nothing else for them to do. I wasn't speaking. I was just sitting on the sofa, staring into space, buffeted by flashes of my father, the father from my early years, not much older than myself now. My head was full of giggles and movement and colour, my father smiling, looking trim and young, happier, my mother in the background. It was a million times removed from the cold and empty house I sat in.

I'd expected more whenever I'd thought about this moment. As a reporter, I'd often had to speak with grieving relatives, intruded on private pain. I've seen people scream, collapse, be sedated. I never thought I would go that way. My mother's death had taught me that life does carry on, that pain does become manageable, but I still expected more. All I had was a sudden emptiness, which is just a nothing, a blank, so all I could do was curl up and let the sounds of the house take over. The refrigerator hummed into life occasionally, competing with the occasional creak and knock of the house as it settled and cooled. A clock ticked, relentless, time slow-marching itself in light metallic knocks, each tick pushing me further away from when I last saw my father; from our last conversation, when I had questioned him, asked him to justify himself. Sirens wailed somewhere in the distance.

It was the growing daylight that hurt the most. The room became lighter and I began to hear birdsong outside. Each dawn always felt like a new start, and it was that which made me realise that I was moving into a new stage of my life; a day had started that my father would never see.

That's when the tears came.

The tears wrung me out and so I must have fallen asleep, because I woke up and felt empty and cold. The house was lonely and bare, and I wondered whether my father had felt the same way every day when he woke here, my mother gone and me in London.

There was no warmth in the house at all. It lacked all those touches that my mother had brought, those artistic flourishes, flashes of colour. I glanced over to a photograph of my parents on the wall and felt another rush of sadness when I saw her smiling face. I wanted her back at that moment more than any other time. I'd forgotten the cancer years now. The woman I remembered was the one before the illness, the one who would hug and kiss me and call me her treasure. If she knew that my father had been taken away too, that I would be left all on my own, she would be heart-broken. Then I wondered whether she did know, whether they were together again and could look after me together once more, keep a constant watch.

That comforted me at first, but the more I looked at the photograph, the more I realised that this was it. There was no one watching over me. My parents had gone and it was all down to me now.

The short sleep had helped, though. It had somehow

built a paper wall between the news of my dad's death and the start of the next phase of my life. It was only a few short hours since I had found out, but the news didn't feel new any more.

As I came round, I was surprised to find that I was angry. Not at anyone, just at the injustice of it all. A man like that just cut down. All he was doing was earning his pay, just like most other people in town. I had a flash that I wanted to do something about our recent indifferences. That thought made me feel stronger, so I nurtured it, grabbed at it like a drowning man at a sliver of air. I thought about the need to mark the man's life, so that somewhere, somehow, he could watch me and know that what had once been there as a birthright, unconditional love, had never really gone away.

I remembered the conversation we'd had about David Watts. I wasn't going to write about that, but I remembered my father lamenting his wasted police career. I could do something about that. I knew he'd been a good policeman. He didn't have the stripes, but I knew he had the town's affection, and that must somehow count for more.

I decided to mark his life in the only way I knew how: I would do all I could to get a front-page tribute to him. His death would make the front page of the *Post*. His life might as well join it in the headlines. The town owed him that much at least.

TWENTY-NINE

As daylight broke, the American lay on his bed in the hotel room, a country hotel on the road into Lancashire. The air-conditioning was a constant hum, a faint draught.

He closed his eyes. He thought about the dead cop and smiled. It had been too easy. A quick flash of a stolen warrant and the man had wandered to his death like he was going outside for a smoke.

That was just part one of the plan. DI Ross would complete part two, although he didn't know it yet. The American had Ross's numbers and he thought about calling him at home, but he knew Ross would be at work, his heart rate a drum solo, anything to keep himself moving and not thinking.

The American rolled over and checked his watch. Seven thirty. Time to book in.

He reached for his phone and called David Watts. It rang twice, but then a drowsy 'yeah' told him that his client was at least sleeping.

'Good morning, Mr Watts. Did I wake you?'

He heard movement and then David's voice sounded

249

more alert. 'Yeah, I'm sorry.' A pause to collect his thoughts, and then, 'How are you doing? Are things going okay?' His voice was a mixture of panic and enquiry.

'It's going well, Mr Watts. The inspector is being very co-operative, although one cop was making trouble, had worked it all out.'

'Who was that?'

'PC Garrett.' He smiled. 'Not one of your fans.'

'Shit. What's he saying?'

'Nothing, Mr Watts. It seems he died during the night.'

There was silence at the other end. He thought he heard a faint gasp.

'Mr Watts?'

There was another pause, and then a quiet voice said, 'What the fuck have you done?' The dryness of David's mouth came through thick and clear.

'What you asked me to do,' he replied, his voice full of mock-innocence. 'You want me to shoot the messenger. Sometimes, there's more than one messenger.'

'You've killed a policeman.' David sounded breathless. 'You've killed a fucking policeman. Oh Christ.'

'Wrong, Mr Watts. *We* killed a policeman, not me. *We*. Do you get the drill?'

David Watts was silent for a moment, and then he asked, 'What now?' His voice was low and scared.

'I have a plan. We're only a day or so away from the end of your problem. It might even end sooner if the inspector does as he's told.'

'What does he have to do?'

The American paused, then answered, 'Let's just say

that PC Garrett sought to unburden himself before he died.'

And with that, he clicked off David Watts. Then he dialled Glen Ross's office using his direct line. When Ross picked up the phone, he whispered, 'Wakey wakey, Inspector. Meet me in an hour.'

He smiled to himself when he sensed the tension in Glen Ross.

'What do you want?' was all Ross could say.

'Just be patient, Inspector. Meet me in an hour and you might find out something to your advantage.'

'What like?'

'Be patient. Eight thirty. What was that dingy little place I passed on the way into town? I've worked up a real hunger overnight.'

'The Sunshine Cafe?'

'That's the place. One hour, Inspector.'

'I'm going to arrest you,' Ross snarled down the phone. 'You killed a police officer, you bastard.'

'Okay, whatever you want. If you want to find me, I'll be in the Sunshine Cafe at eight thirty. Send your boys along.' He paused, smiling, enjoying Glen Ross's anger. 'Hey, some of them might recognise me from my trip to your office yesterday.'

There was complete silence from Glen Ross.

'Be there, Inspector, or I'll come and find you.'

And then the American clicked off. He laughed to himself and got up off the bed. He checked his watch again.

Time for a run before breakfast.

*

Laura was at home, a four-day stretch of no work ahead, a mix of rest days and accrued overtime. She'd spent the previous day trawling through the undetected street robberies, trying to match descriptions to see if they were isolated incidents or part of a gang. She'd made some progress, and thought she had worked out the description of the main offender in the West End. But she had been working on her own, everyone else on the Dumas case, so the day had dragged and she felt ready for the time off.

Bobby was with his father, part of the arranged access, heading out to a zoo or some other treat. He'd be dropped off at the end of the following day, and that would be it for another two weeks. Bobby would miss his dad, but there'd be no more calls. Just the everyday routine of living with his mother, as she frantically fitted everything in around her job. The trips to the supermarket. The childminder pick-ups. The arguments over bedtime.

She was lying in bed, watching breakfast television, thinking how to occupy herself, how to take her mind off the thought that Bobby wasn't with her, when the news came on about the shooting of Bob Garrett in Turners Fold.

She sat up quickly.

There was only one place she was going now. She was going to Jack.

David Watts stayed in bed after the call. He lay back and looked at the wall. His apartment was silent.

He felt sick, tense, edgy. He wanted to get up, walk

around, but he felt trapped, events moving too fast, out of his control. He couldn't get hold of Karen. Every time he called, her phone just rang out. The weekend games had been postponed, the football authorities worried about a shooting live on television.

He should have gone to the police, to the London police, but he hadn't. He had been a coward, thought only of himself, and now more people had died. He knew now that he had to see it through, he had gone too far to go back.

He felt his forehead go damp. He needed to get through this, to make his life right again.

He remembered the bag of cocaine. He knew that would help. Just a bit more, just until this was all over. He could put it all right later. Maybe do more charity work, put something back. His Trust Fund did some of that, but perhaps he ought to expand it. He could work on his relationship with Emma, maybe get her to cut down on the travel.

He took out the cocaine. It would be over soon and he could throw this away, start over.

THIRTY

Glen Ross parked his car at the back of the Sunshine Cafe. He was wearing his best suit, a press conference expected, but his face was ashen, as if he hadn't slept. As he went in, all eyes turned towards him. He saw some familiar faces. One or two nodded, the news now through that a policeman had been killed overnight, but it seemed like no one knew what to say. They returned to their food and conversations, the noise level quieter.

The cafe was busy. He looked around hopefully; he couldn't see the American at first. But then he noticed the black shirt, the bald dome, at a table in the corner, his face turned towards the window.

'What can I get you?'

He turned around and looked blankly at the waitress. He thought she sounded quiet, looked upset, but then he remembered Bob Garrett had breakfast here most days. He flicked a hand towards the menu on the board behind her. 'Just a coffee.'

He waited for his drink and then he walked over to

the American, who didn't look up until he sat down, the vinyl seat squeaking as he shuffled across to the window.

'Good morning to you, Inspector. Working solo this morning?' he mocked.

Glen Ross took a deep breath. He wanted to throw his drink over the bastard, hear him scream.

'Don't be a smartarse,' was all he could muster, hissed through gritted teeth.

The American pointed at his plate and said, 'Good food,' but then he patted his stomach and glanced around. 'Doesn't do much for the waistline, though. Maybe I'm used to some city finesse.'

'It's nice and simple,' replied Glen Ross, his voice terse. 'It's how we like it round here.'

The American smiled and nudged the plate further away. 'I'm sure you do. Now, on to business.'

'Just you wait there,' Ross snapped, reaching forward and gripping the American's hand. 'You killed a police officer last night,' he whispered. 'You will go to prison for the rest of your life if I take you in.'

'If, if, if. You've got your head so full of negatives, Chief, you can't see the positives.'

Ross gripped the hand harder. 'There aren't any positives, you cop-killing bastard. You murdered a man I've known for years.'

The American sat back, leaving his hand on the table inside Glen Ross's grip, and smiled. 'Don't create a scene, Inspector. It doesn't look good in public.'

Glen Ross started to squeeze, trying to get a reaction. The tendons in his hand stood out like dorsal fins, his mouth set in a grimace.

The American took a drink of his coffee. He looked at his hand as an afterthought and said, 'You move your hand now, or else I'll pin it to the table with a knife. You've got ten seconds.' A pause. 'Ten, nine, eight . . .'

Glen Ross thought about keeping it there, but something in the American's eyes told him otherwise, so he pulled his hand away and sat back. His complexion was red and hot. He flexed his fingers, his face flushed with suppressed anger, and looked at the table. He was losing control.

'That's better. Now, more coffee? I've finished mine.' The American looked up and caught the eye of the waitress, asking for another. He noticed a few people were watching. When the waitress came over, her hips rolling, he thanked her loudly. When she'd gone, he took a sip and said, 'This is a good town for me.' When Glen Ross glanced up, he continued, 'No one knows who I am, but the accent stands out like a tree on the prairie. Better than London, where I'm just another tourist. Here, I could get myself a profile.'

'What are you talking about, you fucking murderer?'

'Is that what you said to David Watts when he killed that poor girl?'

'David Watts didn't kill anyone.'

'Well, he's sure panicking a lot for an innocent man. Anyway, wasn't I with you when I set up the meeting with Bob Garrett? Come to think of it, aren't we in a conspiracy?'

Glen Ross's complexion peaked into a pale grey, his breathing heavy.

'Are you okay, Inspector? You don't look so good.

Maybe it's all that simple food catching up on you?' The American shook his head dismissively. 'No, Inspector, I think a profile is good.' Then he slipped in a glacier-sharp look behind the smile. 'I could have just sneaked into town, done what needed to be done and then sneaked out again. But now, I've been seen around. If people talk about an American as a suspect, they will say, 'Hey, he was in Inspector Ross's office. And didn't PC Garrett also arrive? And didn't Inspector Ross dine with him when PC Garrett's corpse was still cooling?' He paused to let the simplicity of it sink in. 'You see, Inspector, our fortunes are now inextricably entwined,' and then he laughed, making sure that everyone in the cafe turned round again.

'I could arrest you,' snarled Ross, his voice low. 'You've confessed to a murder.'

'But you won't. I know that. You know that. So stop shitting me with empty threats.' He took another drink of coffee and watched Glen Ross through the steam. Then he put the cup down and continued, 'I can offer you two ways out of this mess. Easy or hard.'

Glen Ross said nothing for a while, instead just thinking about what he should do. He realised pretty quickly that there was nothing he could do.

The American took the silence as a come-on.

'Good to have your ear, Inspector.' He put his fingers together and rested his nose on their tips, looking thoughtful. 'Tell me this: was Bob Garrett on his own that night, the night the young girl died?'

Glen Ross looked puzzled. 'No, not as I remember. He was with James Radley. But he's dead now.'

The American smiled. 'Good. So the easy way out is this. Bob Garrett unburdened himself yesterday afternoon.'

'Did he?'

The American nodded. 'That's right. He came into your office and confessed to feeling responsible for the death of that young girl. He saw her, walking on her own, and thought about giving her a ride home. But he did nothing. And he saw the murderer lurking and did nothing.'

Glen Ross paused for a moment. Then what was being said slowly dawned on him.

'That's disrespectful. He has only been dead a few hours and you want to use him as a scapegoat.'

The American leant forward, trying to catch Glen Ross's eye, and with a voice packed full of menace, said, 'Let's not pretend you have ever cared for that poor girl, so cut the bullshit.'

Glen Ross said nothing.

'That's right, Inspector, you look away, and you keep your eyes dancing, because you're going to have to watch your back every day for the rest of your life if you don't go along with me.' He paused, then continued, 'You are going to give a press conference in an hour's time, and you are going to tell the good people of Lancashire that PC Garrett was a depressed man. You are going to tell them how PC Robert Garrett, recently deceased, came into your office yesterday and confessed to seeing Annie Paxman walking on her own, and that he had seen the guy who killed her, the one locked up in jail, walking behind her, but he did nothing. Garrett did nothing because he thought he was just a harmless old drunk. But he could have been stopped. And Garrett didn't tell anybody, because everyone would know that he could have stopped it. He told you all this, and then went up to that park and blew his own brains out.'

Glen Ross shook his head but said nothing.

'Don't fuck me about, Inspector, and let me give it you straight: I don't like you, and I would hurt you with a smile on my face. So don't give me the pleasure. You are going to give that press conference, and you are going to take the heat off David Watts. Then, if the shooter gets caught and tries to blame Watts, no one will believe her.'

'And if she doesn't get caught?'

The American shrugged. 'I'm going to kill her, but it means no more heat on you if the shootings stop. But I'll catch up with her, and when I do, she will die.'

Glen Ross looked out of the window. It looked like he might have been fighting back tears, but it could just have been the reflection from the sun beaming into the cafe.

'What if I say no?'

He shrugged. 'There's the "hard" way I mentioned.'

'Which is?'

'I kill you.'

The simplicity of the response halted Ross for a moment, but then he said, 'I'm arresting you for Bob Garrett's murder. You do not have to say anything, but it may harm your defence if . . .'

The American shook his head. 'No, you're not

259

arresting me, because you're a coward. People like you always are. You want to wear the badge and walk the big man's walk, but when it comes down to it you only care about yourself, and your interests are not best-served by turning me in.'

'What do you mean?'

'Inspector Ross, it's like having breakfast with a child. Pay attention please. You turn me in; I talk. I have one rule in life: never go down, but on the day that you do, take as many as you can with you. If you lock me up, I will tell everybody everything, and everything includes you.' Then he winked. 'And what if I say that you told me to kill Bob Garrett when I spoke to you yesterday? Conspiracy. Remember that word.'

Ross rubbed his chest with his hand, grimacing at sharp pains jabbing him there. 'And what if I just ignore you?' he said, sounding uncomfortable.

The American shook his head.

'You can't. I'll come and kill you. Either way, you lose. So go public. One hour. You might want to call your officers together first. You want them with you for this one.'

Glen Ross looked down at the table. 'I can't sacrifice one of my officers.'

'You didn't mind sacrificing that poor girl for the sake of a football career, or should I say *your* career and the chance to get close to David Watts.' The American checked his watch. 'And don't forget: I need details about the girl's family. I'm going after the shooter soon. I can't wait any longer.'

And then he dismissed Glen Ross with a flick of his

hand. He pulled out a newspaper and spread it on the table.

Glen Ross slid out from behind the table and walked slowly towards the door. He looked at the floor as he went, now oblivious to his surroundings. He didn't notice everyone watching him as he walked out.

The American made a play of reading the newspaper, but he watched the inspector's car pull away from the cafe. Once he had gone, he slid out of the booth himself and headed back into town. He had the feeling that today wasn't a day to stay still.

THIRTY-ONE

Glen Ross was behind his desk, sitting back and staring into space.

He glanced over to the photograph of his wife and children. He reached forward and touched the picture, enjoying his wife's smiling face, looking proudly at the camera, his three girls wrapped around her, all in their teens. They were splashed by innocence, not aware of the compromises they would have to make as they went through life. Life wasn't just about parties and clothes and boys. It was about choices. He'd had to make some tough ones. He had a family. He had a position. Most importantly, he had a responsibility to the town he served.

He ran his hands over his face. He felt tired. He thought about the American and his insides churned.

He had four choices.

He could go along with what the American said: tell the whole world that Bob Garrett had let Annie Paxman walk to her death, shatter his memory forever. But where would that get him? Just demand after demand, always putting himself at greater risk.

He could ignore him.

That thought made him nauseous. He didn't doubt the stranger had the ability to kill him. He only had to think of how he'd felt when he'd looked down at Bob Garrett's body. One shot to the head. Gun pressed up against the skin, starfish wound, scorch marks. Cold blood. The thought of it made him feel sick. One of his officers, killed on duty. He knew he couldn't ignore him.

He could call the police in London and tell them everything he knew. That might save some lives.

He looked at the photograph of his wife and children again. He thought about his house just on the edge of town. A detached box, new-build, with a mock-Tudor front and stripes in his lawn. He had worked hard for that, and for the gleaming décor inside, and the new car on the drive. And what about the respect of his neighbours, people who looked up to him? He would lose everything. He stared at the floor. He knew he couldn't involve the authorities.

Or he could kill the American. Then he could tell David Watts that he would sort it out his way.

That was the best option. It put him back in charge, something he hadn't felt since he'd received that call from David Watts a couple of days before.

He put his head back and covered his eyes with his hands. He felt like screaming. He didn't know how to resolve it, that was the problem. How could he put himself back in charge of a situation he didn't know how to control?

There was a fifth option, another way out – a

coward's way out, but he saw again the photograph of his wife and children. He should spare them the shame. He owed them that much at least.

He looked to the room outside and saw a buzz of activity, the resources of the station running at capacity following Bob Garrett's death.

He guessed it was time to call them together and tell them about Bob Garrett's confession.

I walked all the way to Tony's house with my head down. I felt dazed, like I was dreaming, and that I would wake up at any time in my flat in London. But I knew that it wasn't true. I knew it from the eyes I could feel staring at me as I walked, as if every passing car, every curious shopkeeper, was watching me, too uncomfortable to say anything.

I only looked up when the door opened and I heard Tony's voice.

The house felt inviting as I went in, and as I passed him I felt Tony's hand on my shoulder, strong and supportive. Then I felt lighter arms, a softer hold. I squeezed into Eileen and put my head on her shoulder briefly, but then I stood up straight and took a deep breath.

'No need to be strong with us, Jack,' said Eileen. 'You're with friends.'

I smiled weakly and patted her arm. 'Thank you, Eileen. I appreciate that.'

Tony smiled. I asked if I could speak to him. He nodded agreement and then led the way to his study. I felt Eileen's eyes following me.

'I've come to ask a favour,' I said.

'If you want somewhere to stay, that's okay. Stay here as long as you want.'

I was taken aback; it wasn't something I had considered. I knew how hard it was going to be in the house, that I would hear my father's voice, my mother's laughter, coming at me from every room, just my memories to keep me company. But I wanted that, to hear it, to feel it. I never wanted to forget it.

'Thanks, Tony, but it's not that.'

He looked surprised. 'Okay. What can I do for you?'

I looked down at my hands and saw that small streaks of blood decorated my middle finger, that I had picked the skin from around my fingernail until it bled.

'I just want to do one last thing for my dad,' I said quietly.

'Go on,' he said.

'Your paper will be full of what happened to him,' I continued. 'I know that. There'll be a piece about how he died, and there'll be a piece about his career.' I took a deep breath. This was harder than I'd thought it would be. 'I think that maybe there'll be less about my dad as a person than there ought to be. I was just hoping that you'd do a decent tribute. Maybe front-page. Make people remember his life, not his death. Make him more than just a dead policeman.'

Tony nodded, but he looked away.

'Tony?'

He looked back at me. 'It's about your father, Jack.'

I felt myself take another deep breath, my insides

turning over again, not sure how much more I could take.

'Go on,' I said nervously, even though I was far from ready.

Tony bit his lip. 'I've had a call from my boss. Glen Ross has just made an announcement that your father made a confession before he died last night.'

I closed my eyes. 'Keep going,' I whispered.

'He says that he confessed to seeing Annie Paxman before she died.'

I hung my head.

'He says that your father saw her walking on her own, and saw her killer, Colin Wood, walking not far behind her. He did nothing, and then Annie Paxman was killed.

'Glen Ross said that he made this confession last night, and then in the middle of the night he was found at the aviary. He'd shot himself.'

I looked at Tony in confusion. 'He was killed at the aviary?'

Tony nodded.

I felt the world swim around me again, twirling me with uncertainties. Was all my father had told me lies?

'No one told me that,' was all I could say.

Tony stayed silent.

I put my head back in my hands and moaned. The last cherished thing I'd had of my father was my memory of him. Had that vanished too?

I sat down, defeated. Everything had seemed so normal a couple of days ago. How could a story have led to this, my father dead, and now his good name killed off by Glen Ross?

'Are you all right, Jack?'

'You believed my dad, Tony. That's right, isn't it?'

Tony looked down. 'I don't think he told lies.'

'That's not the same thing.'

Tony shook his head. 'I think your father believed what he saw.'

'But either he lied to me, or Glen Ross is lying?'

Tony shrugged. 'But why would he go public? What has he got to gain?'

I sighed. 'Because my dad was trying to talk me into writing about the Annie Paxman murder. He told me that Glen Ross had covered it up.'

Tony sat down on a chair opposite me.

'But you hadn't begun to write the story; you said you wouldn't,' he said softly.

'Well, maybe I'll change my mind now.'

'That's not a good idea.'

'Why?'

Tony held out his hands. 'For the same reason we had all those years ago. A man is in prison, caught on good evidence.' He paused, and then said, 'Jack, I liked your father. I didn't know whether he was right back then, and now I just don't know any more. People say things to protect themselves. Maybe he was trying to protect himself all these years.'

I sat back, angry. 'Jesus Christ, I thought you were my friend, Tony.'

'I am.'

'So maybe Glen Ross is lying to protect himself.'

Tony shrugged. 'Maybe, but why go public, now that your father is, well . . .'

'Dead?'

He held out his hands in apology and nodded.

I felt a tear tingle my eye. 'Because my dad was going to get some evidence so that I could run the story. Maybe he confronted Ross?' I took a deep breath. 'Nothing I write now will have any credibility anyway, because I have a vested interest in clearing my dad's name.'

Tony said nothing for a while, and then asked, 'What proof did your father have?'

'Not much,' I said, my voice filled with sadness. 'Just what you already know. When my dad found Annie, she was dead, and David Watts was running over the fields.'

Tony rubbed his cheeks and looked tired, like he was setting himself up for a fight he didn't have the energy for. He exhaled. 'One thing bothers me.'

'What's that?'

'If Glen Ross has made this public statement and it's not true, then your father's death must be linked to whatever he said to Glen Ross last night.'

I thought about telling Tony about the links with the football shootings, the inscribed neck-chain, but then I wondered about *his* motives now. He was asking too many questions. I wondered whether I could trust anyone in this town and decided to keep some things to myself.

Tony shook his head, answering his own theory. 'But that can't be right, because the only conclusion from that must be that Glen Ross had your father killed to keep him quiet.'

'So why can't that be right?'

Tony looked doubtful, and then said, 'Glen Ross isn't a nice man and I don't like him. But', and he smiled ruefully, 'he's no killer. He hasn't got the balls.'

'So maybe he's telling the truth?'

Tony nodded. 'Maybe. And maybe Neil Armstrong didn't really walk on the moon? Maybe he just roamed around a TV set in a spacesuit, with starched flags and fake moondust? Life is full of maybes, but more often than not they are unlikely maybes. Think about it. Your father challenges Ross about Annie Paxman. A few hours later, he's dead from a single gunshot wound, and then his confession comes out before you've even had chance to buy him a coffin. They seemed linked, but I don't believe Glen Ross is a killer. Coward, yes. Killer? No.'

'What about James Radley?' I asked.

Tony looked confused. 'James Radley? What's he got to do with it?'

'He knew. And a few years back, he died in a fire, still in his bed. Maybe he was going to talk? Maybe that is what happens to people who try to talk?'

Tony shook his head. 'I don't know. It's a coincidence, but I don't buy Glen Ross as a killer. And neither will anyone else.'

'And they'd believe my father was a liar?' I asked bitterly.

'Which is most likely: that a lonely widower confessed to an old lie he told to protect himself, and then shot himself out of guilt, or that Glen Ross had a fellow police officer executed a few hours after an argument about a case that has been dead and buried for over a decade?'

I rubbed my eyes. I could see how it looked, but it didn't make me feel any better.

'I'm sorry, Jack, I don't mean to be cruel.'

I looked Tony in the eye. 'So which story are you going to run?'

He looked confused.

'There are only two, Tony,' I continued. 'The tribute he deserves, or Glen Ross's story.'

Tony didn't answer.

I was angry now. I was angry with Tony for going against me, but I was angry as well that, even ten years on, the real story behind Annie Paxman's death was going to stay buried.

'Jack?'

I looked at him.

'I'm sorry, we all are. We didn't mean for it to be like this.'

I looked at him, a man I had known a long time, and I saw the sadness. I felt myself relent. 'Okay, thanks.'

'Will you be all right?'

I nodded.

'Your father was a good man, Jack.'

I smiled, breathing heavily at the prickle of tears.

'And I'll do him a fine tribute,' he continued. 'Front page. And they'll print it, or there will be hell to pay.'

I smiled again, tears now streaming down my face. I stood up to leave, and as I did so I nodded at Tony. It was all I could manage. I spotted tears in Tony's eyes, but he was smiling too.

I almost made it to the door when Tony asked, 'And what are you going to do?'

I stopped and thought for a moment, and then turned and said, 'I don't know.'

THIRTY-TWO

I hadn't been home for long, trying to work out how to calm the kick I felt to my stomach, when there was a knock at the door.

When I opened it, I saw Laura standing there.

'Laura!'

She walked in and held me for a few moments. I buried my face deep into her shoulder. I could smell her hair, her clothes. I could smell London on her and all of a sudden I wanted to go back there.

'I heard it on the news,' was all she said.

When we pulled apart, I looked over her shoulder and saw someone watching from a distance. It was Martha, Jake's wife. As I looked, I thought I saw her wipe her eyes. She watched me for a few seconds, and then she turned away.

'You okay, Jack?' I heard Laura ask.

I watched Martha get into her car and drive away. There was more than grief in her face. There was something else.

'I don't know,' was all I said, and then I looked at

Laura and added, 'I've got to go out.'

She looked shocked as I brushed past her, climbed into my car and drove away, heading after Martha.

David Watts ignored the phone at first.

He was still on his bed, his knees up by his chest, staring out into space. The ringing didn't register for a while and when it did he didn't move. All the phone had done so far was bring bad news. Why should now be any different?

But some kind of reason kicked in and he wondered whether it was the American with some better news.

He lowered his knees slowly and reached across for the handset. 'Hello?' he whispered.

There was silence at first. He started to panic, worrying whether it was her again, the voice from his past. Then when he heard the electronic distortion, his breathing quickened.

'You haven't done it yet, David. I've heard nothing.'

She wouldn't leave him alone. She was going to keep going until one of them broke their cover. He felt his anger come quickly, his fury at the invasion of his life beating down any fear he had left in him.

'You bitch!' he shouted down the phone. 'You fucking little whore!'

'Emma not back yet?' She laughed, cold and harsh. *'Looks like she got the wrong taxi at the airport.'*

That stopped him dead. It was the calm way she said it, almost whispered, like she was talking about a seating plan for dinner. He thought he was about to pass out.

'You heard it right.'

He started to panic at the harsh anger in her voice.

'*Who is going to look after you now?*' she continued. '*You are a fucking cop-killer now. I heard it on the radio. Not even the police will help you now.*'

He sat back down on the bed.

'*But I'm done with random footballers now, David. I'm coming after you. You can still stop it at any time, but I'm coming after you, and I'll keep on coming after you until I get you. Emma's first, then your family, and then you. And I'm a patient woman.*'

The sound of a dead line flooded the bedroom. David fell back onto the bed, his mind reeling, his arm going across his stomach to comfort the cramped feeling he had there. Where was Emma? Did she have her? What could he do now? He could tell the press about Annie Paxman, say what she wanted him to say, and then just leave the country. He had enough money to go wherever he wanted, maybe eventually play for another team in some far-flung corner of the globe.

He closed his eyes, tried not to think about what might be happening to Emma. He could see her smile, her face. Anything else was too much.

He knew what would take away the pain. That's all he needed right now. No more pain.

THIRTY-THREE

I walked into Jake's shop.

Jake was behind the counter, just staring out of the door. He didn't say anything to me. He just nodded at me and then turned towards a door which I knew led to a back room.

As I passed him, I felt his cold hand wrap around my forearm. When I caught his eye, he smiled, warm and tender.

Nothing more was said. Nothing else needed to be said.

I went into the back room and saw Martha. She had been crying.

'You okay, Martha?'

She looked down and shook her head. 'I heard about your father, and I'm sorry.'

I nodded. I didn't know what else to do.

'And I've heard what Glen Ross said,' she continued, 'and I know that is wrong.'

'I know that too,' I said, 'but other people won't.'

Martha looked up and wiped her eyes. 'Not if we can help it, Jack Garrett.'

I looked at Martha. I saw a steel in her eyes I had never seen before.

'What is it?'

I sensed Jake behind me. I looked round, and I saw him nod, smile, show some strength.

'Tell him, love,' Jake urged.

I looked back at Martha. She definitely knew something.

'Tell me.'

Martha looked me right in the eye and said simply, 'I can prove Glen Ross is lying.'

'What do you mean?' I asked, quiet and nervous.

Martha took a deep breath, gathered her thoughts, and then continued. 'I can prove it. Glen Ross thinks I just put files away, but I know what is *in* those files.' She looked me in the eye. 'And I knew what was in those files ten years ago.'

I stood up and looked at Martha. So she knew about Annie Paxman as well. It seemed like everyone knew. Tony, Martha, and I guessed Jake too. But no one had done anything. A young girl had been killed and they had all stood aside to let the killer walk out of town just so he could chase fame.

'What have you got?' I asked.

Martha watched me for a few seconds, and then reached into a drawer. She pulled out a brown envelope.

'That's from the file,' said Martha.

It was a buff envelope, simple and unassuming. I

asked the question to which I already knew the answer. 'Which file?'

'The Annie Paxman file.'

'Why have you got it?'

'Because I was asked to get rid of some things from it a few years back, just to make it thinner. I kept it instead.'

'Who asked?'

'Glen Ross.'

'Why did you do it, Martha?'

She began to cry again.

I let her compose herself, and then asked again, 'Why?'

Martha shook her head. 'Just because it was the right thing to do.' She looked at me. 'I want you to have it. If there is anything in there you can use to clear your father's name, you take it.' Her chest heaved as she sobbed. 'I don't know about that poor girl, but he's not taking your father's good name away.'

I looked down at the file and then back up at Martha. I saw the plea in her eyes, and I felt it grow in my own.

But I couldn't work out one thing: how had it stayed buried for so long?

Martha must have spotted the question in my eyes, because I saw her shrug.

'I just didn't say anything,' said Martha. She looked at the floor in apology.

'Why not?'

She looked up again, her eyes more focused this time. 'Because we thought we were doing the right thing. We had the killer, but if your father's account got out, the killer would go free. It would create reasonable doubt in the minds of the jurors.'

'You could have said something, Martha, you could have changed something.'

'But what could I have done? I didn't know whether your father actually saw what he thought he saw, but Ross knew that what your father was saying would get Colin Wood his acquittal.'

'So he suppressed evidence.'

Martha looked at me and smiled, but it was filled with sadness.

'No, Jack, he suppressed a mistake, to make sure we got the killer.'

'You should have spoken out. What Ross did was wrong.'

She shook her head. 'I couldn't, because I would have lost my job, and so would others. Glen Ross, your father, James Radley. The defence would have used what we had to get the killer off. It would have felt like just about everyone in the town hated me.' She wiped a tear from her eye. 'I felt trapped, and I know everyone else did.'

'Except David Watts.'

Martha nodded. There was nothing else to say.

'What's changed, Martha?'

'Glen Ross. He's told a lie, and I don't know why.' She pointed to the envelope. 'What he said this morning, about your father seeing Colin Wood, wasn't true. Your father could make mistakes, and maybe he made a mistake about David Watts, but I have never heard him tell a lie. Glen Ross told a lie. He told a lie then, and he told a lie this morning.'

She looked down at the envelope. 'If you can use it, don't worry about me. Just do the right thing by your father.'

I looked at the envelope in my hand. 'If I can, I will. This story will be written, Martha, but some people might get hurt by what I write.'

She nodded. She knew that meant her, and everyone else who knew.

'You do what you need to do, Jack.'

Then something occurred to me, a line of enquiry.

'Does Colin Wood have any relatives left in town?'

'His mum lives in that new estate just off the Accrington Road.'

'And what about his lawyer?'

Martha went quiet as she thought back, and then it came to her. 'Duncan McAllister. He's still got a small practice down by the canal.'

I nodded, and then had to ask the question that was tearing me apart. 'And did you see my father last night?'

Martha nodded.

'How did he seem?'

Martha shook her head. 'I don't know, Jack. I saw him go into Glen Ross's office. He went in looking angry, but there was another man in there. American, tall, moody-looking.'

'Did he say who he was?'

'Not to me. He said he was there to see DI Ross, and that's just what he did. Your father came in, and then left shortly after.'

'When did the American leave?'

'Just after your father.'

'And how did Glen Ross seem last night?'

Martha exhaled. 'Distracted, but he has been the last couple of days, ever since David Watts starting calling him.'

That figured.

I thanked her and turned to leave. Martha hugged me.

I went outside into the triangle. As I walked, I looked towards the police station. I could see a figure watching me. I lifted my hand, clearly showing the file.

The figure moved out of sight.

THIRTY-FOUR

Laura was looking at the pictures on the wall when I walked back into the house. She turned to face me and I saw that she looked worried.

'You okay, Jack?'

I thought for a moment, and then said, 'Maybe, yeah, better.'

Then I thought about how far Laura had come.

'Are you here for work?' I made it sound like an accusation, something dirty.

I noticed the look in her eyes: rejection, anger, I couldn't tell. And then I saw her soften. She reached out her hand and touched my face, running a finger down my cheek. It took me by surprise. I felt a tickle down my back and my stomach jumped.

'I came here because I heard about your father,' she said. 'I just thought you might need someone.'

My eyes filled with tears and I bit my lip. 'Thanks,' was all I could manage. I took a deep breath to compose myself and came up all businesslike.

I held up the buff file I had brought back from Jake's store.

'I need to read this.'

'What is it?'

'The answer, I hope.'

Laura walked up to me. 'Am I allowed to see it?'

'When I've seen it.'

Laura sighed. 'C'mon, Jack, trust me. What's going on?'

'Are you still off the Dumas case?'

'So this is to do with the football shootings?' she responded.

'So you are here for work?'

She smiled and shook her head slowly. 'I came here for you, Jack,' she said softly, 'but I'm still a cop.' She looked at the file. 'What's it all about, Jack?'

So I told her.

I watched as her face changed, from surprise to anger to excitement, as I told her all about Annie Paxman, about David Watts running from the scene, about how he was never arrested, and about how Glen Ross had told the good people of Lancashire that my father had shot himself out of guilt. When I told her that someone was calling David Watts and pretending to be Annie Paxman, telling him to confess to the killings, I saw that she looked intrigued. I was angry by the time I had talked it all out. Laura just looked shocked.

But I hadn't told her about the neck-chain. Even to Laura, I couldn't tell the whole story.

'Your face tells me that David Watts didn't call it in.'

Laura shook her head, and then pointed at the file.

'So you think that might contain something to prove his innocence? Or his guilt?'

I shrugged. 'I don't know. But I'm going to look for it, and keep looking for it until I find it.'

I opened the envelope, deep and filled with paper. I scattered the contents on the floor. There were photographs of the scene, and plenty of Annie Paxman, naked and bruised, prostrate on the ground. I winced at those, found myself staring at them. She was dark and slim and young and beautiful. Her black hair kinked up at the back, spread over the aviary floor by the struggle, and then over her shoulders like scars. Sharp cheekbones were fleshed out by young pert cheeks, but they looked damaged and bruised.

I searched through the file and found the statements made by my father and Glen Ross. By the time I'd read them, I was burning with rage.

My father's first statement told the story he had told me the day before. But there was a second statement, dated the same day, or so it said. My father no longer described how he saw David Watts running across the fields, his long stride as familiar to my father as maybe mine had been. His second statement told the same story as Glen Ross's, that someone had been running away, but it was someone larger, older, slower.

I felt a burst of sadness looking at the handwriting. It wasn't just that it was my father's handwriting, sloping, light, sweeping across the page like a loose thread. It was the handwriting in the second statement that saddened me. It was smaller, reluctant, as if I could see his helplessness as he changed his story, made the facts fit the end, not the other way round, the way it was supposed to be.

I thought of Martha and thanked her silently. She had played her part, kept the originals, filed them away so they couldn't be destroyed, just in case.

I searched around the pile, pushing aside scraps of paper, until my fingers came across something hard. There were two audio tapes. One marked 'RGAP1 – call 1'. The other was marked 'RGAP1 – call 2'.

I looked at Laura, who had been watching me all the while, and then ran upstairs to my room and rummaged around. When I returned, I held a Walkman in my hand.

'When my dad told me that he hadn't touched my room, he wasn't joking. Still there, in my bedside cabinet.' A lump filled my throat as I thought about how he'd kept everything just how it always had been.

I placed the first tape inside the machine and held it gingerly in the palm of my hand. I pressed play and the machine whirred in my hand, like the flutters of a butterfly wing.

The first thing I heard was static, and then electronic bleeps. I watched Laura's face as we listened.

And then I heard my father's voice.

A tear ran down my face when I heard it. He sounded younger, less gravelly, more of the man I wasn't far from becoming.

'I can see a girl. We're just going to investigate, but I think she's deceased. Get an ambulance here quick though.'

'What's your exact location?'

'Victoria Park, Turners Fold. I can see a naked girl on

284

the floor of the aviary in Victoria Park. Otherwise, scene is quiet.'

'Got that. Scenes of crime are on their way. I'll contact MCU.'

I looked at Laura. 'MCU?'

'Major Crimes Unit,' she said.

The tape went quiet for a while. Laura looked puzzled, and I knew what she was thinking, that if this was London the radio would be crackling with officers giving their locations, promising to get down there. This was Turners Fold. On a night shift there were maybe six police officers on duty, with a couple in the station and the other four out in two cars. If the transmissions went quiet, it was because there was no one around to interrupt.

Then I heard the sound of someone running. It was my father, his voice ragged. *'Comms, do you copy?'*

'I copy.'

'We've got David Watts leaving the scene. Did you get that? I've got him about a hundred yards from me, heading towards Pendle Wood.'

I looked at Laura. She was transfixed, listening to something playing out that had lain hidden all these years. I felt anger instead. I knew that whatever was playing out on that tape had ended in my father's death. He was still alive on the tape. He was out of breath, but he sounded measured and calm.

And he hadn't lied to me.

'Did you say David Watts?'

'Yes, David Watts. Eighteen years of age. Resident of Turners Fold.'

Laura was tugging at her lip.

Then there was silence for a few seconds. Laura still couldn't take her eyes off the tape.

'*Do we have an ID on the body?*'

'*Young black female, maybe eighteen or twenty. Can't see any identification, but I recognise her. She's local.*' Then a pause. '*Hang on, there's something in her hand. Some kind of a chain, might be gold.*'

I watched Laura's face. Her eyes seemed keener now, more intent. She looked like she was holding her breath. She looked back at me and then held her hand out. As I took hold of her fingers, she squeezed.

Then I heard another voice.

'*David Watts heading towards the school. Running that way.*' I recognised the voice as James Radley, and then more static.

'*Any identifying marks on the chain?*' the radio voice asked.

I looked at Laura. She stared at me. I felt her hand squeeze tighter.

'*Yeah, there's something on it, but hard to make it out. Will spell it. Romeo-alpha-tango-hotel. Delta-echo. Oscar-romeo-tango. Echo-whisky.*'

I watched Laura's mouth drop open as she converted the symbols into words. *Rath Dé Ort EW.*

'Jack, you knew.' Her words snapped out, and she dropped my hand. She was angry.

I shook my head. 'Only since yesterday.'

'Why didn't you tell me?'

I sighed, ran my fingers through my hair.

'I don't know. Something stopped me. Maybe I was just protecting my father.'

When Laura didn't answer, I reached for the other tape. 'Let's try this one.'

We listened to the same succession of bleeps and static at the start of the recording, and then there was the noise of radio traffic, snatches of jargon and isolated conversations. Then I heard my father's voice again.

'*2199 Garrett calling in for an update on the suspect?*'

'*Copy, officer. Suspect ruled out.*'

There were a few seconds of silence.

'*Could you repeat that?*'

There was a pause, then the voice of the operator again. '*Named suspect no longer a suspect, 2199 Garrett.*'

I sensed my father's frustration, because when his voice came back on he was speaking slowly, like he did when he was controlling his anger.

'*I saw him. Repeat, David Watts was running from the scene.*'

'*Copy, officer, but I repeat, named suspect ruled out.*'

Then the tape descended back into static. I clicked off the machine.

'Who else knows about the neck-chain?' she asked. 'Your father knew. That other policeman knew. Anyone else?'

'It seems like half the town knew something about David Watts' involvement.'

'And they did nothing?'

'Seems that way.'

Then I remembered something my father said.

'Her parents knew, Annie's parents,' I said. 'My father went to see them a few weeks later. He might have said something. And it would give them a motive.'

'So where are they?'

'I don't know.'

Laura exhaled loudly. 'I need to call this in. Shit, Jack! We are trawling the whole country trying to find a reason for the shootings, and the reason is here, in this room, on that tape. I need to know where it came from.'

That made me go quiet for a moment. I looked at Laura and knew how much I wanted to help her, but there was an even stronger feeling taking over, the feeling that I was going to make it right my way.

'These tapes are mine,' I said. 'It came from my source, and I won't reveal a source. If you want them, get a warrant.'

'Like hell!' Laura exclaimed. 'I saw you go after her. Sweet little old lady. I'll go speak to her myself.'

'Who was she then?'

Laura didn't answer.

'There you go. You've got a lead, not a suspect.'

'I've still got to call it in.' Laura turned away from me and pulled on her lip, thinking hard. 'So what are you proposing to do?' she asked eventually.

'It's simple,' I replied. 'I'm going to find whoever has been shooting these footballers, and then I'm going to write about it.' When Laura looked uncertain, I added, 'My father died because of this, and now his old boss is trying to kill his good name as well. I owe it to my father to write the story.'

Laura sighed. 'I can see that, Jack, but there is one thing that bothers me.'

'What's that?'

'That David Watts might be innocent.'

I shook my head, but Laura persisted.

'You've got a sighting at a distance, at night, from behind. Imagine what a defence lawyer would make of that.'

'I've heard that before, and I know my father had. And what about the neck-chain?'

'Maybe David gave it to her? What about EW?'

'Eugene David Watts. He's dropped the Eugene.'

Laura went quiet again.

'Where do we start?' I asked.

'We?'

I nodded. 'I've done better than the police so far, so maybe you ought to stay with me.'

She shrugged, and then said, 'Annie Paxman is the start, I suppose.'

'We know what happened,' I said. 'She was found dead at the top of the town.'

'Yes, but the story doesn't start there. She had a life before that.'

'What do you mean?'

'It's simple. I know about the murder. I know about David Watts. But what do we know about Annie Paxman?'

'She's dead. We know that much.'

'That's right,' Laura answered, 'so we know that Annie Paxman isn't the one making calls to David Watts.'

I exhaled and ran my fingers through my hair. I felt tired, but my mind kept flashing back to my father. He was everywhere I looked. It was those little things, like the spare set of keys I could see on a hook by the door, or the cigarette lighter on a shelf in the kitchen. Yesterday's newspaper was by the side of my chair. I saw a half-completed crossword.

I saw Laura lift something out of the file.

'What's that?' I asked.

'It's the crime-scene photographs.' Laura was peering hard at one, and then she pointed. 'There's some bruising on her palms, like her skin had torn on something.'

'What, like a chain being pulled off someone's neck?'

Laura nodded, and then she began to smile like we had discovered buried treasure.

Suddenly something occurred to me. I had an idea. But I wasn't going to tell Laura, no matter how much I wanted to.

'I need to make some calls,' I said, turning away.

'So do I.'

I took out my phone and went upstairs. I had to call Tony. And then I had to speak to a lawyer.

THIRTY-FIVE

I stood outside Duncan McAllister's office, wondering how to play it.

Duncan McAllister was well-known in town. He had been the main local solicitor for the good and the bad of Turners Fold for as long as I could remember. He had a hand in most crimes and divorces in the town, and if anyone knew every grubby secret in town, he did.

But I also knew that he was as cold and ruthless as anyone you could meet in a courtroom, not scared to bring anyone down. I didn't know how he would treat me.

When I walked in, a young receptionist looked at me with disinterest. This wasn't doctor's surgery coldness. This was just low-pay boredom.

She flicked the corners of her mouth into a half-smile. 'Can I help you?'

'I need to speak to Mr McAllister.'

'Can I ask what it's about?'

'It's about a murder.'

She started to speak again, but then stopped, unsure how to answer.

I knew what she was thinking. That maybe I was a madman – most of those end up in a lawyer's office at some point – or maybe I was the key to a few thousand pounds.

She placed a call and asked me to wait.

I sat down on a soft couch, surrounded by plastic palms and Pennine watercolours on the walls. I knew it was pretence. Every solicitor's office I have ever been in starts elegantly in the reception and then descends to wood-chip and scuffed desks once you get behind the scenes.

When he came in, he looked exactly as I remembered. Marbella bronze, dyed chestnut hair, with a navy suit and polished loafers. He knew he looked bad, but it was more important that he looked like he had spent money getting that way.

He looked me up and down, and then asked me for my name. When I gave it, his eyes flickered, computed it and realised my link with a dead man found the previous night.

'I don't mean to be rude, Mr Garrett, but I'm on my way out. Let's walk and talk.'

I knew I had to sell myself quickly. I was walking behind him as we left his office.

'You represented Colin Wood, over ten years ago,' I said to his shoulder. 'Allegation of murder.'

He nodded. 'I remember it. We don't get many murders in Turners Fold.'

'I'm trying to find out if someone else could have done it.'

'Why?'

'Because it's important.'

He sighed and rummaged for his car keys. When he looked up again, his patience had clearly run out.

'I'm going to court now. If you want to make an appointment, speak to my receptionist. She'll tell you my hourly rate.'

And with that, he opened his car, a blood-red Jaguar.

'Did you know that a police officer saw someone else at the scene, running away? Named him.'

He paused and looked back at me. He considered me carefully, and then asked, 'How do you know this?'

'Because I've heard the radio transmissions.'

'Who are you?'

'I'm a reporter. And my father was the person who made those radio calls.'

McAllister looked towards the hills that surrounded the town, and then up towards Victoria Park. I did my best not to follow his gaze.

'Bob Garrett?'

I nodded.

He leant back on his car. 'What do you want from me?'

'Just your ear, and your help.'

'Neither is free.'

My frustration must have been plain on my face, because he said, 'Look, son, murders can be more trouble than they're worth. They're the cases that keep you awake, but they don't bill so well. Think about it: they're just assault cases with one less witness. But this was a lost cause.'

'Why?'

'Because Colin Wood spent so much of his time drunk that he couldn't remember which day it was, let alone where he had been. He couldn't tell me anything, and once he realised what he had done, he didn't say a word to me.'

'So you think he did it?'

'The DNA says he did.'

'Is it infallible?'

He shrugged. 'Seems that way. If the police can pin someone's DNA at the scene, and then put that person in the same town at the right time, no court will let him go.'

'How do they prove it's a person's DNA?'

'Simple. If he is on the DNA database, they will take another sample just to make sure, like a cotton bud on the inside of the cheek.'

'And if they're not on the database?'

'They take two swabs, and send one off for comparison.'

'Who does it?'

'A police officer.'

'Who took Colin Wood's DNA swab?'

'It was over ten years ago. How the hell would I know?'

'Was DI Ross there?'

He smiled. 'Oh yes, he was there, keeping a close eye on everything.'

'Was Colin Wood on the DNA database?'

McAllister stalled for a moment, and then said, 'No, I don't think so. A drunk? Yes. A criminal? No.'

'Did you have his DNA compared to the sample held by the police?'

He stepped towards me. 'If you've come here to tell me I did a bad job, you'd better be going.'

'Tell me, Mr McAllister. Do you think Colin Wood is guilty?'

'At least be original, Mr Garrett. I am asked a version of that question at every dinner party I go to. And the answer is always that I don't think about it. There aren't many crusading lawyers out there, and there are even fewer innocent clients. My job is to represent people, because someone has to. If that means setting rapists free to rape again, well yeah, that's my job. And after a while you stop caring. Justice ran its course and I moved on.'

I saw him soften.

'I was sorry to hear about your father.' He climbed into his car. 'Despite what you might think, most defence lawyers get on well with the police,' he said out of his window. 'At least the ones we trust. And I trusted your father.'

'And what about Glen Ross?'

He shook his head slowly. 'I've heard too many things from too many clients. They can't all be lying.'

'What if I could get you evidence you hadn't seen before, evidence that had been withheld?'

'I wouldn't get excited. I would just do my job and try and get him out.'

'Whether he was innocent or not?'

'Whether he was guilty or not, I would do it just the same.' He started his engine. 'Goodbye, Mr Garrett.'

295

As he was about to pull away, I tossed two tapes onto his seat.

I walked away, knowing that I could say no more to him. As I did so I heard the static on the tape. He was already listening.

THIRTY-SIX

The landlord of the Swan looked surprised when I walked in.

Laura and I arrived at the pub later than I'd expected, and it was now creeping into late afternoon. I had copied the radio logs onto a few tapes, and I was carrying them in my hand as we approached the bar. I nodded at the landlord and asked for two lagers.

He looked awkward, but, after a brief pause, he reached for two glasses. When he put them on the bar, I asked, 'My dad was in here last night, right?'

The landlord tried to give nothing away, but his discomfort shone over the polished wood of the bar. 'Look, Jack, I don't know what to say.'

'Well don't say it then.' I took a drink of beer. 'Just give it a couple of days before you come to any conclusions.'

He looked uncertain, then nodded and walked away and began to wipe the bar top. 'It's the least I can do,' he said over his shoulder, almost to himself.

I put my beer down and asked again, 'So was my dad in here last night?'

He turned and nodded. 'Yes, but he was quiet.'

'What do you mean?'

He shrugged. 'Just that. He wasn't the noisiest bloke who comes in here, but last night he might as well have stayed at home. He just sat on that stool,' and he nodded to the stool I was stood next to, 'and stared into space.' I felt my hand go to the stool and grip its back. 'Until the news came on about Liverpool, you know, the shooting there.'

I raised my eyebrows. 'What happened then?'

The landlord leant against the bar and shook his head, his face full of sadness.

'He was just looking towards the TV, and then when they started to report the Liverpool shooting, he sat up and paid attention. I suppose most people did. Then when they showed those pictures of the bitch who has been doing these shootings, well,' and he waved his hand, 'he dropped his beer and left like someone had set fire to his fucking arse.'

That stopped me dead for a moment. Who could he have seen? Then I asked, 'What, you think he knew her?'

He shrugged. 'What the fuck do I know, but it was when they showed those pictures that he ran out.'

'Who else was in here last night?' asked Laura.

'When?'

'When Jack's father was here?'

I stayed silent. It was a canny way to ask the question. Martha's mention of the American had put me on edge, but if he was an important part of it, I didn't want the landlord to know.

He stepped back from the bar and thought hard. Then he stepped forward again and said, 'Your father was just there,' and he indicated again at the stool I was now leaning against, 'and there were some regulars just down the bar. There were some others by the door, but on the whole it was a quiet night.'

'Anyone else?' I tried to hide my impatience.

He paused for a moment, and then said, 'There was some fucking Yank, but he didn't stay too long.'

'American?' said Laura, with feigned surprise.

'What was he doing here?' I asked.

'Didn't say. On the whole, he didn't have a fucking lot to say for himself.' The landlord looked like he had a bad taste in his mouth. 'I didn't take to him. Something not fucking right. Too measured, too controlled.'

I glanced at Laura and caught her eye.

'Did he say where he was staying?' asked Laura.

He shook his head, his expression showing that he was getting a sense of where the conversation was going. 'He didn't say anything much, so no, I don't know where he's staying. He hasn't been in here since.' A pause. 'Why? Is he important?'

I shrugged. 'Probably not, but thanks anyway.'

The landlord was rescued from any further questions by the arrival of Tony.

Tony went straight to a secluded table in the corner. He sat so he could see out of the window, so I got him a beer and we went to join him.

I introduced Laura to him. She gave his jumper a quick glance, bright green and brown hoops. He smiled and nodded. I'd called him after I'd spoken to Duncan McAllister, told him what I wanted.

'How did you do?' I asked.

He smiled, looking pleased with himself.

'I did all right.'

'What have you two been cooking up?' asked Laura suspiciously.

Tony flashed a look at me, and when he saw my eyes he turned to Laura. 'Jack asked me to bring in some clippings from ten years ago.'

'What else has he told you?'

Tony looked at me, but when I nodded that it was okay, he said, 'Everything.'

He pulled out a large envelope, which he had kept hidden under the table.

'These are the clippings from Annie Paxman's murder.'

He took one from the top of the pile. I remembered his legendary organisation. Everything looked a jumble, but it always seemed to fall into some kind of order.

'This is the one from the day after the killing,' he said, and he pushed it across the table towards me.

I looked down at the yellowed paper. It looked fragile and dusty, but the headline was still as stark as it had been ten years ago: '*KILLED.*'

The headline didn't say anything more than that. It didn't need to. As I looked at the photograph, I wondered how much different tomorrow's edition would be. The discovery of my father's body had arrived too late to make that day's paper, but tomorrow the picture would be pretty much the same: a stone ground, a corpse, police swarming around. Only the year and the victim had changed.

'Are you all right, Jack?' It was Laura. She must have seen something cloud my eyes.

I looked up and smiled. 'I've got to do this.'

She smiled back, but the clipping underneath drew my attention. I pulled it closer to me. It showed Annie Paxman on the night of the party, in the last few hours of her life. She was smiling broadly, surrounded by other laughing, happy faces, high school now behind them, the future ahead. Her face was the only one in the picture, the rest reduced to arms on either side of her and a couple of collars of the men stood behind her.

'I know what you're thinking,' Tony said quietly. 'I thought the same thing.'

I knew what Tony had been doing. He'd been through the picture archive at the *Post*.

'Okay, show me,' I said.

And he did. He produced another envelope and spilled some old photographs onto the table. He quickly rummaged through and pulled one to the top. When he turned it over, I saw a bigger version of the picture from the newspaper. And as I looked, I saw him. David Watts. Ten years younger, and just some kid from the north, but definitely him. Only one other person was between him and Annie. In the picture, he looked relaxed and confident, sure of himself, where he was going and what it all meant. It was a happy shot, just a bunch of kids eager to get started in life.

I looked up.

'Look again,' Tony urged.

I realised straight away that I hadn't looked closely enough. I picked up the photograph again and peered into the image. Then I saw it, just a glimpse, a line against his neck, and the more I looked, the more I thought I could see links, a chain.

Tony passed over another photograph and I felt my thoughts swirl, the reality of what I could see rushing at me.

In the second photograph, evidently taken just after the first, Annie Paxman was looking away, out of shot, as if something had distracted her. David Watts was looking towards her, a beer bottle in his hand. As he looked, he was straining, and as he strained he was pulling his shirt open.

I felt my hands go damp when I saw it. There it was, the thin line in the first picture exposed as links, just as I'd thought. And right in the middle, stretched across his throat, was a circle. Something was etched on it, and I saw that it was enough. Three curls, in a Celtic design. It was enough. It had to be.

He passed me another photograph.

'One of the graphics guys enlarged that part,' he said.

As I looked, I saw the Celtic curls come to life.

I passed the photographs to Laura.

'Anything like yours?'

I watched her eyes as she looked at the photos, her pupils enlarged, taking in every detail. Laura stayed quiet at first, and then said, 'Oh shit.'

'Any doubts left?'

Laura shook her head slowly.

'And these pictures were taken on the night of her death,' I continued, before sitting back and thinking about how my life had changed so quickly. A few days before, it was simpler, just the life of a jobbing journalist, chasing page-fillers. Now I had a dead father and was about to break the biggest story of my career.

'You don't need to write the story,' Laura said quietly.

Tony looked at her, surprised. 'What, just pretend like we never knew it, and let the shootings go on?'

'No,' she replied, shaking her head. 'There's a hundred thousand pounds reward on this woman. You could go to the police with what you have and claim the money. I'll back you up. You could retire, Tony, and Jack, well, you could afford to chase the stories you wanted to chase instead of working nights for rent money.'

Tony shook his head. 'Jack will never have a bigger moment than this. Afterwards, he could just about pick his career.'

'It's not just that,' she said. She took a deep breath. 'Do you think I'm going to ignore what you've found out? I'm a policewoman, and all I want is for this killer to be caught. I'm going to call my office now and tell them what I know.'

I caught a look from Laura, and I wasn't sure if it was sadness or apology. I felt disappointed, as if she was going to take the story away from me, but I sensed that she felt the same thing, because my need to write the story came before catching a murderer.

Tony sensed what was going on so he coughed lightly and asked, 'So how much more do we know?'

That stalled Laura for a moment, but then she stood up. 'A damn sight more than I knew yesterday.' She picked up the photograph. 'And we've got David Watts with the neck-chain just before the killing.' And then Laura looked at me, 'And on the crime-scene photographs I could see marks on Annie's hands, like the imprint of links, made as she pulled. I bet they match perfectly with the links on that neck-chain. And I saw a circle, just part of the imprint.'

'I didn't notice that on her hands,' I said.

Laura smiled. 'You're a journalist. You were looking at the story, the tragedy, taking in the face, the youth. I'm a cop, and I was looking for evidence.'

Tony and I stayed quiet as Laura walked out, her hand flicking open her phone even before she reached the sunshine.

'Is that your exclusive being phoned through to London?' he said.

I glanced out of the window and shook my head. 'I'm keeping some things back. I just need to see someone. Will you look after Laura until I get back?' When he started to preen, I said, 'Don't get too excited. Not in that jumper.'

I had one last look out of the window and then made myself leave, walking quickly towards the side door of the pub. It took me into a cobbled alley, which brought me out just a few yards from where I had parked my car.

As I drove past Laura she looked up, and when she saw me I thought she cursed. The phone dropped away from her ear as she became small in my mirror, and then she was blocked out completely by a car pulling out just after me.

I knew where I was going. It seemed the car behind me was going the same way.

THIRTY-SEVEN

I stopped my car outside a small redbrick bungalow. It was too new to be pretty. The lines of the house were too straight, too sharp. They hadn't started to creak yet, no sign of the house wearing itself in. But it was neat and tidy, with white window frames, quarter panes, and a single garage at one side. The driveway was short and uncluttered.

I didn't get out of the car straight away. I felt nervous, much more than I'd expected. I'd done house calls before, unsure of the reception, but this felt different. Maybe because I cared more about the outcome.

Then I remembered the conversation I had had with my father when I first came back to the Fold, when we had talked about the shootings. He'd said it was all about a ransom, that these things always are. I'd thought he was wrong for a while, because no one ever mentioned one, but I realised now that a ransom doesn't have to be about money. This one was about atonement.

I set off walking up the driveway and noticed the curtains twitching in the house next door. A face appeared at the window and seemed to watch me. I smiled out of politeness. The curtains moved back and the face disappeared.

I rang the doorbell. I was met with nothing but silence for a while, but then I saw a shape through the net curtains. The shape got larger and then there was a fumble with the key. The door opened and I smiled. She looked suspicious, wary, as if she had got used to receiving bad news.

I pulled out my press ID and flashed it at the face peering through the part-opened door. I kept my finger over my name.

'Rose Wood?'

'Can I help you?' Her voice was quiet, nervous, her eyes still wary.

I waved my press ID again. 'I'm sorry to bother you, but I want to talk to you about Colin's case.'

The American put the binoculars down as the door closed. He looked around. This was a neighbourhood without excitement, not aimed at young families, none of that family rattle to act as a distraction. He looked at the house. The street kinked just after it, so that the houses further along looked at the front of the house even more, like the front row of an amphitheatre. He reckoned on there being at least twelve homes with a view of the front of the old woman's house.

He picked up his mobile phone and dialled Glen Ross. The delay in answering was longer than he expected. The voice that eventually came on the line sounded quiet and withdrawn.

'Inspector, good to hear your voice. I need your help.'

There was no response at first, and then a dry voice asked, 'What do you want?'

'I'm at an address a couple of miles outside of town. The street name is,' and he looked around for the sign. He was parked just on the next street, near the junction. He spotted the street name on a lamppost. 'It's Green Meadow Close. That cop's son is in there, the journalist, inside number eight. I need to know who he's seeing. Who lives there?' A pause. 'That's all.'

No response.

'Can you do that?'

'Okay,' Glen Ross replied, sounding jaded. 'Give me ten minutes to run some checks.'

He wasn't long. When the phone rang again, the American listened carefully. He recognised the name.

He knew his list of targets was getting longer, but he realised he couldn't ignore her. He sat back and waited.

When I was shown into the house, I was surprised. It was neat and clean outside, and I'd guessed it would be the same inside. It wasn't.

Clothes were all over the back of a chair near the front of the window, with cups and glasses dotted around the room, some with dried stains that must have been days old. And there was a smell, cloying in the heat, strong and pungent. Rose Wood either thought everyone lived like this, or else she had stopped noticing.

She offered me a drink. 'That would be great,' I said. That bought me at least twenty minutes with her.

When the tea came, it was in a stained mug and looked stewed. I made a point of taking a sip, but turned the mug around to get to a clean part.

Rose sat back. 'Why is Colin important again?' she asked, her eyes filled with missing him.

'Tell me about him,' I replied.

Rose took a deep breath at that. I saw her flick a glance at the photographs along the mantelpiece, and I could tell they were of Colin, just from the way he held his mother. She was leaning into him in all the pictures, her arms wrapped around him. He wasn't doing much, just looking at the camera, unsure, confused. But he gripped his mother, his big arms surrounding her. He had been a big man. I guessed that Rose loved him to death and fed him just as well. I couldn't imagine that the prison would be as generous.

'He was all I had,' she said. 'My husband was taken away from me when Colin was very small, hurt in an accident at work, so Colin just became everything.' She smiled at me, although I didn't think she was focused on me. 'I know people would make fun of him because he wasn't very clever at school, and he didn't want to go out and play football, but he was always a very good boy for me. He looked after me.'

'Tell me about the night he was arrested.'

Her smile faded. 'He'd gone to the pub. He went there most nights. Everyone knew he wouldn't hurt anyone, not ever, but they all think he's a killer now. And that isn't right.'

She wiped her eyes, the lashes damp with tears.

'He was arrested for being drunk, and then he came

home. A few days later, Glen Ross arrested him, said that he'd raped that girl.' She shook her head. 'He wouldn't rape anyone. He wouldn't hurt anyone.'

I thought that she was bound to say that, she was too close to Colin; but didn't that also apply to me when I thought about what my own father had said?

She wiped her eyes again and focused on me, as though she had remembered where she was. 'So why is Colin important again? You didn't tell me.'

I ran my fingers through my hair, tried to think of a way to phrase it. I realised that she would appreciate me being direct.

'I think I may have found some evidence that wasn't brought up at his trial. It might help get him out of prison.'

Her chin trembled, and I saw rings form in her tea as she started to shake. I took the cup off her and placed it on the small table next to her. I held her hands, and when I looked into her eyes I saw years of loneliness. For a moment, I resented my father, even the day after he died. Annie Paxman hadn't been the only life destroyed.

'It's not much,' I said, 'but it shows that someone else was seen running away from Annie that night.'

She took a deep breath and then dropped my hands. She turned her face away, and I followed her gaze to the mantelpiece and back to the line of photographs.

When she turned back to me, I saw that her eyes looked harder.

'I've heard this before,' she said, her voice quiet.

'When?' I asked, startled.

310

'Oh, for the last five years.'

'What have you heard?'

She sat back, and I thought that she looked suddenly dejected.

'About David Watts.' She was looking at the ceiling.

I said nothing for a while, feeling disappointed, and then I nodded.

'Who told you?' I asked.

She looked back at me, her eyes narrowed. I could see her weighing me up, wondering what she could tell me.

'A girl called Liza Radley,' she said.

I looked at her confused. 'Liza Radley? James's daughter?'

She nodded. 'Yes, whatever that useless drunk of a policeman was called.'

I tugged at my lip. I hadn't seen Liza Radley for years. My father had been friendly with her father, I remembered that, but they had drifted apart. And then he'd died in a house fire. I'd heard the rumours that he was a drinker, and that he had fallen asleep in his chair after putting on the chip pan. But he had been at the scene with my father. He had seen Annie Paxman, and he had seen David Watts as he ran from the scene.

'He used to come to the house,' she said, 'all drunk and crying, saying he was sorry. I felt pity for him at first, but then it seemed like it wasn't me or Colin he cared about, just himself. He was selfish. Drunks are like that. He said he cared, but he didn't do anything to help Colin.'

'So why did Liza start coming round?'

My mind started to work fast, filled with images of young Liza. I had only met her two or three times, just a noise in the back of her father's car, but that had been years ago.

The old lady shrugged. 'I don't know. She just turned up one day and started to tell me how her father had seen David Watts when that girl was found. She was always talking about getting Colin out of prison, like it was her job to rescue him. But there was no new evidence. It was just her, dreaming. She was like that, a dreamer.'

I started to feel excited. Liza Radley knew. And, more importantly, she might have known about the necklace. I felt my heart beat faster, my mouth dry up.

'When did you last see her?' I tried to sound relaxed, but my mind was whirring, a collection of images coming together. Liza as a young girl. The security camera picture. The neck-chain.

Rose put her head back and started thinking. 'About a year ago. She said she was going to make it right, and then she stopped coming round.'

That came at me like a door slamming shut. *She was going to make it right.*

'What was she like?' I asked, my voice sounding keener.

Rose smiled. 'Something not right about that girl. It seemed like she was too busy having rows with herself to get out and make friends.'

'Did she talk about her parents much?' I knew I was sounding too eager, snapping the questions out, but I couldn't stop myself.

Rose shook her head. 'If I ever mentioned her father,

she would just look sad. She said once that he was always drunk, and it seemed like she hated him for it.'

'Do you know where she is?' I was leaning forward, my eyes wide.

Rose looked at me, vacant for a moment as her mind went back in time. 'She moved away. She got some insurance money, and she sold the house, what was left of it, to a builder, and then she left.'

'Her address. I need her address. Do you have it?' My nerves were taut, my breath getting short.

Rose thought for a moment, and then stood up. 'Wait there,' she said, and she shuffled over to a roll-top bureau in the corner. When she opened the drawer, silhouetted against the light coming in through the window, I could see papers spilling out, springing up like a jack-in-a-box.

I felt my phone vibrate in my pocket. I took it out to glance at the caller ID. It was Laura. I clicked off the phone and glanced over at Rose. She was still wrist-deep in the drawer.

'Here it is,' she said and she walked over with a scrap of paper. It had an address scribbled on it and a phone number. It just said *Liza* underneath it.

I looked at the paper, and I wondered if it was the key to the mystery. I could see my hand trembling as I held it.

'Talk with her,' said Rose. 'Ask her how she's keeping. She always seemed a little bit lost.'

I nodded. 'I will.'

THIRTY-EIGHT

The American was thinking of a drive around the neighbourhood to allay suspicion when his phone rang. He pressed the answer button and barked a sharp, 'Yes?'

'Get out of town!' It was Glen Ross.

He pulled the phone away from his ear, surprised. Then he heard the distant squeak of Glen Ross saying, 'Answer me, you bastard.'

'Calm down, Detective. You sound tense?' He smiled. He thought he could hear Glen Ross breathing hard and fast, wasn't sure if the rustle was interference on the line or Ross's hands grabbing at his own shirt. 'Mr Ross?'

'New Scotland Yard have just called me.' His words were spat out, his heaving breaths throwing them like bullets. 'They're coming to Turners Fold.'

The American pursed his lips and looked towards the house. If he had to walk away from a million, he would take a few people out as revenge.

His deliberations didn't take long. One million was more money than he would get in ten years from Marky.

It was early retirement. Or he could keep doing the work for the fun of it. Job satisfaction was a wonderful thing.

'What do they know?'

'I don't know,' Glen Ross screamed. 'I just got a call from a friend in headquarters. They're coming up here.'

'Just do as you're told and everything will be fine.'

There was more heavy breathing, and then it started to slow down.

'Now listen to me,' the American said. 'Just tell them about the girl's murder and then act dumb. Spin all that self-justifying bullshit about why you didn't haul in David Watts, and then tell them what you told me, that you didn't know where the family went. Let them do the rest. Can you do that?'

More deep breaths, then, 'Yes, I can.'

'Good. Co-operate with them. If they don't suspect you, they won't grill you. I'll deal with David. I'm hoping I'll have it sorted out soon.' He looked towards the house. 'Very soon.'

He hung up on Glen Ross and dialled David Watts. 'Yeah,' came the answer.

'Mr Watts, get out of the apartment. The police down there are asking questions about your situation.'

'You fucking prick. I'm paying you to end it.'

'Don't worry, I will, but you need to get out and keep your phone with you. I'll give you instructions later.'

And then the American clicked off the phone. He closed his eyes and took a deep breath of his own. It was time to get serious. He thought about the people in the house. And the woman he had seen talking on the phone back in Turners Fold. The job was getting harder, more targets by the day, but one million was one million.

The face at the next-door window turned away and walked slowly over to the television. He flicked it on to find something to watch. There wasn't much. He looked towards the back of the house. His wife was doing needlecraft through a large reading glass.

'He's come out now,' he shouted over.

His wife didn't look up. 'Who?' she asked, only half-listening.

'Bob Garrett's lad.'

'You're an old gossip,' she said, still looking at her needlecraft. 'Get a hobby.' She looked up. 'Are you sure it was him?'

'Course I'm sure. I worked with his father for ten years, so I know his lad. Poor sod.'

His wife sat back in her chair and ignored him. Policemen were all the same. They never retired. They just worked from home.

David Watts was driving too fast. He knew it, tried to stop himself, worried it would draw attention, but he couldn't slow down.

He was heading north, onto the M1, something telling him to head to the seat of the trouble, not away from it. He'd taken some cocaine, enough to get him through the next hour, and there was enough in the glove compartment to keep him up and running for a few weeks. He'd taken another batch from Marky before he left the city.

He was racing past cars, one eye always on the hard shoulder, looking out for police. He had a pocketful of cocaine and he didn't want anyone to know where he was going. Service stations and small southern towns rushed past the windows, mixing with the blur of trees and grass embankments. Cars and lorries were left as he went, each one a shrinking spot in his mirrors, his engine starting to climb, the wheels straining hard to keep tight on the tarmac.

He reached into his shirt pocket and pulled out his phone. He glanced at the keypad and began to key in Emma's number. He felt the rumble of road paint and heard the blast of a horn. He looked up to see himself drifting towards the right and gave the wheel a hard turn to get it back in line. He felt the tyres grip and the swing of the car threw him about for a second. He took some deep breaths to calm his nerves before he carried on punching in the number, taking longer now, constant glances up to check the road ahead.

He held the phone to his ear, but all he could hear was the ring, playing out to no one.

He gripped the phone and felt his foot press down harder on the accelerator. The countryside he was now travelling through began to rush at him.

'Answer the phone!'

There was still no response.

He pressed harder on the pedal. The needle was touching past a hundred. He was shooting past cars, swerving to overtake on the inside when they came into his lane.

He clicked the off button and then jabbed his finger

at the redial button. Same response. He pressed it again. Same result.

He looked up and saw the rear of a car coming up fast. He stamped on the brake pedal and felt the rear begin to slide, the noise from the tyres taking over from the engine. He steered into his slide and slowed down just enough to let it pull away. He sat back into his seat and breathed out long and hard. He could feel the flush of his cheeks, the slickness of his palms.

He pulled over into the slower lane and began to drive at a legal speed. His heart and pulse were the only things racing now.

He picked up his phone again and went into its memory. He clicked the key to connect with the American's phone. It only rang once before he heard the voice he now wished he'd never heard.

'Hi, Mr Watts. Have you done as I asked?'

David nodded. 'Yes, I've left London.' He mopped his forehead with his hand. 'Where shall I go?'

'Just out of sight and wait for my call. Avoid hotels. You need to be invisible.'

'Won't it make me look guilty?'

'*Looking* guilty isn't enough.'

'Okay, okay.' He rubbed his forehead again. The air-conditioning filled the car with cool air, but it wasn't getting rid of the dampness on his face. 'I got a call. She said she was going to get Emma. And I can't get hold of her.'

'Who is Emma?'

David took a deep breath. He thought about the last few months with her. The promises, the hopes. Then he thought about the person he was speaking with, some mysterious American with a bent for murder. He wanted to close his eyes, to shut out what he was about to do, but he had to watch the road, the oncoming scenery going out of focus.

'Just a girl,' he replied.

He pulled the phone away from his ear so he could wipe his eye with the back of his hand. He felt a lump in his throat and his eyes became moist again. He thought about her smile, about how she looked when she was asleep in the morning.

'Does she know?'

David couldn't answer. His voice was thick with emotion, his cheeks now wet with tears. He knew the answer. If Emma had been taken, she would know now.

He clicked off the phone, unable to speak. He tried to make out the road ahead, but it was difficult. It was made harder because he didn't know where he was going, but it all blurred behind tears now.

He'd just killed Emma.

The American put down his phone and stepped out of the car. He looked around. He couldn't see anyone watching him, so he felt for his knife. He knew he couldn't use the gun. If he started pumping bullets in there, there'd be a witness in every window for the first mile of his escape route.

He walked quickly up the street and then onto the drive. He rapped on the door, and Rose answered within a few seconds.

She smiled and looked at him. 'Can I help you?'

He reached into his pocket and pulled out a wallet. He flicked open a flap, showed the police warrant card.

'Good evening, ma'am. Was that a reporter I just saw here?'

Rose nodded. 'That's right.'

He smiled sympathetically, like he knew how easy it was to be taken in.

'I'm sorry, ma'am, but he is not what he appeared to be.'

Rose looked shocked.

He nodded. 'Can I come in, please? I'll need to take some details.'

'Yes, thank you,' said Rose, and moved away from the door to let him follow her in.

He closed the door with a soft click and smiled to himself. He followed Rose into the house. As she walked, he saw the long hair, watched its movement as it danced in time with her walk.

Rose turned around, oblivious, polite. 'What has he been doing?' she asked, her face creased by worry. 'He seemed like a nice man.'

He smiled. It came easy, the charm relaxed and warm. 'That's what worries us. He's so convincing.' He reached out and held her hand for a moment. 'It's not your fault. Others have been taken in.' When Rose put her hand to her mouth, he nodded towards the couch and said, 'You ought to sit down.'

Rose's mind was racing, wondering what was going on, but his calmness, his authoritative air made her obey.

He sat down next to her. He leant forward so that

he appeared concerned, not relaxed. 'What did he want from you?'

'Just wanted to know about my son, Colin,' she said.

He feigned concern. 'I'm sorry to tell you this, ma'am, but I believe that the nice young man is out to harm someone. I raced up here when I heard he was in the neighbourhood. Did he say what he wanted?'

'Yes,' she said, 'he said he wanted to help me with my son's case. Then we talked about Liza Radley, a girl who used to live round here.'

The American blinked but gave nothing away.

'Did he say why?'

Rose shook her head. 'Not really. We were just talking.'

He stood up and walked to the window. He looked out over the street, trying to see faces behind glass, or people tending their lawns, maybe with too much time on their hands, so that they spent it plotting the coming and goings of people in the street. He could see nothing unusual.

'Funny, though,' Rose continued, 'he seemed as bothered about Liza Radley as he did about Colin.'

The American's thoughts started to slot into place. He tried to force down the crinkles of a smile around the corners of his mouth. He turned round slowly, feigning mild curiosity, but his eyes were burning with determination.

'You knew this Liza?' he asked innocently.

'Yes. She used to visit me a few years ago.'

He thought back to the security footage of the shooter. The dead cop ran out when he saw the security pictures.

He faked a worried look. 'Did you tell him where Liza lived?'

'I did,' Rose replied. 'I gave him her address.'

He turned back towards the window and stroked his cheek with his hand. His eyes narrowed. He might be on his way there now. Or he might be on his way to the police. Glen Ross won't be able to bluff his way out if the reporter could link all this with a local girl, one who matched the security pictures. And the quick route back to David Watts was obvious. He scratched his cheek and his mind listed the options. Had that cop told his son about David Watts? Had he told his son about the phone calls to David Watts by the shooter? There had been an hour or so between their meeting at the station and their meeting in Victoria Park. He started to get angry. He was having to factor in the unexpected, and the unexpected might cost him a million.

He started to do some calculations. The cop's son had to be taken out of the picture, no doubt, and the woman who was with him in the bar before. And there was the old guy from the paper. Those three taken care of would slow down the connection to David Watts. He didn't need to stop the connection. He just needed to slow it down enough to let him get his million pounds. Then he had to take out the shooter. That would stop the shootings and no one would ever know.

He realised it had to be that night.

He turned back to Rose, whirling lightly on his heels as he turned away from the window. 'Do you still have Liza's address?'

'Yes.' And she went to the table by the window. She walked back to him and handed it over. 'He copied it off this.'

The American looked down at the address. It meant nothing to him, but he knew he would be able to find it.

'Who lives there with her?'

Rose shook her head sadly. 'I don't know, but she didn't seem the marrying type.'

He smiled. Just the answer he wanted. He could just make her go missing. No one would even know she was dead. Not if he did it right.

He looked at Rose and smiled warmly. 'Thank you so much. You've been a real help.'

She looked grateful, almost bashful.

He nodded towards the door. 'I'm going to have to go, ma'am. There's a lot of work to do.'

She understood and stepped aside so he could walk past her.

'No, after you, ma'am.'

She smiled, blushing slightly.

She walked in front of him towards the door. Her hair swished gently as she walked. He watched it like a hypnotist's prop, side to side, brushing against her back, old grey strands catching in the static of her shirt. He flexed his fingers and took a deep breath. The hair looked brittle and old, but she didn't look heavy.

He lunged forward, his movement quick, his arm outstretched. He gripped her hair. He felt his hand take the tension as the ponytail stretched tight. She gave a yelp of surprise. He yanked her ponytail upwards and forwards fast, so that she was on tiptoes, trying to keep her balance. She tried to pull away but his grip remained strong, his arm locked in front of him. Every struggle brought out hair and made her cry out.

'What are you doing?' she yelled, her pitch now more of a scream, half-panic, half-pain. She had tears in her eyes. Her arms were flicking upwards, trying to get free, but the loss of balance caused too much pain. He began to twirl her around. Her feet skipped on the floor as she tried to keep her balance. The nerve endings in her scalp stretched and tore, like tiny fires, the pain making her catch her breath.

He flicked his leg up to put the knife holster in reach. He reached down with his spare hand and pulled it out, the blade gleaming in the sunset streaking in from the front window. He held the knife in front of her, and yanked a little harder on her hair.

Her eyes widened, her mouth opened in pain. He thought he saw piss on the floor. She took a deep breath to scream so he thrust forward with the knife. He pushed the knife in hard, getting her just below the ear, at the end of the jawbone. It sank in up to its handle, her eyes wide with shock. He gave it a quick twist and then pulled it out. The blood supply was cut to her brain and it shot out of the gaping wound instead, following the blade and soaking his hand. It was like cutting off an engine's fuel supply. She shook, quick spasms, and then grew heavy in his grasp. Within ten seconds she had gone limp, her eyes lifeless and cold, her feet now trailing on their toes, her body spinning lightly in his grip.

He threw Rose's body towards the corner. It landed with a thump, a scattering of blood on the carpet showing its path, the wound face down. Gravity did the rest, a slow leak from her neck.

As he went, the neighbourhood was still and quiet. No sirens in the distance. No neighbours coming out of their front doors. No one saw him leave.

THIRTY-NINE

As Turners Fold came into view, it looked isolated. Nightfall had come around during my visit, and the journey back brought me into the valley from the north, so I was looking at the town from a side I hadn't seen in a couple of years. My route from London had brought me in from the south, where the urban clutter of Manchester petered away until the town just appeared. The northern side of town was different, as it just disappeared into the hills, so at night it was smothered by darkness. As I drove back, I could see Turners Fold as just a collection of houses and street-lights surrounded by nothing. In London, nightfall just made the noise echo more, the sunlight replaced by headlights and shop-fronts. In Turners Fold, nightfall brought on a shutdown. The streets were empty as I drove into town, and when I got back to my house it was in darkness. It looked a lonely place, living off memories.

I kept on driving. I wasn't ready for that yet. I drove to Tony's house instead.

Tony was on the back patio, drinking a beer. He was staring into his dark and quiet back garden. He didn't look round when I joined him; he just reached into a bucket of ice and held a beer in the air. I had the cap off before I noticed Alice sitting further along the porch.

She looked up at me, her eyes deep and moist. 'I'm sorry about your dad, Jack.'

I nodded a thanks, feeling suddenly choked, when I became aware of someone behind me. As I looked round, I saw it was Laura.

'Has Tony been looking after you?'

She smiled and nodded, and then surprised me by coming up behind me and putting her hand into mine.

I swallowed. I felt my skin tingle when I felt her hand give mine a squeeze.

'You keep on leaving me,' she said, and I sensed the mischief in her voice.

She was cajoling me, keeping my spirits up.

'It's just to remind myself how much I miss you,' I replied, playing along.

I noticed how Alice looked away.

For the first time that day, I felt still, as Laura's hand warmed up in mine, her fingers soft and light.

As I stood there, I thought about my visit with Rose Wood. Liza Radley would fit. She was the right age, a few years younger than me, and had the right colour hair. But was that enough?

I glanced over at Tony and gestured with my eyebrows that I needed to talk. He nodded, almost imperceptibly.

I dropped Laura's hand and went inside. She presumed

I was heading for the bathroom. I heard Tony say that he was going to get some more beer.

I waited for him in the kitchen.

'Where did you go?' he asked, his voice quiet.

'I went to see Colin Wood's mother, Rose.'

'How is she?'

I thought about her, how she was surrounded by pictures of him. 'Still missing him.'

'Did you discover anything?'

'Maybe.' I checked behind me that no one was listening. I could hear Laura making small-talk with Alice. I wondered if they were talking about me. 'Do you remember Liza Radley?'

'James's daughter,' he said, nodding. 'Why?'

I could see him thinking, maybe the same way as I did.

'Because Liza spent a lot of time at Rose's house, talking about making it right.'

Tony turned away, his hand over his mouth.

'Tony?'

When he turned back, he said, 'Liza used to place a notice in the paper on the anniversary of Annie's death. Nothing special. Just a "*You're not forgotten*" kind of thing.'

'For how long?'

He exhaled as he thought, then he said, 'Until last year. She did it for the first few years after her parents died. I remember it, because people used to comment on it. She was known for being quiet, like she didn't fit in, staying out late on her own, just driving around, or sitting in the town square, watching the town move.'

He stopped suddenly, his eyes wide, and then he said, 'Wait there.'

He rushed out of the kitchen, and I listened to Alice and Laura talking. I could hear Laura asking about me. That made me smile.

When Tony returned, he scattered the newspaper clippings he'd had earlier over the old wooden kitchen table. He rummaged through until he found what he was looking for.

'What do you see in that picture?'

I looked at it, and I saw that it was a photograph of mourners walking behind a coffin into the church, the text below it yellowed with age, the corners of the clipping turned-up and dry. I looked at the photograph. I hadn't gone as far back as the funeral. There were two people virtually holding each other up. Annie's parents, I guessed. Behind them were a collection of men and women of all ages, dotted with children here and there, mixed in with people around Annie's age.

'Is David Watts in there?' I asked.

Tony shook his head.

'No, he isn't, but do you recognise her,' and he pointed to a young girl stood away from the gravesite, strangely alone, in her hands a small posy of flowers. She was a blurred dot, but some of the features were recognisable.

I couldn't place her, not at first, but I definitely knew her. I looked at Tony, who was raising his eyebrows.

'Liza Radley,' I said, my voice hushed.

Tony rummaged some more. He found another press clipping, this time from the funeral of Liza's parents.

'Why did you get this?'

'I don't know. James Radley found Annie Paxman, along with your father. I just thought it might be useful in some way.'

And then he threw onto the table the picture released from the CCTV in the apartment building in Manchester. It was grainy and indistinct, the woman hiding behind a baseball cap, but I could see the blonde hair.

Then I looked at the picture from the Radley funeral.

It showed people coming out of the church. There were police officers, and I could see my father and Glen Ross in the background. But at the front was a blonde girl, hair long and streaming down her neck, with a face still and composed, her eyes deep and shadowy. She had spotted the camera and was staring it down.

I looked back at the CCTV-still, and then, as I held it next to the clipping, I gasped. It was her, just from the way she looked at the camera, like a challenge.

I couldn't put the picture down. I was shaking, knowing that I was looking at the most wanted woman in the country, not far from where she grew up. I felt my mouth go dry, my hands were slick, the biggest story of my life was spread across the table in clippings and old photographs.

I looked at Tony. He looked shocked.

'What do we do now?' he asked.

I stroked my cheeks, felt my palm rasp against the bristles coming through my skin.

Then I looked at Tony, and I knew exactly what I was going to do. 'I'm going to visit Liza Radley.'

'You got her address?'

I nodded.

Tony exhaled and reached for another beer from the fridge.

'Do you tell your London friend about her?'

'Laura?' I queried. I thought about it, and then I realised what I had, and how I could use it. 'No,' I said. 'My father went to the police, and he's dead now.'

'You can't go on your own,' he said, sounding worried.

'I can if I have to,' I replied.

'And if she shoots you?'

I wiggled my nose as if I had an itch. 'I suppose you'll tell the police.'

Then I remembered the tapes I had made of the radio traffic from ten years ago. 'Remember the radio calls? Use them wisely. Send one to your house. One to your work. Make sure that there are enough copies out there, so that if you lose a few, there are still others around.'

'And one to Glen Ross,' Tony added.

I looked at him. 'Why?'

Tony's grin slowly spread. 'If we make him sweat, he might do something stupid.'

'But if we do nothing to him, we might catch him unawares.'

Tony thought about that, but then shook his head. 'I reckon it's time to smoke him out.'

'Agreed,' I said, and then grinned. 'Let's get to work.'

The American's car was the only one on the street. The shop windows were all in darkness, the only movement coming from the traffic lights mapping out the corners of the triangle. They had been flicking between red and green as he approached town, colours winking in the distance, but as he reached them, they stayed green. He kept on driving, no need to stop anywhere.

Along the street, everything was still. He took it slowly, and as he went past he saw that the house was in darkness. He drove to the end of the street and around the block, looking for signs of police activity. There were none. Just a quiet suburban street in a quiet town in the middle of nowhere county.

He drove to the end of the street and waited, parking just where the houses ended and darkness began. He could be patient.

The black Mondeo drove slowly into town. It stopped at the lights while the occupants looked around. Two London detectives. A woman driving, Nell. Late thirties. Dark hair, white skin, figure covered by a dark suit, tapered pants hiding an athletic physique. Mike sat in the passenger seat. He was black, cropped hair, sharp nose, almost European, but his eyes were dark. He looked around, trying to get a sight of the police station.

'See anything?' she asked.

He shook his head then looked through the front window. The town petered out to nothing, so it couldn't be far away.

'Turn down here,' he said, pointing along the side of the town hall.

She swung the car to the right, a slow, steady turn,

the way dark apart from the dim glow of the street-lights. 'Small towns make me nervous,' she said. 'Whatever went on here all those years ago, someone in the police station will know the suspect. Someone else will know the victim. Whatever, it makes things dirty, and I don't like dirty investigations.'

She was silent for a while, just looking side to side out of the window, her forearms resting on the steering wheel, leaning forward. Then she pointed. 'There it is.' Mike followed her gaze and saw the police station sign illuminated by a spotlight.

They parked the car just down the road from the station. They didn't want anyone else to know they were there.

They got out, the two clunks sounding loud as the doors closed. She looked up and down the street. There was no one to be seen. The late-night shop on the other side of the square was open, but there were no customers, no cars, no people.

'Exciting place,' Mike said, looking around.

She twitched her nose. 'Hmm, don't believe it. These small places have more crime per capita than the big cities. It just never gets reported.'

'It's not crime if it doesn't get reported.' He looked up and down the street. 'It's just life, that's all.'

Nell set off for the police-station steps, Mike trotting to catch up. They took the steps together, just three small ones, enough to make it an entrance, something above street level. When they got into the station, he hung back, letting her take her place at the front of the charge.

The station only had a small foyer, with a glass screen at one end. There were two rows of chairs facing it, orange and hard and unwelcoming.

Nell introduced herself to the civilian behind the glass, a flash of their badges enough to get everyone's attention, and then asked to see whoever was in charge. The lady said it was Glen Ross, who wasn't normally in at this time, but he'd been working late the last few days. The London detectives exchanged glances. A change to the routine. The first sign of anything suspicious.

They were allowed through and taken to a door marked by a brass plaque that said, '*Detective Inspector Glen Ross*'. Mike knocked on the door, two light taps.

They knocked again and a quiet voice said, 'Come in.'

As they walked in, Glen Ross was sitting behind his desk, his hands gripping the chair arms. They walked over so he stood up to greet them, and they shook hands and sat down. Nell noticed the marks Ross's hands left on the polished wooden chair, clammy and damp. When he sat back down again, she noticed another brass plaque on the desk, sitting right in the middle, so that any visitor would know straight away who they were speaking with. Then she noticed the photographs, the detective grinning and posing, enjoying brushes with fame.

She glanced over at Mike, who knew what she was thinking: that he was no public servant, no career cop out to do the right thing. He was a career arsehole.

Nell smiled. She already felt in charge.

'What can I do for you?' he asked.

Nell thought she detected a tremor.

'We called earlier.' She paused, watching him. 'We've had a tip-off.' She paused again, trying to make him anticipate their reason for being there. 'I don't know if you were around then, but have you ever heard of the murder of Annie Paxman?'

Mike and Nell looked at each other as Glen Ross went instantly white, the colour gone from his cheeks. He seemed to grip the sides of his chair again. Mike made a mental note to ask for reinforcements. He reckoned they might be around for a while.

Rose's neighbour was at the window again, bored, looking around.

His wife sat back from her needlecraft, the artificial light now starting to make her eyes strain. She took her glasses off and rubbed her eyes.

'Are you still spying on Rose?'

'Her curtains are still open,' he said, 'but I haven't seen her go out.'

That seemed unusual. She thought about ignoring it, but she could tell by his fidget that he thought something was wrong. Cops survive on instincts. She trusted his.

'Go round,' she said, 'just to make sure.'

He got up quickly and went out of the house, glad to have something to do.

She'd just got back to her needlecraft when her husband burst into the room.

'What's wrong?' Her chest took a leap, the look on her husband's face telling her that something bad had happened.

He waved her away, his breathing fast, his cheeks flushed. She watched him pick up the phone and press 999.

She took off her glasses and stood up. She went to go next door, to check on Rose, but when her husband shouted at her to stop, when she saw the look in his eyes, she did as she was told.

FORTY

Glen Ross was staring at his two visitors but his eyes weren't focused on them. The detectives were speaking, but it was as if they were speaking in whispers. He could hear his heartbeat, could hear the laughter of his children, could hear his breathing, fast and heavy. He could focus only on the photographs on his desk: his wife, his daughters. Everything else was a haze.

'So do you remember the Annie Paxman murder?' the male Londoner asked, as if he had been sat waiting for an answer.

Ross licked his lips and thought about the file. If they asked questions around the station, they'd know he had asked for the file not long before. There was no point in lying about anything they could find in it. Any quick check of the records would tell them that he knew all about it.

'Yes,' he said, his voice nervous and hesitant, his throat and mouth sandpit-dry. 'I remember it. About,' and he bought some cooling-down time by pretending to think about the date, 'say, eleven, twelve years ago. A girl found dead in a park.'

He saw them exchange glances, could tell that they knew that much. They turned to him and the woman asked, 'Who did you get for it?'

He shrugged, his hands gripping the chair arms tightly again. He felt warm and he could feel moisture on his forehead. 'Colin Wood. Local man. Not all the tools are in the shed, if you know what I mean.'

He tried to meet her gaze. She made him nervous. She was staring at him. He couldn't remember her name, but it felt like she knew all about him, already knew the answer to every question she asked and was waiting for him to slip up.

He coughed, couldn't stop himself. He felt his chest become warm and tight. He fought the urge to rub his hands on his chest, to free some kind of a blockage.

'Did you speak to David Watts about it?' she asked. 'He was with her that night, wasn't he?'

He took a deep breath. His mind raced for ways out of this.

'It's a long time ago,' he said, floundering. And he thought for a few minutes, realising that vagueness was the only option. Do not say anything. It will only ever be used against you later. 'He was just the last person seen with her. We spoke with him, he satisfied us about his movements that night, and he left town to become a football star. That's it, nothing more.'

'The reason we are here,' the male officer said, but he didn't go any further. Her hand reached across and touched his, just enough of a brake to stop his words dead.

'Have you discussed this with anyone recently?' she asked.

Ross shook his head. 'No, no one.'

'Has David Watts spoken to you about this?'

He nodded, uncertain about what was coming. 'Yeah, way back then, when it happened.' He coughed again and rubbed his chest.

She looked him in the eye but stayed silent. She wanted him to fill the silence, but he wasn't about to do that.

'Not since?' she asked eventually, her voice low and clear. Her eyes narrowed slightly, as if to warn him not to lie.

'Recently?'

'You said recently. I said since. But we'll try recently.' She shrugged. 'Say, during the last week?' She tried to sound casual, but there was steel in her voice, some anticipation of the answer that put him on edge.

He cleared his throat and shifted in his seat.

'No,' he said, his chin trembling lightly with nerves. 'No, he hasn't.'

'When was the last time you spoke with David Watts?'

He exhaled and gave a nervous laugh. 'Years, maybe. I hardly know the man, except what I see in the papers.'

The male officer leant forward, but again he was stopped by a light touch on the arm.

'Thank you,' said the female officer. She smiled and stood up. She held her hand out to shake his again. The male officer looked surprised, but stood anyway.

Glen Ross was equally surprised. He'd expected more, some revelation, some damning piece of evidence. He stood up slowly and shook her hand again. He knew his hands were wet, but he had no choice. He felt himself blink as sweat got into his eye.

'Is that all you want?' he asked, sounding nervous about the answer.

She smiled and nodded, and gave his hand a squeeze. 'You've been very helpful.' She let go of his hand and turned to go, then stopped and said, 'Can I take the file with me?'

'The file?'

'The Annie Paxman file. Can I take it with me?'

He stood up straight, tried to assert himself. 'It will be stored away somewhere. It might take some finding.'

She shrugged and said, 'Okay then.'

Mike and Nell exchanged glances, slight smiles. They knew they had work to do in the town. They both left the room, leaving Ross asserting himself to a closing door.

As the door slipped back into its jamb with a click, Glen Ross's knees weakened and he sat down. His breathing was too fast to be healthy. He sat back in his chair and looked at the ceiling. His hands went over his face, his fingers kneading at his eyes, the skin around them loose and tired.

He was only like that for a few seconds when there was a knock on his door. He looked down and said, 'Yeah?'

The door burst open. It was a young constable. He looked anxious.

'What is it?'

340

'There's been a murder, sir.'

Ross's stomach lurched. 'Where?' The patrolman looked towards the window and nodded. 'Green Meadow Close.'

Glen Ross shut his eyes. 'Who's dead?' he asked, trembling slightly. He was clenching his teeth to fight back the taste of bile.

'Someone called Rose Wood. A retired woman. Lived alone. Found dead by a neighbour.'

Glen Ross nodded but couldn't speak.

'And sir, get this. The neighbour said the last person in the house was Bob Garrett's son.'

Glen Ross reached for his waste bin and held it to his mouth as he vomited. When he put it down, his chest heaving, he was aware of his room getting busy as people came in to see how he was.

He knew he wasn't good.

As Nell and Mike began to make their way through the police station, a constable bustled past them. He looked harassed, worried.

Mike turned to Nell and asked, 'What are we doing now?'

Nell had a half-smile on her face, a distant look. 'We're calling for reinforcements,' she said. 'I thought that this was some crackpot theory, but that detective was lying, and I want to find out about what.'

'Are we going back to London?'

Nell turned to him. She shook her head. 'Call your girlfriend. We're staying overnight, but we need to call the office. We need some more people.'

Mike understood now. 'So what do we do right now?'

She looked around. 'We make trouble around here for a while, ask about Annie Paxman, and then wait for the detective to move. Someone ran in there with some news. That must mean something is happening, and once it does, we follow. Might get him sweating a bit more.'

Mike raised his eyebrows. 'Is that possible?'

She grinned.

As I pulled up to my house, I looked across at Laura. I could sense that she knew what I was thinking, that the house felt nothing like the one I had grown up in. It felt like bricks and mortar, little else.

'You'll be all right,' she said softly.

Our eyes met for a moment, and I got the feeling that she was about to lean across and kiss me. It was the way her eyes closed, just for longer than a blink, and that sense you get when you know it's going to happen. The sound of our clothes rustling in the car, of our breathing, was all we could hear.

'Let's go inside.'

I stepped out and went to the door. I felt like a stranger there. I turned to Laura.

'What made you come up here?'

She smiled coyly. 'I had a rest day.'

I turned the key and went inside. It felt cold and dark.

'You know some detectives are on their way here?' she asked.

I put the keys on the table. 'I saw you making the call earlier.' I looked at her, tried to gauge her thoughts. 'It's not about us any more, you being here. Am I right?'

Laura looked at me. 'I've got a child, back in London.'

'I know that.'

'He's with my mother, because I'm still here, in Lancashire.'

I didn't answer.

Laura looked at me, challenge in her eyes, but then I saw her relax.

'Do you think I'm doing all of this because of Annie Paxman, or the football shootings?'

'Aren't you?'

She sighed. 'I could have called it in and headed back to London.'

I caught a look in her eyes, but I wasn't sure I wanted to recognise it.

'But there are still things I know which you don't.'

Her eyes said that she knew. 'What are you going to do now?' she asked.

'Right now?'

'Yes.'

'I'm going to write that story.'

'I'm not here for Annie Paxman,' she said and looked nervous. 'I'm here for you, Jack Garrett.' She looked upstairs. 'And I'm not driving back to London this late, so you'd better decide where you want me to sleep.'

I wanted to hold her right then, like I had always wanted to hold her, since I had first seen her back in that bar in London.

'I'd like you to stay,' I said, before I'd had chance to think about what I was saying. 'If you want, that is.'

She paused. 'I'd like that.'

FORTY-ONE

I was still at my computer, tapping the keys like I was wired, when Laura came down the stairs.

I heard her footfalls, and as she came into view I saw she was in one of my shirts. She was tall and leggy, so it just crept down her thighs. Her legs were bronzed and lean, and when she came to the bottom of the stairs, she crossed them at the ankles, coy and cute. She looked at me, and I found myself looking back. Her hair curled and waved and streamed over the shirt collar, teasing around the buttons, and the cuffs hung over her hands, just her fingernails showing.

'I've made up the sofa,' I said simply. 'I'll take that. You get some sleep. We need to be alert in the morning.'

Laura glanced at the couch, the twist of her body making the shirt ride up her legs. I noticed she was wearing an ankle bracelet, fine gold blinking in the light. It made her look young, pretty, took her back to the woman she had been before there'd been a child and a husband. Maybe that woman had never gone away?

344

When she turned round, I looked back up, and her eyes glimmered as she caught my gaze.

'I was hoping you'd be up there too,' she said, her eyes flicking upwards.

I didn't reply.

'You need someone with you, Jack.'

I looked at her and spotted a glare in her eyes that I'd never seen before. I knew what it meant, that she was taking a risk, worried that I might reject her, make her feel small, but that this was the moment for it. We had crossed the line that had kept us as friends.

She came over to me. My arms stayed by my side, uncertain. She leant forward and kissed me lightly on the cheek, and then took my hand. She led me upstairs without saying a word, and then when we got into the bedroom she flicked off the light. I watched her make her way across the room, her movement caught by the moon outside, her body cast in silver streaks as she climbed into bed.

I got undressed and climbed into bed with her. We didn't say anything. I turned away from Laura. I wanted to feel her in the bed with me, feel someone close behind me. I wanted to be held.

I pulled the sheets around me, and as I did so, Laura came up behind me. She put her legs into the space behind mine and put her arm around me. It was tender, not passionate, and her legs felt warm and soft, kind of hooked behind mine. Her body fitted against me. I could feel her breasts against my back, and her hand rubbed my shoulder, comforting, her touch paper-fine.

I felt the strain of the last day come to the surface,

and I closed my eyes. I sank back into her, felt her arm wrap around me, felt her pull me close.

I turned around to face her. I put my hand to her cheek and brushed my thumb against her skin. She blinked, and in the moonlight I saw her eyes sparkle. She put her hand over mine and held it for a moment, and then brought it to her mouth. She kissed it, a soft caress of my palm. Then she pulled herself closer, slowly, her eyes closing. She brushed a kiss across my lips, hardly a touch, and then kissed me again, this time with more urgency. I put my hand behind her back and pulled her towards me. I felt myself gripping her hair lightly, kissing her, wrapping her closer into me.

She stopped me for a moment and then pushed me onto my back. She was silhouetted against the moon-light. She raised her hands above her head so I could lift the shirt off her. My hands ran slowly up her body as I did so, and when I had tossed it to the floor, she was naked with me. She stayed like that for a moment, her hair cascading onto her bare shoulders, her hands on my chest. Then she leant forward to kiss me again. I became lost in her, and as I drifted with her, I felt my pain melt away.

Liza Radley sat in her chair, looking out through her open window, checking for the twist of headlights along the road leading to her house or the slow purr of an engine. There was a shotgun across her lap. She was still; she hadn't made a sound for hours, her head tight with tension.

The television was blaring, but each new bulletin,

346

each retelling of the story so far just cranked the tension up further. She rubbed her forehead. Nothing from David Watts. She closed her eyes and put her head back. Her chest tightened and she blinked back tears. Voices fluttered in her head, soft laughs, whispers, sometimes shouts.

She stayed like that for a few minutes, and when she put her head back down again, tears ran down her nose and dripped onto the stock of the shotgun. She reached out and started to wipe them off, but another one joined them. Her chest got warm with emotion, and she began to shake as more tears came. She put her head back and cried out, tears streaming down her face, her hands gripping the stock hard, the barrels shaking as she sobbed.

'How many more?' she wailed. She slid off the chair until she landed on her knees on the floor. She put her head down. 'How many more?' Her voice was distorted by pain.

She lifted her head and looked back at the television. It was replaying the scenes from Liverpool, showing clips of grieving Tottenham fans, and then a media camp outside the player's home. She looked out of the window. All she could see was darkness.

She shut her eyes again, but the tears still crept out, her lashes wet. She put her head to the floor and began to scream, started to thrash her head around, banging her toes on the floor. She lifted her head up and screamed, 'No, no, no, no,' her throat pulled taut, her eyes wide. She sank back so that she was kneeling down. She looked again at the television, blurred through tears. The news had moved on to something else.

She gripped the shotgun harder and pointed it at the television. She was shaking and crying. She stood up and let out one long scream, knowing that there was no one within miles to hear her. She squeezed the trigger, paused for a moment, and then shot a blast at the television. The glass shattered; there was a bang, and then smoke from the television mixed in with the smell of gunpowder. The noise echoed round the house, the only sound to fill it for hours.

She sank to her knees, her arms around the barrels of the gun, hugging them. The heat burnt onto her cheek, but she didn't let go. She began to rock, backwards and forwards, her hair dancing lightly in the breeze coming in through the open window.

FORTY-TWO

The American waited until a car drew near so that he could drown out the sound of his car door closing.

He walked slowly, careful that no one heard the crunch of footsteps coming to a stop outside the house. His eyes flicked to both sides of the street as he walked, checking for signs of neighbours checking on other neighbours. There was nothing. Just dark houses and the occasional streetlight, the wrap of a cool breeze making the leaves on the trees rustle and whisper.

When he got to the Garrett house, he didn't stop. He turned and walked casually up the driveway, not pausing, not looking around, not panicking, just making like someone returning home. He walked up the side of the house, his steps silent, his movement fluid and invisible, melting into the darkness. Once he was at the back of the house, he paused. He was hidden now, the only light coming from the moon at the front. The house blocked out most of that, except for where the shadows shimmered at the end of the garden. He was still for around five minutes, his breathing light and measured, checking for the sound of doors opening, neighbours wondering who he had been.

There was nothing.

He moved slowly along the back of the house and got himself under the window. He knelt down and listened. He was low down so he would have a head start if anyone came to the door, not in their immediate line of vision.

He waited another five minutes. Still nothing. Not even a bored dog howling.

He checked his knife in his sock. He had cleaned some of the blood off it, but it had less of a gleam than earlier in the evening. His pepper spray was still in his pocket, and the handgun nestled snugly in the holster at the small of his back.

He stood up and put his hand on the door handle. He gave it the gentlest of pushes. It opened an inch, no locks, a light click the only noise. He stopped and smiled. He loved country people.

David Watts was in Manchester. He had felt himself drawn in. There were hotels by the motorway, and a retail park with American restaurants and English shops, but he wanted something more private. Traffic lights punctuated the flow of vehicles every fifty yards or so, and as he looked around he saw movement, the shuffle of traffic heading in or out of the city.

He drove on until commerce turned into housing, and then the closer he got to the city, the closer the houses got, until they were either lined up in rows or boarded up and derelict. He swung into a street he hadn't driven through for more than two years, a long stretch of terraced housing, heading for a house that used to welcome him whenever he played in Manchester.

When he knocked on the door, he didn't know what response he would get. When she opened the door, she looked surprised, pleased at first, but then her look clouded when she remembered how he had stopped calling.

'Hi, David. Long time no see.'

He shrugged, smiled, tried the charm. 'I was passing. Thought I'd see how you were doing.'

She looked suspicious, reluctant. 'How do you know I'm not with someone?'

David was about to answer when a voice came from the top of the stairs.

'Who is it, Mummy?'

She turned around. 'Back to bed. It's no one for you.'

'I just guessed,' said David, looking towards the stairs.

She turned away, looked angry, but left the door open so he could follow.

David followed her into the back room, trying to remember her name. He used to have a girl near every club, but he'd given it up when a girl from Newcastle sold a Saturday night to the papers.

Then he remembered.

'How's life, Julie?' he asked.

She sat down, and then leant forward to the bottle of Smirnoff on the table. 'I get by.'

David didn't answer. He just reached into his pocket and tossed the bag of white powder onto the table. 'We could have a real party.'

She smiled properly for the first time.

'Sounds good,' she said. 'Sounds really good.'

I didn't hear the noise.

I was hard asleep, my mind flitting through impossible scenarios, the sheet tangled around my body. I'd tried to stay awake so that I could go back to the story, get it finished before daybreak, but the wrap of Laura's arms was too warm, too safe.

I woke when I felt Laura lift my arm and put it down on the bed. I felt her move and sit up, and then pause. I opened my eyes, the images coming in blurred at first. When it cleared, I saw Laura was still, her head tilted, as if listening for something. I reached out and touched her back, but she held up her hand so I stopped.

I rubbed my eyes and watched her stand slowly, her naked body framed against the window, curved and sweeping. My mind began to clear, sensing something wasn't right. She pulled on her jeans, quickly and silently, and then slipped on her T-shirt. She put on her shoes and then crept towards the door.

I was about to ask her what was wrong when I heard it. It was a creak. Downstairs. But it wasn't just that. It was a creak followed by nothing. A creak that had made whoever was down there halt, waiting to see if we had heard anything. Had they heard us? Had they heard Laura creep out of bed and put on her clothes?

She turned round to look at me. My eyes were quickly adjusting to the darkness. I put my finger to my lips and then beckoned her back to me. She crept over to me, her light steps not making a sound, and knelt down by the side of the bed. She reached to the floor and passed me my clothes. I looked at her. I could see the fear in her eyes, could sense it in her urgency. Someone had killed my father. Now there was someone in the house.

I slipped on my pants, the bed springing as I did, and then put on my shirt, the one worn by Laura earlier in the night. I could smell her on it, a faint perfume.

I pointed at my camera, which had been on top of my bag on the floor. She looked at me, curiosity in her eyes, and then crept across to get it. When she was there, I whispered that she should open the window. She looked back at me, then at the window. She held her hands out and hunched her shoulders in query, but when I pointed again, she reached across the table and pulled on the window catch. It gave easily, and she was able to open the window, only a slight squeak giving her movements away.

She had a quick glance out and saw why I had asked her to do it. My room was above the bay window, giving a tiled slide to a seven-foot drop to the floor.

She crept back across the room and knelt down beside me. I explained what I wanted her to do. She shook her head, giving me the cop's answer. I hissed at her that someone was in my house, and that gave me rights. She thought for a moment, and nodded.

Then we both heard a creak. I knew that one. I had heard that creak throughout my adolescence, an early warning to throw the cigarette out of the window, or for a girl to sit up quickly, to look like we hadn't been doing anything.

Whoever was in the house was at the bottom of the stairs. We kissed, and then stood up. We knew what to do.

As David Watts lay back, he sensed how high Julie was getting. He had an urge not to get there with her.

He looked around. He'd forgotten how bad some of the bad places could be. The cream walls were browning with nicotine and the carpet looked worn, covered in stains. The kitchen stretched out into the back yard, an eighties extension. The wood-effect furniture was cracked and dirty, and when he looked down at the sofa he saw the holes where Julie had relaxed too much with a joint hanging from her fingers. She used to be fun, a party girl. It seemed like she hadn't realised that the party had ended.

He thought about the American, wondered how he was getting on in Turners Fold. He couldn't stand that he wasn't in control. He sat back, looking at the ceiling. His eyes flitted around the cobwebs.

Julie came into view. She was smiling, swaying, dancing, her eyes closed, her dirty blonde hair swishing over her shoulders. He noticed the dark circles under her eyes. She gave a smile intended to be flirty. The glazed focus in her eyes made it look seedy and cheap.

He pulled out his phone and rang the American's number. He needed to know. He heard two ring tones, and then it was clicked off.

He looked at his handset before throwing it into the corner.

*

We both heard the phone ring. We froze. The sound was clear and near. It was on the stairs. There was a rustle of clothes and a muffled curse. No hesitation. I hissed, 'Now!' and bolted for the door.

I could hear Laura running behind me, her breaths frantic and scared. She had to be right behind me. That was the plan.

I flung open the door and dashed across the landing, only as wide as the stairs. I was past in a flash and then I heard feet on the stairs, starting to run, missing out steps. Laura stayed in my room.

I crashed through the door into my father's bedroom, my bare feet stumbling as I stopped to avoid the bed. My heart was thumping. All I could hear was the sound of my pulse and the blood rushing through my head. Time had slowed down. The footfalls on the stairs were loud, each step crashing as I scrambled round the bed and towards the window.

I saw the camera flash. Laura must have put her arm round the corner and fired the camera, the blue light making the stairs seem as in daylight. I heard a voice say, 'Shit,' and a stumble. I heard Laura rush back into my room. I heard a rush up the stairs, the flash had only halted the steps for a second, and then a slam as my bedroom door flew open. I heard Laura's feet land on the table and then light screams. Laura was heading for the window. There was a crash as something hurtled against the window frame, and then I heard a thud on the roof outside. There was a shout of 'Fuck' from my bedroom, and then I heard the table clatter as it took a kick. It was a male voice. Laura had got out.

I rushed to my father's window. That was the plan. Get a picture and split up. Laura would have the easier drop. I would have a straight fall from the window. But it was onto grass.

I grabbed at the window and pulled it up, expecting it to spring upwards.

It didn't move.

I looked down, panicking. There was a window lock. Shit.

I looked around for the key, scrambling through the drawer unit next to the bed, my hands flicking through clothes, throwing them around.

I couldn't find it. I could hear pacing in the next room. I was trapped, cold sweat gathering on my lip. I opened the next drawer. If the key wasn't in there, it was stay and fight or throw myself through the glass.

My hands scurried through the next drawer. Nothing there. I was starting to panic. The noise from my room had stopped. He had heard me. It made me pause for a moment and I looked around. There was no way out. A square room, a square bed, and one door out.

I opened the bottom drawer and tipped out the contents, my hands fumbling now, desperate. I dropped to the floor and pushed aside papers and photographs.

He entered the room slowly. He made no noise, but I could sense him blocking the doorway. The door was on the other side of the bed to me, and I was exposed, cornered.

I looked around my feet, at the mess I'd made on the floor. Then I saw something. It was a can of deodorant. I picked it up and shook it. There was some left in.

I rummaged through the clothes I'd thrown over the floor, looking for a cigarette lighter. There must be one in there. Dad had smoked in bed. Always had. I'd tried to tell him to stop. I hoped he hadn't listened to me.

Then I felt it, a knock against my knuckles. My hand closed around it and I felt empowered.

I shot to my feet, pointed the aerosol, and pressed, my finger clicking the lighter alive.

My mouth dried in an instant. Nothing. No flame. Just two clicks. My eyes shot to the floor but there was nothing I could use. Just papers and pictures.

The intruder stood up straight and reached into his pocket. He filled the doorway and a sliver of moonlight from my room flickered against the knife he held in one hand. His other hand produced a canister. I thought I saw a grin, and then I noticed him put his arm across his nose.

'This is what you want,' he said. I spotted the American drawl.

He pointed the canister into the room and sprayed.

I copied him, covered my mouth with my arm, and fell to the floor, not knowing what it was. I dropped the canister I'd been holding.

It hit me straight away. My eyes began to burn, my nose streamed, and I began to cough. I tried to take a breath, but my throat flared up with fire. I spluttered and roared, and started to rub my eyes, but it made it worse. I felt like I was melting, my eyes pouring water, my throat burning. I buried my head in my father's bed, tried to wipe it off, but it didn't work. I was shrieking and coughing and wiping my eyes, my finger-nails scraping at my face.

Then I heard footsteps. He was coming into the room. He was coming to get me.

I reached behind me on the floor, looking for some-thing, anything, my hands scrabbling around under the papers. The footsteps got nearer. My search became frantic. I scattered whatever was there, and then I felt it, cold and round. A paperweight, nothing special. Just heavy and a good shape for the hand.

I shot to my feet, unable to see, and drew back my arm. There was one more footstep and I was able to get a bearing.

I threw the paperweight hard. A fastball, straight and high. I heard a yell, and then it dropped to the floor. I could make out a shape on the other side of the bed, bending down, holding his head. He was all in black, but I could see the pale skin, his hands over his fore-head. The spray must have been clearing, because I could make out a dark patch around his hands, could hear him cursing, saw him trying to stand up straight.

I jumped onto the bed, screaming with rage now, and ran across in two steps. His head was still down, his face towards me as I got to the edge, so I swung my right leg and jumped off with a volley. I felt my foot hit something soft, my leg jarring, and heard a crash as he fell backwards. I fell on top of him, so I began to punch and elbow my way off him, stumbling over the falling body and landing just in the doorway, my feet scuffing at the floor, trying to get away.

I heard a rumble of movement and I caught sight of the shadow moving, something swinging through the air. I felt a slice on my leg, wetness, and then heat. I shouted in pain and kicked out in instinct, my foot finding his head again.

I rushed to my feet, a wince of pain, and then I heard another burst of movement towards me, so I kicked out again, catching just enough shoulder to stop him.

I ran across the landing and into my room. Instinct told me to avoid the stairs, too much like a shooting range, even a flying knife wouldn't miss. I kept running, the footsteps behind me starting up again, fast and earnest. I jumped onto the table and made a leap for the window. The table moved as I jumped. It rocked on its legs and my kick for the window pushed it backwards. I heard running footsteps enter the room. I made it into the open window, my ribs hitting the window frame hard, and I fell forward, my feet kicking out at the sills to get away. I felt something hit my foot as I went through.

He had missed. Just.

I landed with a thud, my head crashing against the tiles. I kept rolling, and then I was falling through the air, landing with a jar on the driveway. My head hit the ground as I landed and I grunted in pain. I was dazed, the graze stinging, but I knew I couldn't wait.

I picked myself up and began to run. I had no shoes on, so I ran across gardens, shouting in pain as I hit each driveway, shingle and concrete shredding the soles of my feet. I heard his feet on the bay window and then a neat thud as he landed feet first. Then I heard running.

I was fifty yards away from the end of the street. I knew where I was headed. I'd told Laura to head for the fields on the other side of Accrington Road. Lie low and wait. Once in there, it would be easy to lose a stranger. I had my head back, going as fast as I could, heading for there. I gritted my teeth as the tarmac cut into my feet.

I looked back. He was running. Then I saw him stop suddenly and reach behind his back. He came up with a gun. I saw him raise it, taking aim.

I looked forward and tried a surge. The end of the street crept closer.

I cut across a lawn and then onto the street, making a sharp left. I screamed as I ran, hollering, bawling, trying to get people to their windows. The tarmac on the road was tearing my feet up. I could feel the skin getting raw, but still I ran, moving from side to side, trying to make a hard target. I was twenty yards away. My lungs were screaming at me, mouth open. Just a few seconds more. A light went on. Then another. I carried on yelling.

Then I stumbled.

I went to my knees, the road cutting through my pants, my knees scraping on the floor. I just hauled myself up again, making a swift dart to the left as I did.

A gun was fired. A car windscreen shattered where I'd just been.

I sprinted for the main road and a dark patch

between two houses. I knew that behind those were the fields. Once in there, it would be darkness. It would be soft underfoot. The moon would cast shadows, would light up the open spaces, but I knew where there was a line of trees.

I could hear engines on the main road, a lorry, moving slowly. I could tell it wasn't far away. I looked through the gaps in the houses, and I could see it would pass me at the same time as I reached the road. It would block me off, make me stop.

I tried one last burst, a bolt for the road.

The wheels rolled into view, the front of the cab large and red, chrome grilles, all moving towards me. I couldn't stop. The truck kept moving, and I screamed, my feet tearing, my legs pumping, chest heaving. I ran into the road, my bare feet skidding over the tarmac, my toes scrubbed raw. I felt a rush of warm air, heard the blast of a horn, and then the wind from the passing truck shoved me just out of the way, its cab missing me by inches.

I was in between houses on the other side of the road before the dust in its slipstream had settled. I ran through the yard and vaulted the wall at the back, my hands slapping at the dark coping stone. A dog barked in the yard and ran towards me, jumping against the wall.

As I hit the grass, I stayed down. I took deep breaths, sucked in air, tried to get calm. I looked back, peering over the wall. I could see him running so I got to my haunches, ready to go again, but he wasn't coming for me. He had his gun in his hand, pointing upwards but visible, a warning to the neighbours. He looked in my direction, but then turned away and walked back down my street. He walked to a car at the end, jumped in and fired up the engine. I saw neighbours on my street at their windows. He left the car lights off and reversed hard until he got to the Accrington Road, swinging it around with a hard left lock, and then screeched his tyres as he floored it, the car disappearing quickly into the distance. The rear lights flicked on as he got to a red light, but he didn't stop. He went through it at around seventy miles an hour, his rear end sparking as he bumped over the junction, lighting up the street for a second.

I sat down in the grass and put my head in my hands. I stayed like that for a few minutes, coughing, retching, the taste of the gas still hot, and then the pain from my calf began to creep through. I reached down to where it hurt, and I yelled when my hand found the spot. I felt warm liquid on my leg and I knew I'd been cut.

I stood up and gasped as the pain shot through my leg, the adrenalin subsiding. I knew I had to find Laura. But then something struck me, and it made me sit down.

I realised that I had just seen my father's killer.

FORTY-THREE

Mike and Nell were drinking more coffee, trying to stay alert until the back-up from London arrived.

'I don't like this place,' said Mike.

'We don't have to like it,' Nell replied. 'We just have to comb it.'

'Do you think the shooter is nearby?'

Nell shook her head. 'She's travelling. Whether she started here is something we need to find out.'

'What does the office say about Glen Ross?'

Nell shook her head. 'Local boy, nothing known.'

'Well, something's got him jumping.'

Nell smiled. 'He might just get worse. I got a call half an hour ago telling me that two detectives from local HQ have landed in town. They're watching his house.'

Mike grinned, but then asked, 'Where do we start tomorrow?'

Nell tugged on her lip. 'The local law firms,' she said. 'Running round for criminals gives them the inside line on rumours. If there is anything to this, they should know. They'll at least have a line on Glen Ross.'

'Will they tell us?'

Nell nodded. 'They'd better.'

Then they heard noise behind them, excited chatter, bursts of radio, talk of a shooting at Bob Garrett's house.

Nell and Mike looked at each other.

'Dead copper, right?'

Nell nodded.

'Time to wake up Mr Ross,' she said. 'This town is getting awfully busy.'

The American headed north, Turners Fold disappearing over his right shoulder, the roofs now vivid blue as streaks of sun peered over the horizon. But there was some redness to the sky, storms ahead.

He gripped the steering wheel tightly as he drove, his mouth set in a firm line, his anger controlled, but only just. He wanted to press hard on the accelerator, burn off his frustration.

He was keeping off the major routes. There was a risk of a stray patrol car picking him up, the police airwaves broadcasting his number plate. He struggled along country roads instead. They had no lighting, no signs, no numbers. Just rolling expanses of hills and farms, the occasional stone bridge and two-street village, broken only by ninety-degree bends and hiking trails. It was only the rising sun that gave him any bearing: as long as the sun was to his right for the next couple of hours, he reckoned he would be okay.

But the frustration was making him tense, and he couldn't afford to be tense. He needed to be relaxed, focused, in control. He had never been driven by emotion. That was a negative. People make mistakes in anger. But he had ended up with too many loose strands, frayed corners dragging him down.

He should have turned off his phone, he realised now, but he was even angrier with David Watts for calling him.

He sat back in his seat and took a deep breath. He had to stay calm. He was a perfectionist, and on this, his most lucrative job yet, he needed it to be just that: perfect. That chance had gone now. The police would be watching the grieving son. His father had been found dead and then within twenty-four hours a gun-wielding stranger broke into his house and chased him down the street. Made Glen Ross's suicide announcement pretty worthless.

He slowed down to take another sharp bend, the road zigzagging around.

He checked his watch. Just after five. He needed to be there before Liza Radley woke up. No more mistakes this time. No more leaving his phone switched on. That was his only mistake so far. Not any more. His phone was off and it wouldn't go back on until he wanted to make a call. David Watts could sweat it out for a few hours. A taste of defeat would do him good. See life from the other side.

He leant forward and squinted through his windscreen. He had to be focused. He didn't underestimate the enemy ahead. She had already carried out three perfect assassinations and three protection killings. This was no little lady, hunched over an apple pie or filing her nails. She would be armed, she would be wary, and she would be prepared to kill anyone who got in her way.

He smiled to himself. It was a shame he had to kill her. He reckoned they would have got along just fine.

David Watts was lying on his back, naked, thinking about the American. There had been no call for some time, and he was not answering calls either. How long now?

He felt dirty and cheap, the post-sex comedown. But it hadn't been about sex, he knew that. He had done it to hate himself, to remind himself what lay behind the fast car and Chelsea Bridge apartment. He could smell the cheap life, reminders of where a bad right foot might have left him.

Then he thought of Emma, wondered where she was. Maybe she was okay, on a flight somewhere, just wondering where he had gone. His chest took a heave. She wouldn't be there when he got back. He knew that, could feel it. She might even be dead.

He covered his eyes with his hands. Why hadn't he called the police? Or even the airline? They would confirm that she was safe on a plane somewhere. But what if they recognised his voice, or wanted to know his name?

His nails dug into the skin around his eyes and he began to pull down, bringing blood to the surface. He thought about Emma some more and felt his stomach turn over. He took some deep breaths to cool down the nausea, his nerves eventually slowing, the grip of his fingers easing off.

He felt tired. He rubbed his face with his hands and then messed with his hair, scruffing it up. He glanced over at Julie, sitting on a chair by the bathroom door. She'd taken some cigarette papers out of her bag and was licking three, joining them together for a joint.

She was still naked. Her body was thin and pale, not toned and golden like she used to be. He could see bruises on her upper arms, finger-marks, and her shins and thighs were mottled and pink. She had no form, no shape, just up and down, sagging where she was supposed to curve, hanging where she was supposed to be pert.

He rubbed his eyes again and thought more about Emma. When she was naked, it was like looking at a masterpiece, all curves and grace. And she made love like she had spent all day thinking about him, hungry and fast.

Julie was looking at him, raised eyebrows, holding a small lump of cannabis in her hand. He heard the small child in the room next door begin to stir. Julie didn't flinch. Was this what he was going back to?

David got off the bed and took out his phone. He pressed the auto-dial number, trying to speak to the American again. There was nothing, just a recorded message saying that the phone was switched off.

He closed his eyes. It wasn't supposed to be like this.

Detective Inspector Ross was just plain old Glen at home.

He was lying in bed, his eyes wide open, looking at the ceiling. He hadn't slept for a couple of nights now.

His wife was breathing lightly next to him, looking tranquil. His daughters were all inside, soundly asleep in their rooms, as ever.

The telephone rang next to his bed. He picked it up, nervous, twitchy.

He listened as the news came through, his expression unchanging. Just something he ought to know. Might affect the Bob Garrett enquiry, scaled down when the announcement about the suicide was made. There had been a shooting on Bob Garrett's street. A tall male, all in black, running after Jack Garrett, taking shots. He just nodded and listened, rubbed his chest with his hand when he heard that Jack Garrett had got away.

Then there was something else. There were more detectives in town. They had been to Rose Wood's house, and now they were heading to Bob Garrett's.

He put the phone down, and when he looked round his wife was awake, watching him.

He patted her on the arm. 'Just work, sweetheart. Nothing for you to worry about.'

'You look awful, Glen. What's wrong? Are you sleeping all right?'

He smiled and patted her on the arm again. 'I'm fine. Go back to sleep.'

She looked at him for a moment before turning round and curling up again. He returned to his view of the ceiling. It was blurred now, knocked out of shape by the tears in his eyes. He knew now how it would end. He knew that all this would be gone for him soon. He'd thought it had been dead for over ten years, as lifeless as Annie Paxman herself. It hadn't. It had just been dormant. And now it was alive again and spinning out of control, and it was going to spin all the way back to him.

He tried to swallow but it was hard. His breaths were tight and ragged, and when he looked down he saw that his fists were clenched. He closed his eyes, as if darkness would help. It didn't. The shadows were still there.

He heard a car outside, two doors open and close. He knew who it was: the two London detectives coming to speak to him.

He reached over and wrapped his arms around his wife. She was content, smelling of warm nights, and when he pulled her to him, she murmured. As he buried his face in her hair, he wondered if this would be goodbye. He gave her a kiss and then climbed out of bed.

FORTY-FOUR

I was aching as I sat in the grass, my brow damp with sweat. The sun was low and I could just make out my feet, shining silver. But I could see a patch of darkness, and by its warmth, its stickiness, I knew it was blood.

I ran my hand down my leg and felt my trousers. They were damp. I had a deep slash in them, neat and easy to stitch, and I guessed that my calf wasn't much different. I had tried walking but it had been too painful, each step making me wince and grit my teeth.

I sat down for a moment to rest my feet. They were red and scrubbed, but the walk through the grass had helped, the dew cooling them down and softening up the scrapes and scuffs. I looked around and checked for movement among the shadows.

I checked my watch, wondering how long I would have to wait. I couldn't make out any houses, just fields and trees, and I realised I was the only glimmer of life as far as I could see. If that crazy bastard came back, I was a sitting target, no one to hear the gunshots, no one to see the shooter.

I lay back in the grass. I wasn't sure I cared. I felt drained and exhausted and just wanted to sleep. The grass was wet, and pretty soon my back was soaked. I didn't move. I watched the new day turn a bright cool blue, licked by the red streaks coming from the east. It was like fire trying to reach across to the sky in the west, still hanging on to some hues of night-time.

I closed my eyes and wondered whether I could sleep. I didn't feel like I could walk any more and I was losing the will to stay awake. It didn't take long for the world to fade away, my breaths slowing right down. It felt like I was slipping backwards, away from consciousness.

I jerked awake when I felt vibrations through the ground, and then I heard the sound of grass squeaking under someone's shoes. My heart began to race and I sat up quickly. My head snapped around, trying to see shapes, hints of movement.

I felt shadow fall over me. I started to scramble backwards, but then I recognised the shape.

I grinned. 'What took you?'

Laura looked at me, then down at my leg. She gasped and went to her knees, her hands going out towards me.

'Jack, are you okay?'

I sat up and pulled up the leg on my trousers. She put her hand over her mouth, shocked.

'I thought you'd got away,' she said.

'I did,' I replied, 'but he got a cheap shot in before I got out of the house.' I grimaced. 'I think it was a knife.'

She sat back and put her hands on her legs. 'I saw

371

you,' she said, 'running down the street.' She shook her head. 'I didn't know whether you had made it away or were stuck to the front of that lorry.'

'Where were you?'

'I ran down the side of a house just down from yours. I was just across from you when he fired a shot.'

'How did I look?' I asked, breathing heavily with pain, trying to make light of it.

'Imagine a barefoot city boy running down the road for his life. That's how it looked.'

I shrugged my shoulders. 'You just had a bad seat.'

She smiled and leant forward and kissed me on the top of my head. 'We need to sort that leg out.'

'You any good at needlework?'

She shook her head. 'I was thinking more of a wash and a bandage.'

I lay back again. The sky was getting brighter.

'What do we do now?' she asked.

'We?'

'If you are going to be the hotshot reporter all day, I need to stick with you.'

I looked up at her. My spirits had lifted since she'd arrived, and thoughts of giving up on the story had gone. 'Detective or friend?' I asked.

'Lover?' she queried, her eyes dancing with mischief. When I didn't answer, she kissed me on the forehead. 'For today, I'm a detective, for your sake.' She pointed towards the town. 'If you're going that way, you'll need to get past a police roadblock.'

'Have they been to the house?'

'In numbers. You're starting to interest them now,

and it seems like the road into town is lit up by head-lights.'

I cursed as I thought of my computer, the story I had started to write, and the envelope I had been given by Martha.

Laura read my thoughts. 'They're in the boot of my car.'

I stalled for a moment, and then asked, 'how come?'

'Because while you were running through the fields like a singing nun, I went back into the house to get your stuff.' She shrugged. 'I guessed you would want your things, so I got your work from last night. I got out just before the police arrived.'

'And did you get a good picture of him, the one you flashed down the stairs?'

'Sure did. Right in the face, looking up.'

That made my heart surge. He killed my father, and we had a picture of him.

'Lover sounds just fine, by the way,' I said, and grinned at her.

'So what now?' asked Laura. 'Are you going some-where quiet to finish your story?'

I thought for a moment, and then realised that I was going to stick to my plan.

'I've got to go to the Dales. There's someone I need to speak to.'

FORTY-FIVE

The American smiled as Kirkby Askham came into view, a small cluster of life a few miles on from Skipton, in the heart of the Yorkshire Dales.

There wasn't much there, just a pub, a church, a couple of small shops, and miles and miles of natural beauty. The buildings looked like the stones that bound them had just tumbled together and then bonded over time. This was picture-postcard Yorkshire, with rolling fields, the occasional burst of woodland, and a sea of open rough pasture, sheep grazing lazily over the village.

But he wasn't there for the view. He had been touring the roads around it, checking out the area, but it was Liza Radley's house he was after, a converted barn a couple of miles into the hills. He needed to get to it on foot and not arouse suspicion. He had driven round and round for half an hour, looking for ways in. He thought he'd found one.

He set off, a thin grin on his face, and then took the left turn just after a bend in the road. No one saw him. The road closed in straight away, dry-stone walls lining a narrow tarmac track, the stones a lighter lime-stone grey than the blackened walls he had seen in Turners Fold. Beyond those, the fields pitched and rolled, broken into squares, the sound of his engine loud in the peace of the scene. The road twisted, rolled and climbed, so he guessed it was an old track. There was no other traffic, no signs of any buildings, life, industry.

He climbed a slight rise with the brow fifty yards ahead. It was hard to call it a hill, but it was enough of an incline to provide a horizon, a spread of blue just a few seconds away. He slowed down, tried to cut his engine noise, and as he crawled over the top of the slope he looked into a green valley. It wasn't deep, more of an undulation, a couple of fields sloping down to a narrow river, trees lining the banks, and then a long field rising away from it. In the dip was a house, the rise and fall of the land just enough to make it secluded. It sat on its own, grey, isolated, dotted by windows picked out in white. It would have once been a lonely barn, somewhere to store straw and food when the snow kicked in. Now, it was just some house stuck in the middle of nowhere, hidden in a cleft, undisturbed by outsiders.

He backed up twenty yards, to just before the brow of the hill, and stopped. He reached into the glove box for his field glasses and then got out of the car.

He walked slowly back to the brow, his ears straining for the sound of activity at the house, making sure she wasn't setting off after him in her car. This was his show, not hers. He couldn't hear anything, so he kept walking, slowly, steadily, until he could see into the dip in the landscape, could see the top of the house. He knelt down and shuffled forward, crouching just behind a clump of rough pasture grass. He put his field glasses to his eyes and looked around.

He focused on the house. It looked empty. He didn't mind that. If she wasn't there, he would wait until she returned. She would have to come home eventually, and he thought it would be soon. She was shooting in the north now, quick darts out and then quick darts back. All the curtains in the windows were closed. He could see the front wing of a car, parked at the back of the house.

He brought his glasses further down from the house, then swung them back. He'd seen something near the porch. His eyes had caught something that he ought to take notice of but his brain hadn't been quick enough to tell him what it was. He ran the glasses up and down for a few seconds before he saw it. It was a drinking glass, one that contained some liquid, maybe half-full.

He put his glasses down. Who goes away leaving a glass outside?

He picked up his field glasses and scanned the house again. He looked at every window, checking for movement inside. He couldn't see anything. Just the closed curtains.

He looked around the rest of the property.

The road that snaked down to the house was interrupted by a cattle grid, a ten-foot-wide rattle of metal bars. He couldn't see a path across it. On foot it would be tricky, and would slow him down enough to make him a good target. Driving over it, he might as well call her in advance. He could wade through the stream, it was too wide to jump over, but the water would slow him down and make his footsteps noisy when he was in the house.

He ignored the back of the house, as his searching that morning had hinted that there was nothing behind the house for miles, so he would have nowhere to leave his car. He had no intention of starting his search again. The locals would only see a car so many times before they found it suspicious.

It was the land to the left of the house that interested him most. The house was only around twenty yards from a small cluster of trees, the southern edge of a windbreak. Behind the cluster were more fields, running to a rise similar in height to the one he was on. From his searches that morning, he knew there was a lane on the other side of the rise, with gates providing a space to park in. If he could get into the fields without being spotted, it would be the most anonymous way of closing in. He wasn't worried about the registration number being identified after he had gone. He was driving on false plates and the car would be going in the crusher once he had the million pounds in his hand. If he was successful, he would use her car to leave the scene.

He backed away, satisfied, checking all the time that he hadn't been spotted. It didn't seem that way. He got back to his car, and once in it he released the handbrake. He rolled gently backwards for a hundred yards, and then when his speed slowly disappeared as the road levelled out, he put on the brakes and started the engine.

He turned back towards Kirkby Askham as quietly as he could. He was going to work.

FORTY-SIX

We stopped for breakfast at an old trailer, hot food served out of a hatch, the spread of the Dales the view.

I was clean again. A supermarket had provided the clothes, just a white T-shirt and jeans, white deck shoes on my feet. I'd raised my eyebrows at them when Laura handed them to me. I'd expected better from a city girl.

I had a roll-bandage over my leg, nice and tight. I could stand better, but I hoped I wouldn't need to run.

We'd headed north again, but when we saw the trailer we knew we had to get some energy and convince ourselves that we were doing the right thing.

We were halfway through bacon sandwiches when I heard the ring of Laura's phone.

I was nervous about who it was, but I relaxed when she mouthed 'Tony' at me. I watched her nodding and listening, but it was only when I heard her gasp that I really paid attention. She put her hand over her mouth and shook her head, looking shocked and pale.

I raised my eyebrows in silent query.

She held her hand up to me to ask me to wait a moment, and then passed me the phone.

I dabbed my mouth and then when I put the phone to my ear, I heard Tony's voice.

'Good to hear that you're all right, Jack.'

I guessed what he was talking about. 'News of the raid on my house slipped out then?'

'More of a shootout is what I hear. Your name is the talk of the wire in Lancashire this morning, and the police have swamped the town.'

'That was no shootout. That was an escape.' I shook my head and sat back. 'Someone is after me, Tony. He has killed my father, and now he's after me.'

'Was it the American man people are talking about?'

'Who else could it be?' I answered wearily. 'To do with David Watts, I guess.'

Tony didn't respond. I looked back up at Laura, who still had her hand over her mouth, but was now looking down, thinking hard.

'Tony?'

I heard Tony sigh, and then he said, 'It isn't just the American hunting you.'

'What do you mean?'

Another pause, Tony thinking how to put it. In the end, he went for simplicity.

'Rose Wood died last night,' he said, his voice low and sad.

I paused, lost for words. I thought about her, polite and lost, but I sensed the danger in the message.

'How did she die?'

I heard Tony breathing hard, trying to work out how to say it. There was only one way.

'She was stabbed,' he said, his voice flat, letting my own mind do the equations.

'Stabbed?'

'Uh-huh. A knife, they reckon, jammed into the neck, just below the ear. A neighbour called it in.'

I thought about Rose and it made me angry. And I thought how it was changing my day. That made me angrier.

'So the police want me to call in and give them the low-down on our meeting?' I asked.

'It gets worse than that.'

'Can it?'

'Oh yes, it can.'

Seems that I was slow on the uptake.

'Follow the trail, Jack.'

'What do you mean?'

Tony didn't say anything for a while, just static filled my ear, and then he said, 'The police want you because they think you might have killed her.'

My mouth dried up. I wasn't sure how many shocks I was supposed to take in a week.

'Me?' I queried, my voice shrill. 'She was alive when I left her.'

'Yeah, I know that, but the neighbour who found the body told the police that you were the last person to visit the house.' He coughed lightly, and then continued, 'The neighbour knew your father, so he named you. He went round after you'd gone and found her.'

'So I'm a murder suspect?'

I sensed Tony nodding. 'Number one,' he said.

I dropped the phone from my ear for a moment and looked at Laura. I could tell she was going through the assessments in her head: what would happen to her if she didn't take me in? I was a wanted man and she was a police officer.

I put the phone back to my ear.

'We have to get Glen Ross,' I said, a snarl creeping into my voice. 'We have to do it today. Use those tapes.'

'It might not be Glen Ross calling the shots.'

'Who else? David Watts?'

'Why not?' Tony replied. 'He's got a hell of a lot more to protect than Ross, and he's the only one who could afford a contract killer.'

'C'mon, Tony. He's a footballer, that's all.'

'Yes, I know, but he's got millions of pounds to protect. That can do strange things to a man.' He paused for a moment, and then said, 'It might buy you some leverage with Liza Radley if we wait.'

'How so?'

'Think about it, Jack. She wants the story told. If she knows that if she doesn't tell it soon, she might be silenced for good, then she might tell it to you.'

I thought about that for a moment.

'Okay, you're right, Tony. Just wait a while.'

'But you better go quickly,' he said. 'Go now.'

'Don't worry about me, Tony.'

'It wasn't you I was thinking about.'

I was confused.

'Whoever killed Rose Wood', he continued, 'went to

382

her for the same reason you did, and whatever you got, I bet he got it too.'

'Shit!' I exclaimed, the connections fusing in my head. 'He's gone after Liza.'

Nell clicked off her phone.

'Any joy?' asked Mike.

She shook her head. 'David Watts hasn't been seen all night. We checked his apartment last night, but there was no one there.'

'Has anyone spoken with his lawyer?'

'I don't know if he's got one. They spoke with his agent this morning. Some cold fish, so they said, worried she might have lost a client.'

'Had she seen him?'

'She wouldn't talk at first, but the rattle of the handcuffs changed that.'

Mike exhaled. 'What did she say?'

Nell smiled. 'She confirmed the phone calls, that someone was saying that unless he confessed to the murder of Annie Paxman, she would shoot more footballers.' She raised her eyebrows. 'That detective was right.'

'Shit!' And then something occurred to Mike. 'Where *is* DC McGanity?'

At that, Nell didn't look as happy. 'As far as we can tell, she was last seen jumping out of a window, with someone firing shots at her.'

David Watts was in the shower, washing himself down. He wasn't sure he'd be any cleaner once he'd used the towels, but he had to wash her out of his hair. The water came out at barely a trickle, but at least it was warm.

Once he'd dried himself off, he stepped back into the bedroom. He was surprised to see her still there. She was sitting on the end of the bed, looking at the floor.

'I thought you'd taken your little girl to school.'

'She went with a neighbour.'

He dropped his towel and began to get dressed. 'What's up? Want some more?' He pulled on his shirt and shook his head. 'Sorry, sweetheart, no gas left in the tank.'

She was on the bed. Her robe fell open. She was naked underneath. She looked at David, and reaching to her left she pulled out the bag of cocaine David had passed her the night before. She tipped a thin line onto her stomach, just a sliver, a white trail leading down to her pubic hair.

He saw her and wanted to look away. He saw the powder and wanted to go to her.

Then he thought about what lay ahead and realised he needed the kick-start.

He went over to her and knelt down, his hands on her, his face getting down for the powder, Julie with her head back, her eyes closed.

Then he saw it. Just a small red light, hidden behind some clothes.

He jumped up and snatched the clothes away, throwing them around. A camcorder. Cheap, but good enough to record whatever had gone on in the room.

He knew straight away what this was all about. Money. It was only ever about money. She was selling him. And he thought he had bought her. His mind flashed back to the few hours they'd just spent together. Cocaine. Sex. Images of Emma flashed through his head, pictures in magazines, gossip.

He felt tears in his eyes, rage, anger. His nails cut into his palms as he looked at her. She was backing up on the bed, scared, crying.

'How much were you going to get for this?' he asked, barely able to speak, his mouth dry.

She tried to cover herself. 'I don't know,' she cried. 'You came to me, remember. Maybe enough to give Abi a better life.'

'I knew I was getting a whore,' he said, his voice snapping the words out. 'I just didn't know I'd be paying for it.' He went towards her, laughing, low and mean. 'Because a brush with fame seems to be worth losing every bit of self-respect you have left.'

'It's easy for you,' she said, her voice rising, getting angry. 'You've got it all, always had it all. This is as good as I'm going to get, and you have no fucking idea.'

'Well, maybe you're right, because you live like a dog, and you look like a dog. Christ, you even fuck like one.' He gripped her round the throat, his right hand squeezing, pushing her down. 'Fucking me like that, doing all of that, with your precious baby asleep in the next room. And you say this is for her.'

She gulped, tried to cry out. 'Don't, you're hurting me.'

He gripped her breast hard. 'You still like it now?'

She had her eyes shut, clamped tight, a tear squeezing out.

He pushed her down onto the bed. He could feel himself against her, pushing, felt the excitement as she struggled. His knee nudged hers apart.

One good thing about losing everything was that he had nothing left to lose.

The American had been right about the lane. He had walked less than a mile when he'd reached the top of the rise and found himself looking down towards the cluster of trees that shielded the house from view. He stopped to check his weapons, coldly calm now. His knife was in its sheath on his leg. A new pepper-spray canister was in his pocket. The gun was in its holster at the small of his back.

He was walking fast, anticipation making him smile. And he had something else: a short piece of nylon rope.

If he had no choice, he would shoot her. If it came to hand-to-hand fighting, he would use the knife. But what he really wanted to use was the rope.

She didn't deserve quick and painless. As he walked along the fields, he'd started to imagine her with the rope around her neck, his hands making the circle, pulling tight. He could almost hear the bones creaking as he pulled, could almost feel her struggling and kicking and thrashing as she pleaded. He wanted to see the terror in her eyes. He wanted to feel her scratching at his arms, her legs banging on the floor as she tried to release his grip. She wouldn't match his physical strength, so he could release and tighten it at will, prolong the moment, let her know that every last second of her life was just that, the end. When she did fade away, he wanted to be looking into her eyes, wanted to see the coldness creep in, wanted to make sure that the last moments she spent were bound up in terror.

His cheeks flushed. He was erect. He was ready for this one.

He approached the cluster of trees. It wasn't thick woodland, just a thin screen, so he tried to keep low, his view of the house obscured, hoping her view of him would be obscured too. His eyes scanned the ground as he crept, looking out for tripwires or sensors, some way of knowing that someone was on the property. It seemed normal.

He got in among the trees and knelt down. He got out his field glasses for another look at the house, to see if anything had changed. Whether any blinds were open, or whether the glass near the porch had moved.

As far as he could tell, it was all the same.

Showtime.

FORTY-SEVEN

Laura was driving fast and I kept a lookout for police patrols. The roads were quiet, no one around, so she nudged the speed higher, the trees and lay-bys blurring past.

I was looking at the map, trying to work out where we were going. We needed to be at a small village called Kirkby Askham. Liza Radley's house was just beyond that.

I started to get nervous. I was chewing my lip, thinking about what lay ahead. Laura interrupted my thoughts. 'Where are we going?'

I turned to look at her. She was staring straight ahead, concentrating on the road, as if it was just a thought spoken aloud.

I returned my eyes to the road, realising that there was no way to dress it up.

'We're going to talk to the woman who has been shooting footballers.'

My leg screamed with pain as the car screeched to a halt.

'What!'

I smiled through the pain, enjoying the effect.

'You heard me,' I said.

'Who is she?'

I watched her. Laura was a policewoman. Would she stop me if I told her? Then I thought about the night before. That wasn't about the job.

'She's a woman from Turners Fold obsessed with Annie Paxman's death. Called Liza Radley.'

'That's bullshit,' she said, and then she paused. 'How do you know this?'

'Old photographs, guesswork, that kind of thing.'

Laura stared straight ahead for a while, gathering her thoughts, before she said, 'Jack, let me tell you one thing: people don't just start killing footballers. They build up to killing footballers. A person's first murder makes them pause, take stock, even panic a little. Sprees come later, much later.'

'So you're saying I'm wrong?'

Laura looked at me, disappointment in her eyes. 'I'm saying that you're too wrapped up in the story to see the truth. And you're not being fair to me, Jack. You knew all this last night, as we were making love, but you didn't say anything. Maybe you're thinking too much about the story and not enough about yourself. You're putting yourself in danger.' Laura clicked on her phone. 'I'm calling it in.'

I grabbed her wrist. 'And maybe you're thinking too much about an arrest? I'm thinking only of the story, and for that I need to do what I need to do. I'll worry about me later.'

Laura started to answer, but then she stopped. I could almost see the thoughts flashing across her eyes as she tried to decide whether she had the killer in sight. She tugged at her lip. 'Who is she?'

'Her father was James Radley, the policeman who arrived on the scene of Annie Paxman's murder with my father.'

'The other cop on the tape?'

I nodded. 'He knew and hated himself for it. He saw the same thing my father saw.'

Laura exhaled. 'And his daughter started hating him for it too?'

'Something like that, I guess. I'll let the head doctors sort that one out, but my take is that she hated the town and hated David Watts for what it did to her father. She puts her father out of his misery and then goes after David Watts.'

'And when it all comes out, she'll bring the town down with her.'

'Seems that way. I'm guessing that she won't mind an interview.'

'I'm calling this in, Jack. Now.'

I made a play of reaching for the door handle. 'You can, but we aren't far away now. I'll walk. I just hope I don't tip her off.'

Laura grabbed at my hand. 'You bastard, Jack Garrett,' she snapped. 'I'm a police officer. Are you trying to end my career?'

I looked down and thought for a moment. When I looked again, I was steely and determined. 'I'm doing this my way, because this story is going to be written.

But Laura,' and I put my hand over hers, 'we're past the cop–reporter thing now. We need to talk when this is all over.'

Laura looked into my eyes and saw that I meant it.

'You'll cover for me, if I get in trouble?' she asked.

I smiled. 'I'm making you the hero of the piece.' And then I kissed her.

I felt her move into the kiss, her hand falling away from mine. When I opened my eyes, she said softly, 'Okay, you win.' She paused, and then said, 'But I'm calling it in as soon as we get there The reinforcements might just arrive before she kills us both.'

'Do we tell her about Rose Wood?'

Laura sighed. That was a tough one.

'Maybe,' was her reply, 'but let's not get her angry.'

FORTY-EIGHT

He walked quickly across the open land between the trees and the house. There was no sign of movement as he went, his footsteps silent. As he reached the house, his back flat against the gable, he listened out. There was nothing.

He eased himself around the corner of the house and crawled to the first window, listening again, his ears cocked for any noise. Still nothing. He had a quick look into the window. He saw it was broken, shards of glass hanging down.

He ducked back down again and pulled the gun out of its holster. She could surprise him, unless he got his shot in first. He walked along the front of the house, looking out for debris that might give him away. He made it without a sound. When he was at other end, he carried on down the side of the house, the side that looked down towards the cattle grid. He walked quickly to the back corner, trying to keep out of sight of anyone who came down the road.

As he got to the corner of the house, he peered

round. No one there. Just the car he'd seen earlier and a garden seat. He smiled. This was no farmhouse. It was just a house on its own, for people who wanted to be on their own.

He walked to the door at the back of the house and looked through. He was looking into a kitchen, cast in semi-darkness by the closed blinds. He tried the door handle. It turned in his hand, no squeak, but when he pushed the door didn't give. It was bolted.

He cursed and walked over to the kitchen window. It was an old sash window. He put his gun away and pulled out his knife. He was able to get it between the two panes and ease the catch round until the two frames just settled in their runners. He started to ease up the bottom half of the window, pushing against it as he did it, not allowing it to move in the frame, until there was enough room to get his body through. He took a deep breath and let go of the window, holding his hand underneath, anxious that it would crash down and wake her. It held, decades of paint making the sash-rope tight and stiff.

He put his head through and looked around. There was nothing in his way, so he put his knife on the sink and then put his shoulders through, grabbing the edge of the sink and slithering onto the floor. He listened out. There was nothing. Just the clunk of an old clock on a shelf by the door and the occasional creak of the house timbers. He looked around the kitchen. It was bare, nothing homely. No flowers or plants, no pictures on the wall. The house smelled cold and unwelcoming. It was as if no one lived there any more.

He started when he heard the noise of a car engine. He moved against the wall and pulled his gun out of its holster again. His breaths matched the steady beat of the clock, but there wasn't much else.

Then he thought he heard something upstairs.

We were squinting through the shadows, looking for the house, trying to drive normally, when suddenly we emerged into sunlight and were overlooking a low green valley and an isolated grey-stone house.

'Is that it?' asked Laura, as we began to descend the light slope towards a covered bridge.

I looked ahead, holding my hand out for Laura to slow down. 'I don't know. We'll need to check.'

'I'm not stopping, it'll be too obvious. We'll drive past and then turn around further on.'

We carried on down the hill, and then our tyres rattled noisily as we crossed the cattle grid, the engine noise bouncing around the early morning.

Laura stopped the car, the tyres kicking up dust.

I looked at Laura in surprise. 'What's going on?'

Laura pointed ahead, tight-lipped. 'We've run out of road.'

I looked in front, and then saw that the road just turned into a track.

'Shit, it's just for this house,' I hissed, angry with myself for not making us more careful. I looked up at the house. We couldn't get any further.

'This must be it,' I said. 'We just have to make like tourists. Get some maps out, point, that kind of thing. We'll do that for a couple of minutes and then I'll go up to the house. I'll pretend to be lost, and then ask her questions when I've got her to the door.'

'No more secrets.' It was a command, not a question. I held up my hand in agreement.

Laura turned to look at the house. 'If we get out of this car so near to the house, she might just shoot us.'

'Yeah,' I replied, feeling the adrenalin beginning to pump, 'and she might just blow my head off through the front door, but it's a risk I'm prepared to take.'

I grabbed the maps and stepped out. I walked round the car to put it between the house and us. I put a map on the car roof, drew a line with my finger, but all my attention was on the house. As I play-acted, I could feel the stares of every window on me, each one maybe hiding a rifle, pointing right at me.

FORTY-NINE

Liza Radley snapped awake.

The room was in shadow, but she sensed something wasn't right. She was in a bedroom at the front of the house, with a view over the approach road. She could hear something, an engine noise getting louder.

She lay still, silent, trying to work out how far away it was. The engine got closer, the crunch of the tyres on the road outside, her road, and then she heard the car rattle over the grid.

She sat bolt upright, and then looked towards the window. She could hear voices, hectic voices, whispering at her to get out, like mocking laughs, scratches at the door.

She jumped out of bed and ran to the window. She was wearing her clothes from the previous night. She inched open the blind and looked out. Her eyes squinted against the sudden brightness, and then when she saw the car, she let the blind drop back into place.

She turned back to the window and peered out again. They were getting out of the car. It was a young couple, a man and a woman. They didn't look at the house.

Liza watched them for a while, calming down. They seemed okay. People did get lost up here, and when they did, that's all they did: they got out a map, pointed, sometimes argued, and then turned round and drove away. She looked around her land and then up the track, back towards the main road, but it all seemed the same. Maybe check the television, she thought. If the police were on to her, there were bound to be pictures of a stake-out. She looked again at the couple by the car. It didn't seem like a stake-out.

She turned around, thought she heard a whisper. Nothing there.

She reached for the remote control for the television, the only one she had left, the set downstairs destroyed, and flicked it on. It went straight to the sports news channels. Nothing. The headlines were running across the bottom of the screen.

She threw herself onto the bed, remote control in hand, ready to channel-hop just to check the latest.

If nothing happened this morning, she was going after David Watts. He was next.

And it would be easy, because she knew he would come for Emma.

He could hear voices, someone talking. Someone was with her. Bad news.

He listened out. He could hear a female voice, just talking, not saying much. He couldn't hear anyone answer.

He edged along the wall, his gun in his hand. He got to the kitchen doorway and looked along the hall.

It was a long one, maybe thirty feet, with a room going off at both sides and the front door at the other end. The door provided the light, and as it came in, it shone up the stairs. He looked along the floor. It was the same as outside. No tripwires or sensors. The floor looked packed full of dangers though. It was wooden boards all through the house and up the stairs, lacquered but old, worn down in scuffs, with every board carrying a creak. He just had to hope he got lucky and only picked the quiet ones to walk on.

He walked as softly as he could, his steps slow and deliberate, keeping to the edges. He could still hear talking upstairs, but then he realised there was a television on. That was good. It might mask any noise he made.

He reached the doorway to the room going off the hall to his right. He peered round, his gun ready. The room slowly swung into view. No one there. He went into the room to give him a view of the room opposite. That slowly came into his eye-line. Empty.

He went back into the hall. He moved with his back against the wall, sliding himself along silently. He paused by the front door when movement outside caught his eye. He looked and saw the two people near the cattle grid. When he saw who it was, he grinned to himself. He could tidy up his frayed ends all at the same time.

He looked back towards the stairs. The noise from the television echoed down. He couldn't hear movement. There was definitely a voice, not just the television, but it was the same voice every time.

He stepped forward and put a foot on the stairs. His foot rested on the step and he began to press his weight forward to begin his climb.

The wood began to give slightly, bending against the force of his footsteps. He realised too late that a creak was coming, too far gone to stop himself. His foot carried on pressing, the wood carried on giving, and then it groaned in the empty wooden hall, the noise like a fired gun, shooting along the walls and up the stairs.

He almost saw the noise reach the room upstairs. It seemed to get there when he heard the voice stop mid-sentence, when the subtle sounds of movement, almost too soft to hear, fell into silence.

He stopped then and waited for more sound so he could decide what to do.

Liza heard something. A creak of wood. The voices halted as if the noise had scared them off.

She eased herself off the bed and crawled across the floor. When she got to the window, she looked outside. The young couple were still there.

She cursed and looked at the floor, her mind waking up fast now. Someone was inside the house. She looked again for signs of the police: cars up the track, snipers in the trees. There were none.

She turned away from the window and slithered back across the floor, her eyes darting to the door as she went. It was open. There was a landing with three more bedrooms going off to the left, and then the stairs going down to her right. At the other side, there was one more bedroom and the bathroom. She shuffled quickly to the drawers by her bed. She found the gun she kept in there, always loaded, a Glock 17, the double-action trigger giving it a quick safety release. She wanted to be able to shoot quickly.

She grabbed the gun and got on the floor behind the bed. It was an old metal-framed bed, so she had a shot at the feet of anyone who came in. She could lie underneath, and then shoot up under the chin when he was over her.

She started to clamber underneath, but when she saw the springs over her head, she realised how trapped she would be if she messed it up. Then she noticed the light on the floor coming through the bedroom doorway. There was some reflected light getting through from the hallway, coming off the pale walls and into the bedroom, giving an opalescent sheen to the boards by the door.

She crawled out from under the bed. She would wait until the sheen disappeared, whereby she would know someone was in the door frame. Then she would begin firing.

She knelt down on the other side of the room, her gun trained on the open door.

FIFTY

I had just pointed out my tenth alternative route on the map and was running out of ideas. Laura was looking edgy.

'It's time to go up there,' I said, stepping away from the car.

Laura looked up at the house. It looked the image of Dales charm: a stone-built box house, set among trees and fields, facing south, roses scattered around the front porch.

She took a deep breath. 'You're not going.'

'Yes, I am,' I said, and set off walking.

'No, you're not,' she replied, 'because it's too dangerous. We're unarmed, and you might get hurt. And I might get hurt. I'm not leaving Bobby without a mum. When we got out of the car, I got my phone to send in our location. I'm sorry, Jack, but some things are more important than a story.'

I paused, took some more steps. And then stopped and turned around. I knew she was right. Was I doing this for the exclusive? I had it anyway. But I felt betrayed.

I thought I was piggy-backing her. Maybe it was the other way round? I looked up at the house.

'I need to go up there,' I said. 'I've got a personal stake in this.' I looked back at Laura and said, 'Professional stakes aren't always worth risking your life over, but personal, well, that's different.'

Laura looked down at the floor, playing in the dust with her foot.

'This is non-negotiable,' she said.

I looked at her, and then shook my head. 'Who said we were negotiating?'

I set off again towards the house.

He moved his foot away slowly and placed it on the side of the step. He put his foot down gradually, but the wood didn't creak.

He stepped up onto the first stair. He put his back against the wall and took each step slowly, his gun pointing up the stairs. The television was still playing, giving him a sound source. After four steps, the door came into view, the muted light from the bedroom showing through. The talking had stopped.

He slid his back along the wall, his clothes making a light brushing sound. He took the remaining stairs slowly, certain he'd been heard. He reached behind his back and pulled out the pepper spray. If she was hiding behind a door or somewhere, a burst of spray would bring her out.

He got to the top step and flattened himself against the opposite wall. She'd have to put herself into the doorframe to shoot him. The light wasn't good on the landing, although maybe it was better than the bedroom, which looked in shadow, just the blues from the television making the walls flicker.

He walked sideways, crab-style, against the wall. His ears were straining for any sound above the television, anything to confirm that she was there.

He went past the closed doors to the other bedrooms and then ended up in front of the open doorway. He had one ear to the gap between the door and the frame. There was only the television. He couldn't even hear her breathing.

Then he heard the squeak of a foot on a shiny floor. She had moved. She was waiting for him.

He smiled and took a silent deep breath. She wouldn't have to wait any longer.

Liza crouched on the floor, trying to hear past the television. Cricket talk, golf news. The room was too full, too loud, crowding out any sounds trying to break through. She'd heard nothing else since the creak on the stair.

Her eyes were fixed on the door, but there was no one there. But then she thought she heard something. Her heart clenched. She crouched down, her eyes fixed on the light on the floor. It was faint, but there was enough of a glow to see. She tensed her finger, wrapped snugly around the metal, the trigger starting to give. She felt the shadows close in on her, could feel darkness creeping in from outside the room. Her eyes flashed to the television. Still nothing from David Watts. She looked again at the door. Was this his message?

She edged slowly around the bed, her knees shuffling, her feet squeaking on the varnished boards. The sheen was still there on the floor. The doorframe started to come into view, a slice of muted light that spread as she moved around. But it was only light. No sounds. No movement.

Then it changed. Her eyes shot to the floor. Someone had stepped across the light. The boards by the door were in shadow. There was someone there. Someone was coming in.

She'd stopped breathing, her panic making everything stop. Her chest beat hard and her mouth went dry and lifeless. Was this it? The end?

Her thoughts gelled in a flash.

She threw herself to the side so that she landed on her shoulder. She drew the gun up quickly at the bedroom door and started to pull on the trigger. She was sliding on the boards, the trigger hard against her finger, fighting back as she squeezed harder, her fall still taking her along the floor, the gun pointing at the door.

The sound was like an explosion in the room. The recoil from the gun shot her hand upwards as she fired, and again, and again. She shot four times into the door. Dust flew up as the bullets hit and went through, wood splintering, the noise still echoing round, the filtered light catching the dust and wood as it twirled to the floor.

There was a rumble of feet, the thump of someone dropping to the floor. She shuffled backwards so that she was out of shot of anyone in the doorway, her feet scrambling across the floor. She shook her head to try to shift the noise of the gun out of it. She could hear a voice, a male voice, snarling with pain. She had hit him.

She sat on the floor, panting, trapped in the room, the only way out through the door or the window. She took a deep breath. She wasn't creeping out. It was her house.

She stood up and began to walk slowly across the bedroom. She held the gun out, ready to fire, letting the doorway come fully into view this time. Her view slowly grew as she moved across the room. She went past the television and reached behind with her spare hand to switch it off. When the room fell silent, she stopped and listened. She couldn't hear anything. She stayed like that for a minute, wondering where the noise of pain had come from. There was nothing.

Then she edged towards the door and saw the spots of blood on the floor. They were for real. Someone was in the house. It wasn't just in her head.

But where had he gone?

I ducked when I heard the first shot.

I turned round to Laura. She had taken cover behind the car. I looked back towards the house. I was in open space, halfway along the path. I quickly scanned the house, but I couldn't see anything. No windows open, no one watching me. The shots sounded muffled, as if they were indoors.

Three more shots, quick bursts.

'Get back here, Jack.'

I ran back, every step a lifetime, the car never drawing near. Every crunch of my feet on the path was shouting out my location, like races on radar. My leg jolted with pain, but I went into a slide as I went for the rear of the car, feet first, flying through the air.

I skidded to a halt, the gravel ripping at my trousers, a cloud of dust surrounding me. I was behind the car. I put my head down and sucked in air, and then looked at Laura. She was in a crouch.

'Ever the drama queen,' she said.

I looked down at myself. 'I think I scuffed my new jeans,' I announced, and then laughed nervously. I pointed up at the house. 'Was that meant for us?'

She followed my gaze and then shook her head. 'It was inside the house, but who was she was shooting at?'

I thought about it for a moment, and then said, 'We know she's due another visitor.'

We both thought about that for a second, and then Laura said, 'You stay here. I'm going up to the house.'

'Not on your own.'

'Don't be the hero, Jack. I'm a cop. Let me be one.'

I sighed. 'And let me be a crime reporter.'

Laura's hand was in the glove box, scrabbling for her warrant card. 'At least you've got a witness for this crime scene.'

She found the card, and then raised her eyebrows. 'Gotta go.'

I followed not far behind.

Liza looked into the empty doorway. Spots of blood dotted the floor. Her eyes tried to track them but they didn't go anywhere.

She edged forward and framed herself in the doorway. She let her hand do a sweep, her gun ready to fire. Still nothing. She sounded alone. But she knew that she wasn't.

She thought she could hear every sound in the house, even the dust settling. She felt flutters of fear in her stomach, her mouth going dry. The gun had a slight tremor as she tried to see along the landing. She squinted hard, just seeing the same old scene. She swallowed, felt frantic, when she saw a chink of something. Her eyes strained towards it. It was a sliver of grey, just a brighter shade than the rest of the light. She realised what it was: the last room along was open. The door was ajar, just, letting out a slice of light.

She stepped onto the landing, her foot landing slowly, her toes spreading on the boards, her footstep silent.

She ignored the first door. She was about to take another step when she stopped, her stance in mid-stride. She'd heard something. It was like a rumble, just light, but she couldn't tell where it was coming from. She stepped forward again, her gun ready, her body poised and coiled to react. She couldn't see anything. Just shadows, dark and long, each full of echoes of Annie, and her own father, his voice slurred and angry from whisky, shouting, hitting, sometimes crying. They grabbed at her, willed her forward, their entreaties mixed in with their cries as they choked on the smoke.

She quickly stepped back into the bedroom and stood there, her chest heaving, her brow moist with sweat. She took a few fast breaths to try to calm herself and then set off again out of the bedroom.

She took one step and closed her eyes, tried to force away the shadows. She had to see what she was doing, had to stay alert, ready.

She opened her eyes and kept on walking, three steps, then four. The door at the end inched towards her, each step taking her closer to it. The slice of light grew larger and the rest of the house grew darker. The door was definitely open. And she knew that it was never open. She had no reason to go in there. But now someone was in her house, trying to wreck all she had left.

She stopped outside the door. She leant forward and tried to listen through the opening. There was nothing. She was listening out for the sounds of someone in pain, maybe even the final sounds of someone dying. There was none of that. There were just the creaks of the house, every one part of the structure now. She had sat in silence so often that she knew them all.

She pictured the room on the other side of the door. There was just a bed, some drawers, and a wardrobe, just in case of visitors. There weren't any. He'd be out in the open or under the bed. The door went right back to the wall. If he was exposed in the room, she'd shoot him.

She tensed herself ready to go. She held the gun against her chest, clenched her finger on the trigger. Once inside, she thought, she'd get low, start firing, try to get some shots under the bed.

She counted to ten, took a deep breath, and then flung herself through the door.

Laura crept up the path, trying to get to the door as quickly as possible.

She hoisted herself up onto the porch and made herself flat against the wall. She stole a glance back at me and then looked up, breathing heavily.

I knew what she was thinking. She was praying that the reinforcements would arrive. She was thinking of Bobby, not wanting him to grow up without her.

She peered round to see if she could see through the glass in the door. Then I saw her try the handle. It was locked.

'People are on their way,' I said. 'Stay put.'

She paused for a moment, and then nodded. Then she looked angry as I walked away.

'Where are you going, Jack?'

'I'm going for an interview.'

Laura looked at the door, and then at me.

'Jack, you bastard!' she hissed.

I ignored her and carried on walking. I was going round the back.

Liza kicked the door open. She swung the gun around. No one there. The door was flat against the wall, still juddering. Her eyes shot around the room, and then she threw herself to the floor. She looked under the bed, ready to fire, but it was empty. Nothing there. Just empty space. Like it always had been.

She put her head on the floor, panting, relieved. She

stayed like that for a few seconds, and then shuffled backwards to lean against the wall. She sat down and put her head back, letting her breathing calm down. Her chest was going fast, her lips were dry, her throat hoarse.

She got her senses back and had another look around. She glanced towards the window. It was getting bright outside, but there was a touch of redness about the sky, as if storms were on the way.

She looked around the room again, wondered if she had imagined it. Maybe the door had always been open. Then she thought about the blood. She hadn't imagined that.

Her eyes snapped back to the window. Something caught her eye. She gasped when she saw. It was open, just a crack, but it was open. She froze. He'd gone out that way. He might have dropped down to the floor and run round the house. He could come back in, through the front, or the kitchen, or he could just be waiting in the trees.

She looked to the door, her nerves creeping back up again. She tried to listen, but she couldn't hear anything over the rush of blood through her veins and the frantic beat of her heart.

She didn't see the foot on the ledge. If she had looked, she would have seen his left foot on the corner of the sill. If she had looked up, she would have seen the fingers of his left hand clenched against the stone, the ends white with the strain. If she could have seen through the stone, she would have seen him straining against the wall, his whole body-weight taken by his left hand and foot, his right hand fixed into a gap in the stonework. He was facing outside, his gun tucked into his belt, ready to swing back in through the window.

Then she heard a noise at the front of the house, someone shouting and banging on the door. She whirled around, her gun pointing.

Then she heard movement outside the window.

I was at the front corner of the house, my head low, trying to keep out of sight, when I heard Laura bang on the door, shouting that she was police.

I stopped and looked up, checking for faces at the window. There was nothing.

I used Laura as a distraction and ran around the back of the house. Just as I got there I heard movement above me, and then came the smash of glass.

Liza Radley spun towards the window, her gun coming up, when his feet crashed through.

She screamed as glass flew around the room. It prickled her face, stung her skin, clattered on the floor around her. She put her arms up and her gun skidded across the floor. She felt wetness on her cheeks, knew she had been cut. She was scrambling backwards as he thumped to the floor and rolled over. She yelped as her hands landed on the glass, but she kept going, her feet kicking away at the floor, trying to get out of the room.

He sat up and grinned. 'Good morning,' he hissed, his voice packed with menace. 'I've come to kill you.'

He went for his gun. It was in his belt. She saw wetness on his right leg, a dark patch. Blood. He was reaching down with his right hand, almost at the grip.

'You bastard,' she screamed and leapt towards him. She wrapped her hand around a long shard of glass, gripping it hard, the edges cutting into her fingers. He was only a couple of feet away, a point-blank shot. She kept moving, flying at him with the glass, the point aimed at his hand, the one going for the gun. He leant backwards and began to pull the gun out. He lashed out with his left hand, catching her on her cheek. It knocked her to one side, but she just lunged again, screaming loud, her eyes wild.

She pushed the glass down into his arm. He shrieked, high and full of pain, and tried to move away. He couldn't, the glass was stuck fast in there. He tried to thrash around, but she held on, her ears full of his screams, the glass slicing into her fingers. She hissed with rage and pain and then gave her weapon one final push, her hands wet with blood, and then she felt the glass hit something hard, maybe bone. He yelled out loud and she heard the gun hit the floor.

She kicked it away and let go of the glass. It stayed in his arm. She began to scramble across the floor again, leaving blood as she went. He screamed and gripped the glass, pulling it out. She tried to get to her feet, tried to run, when his other hand flew to his leg and a knife came out. He lashed out with the blade. She yelped and kicked away, the knife catching fresh air. She made it out of the door and slammed it. A shot was fired and she was showered in wood splinters. And then another. She screamed and ducked down, running for the stairs.

He was grunting with pain. 'You bitch, you bitch,' he kept saying as she heard him get to his feet.

She ran fast for the stairs, too fast. She stumbled at the top and fell forward. She twisted in midair, put her shoulder first, but the impact hit her hard, her arm going dead. She rolled down half the stairway, clattering against the stair-rail, and then came to a stop. She groaned with pain. Her shoulder hurt and her arm was limp. But then she heard the door open upstairs. He was angry, his pain coming out in seething breaths, his left leg dragging behind him. And he still had his gun.

She scrambled to her feet and ran down the rest of the stairs, jumping the last two and then ducking into the room on her right.

A shot rang out as she made the corner, her feet skidding on the floor, the sound of the glass exploding in the front door making her flinch. She heard someone outside scream and scramble away.

I heard the scream too. Laura. I knew it straight away.

I started running, my leg sending flashes of pain upwards, but I didn't stop. The dust kicked up around me as I ran, the front of the house taking forever to reach. My mind was hot, images of Laura, sounds of Laura.

As I reached the front of the house, I saw her. She was lying on her back, wood splinters around her.

I ran again.

*

413

Liza was trapped. Blood was dripping from her hand onto the floor but she had stopped feeling the pain, her mind racing, her heart beating fast. She had dropped her handgun upstairs. She might need something bigger. Her rifle was in the car. Her shotgun was in the bedroom. She looked around, trying to remember where the gun cupboard was, her mind fuzzy, confused. Then she cursed when she remembered it was in the garage, at the back of the house. She could hear him on the stairs, his footsteps slow and heavy.

The only way she could get into the garage was through the other room, across the hall, across his line of vision, in his firing range. If she stayed where she was, she would be trapped.

She didn't think about it for long.

She ran at the doorway and across the hall, heard a shot, then made for the doorway into the other room. She was going as fast as she could, bolting across his path. Another shot was fired and hit the doorframe as she took the corner. Wood splintered around her, but she kept going, her feet skidding on the boards.

His footsteps got louder. He was coming after her. She could hear his grunts of pain. She ran towards the door that went into the garage. Another shot. She ducked and screamed. He was moving faster now, sensing her panic. She could see the garage door ahead. She couldn't remember if it was locked. As she ran, she remembered: it was always locked. She skidded to a stop to get the keys off a hook, and then ran again. The door was just a few feet away. He was in the room.

She could sense his presence, could hear his footsteps, his breathing.

'Come here,' he shouted, snarling.

He could see her now. He was trying to get closer, his shooting hand weak. She scrambled with the key in the lock, her panic making her fumble, wasting time, but then she got the door open, the cold air from the shade of the garage rushing past her.

She ran in and closed the door behind her. The place was a mess. She hardly ever went in there. She had her own weapon store, but that was back in the house, upstairs, right past where he was.

She could hear his footsteps just outside the door. He was getting closer.

She scrambled over boxes and tools to the gun cupboard.

She saw the padlock. She stamped her foot in anger and panic. 'Shit!' She remembered she'd done that so she couldn't tempt herself, so she could fight the urge to stick one in her mouth and blow her own brains out.

She looked around, frantic, trying to see something she could use, her hair thrashing around her face.

Then she saw it.

As I reached Laura, I saw the blood on her chest and flecks on her cheeks.

I jumped onto the porch, skidding to a stop next to her.

'You okay?'

I saw her grimace, and then I sagged with relief when she moved.

'Bloody splinters,' she hissed, and then she sat up. 'Is hanging around with you always this dangerous?'

'It only got spicy when you came to town.'

Laura brushed the bits of wood onto the porch. I saw a look of determination in her eyes.

'I've been shot at now,' she said quietly. 'I don't like that.'

'You going in?'

She nodded. 'You bet.'

Liza stood flat against the wall, a circular saw in her hand.

It was big and heavy, with a large two-foot blade and a bulky orange handle. She used it to cut logs. It was powered by petrol, so she could take it out to the fields. There was some fuel left in there.

Her chest was heaving, her cheeks flushed red. He was just the other side of the door. There was no point in starting the saw now. He would just hear it and get her at a distance. Or maybe he'd sit outside and wait for her. No, she had to swing at him as he came in through the door, starting it up as she swung, hoping it would gather enough power to do some damage.

She thought about what she was going to do. She knew she had no choice. He was right outside the door. He had walked up to it and not gone away. She held the saw up, the handle in her left arm, the one not hurt by the fall down the stairs, with her bad arm on the switch. It became sticky with blood from the cuts on her hand. She squeezed her eyes tightly shut and prayed. She looked up, but saw only a ceiling.

416

Her breath caught as she saw the handle on the door move. It was only a twitch, but it meant he was coming in. The door would open inwards, the hinges nearest to her. He'd get a good sweeping view of the garage, but to see her, he'd need to put some of his body into the doorframe. And then she had him. Even if the saw didn't turn on, the weight and force of the swing might do enough to knock him backwards, the teeth sharp enough to tear at his skin.

The door handle began to move downwards. She could hear it creaking in the silence of the garage. It edged down, inch by inch, until it was almost as far down as it would go. She held her breath, bracing herself against the wall. He had to open the door soon. The saw was heavy. She couldn't hold it there much longer. It was above her head, her bruised shoulder screaming pain at her, but still she held it there, trying to hang on to some advantage.

The door flew open and stayed open. Her hand tensed on the start button. She could hear him breathing, could sense him looking around his field of vision, trying to work out where she could be. There was nowhere to hide. It was a square room, strewn with boxes, but with no large cupboards to hide in. She could hear his feet shuffling forward as he tried to see all the corners. He would have to come closer.

She pushed back against the wall, tried to give herself that extra inch.

His gun arm started to edge through the doorway. The pistol was pointing downwards, but he was just behind it. Time split into fractions. His whole hand was through, and then she saw his foot. He was edging his body in, ready to swing his arm to point the gun right at her.

She tensed, her hand flicked the switch, and then she began to scream, her arm starting to windmill towards him.

We stepped away from the door when we heard the noise.

'What the fuck is that?' I shouted, and pointed along the house. 'It's coming from down there.'

Laura nodded: Go.

His body swung into the doorframe and the gun started to come up. As she was halfway through her swing, the motor caught, and the room was filled with the scream of the saw, loud and deadly. The jagged teeth, shiny steel, became a blur as the saw spun fast. He came into view but began to recoil, his arm pulling away. She didn't stop. Her swing continued, her scream mixing with the saw's and drowning him in sound. He was stumbling backwards, trying to fire a shot. She lunged forward, the swing ending its arc, and the scream became a whine as it made contact.

His gun clattered to the floor. She fell forward as he fell back and out of the way, the saw meeting little resistance, his screams now mixing with hers. She noticed his hand still on the gun, clenched tightly against the trigger, but he was still stumbling backwards, retreating into the house. Then she saw the trail of blood. The door shut behind him and his hand and gun were still there on the floor. A red circle spun on the blade like the swirls on a spinning top.

She grinned.

She went for the door, full of fresh energy, the saw still whirring, and ran back into the house. He was easy to find: she just followed the blood and the shrieks of pain. She ran after him. She saw him shuffling towards the front door. She knew it was locked.

'My turn,' she screamed, and then ran at him across the room.

We lifted the door to the garage, our eyes wild, hearts beating. As daylight flooded the garage, the scream of machinery moved. We saw a door close and realised they had gone.

But we hadn't heard a key. We could get into the house.

Then I saw the hand and had to take a breath to keep down my breakfast.

Laura flicked the severed hand away and picked up the gun.

'C'mon,' she said, and moved towards the door.

He turned around, his face white with shock. His other hand reached into his pocket and pulled out a canister. She was getting closer, the saw held in front of her, the blade shrieking.

He grimaced and pointed the canister towards her as she ran. She was only a few feet away. He pressed the button. Nothing came out.

'Fuck,' he shouted, and then jumped out of the way.

She was still running, it was too slippy to change direction. She tried to stop herself but she started to slide, the saw swinging wildly in the air as she fell. She skidded past him, her arm flailing, and she heard a wet noise and a scream, and then a thud as he fell to the ground.

She came to a stop on her back, the saw skating off the boards, throwing up dust before the blade cut into the doorframe.

She lay back, panting, her eyes wild with victory. She glanced over and saw him trying to get up. He was twitching and trying to move, like still-warm road-kill, squeaking on the wooden floor, but he couldn't get anywhere. He was moaning, trying to fight his pain.

She stood up slowly, gingerly, her own pain coming back now: her bruised shoulder, her cut hand, the spots of wetness where she had been struck by flying glass. When she got to her feet, she tried to suck in some air, and then stood up straight. She went over to the saw and switched it off. The spinning red circle on the blade slowed to smudges of blood, coated in sawdust. She looked over to him, at the base of the stairs, trying to slide away.

She limped towards him, the saw in her hand. When she got near him, he stopped trying to crawl away. He turned his head to look at her. She stood over him and looked down. His foot was at an unnatural angle, dragging on the floor as he had tried to move. She looked up his leg and saw a cut in his trousers. Then through the cut she saw wet redness. She realised that her last swing had sliced through his lower leg, leaving the ankle and foot barely attached. It must have been the leg he

420

used to try to swivel away from her. He was lying on his back now, his breaths coming short and fast, his eyes wild. She noticed that his leg was losing blood badly. He was holding his forearm against his body, hoping it would stop the flow of blood from where his hand used to be. It wasn't slowing.

She smiled at him. He put his head back on the floor. His eyes looked listless, his cheeks hollow. He was fading.

'Who are you?' she asked, her voice soft.

He shook his head.

She watched him, saw the life slipping out of him.

'Tell me. I can get you help, if you help me.'

He shook his head again, weaker this time. A smile teased the corners of his mouth.

Her hand went back to the switch on the saw. He didn't say anything. She turned on the saw, his eyelids just flickering at the noise.

'Please tell me,' she mouthed to him.

He didn't respond. He just looked at her.

She thought about what to do with the saw, what she could threaten him with, but when she looked into his eyes, she saw that he knew he was dying.

She placed the blade over his throat, inches from his Adam's apple. He flinched slightly, but only from the noise. The breeze from the saw made his hair flutter.

'Please tell me,' she said. 'Who sent you?'

He lifted his throat towards the blade, until the spinning teeth were almost skating across the skin. He looked into her eyes, pleading. She saw what he wanted: make it quick, end it now.

She shrugged. Okay.

Then his eyes just flickered with life, his mouth opened, one last effort. He grinned at her, his teeth bared, half a grimace.

'David Watts told me one thing,' he hissed, his voice barely audible over the shriek of the saw.

She moved the blade away.

'David sent you?' she asked.

He exhaled, his chest only just moving, his eyes closed.

'What did he tell you?' she asked, her voice sounding urgent.

His eyes opened. His tongue flicked at his lips. He tried to speak, but nothing came out. She put her head closer. Then he tried to speak again.

'David told me,' he said. Then he grinned again, his last play. 'He told me he liked to jerk off when he thought about Annie's face as he strangled her.'

He sank back. She stood up straight with a jolt. She looked at him. His eyes were wild with rage now.

He nodded weakly. 'One good fuck and left her for the buzzards.'

Tears flashed across her eyes.

'He knew the town would save him,' he said. He smiled, almost contented. He knew he was going.

She shrieked at him, her body straining with rage, and then plunged forward with the saw. She threw all her weight behind it, met no resistance, only stopping when she heard the whine of the saw in the floor.

She sat back, spent, and turned off the saw, leaving it stuck in the floorboards. Her chest heaved with sobs, and then she looked into his eyes as his head turned away from the saw blade and rolled towards the stairs.

Her shoulders hung as she cried. The house was silent, just her tears. She thought she could hear birdsong outside. She put her head back, banged it lightly against the wall.

Then she heard a shout from behind her.

'Stay there! Police, police!'

Liza grabbed at the saw and flicked the switch again. The saw burst into life. She turned around.

A woman was in her house, a gun pointing towards her, a man just behind her.

'Police, don't move!'

Laura was in front of me, her gun arm taut, her stance set.

I watched as Liza Radley put up her hands, the saw in one, the blade still filling the hall with noise.

'Put the fucking saw down!' Laura shouted.

I was just behind Laura, needing to be there.

Laura edged closer.

'Put down the saw.'

Liza looked at the saw, and then back at Laura.

Laura was within a few feet now, still creeping forward, the gun aimed at Liza's head. Then I saw Laura look past her, to the floor. I followed her gaze, saw the head, the mouth open, the eyes closed. Laura's gun wavered, distracted.

Then I saw Liza lunge forward with the saw.

Laura looked up at the sudden movement. She lashed out with her hands, useless, impotent. The blade brushed past her fingers, her fingers jolted as the gun was knocked out of her hand. Laura turned, backed away, tried to get out of the way of the saw, its whine too close, too fast. She fell to the floor, scrabbling backwards, came to a stop by a door jamb.

Liza stood over her, the saw still screaming. Laura sat back, panting, scared. She shuffled against the wall, her hands up in surrender.

Liza raised her arm, ready to strike down.

I went for the gun. It felt heavy, cold. My first time. All I could do was pretend.

'Stop, now!' I screamed, the gun pointing at Liza.

Liza didn't look up, was still poised with the saw.

'She's got a kid,' I shouted. 'Let her go.'

Liza looked at me. She straightened, her stance uncertain. I noticed Laura's eyes were closed, a tear running down her cheek.

'Bobby,' I continued, my voice softening. 'Starts school next year.' I paused, and then pleaded, 'Don't do it.'

I saw Liza take a breath.

'She's not from Turners Fold,' I said, my gun still pointing at her. 'She's just a copper from London, doing her job.'

I saw Laura's eyes flick open. Liza's eyes were still on me.

'Throw me your gun,' said Liza.

I exhaled and looked at Laura. I thought I saw Laura nod.

'Why should I trust you?' I said.

Liza shook her head. 'You don't have to, but if you

miss with that gun – if it still works – or if you just injure me, I'm going to run this saw through your girl-friend's skull.'

'Girlfriend?'

Liza smirked. 'I can see it in your eyes.'

I looked at Laura again. She nodded.

I knelt down and put the gun on the floor, and then skidded it across to Liza.

Liza bent to pick it up. Now we had nothing.

I stayed where I was as Liza backed down the hall, circular saw in one hand, gun in the other. She got as far as the body on the floor, and then she knelt down, the saw at last stopping its scream.

I watched as she looked at the body, which seemed like a pile of loose clothes, soiled and thrown in a heap, blood pooled on the floor. I looked over to the head and caught a glimpse of his eyes. They seemed to follow Liza, dark and glassy, his mouth open in surprise, one last scream.

She crouched down and pulled his jacket to one side, the cloth pinched between two fingers. She searched the material and paused when she found a phone, stuffed into his inside pocket. She pulled it out and rolled it around in her hand for a few seconds, and then she turned it on. It beeped and then the screen lit up blue. I watched as she put it into her bag, along with his wallet. She found his car keys and twirled them from her fingers for a few moments before throwing them onto his chest.

I kept watching as she took a look around the hall. I could tell she was saying goodbye.

I walked over to Laura and held her, felt her grab my arm and then the soft wetness of her cheeks. I looked down, and when she looked up, she smiled. She wasn't watching Liza.

I looked up as I heard the saw being picked up again, the weight of it clunking against the floor.

Liza opened up the fuel tank and ran a thin line of petrol from the body in the hall into the kitchen. She stood over the petrol and looked down. Rainbows twisted in the fuel, like flames just waiting to go. I saw her smile. I didn't know if this was a new beginning, or just the end of everything. Maybe it didn't matter which one.

She pulled out a cigarette lighter. She held it between her fingers for a moment and shut her eyes.

She clicked the lighter. There was a small spark and then a flame curved and twisted. She looked down at the floor and opened her hand, the gold metal shining back sparkles of sunlight as it tumbled down. The flame went out almost as soon as it hit the ground, but not before it had licked the skin on the fuel. There was a faint whoosh and then a low blue shimmer ran down it, spreading along the line. It raced through the kitchen and into the hallway.

I helped Laura to her feet. 'Let's get out of here!' I shouted, trying to inject some urgency. The flames were beginning to eat up the wall, creeping along the floor, the blinds in the kitchen now ablaze.

Laura looked up, her eyes red, and nodded. Then she pointed to the body, just by the stair rail. 'I guess he's the one who shot your father.'

I saw the head again and my stomach lurched, the taste of bile launching itself into my mouth as I dry-heaved. I took some deep breaths, but they were hot, fuel-filled.

I heard the door, a creak above the crackle of the flames, and saw Laura step outside. The living room was ablaze now, the chairs billowing smoke, the lampshades dripping hot black onto the floor. But I remembered my camera, remembered I was a reporter. I pointed it at the head and got two shots, and then pointed it in all directions and got some more, the house further in turning black with smoke.

I started to cough, could feel the heat and smoke drying me up, so I backed up to the door and stepped outside. Laura was already there, wiping her eyes. I joined her and put my arm around her shoulder.

Laura looked at me with the disdain and composure she'd had when we first met.

'It's the smoke,' she said.

I smiled and kissed her on the top of her head. 'I know.'

We stepped off the porch and started to walk down the path. We heard the heat breaking windows inside the house, the fire starting to gain some strength. Every step took us further away, but we only walked about twenty yards. We turned towards the house to watch it burn.

'Do we go after her?' I asked.

Laura looked up at me. Then she looked down again. 'Bobby nearly lost his mum, that's what I'm thinking at this moment. Liza Radley can go to hell right now.'

There was no answer to that.

I looked back towards the house. 'I reckon my interview has gone.'

Laura was about to respond when I heard a car engine. We looked at each other. We had no weapons.

We heard the car at the house begin to move, and then a few seconds later, the noise of the engine got nearer, and we realised that it was coming down the path, the tyres crunching on the loose dirt. As we heard it pick up speed, I got my camera ready.

It crawled slowly down the path, heading for the cattle grid. I got some pictures of a side profile and then cursed when she turned to look my way.

She didn't stop there, though. She drove down to Laura's car and came to a halt just feet from it. I saw her pull a handgun from her lap and point it down at Laura's tyres. But then, for a split second, she turned my way and looked me right in the eyes. She held my gaze for a moment, but then she pulled her handgun back into her car and pressed lightly on the pedal. She approached the grid, the noise of the tyres rumbling like a snap thunderstorm, and then she accelerated away up the hill.

I stood up as she pulled away, my hands on my hips. I shielded my eyes from the sun, and the scene seemed quiet again when the car went out of view.

'You were right,' said Laura.

I turned around.

'About the interview,' she continued. 'It's just driven over the hill.'

As the fire took hold, Laura watched while I took

pictures. As the roof began to crack and crumble into the flames, we decided to leave.

'Aren't you waiting for the reinforcements?' I asked.

Laura looked thoughtful for a moment, and then shook her head. 'I'm seeing this through.'

It was another sunny day. And it was time to go back to Turners Fold.

FIFTY-ONE

Liza Radley pulled into a lay-by on her way through Lancashire. She had to slow down for a moment, take stock. There had been months of planning, but now she was improvising.

She closed her eyes and listened to the sound of traffic rushing past her, felt the car rock with turbulence. She felt her eyes go damp, her throat tight with sadness. There was a fluttering, like wings beating, a light sound just filling her head. It wasn't a voice, more of a heartbeat.

She opened her eyes and looked across the road. There was a diner, stainless steel, American reproduction. She could see faces looking out, fathers, sons, mothers, just happy families passing idle conversation, lives untouched.

She took out the wallet she had taken from the body in her house. As she opened it, she saw a police badge, faked or stolen, and some money. There was a fake ID which showed the head by the stairs, with a casual smile and deep blue eyes. There were credit cards as well, for three different identities: all cloned, she expected. He was a real-life fake. She knew now that this was no friend or fan acting out of some perverse loyalty. He was a professional hitman, hired by a wealthy and famous client.

Next, she pulled out the phone. She looked at it, weighed it in her hand, guessing that she had the key to the endgame. She pressed the button and saw the screen flicker into life again, the screen lighting up blue. She flicked through the options screen until she got to the list of stored numbers. There was only one. The number identification just said 'David Watts'. No code words. No secrecy. She smiled to herself. He was making sure that if he went down, his client went with him.

She put the phone on her lap and watched it for a while. It didn't do anything, so she reached into her glove box and pulled out the voice distorter.

She clicked the dial button and checked around her while she waited to be connected. She felt her chest tighten when she heard a ring tone.

David Watts had pulled into a farm track. He was just driving round, waiting for news. He didn't want to see a police car. The girl in Manchester was eating him up now, making him grip the steering wheel until his fingers turned white, broken only by the blood around his knuckles. He had stopped to top up his nose. The powder had started to fade away, so he was stuck with real life for a moment.

His phone rang. He saw who was calling. Maybe he could go home now.

He pressed the answer button and barked, 'Where the hell have you been?'

He was expecting the measured tone of the American.

Instead, he heard a voice he wasn't prepared for. It was the voice on the calls he dreaded, that flat electronic distortion making him freeze.

'Hello, David.'

He put the phone down and looked out of the window. He felt himself go pale, not knowing how to answer at first. How had she got his number? Then he felt his stomach tighten when he realised that she had the American's phone.

'How did you get that phone?' he asked, his voice quiet and nervous, not wanting the answer. He cringed when he heard her laugh.

'Let's just say that your friend can't come to see you any more.'

David wiped his eyes with the palm of his hand. His thoughts raced as fast as his nerves. His heart tightened when he realised what she meant. 'What have you done?'

'I'm sorry, David, but he just sort of fell apart.'

He swallowed nervously, his stomach crawled.

'Were you close to him?'

'What do you want?' David barked, ignoring her question, angry now.

'I want you, David. Is that so bad?'

He felt his hand go slick around the steering wheel, slippery with sweat. He wiped them on his pants and then wiped his mouth. He needed a drink.

'What do you mean, you want me?' he asked.

'I want to hear you say sorry, David. I want to hear you admit what you did, and when I hear you say it, I want to see the remorse in your eyes, the sorrow, an echo of my pain.' A pause. 'That's what I want.'

David kicked the underneath of the steering column. 'I'm not going on TV,' he sneered. 'You can kiss my arse and shoot every footballer in town, but I still won't do it.'

'I don't want it like that any more, David. You don't need to go public any more.'

'What do you mean?' he asked, his voice quieter, wary now.

'I want to see you on your knees, in front of me, begging for my forgiveness.'

David laughed, traces of hysteria filtering through. 'Yeah, so you can blow my fucking head off. What kind of arsehole do you think you are dealing with here?'

'The kind who did what you did to Annie Paxman,' she snapped.

'Oh, fuck you,' he snapped back. 'She was such a prick-tease. I had to shake that fuck out of her.'

He took a breath and looked out of his car window. If he could get this bitch on her own, he might be able to end the problem his way.

'Where do you want to meet?'

'Where do you think?' she snarled. *'You get to Turners Fold in the next couple of hours and go to where this all started, to that aviary.'*

'And if I don't?'

'I'll kill you. I'll stalk you and shoot you the first chance I get.'

'But you forget that I could just call the police. Get them to swarm around the aviary. Then it's all over.'

'But you won't, David, because you're scared I'll talk.

433

You want me to either die or go away. And I'm doing neither until I get what I want from you.'

'But who would believe a crazy bitch like you?'

'That's your gamble, David. Your choice. And anyway, I've got the one thing you want.'

'You've got nothing I want.'

'Emma. I've got Emma.'

David stopped smiling.

'I said I would get her, and I got her.'

David was silent for a moment, and then he said, 'I don't believe you.'

Then it was her turn to laugh.

'That's not your choice, David, because if you don't come for her, I'll leave her dead where you left Annie.'

'Prove it.'

She laughed again.

'You don't think I'm driving around with her in my car, do you?' She laughed again. *'I'll get her on the phone, and then you'll know. And once you know, get to that field and get on your knees. You beg for my forgiveness and you get Emma back.'*

'You fucking bitch! I'm going to . . .'

'Stay by your phone, David.'

He was about to shout her down when he realised he would be shouting into a silent phone.

He tried to shrug off the prickles of fear. She'd killed the American, and he'd come recommended by one of the meanest bastards in town.

He threw the phone back into the glove box. A quick check of his mirrors and he pulled back out into the road and accelerated hard. He was going to end this

his way. There wasn't a battle in his life he had lost yet. Why should this be any different?

He set his mind on Turners Fold. He wasn't going to leave there until he knew that she couldn't.

Laura was quiet at first as the roads hurtled past.

'You're mad with me, right?'

Laura ignored me for a few seconds, and then I saw her relax, her shoulders slump.

'No,' she said. 'I'm mad with me. I was the policewoman back there. I should have controlled it. I let myself go with you when I should have made myself wait for back-up.'

'So why aren't you still there?'

Laura paused for a moment, and I thought I saw her blush, before she said, 'The same reason.' She flashed a look at me and then asked, 'What's it all about, Jack?'

I rubbed my eyes and wished I had a good answer. All I thought I knew was that we were both surviving on hardly any sleep and pure adrenalin. My leg was beginning to hurt again, and I thought that if we lost momentum now, we would lose the rest of the day. And that wasn't going to happen. Right then, I was a suspect for Rose Wood's murder. If we lost momentum, I'd find myself in a police cell, facing a life sentence.

'She hates Turners Fold,' I said, 'and she hated her father. I suppose it is as simple as that.'

'And that makes her shoot footballers, and anyone else who gets in her way?'

'Seems that way.'

Laura didn't respond, so I carried on.

'She was an oddball, Laura, and small towns don't like oddballs. They like everything to fit together, and people like Liza Radley don't fit into the mix. She hated the town, and then she hated her parents because of what happened to Annie Paxman.'

'So she was striking back at Turners Fold?'

'In part, I guess.'

'And the other part?'

I tugged on my lip for a moment. 'What David Watts was allowed to get away with encapsulates everything Liza Radley hates about Turners Fold. He's the big guy, the next big star. Annie Paxman was nothing. He was allowed to walk away because the town needed him more than it needed Annie Paxman.'

'Are you going to write that stuff?'

I nodded. 'If I get the chance.'

'And you think Liza Radley took up Annie's cause as some kind of revenge?'

'That puts it simply, but that is just about it.'

'But why such a big deal? Why that?'

'Because her father was one of the first at the scene. He did what my father did: he allowed the secret to stay secret, because it suited them that way. But James Radley and my father were different. My father kicked back by hating his job. James Radley kicked back by hating himself, so he got lost in a bottle. My thinking is that she thinks she hates David Watts, but really she hates her father for what he did, and for how it affected him.'

'Phew, sounds like a shrink's field day.'

'What made Liza Radley stop herself from driving that circular saw into your skull?'

Laura didn't answer.

'It was when I said you weren't from Turners Fold,' I continued, 'and when she knew you were a parent. She lost a parent when Annie Paxman died, and lost him for good in that fire.'

Laura just drove for a few miles. I watched the green of Lancashire rush past the car windows as we headed back down south, my eyes bobbing in time with the ebb and flow of the walls. This was away from cotton Lancashire. This was farm country, with shallow streams and patches of woodland, filtering the sun.

'Where next?' she asked. When I looked around, she continued, 'What if we've lost her?'

I shook my head. I knew straight away where Liza Radley was going.

'We haven't lost her,' I said.

'But she started the fire, and that can only ever mean one thing; she isn't going back.'

I thought about that. Liza Radley had played her hand, stared David Watts down, matched and raised. He had sweated and twitched, until his nerve had gone and he had sent someone after her. David Watts had hired a killer to catch a killer, but Watts's mercenary had also killed people he'd met along the way who might cause problems: Rose Wood, my father, and he had tried to get me. I looked to my right. And Laura.

'Oh, she's going back,' I said, raising my eyebrows, 'but back to the beginning. Back to Turners Fold.'

I reached into my pocket and pulled out Laura's phone. I flicked through the recent-calls menu, found Tony's number, and pressed dial.

Laura turned round to me. I smiled and then looked out of the window.

When Tony answered, I told him what had happened at the house.

'Tony, I think it's time to use the recording,' I said. 'Get Glen Ross in good company and play it, see what he says.'

I hung up on him and waited for Laura to speak.

'And what do you want me to do?' she asked eventually. She didn't look at me when she spoke. Her eyes stayed on the road, every minute bringing us nearer to Turners Fold.

I thought for a moment, and then said, 'I need you to create a press storm. Get hold of some TV companies. Get on the newswire. Tell them that the word is going out that the football shootings are tying in at Turners Fold.'

'Isn't that going to wreck your exclusive?'

I shook my head. 'No, because no one else has got inside it like we have.'

'We?'

'Yeah, "we". You got a problem with that?'

She aimed a playful slap at my thigh and then asked, 'What are you going to do?'

'Me?' I scratched my nose and grinned. 'Lie low and wait,' I said, 'and hope it all ends before they catch me. I'll call you if my hunch is right. But get a TV crew on your side, ready to go.'

Laura looked at me with curiosity. There wasn't long to go.

FIFTY-TWO

Nell was on the phone when Tony walked into the police station. She and Mike had been up all night, co-ordinating new people as they arrived in Turners Fold, all of them looking for Liza Radley. What Glen Ross didn't know was that some of them were just asking awkward questions to make him nervous. So far, Turners Fold had been an impenetrable wall.

A local officer sidled up to her.

Nell just put her hands over the receiver and raised her eyebrows in query.

'We've got a reporter at the desk, local. Tony Davies.'

'What does he want?'

The officer shook his head. 'Didn't say, but he's okay.'

Nell and Mike exchanged glances, and then Nell nodded. 'Show him through.'

They watched as Tony approached them, a press badge in his hand.

Nell looked at Mike, who gave a small shrug. She turned back to Tony. 'Tell me what you've got.'

Tony looked towards the police station. 'I need to see you in there, with Glen Ross.'

'Detective Inspector Ross?'

Tony nodded.

'Why with us?' asked Mike.

'No offence, but I'm writing the story of the year, not helping you out. I want to confront Glen Ross with what I have, but not alone. He's dangerous at the moment.'

Nell couldn't help a little smile. 'And what is it in connection with?'

Tony stayed expressionless. 'You know what it's in connection with.' He paused. 'I'd get David Watts down here too, but I'm told he's on the run.'

Nell's eyes flickered, nothing more, but Tony saw it.

Nell considered Tony for a while, and then she nodded and smiled. 'Okay, sounds good. Just give me a minute with him first.'

Tony watched them go and smiled to himself.

Nell tapped lightly on Glen Ross's door. She went in when she heard a mumbled, 'Yeah?'

She was shocked when she saw him. He was paler than before, looked washed-up and wrung out, dark rings under his eyes. She could see a light tremble.

'You okay?' asked Nell.

He looked up and shook his head. 'I've been better. Some bug or something.'

Nell shrugged and sat down. Mike came in and sat on a chair just behind her. She didn't say anything at first. Let him sweat it out for a while.

She noticed he was doing just that. His face was shiny with dampness and the pen he was holding flickered in his grip. She saw that there were no papers on his desk, nothing to show that he had been doing anything before they came into the room, as if he had been just staring at nothing.

'We spoke with some of your staff last night,' said Nell.

He looked up, seemed disinterested, and sat back. 'What about it?'

Nell looked down at her suit, stopped to brush off some loose lint. She looked up and smiled. Spin it out, make him wait. Glen Ross began to shuffle in his chair, started to swallow, blinked too often.

'They say David Watts has been calling you this week.'

Glen Ross looked down and began to drum his pen on his knee.

Nell let the silence sit there until she could tell he wasn't going to answer.

'Well, has he?'

Glen Ross looked up. 'Why are you questioning me?'

Nell shrugged. 'We're not questioning anyone. We're just trying to find out what David Watts has been doing. One area of enquiry is his telephone calls over the last week. You told me he hadn't called. Now, I think different.' She smiled. 'As a fellow police officer, I was hoping I could count on you to help.'

Glen Ross blinked.

'Are you willing to help?'

'Do I have to?'

441

Nell shrugged. 'Are you worried if you do?'

Glen Ross looked down again, his mouth open, breathing heavily. He rubbed his chest, discomfort creasing his face.

'You okay?' asked Mike.

He didn't get a response. Glen Ross just looked at the floor and took some deep breaths.

Nell turned round to Mike, who shrugged and then shook his head. She knew what that meant. They would get nothing out of him without a lawyer present.

'There's a reporter who wants to talk to you,' said Nell. 'He just wants to get an update on what's been going on around here.'

Glen Ross looked up slowly. 'Who's that?'

She held her hands out. 'Never met him before. Local reporter. In his fifties, maybe. Loud jumper. Tony something.'

'Tony Davies?'

She pointed an affirmative. 'That sounds about right.' A pause. 'Do you want to see him?'

He curled his lip, but then said, 'Why not?'

Nell nodded at Mike, who went out of the room to get Tony. When the door clicked shut, Nell asked, 'Is there anything you want to tell me?' There was no answer. 'You might have had your reasons for lying about David Watts, but I don't care about that. I just want to clear up this lead and then get back to London.'

Glen Ross put his head back and looked at the ceiling.

Nell watched him closely. She was getting concerned. He looked under so much strain that he might just snap right in front of her.

Her thoughts were interrupted when Mike walked back into the room, with Tony just behind him. Nell stayed where she was, but Glen Ross stood up briefly to nod at Tony, before slumping back into his seat.

Tony walked to a filing cabinet and placed a small tape player on top. Nell looked at him with curiosity, wondering what he was going to do.

Tony turned round to address the room.

'I know why you two are here. I've been told from a good source that a woman has been calling David Watts claiming to be the person shooting footballers. But the caller claimed she was a girl killed here in Turners Fold over ten years ago.'

No one answered. No confirmation. No denial.

'And I know that the caller told David to either confess to the girl's murder or she would keep on shooting footballers.'

Nell and Mike exchanged looks. He was getting good information from somewhere.

'Things got more complicated yesterday, because you, Glen, announced that Bob Garrett, one of your own men, went to you two days ago and confessed that he had seen Annie Paxman's killer and done nothing about it, that he could have stopped it.'

Nell and Mike turned to Glen Ross, who was nodding, looking uncertain.

'Then later that evening, after this surprise confession, Bob Garrett blew his own brains out by the old aviary, right where Annie Paxman was found all those years ago.'

Glen Ross was still nodding. Nell's eyes narrowed,

443

watching him carefully. This reporter was speaking for effect, part of a build-up. Something was coming.

Tony shrugged. 'Works out just right. Case solved. It gets David Watts off the hook. Seems that the shooter just got it wrong, and maybe she'll stop shooting now.'

'Where is this going?' asked Nell.

Tony smiled. 'There was no suicide, because there was no confession.'

Nell raised her eyebrows. 'How do you know?'

'Because I know that Bob Garrett saw the killer, but I know that it wasn't Colin Wood he saw.'

'Colin Wood?' asked Nell.

'The local fall guy, set up by Glen Ross.'

Tony threw a piece of paper on the desk. Everyone watched it float down.

Glen Ross recognised it first. An incident log. A transcript of the radio traffic from ten years ago. He closed his eyes.

'Bob Garrett saw David Watts running away. He didn't see Colin Wood, whatever Glen Ross said yesterday. But he kept quiet because Glen Ross told him to, because Glen Ross knew all along that David Watts had killed her, but he covered it up, because it would be bad for the town.'

'That's not true,' said Ross, his voice a whisper, his eyes still closed.

'And he knew about the football killings and David Watts, but did nothing about it. And a tall American came to see him, just before Bob Garrett was shot, matching the description of someone trying to kill Bob Garrett's son.'

Nell's eyes snapped to Glen Ross. He was staring at the photograph on his desk of his wife and daughters. He looked to have tears in his eyes.

'Ross?' asked Nell. There was no reply.

Tony pointed at Glen Ross. 'He knew, all of the time, and did nothing. And he let one of his own officers die.' Tony looked at Mike. 'And he thought David Watts was worth more than the life of that young black girl. Or that poor simple bastard sat in prison.'

'You knew, Tony, you fucking hypocrite,' Glen Ross snarled.

'I heard the rumours, that's all. But you told me they weren't true, and I had no proof.' And then Tony smiled, nice and slow. 'Until now.'

Tony turned round and pressed play on the machine. Nell's eyes looked towards the machine when Bob Garrett's voice filled the room.

'*I can see a girl. We're just going to investigate, but I think she's deceased. Get an ambulance here quick though.*'

'*What's your exact location?*'

'*Victoria Park, Turners Fold. I can see a naked girl on the floor of the aviary in Victoria Park. Otherwise, scene is quiet.*'

'*Got that. Scenes of crime are on their way. I'll contact MCU.*'

Nell and Mike swapped looks, Mike's now keen, and then turned back to Glen Ross. There was a gap, and then a fresh radio call came on.

'*Comms, do you copy?*'

'*I copy.*'

'We've got David Watts leaving the scene. Did you get that? I've got him about a hundred yards from me, heading towards Pendle Wood.'

'Did you say David Watts?'

'Yes, David Watts. Eighteen years of age. Resident of Turners Fold.'

'Do we have an ID on the body?'

'Young black female, maybe eighteen or twenty. Can't see any identification, but I recognise her. She's local.' Then the pause. 'Hang on, there's something in her hand. Some kind of a chain, might be gold.'

Another voice came on.

'David Watts heading towards the school. Running that way.'

'That was James Radley,' said Tony, over the static. 'He's dead too.'

'Any identifying marks on the chain?' the radio voice asked.

Mike and Nell had their jaws set, their eyes on fire.

'Yeah, there's something on it, but hard to make it out. Will spell it. Romeo-alpha-tango-hotel. Delta-echo. Oscar-romeo-tango. Echo-whisky.'

Mike and Nell exchanged glances. Mike mouthed 'Oh shit.'

Glen Ross turned to stare out of the window. Then another call came on. Bob Garrett again.

'2199 Garrett calling in for an update on the suspect?'

'Copy, officer. Suspect ruled out.'

Glen Ross reached behind himself and pulled the picture of his wife and daughter off the desk.

'Could you repeat that?'

446

'Named suspect no longer a suspect, 2199 Garrett.'

Nell and Mike exhaled in unison.

'I saw him. Repeat, David Watts was running from the scene.'

'Copy, officer, but I repeat, named suspect ruled out.'

'Inspector?' Nell asked.

Glen Ross reached behind himself again. Nell's eyes followed his hands, transfixed.

'We're getting Colin Wood's DNA tested.' It was Tony. 'We've spoken to his solicitor. They hadn't done that. Tested it, I mean.' He paused. 'It'll still match, won't it, Glen, with the evidence left at the scene?'

Glen Ross opened a drawer.

'After all, you took the samples from Colin, didn't you? Swabbed and bagged.' Tony was barking out the accusations. 'But maybe you swapped them. Colin Wood was lifted for being drunk and you saw your chance. You got David to give you some swabs and you put those into the bag used for Colin Wood's swabs. All you had to do was put those swabs into the database with Colin Wood's details attached, and the database would find the link.'

No response.

'Inspector?' It was Nell again, but this time her voice was more insistent.

Nell watched his hand and realised too late what he was doing. The tape played static in the background, radio bleeps, but she could no longer hear it. She stood up, her hands out. 'No, no.'

Glen Ross pulled out a gun and put it in his lap. He looked up. It was the gun found next to Bob Garrett.

Nell put her hands out, screaming at him, 'Drop it, drop it!'

Tony didn't move. It was all happening too quickly.

Glen Ross lifted the gun and put it into his mouth. He turned round in his chair, looked at the other people in the room. His face was creased in tears. He looked frightened. Nell was still screaming at him. A thin threat against a suicide.

Tony had his mouth open in shock, turned round to switch off the machine. Glen Ross shut his eyes and began to squeeze the trigger. A sound came out of Tony's mouth, a plea to stop.

The noise of the gun echoed around the room. Glen Ross's head knocked back against his seat and then he slumped forward. Glass tumbled to the floor, the sound of it breaking drowned out by the gunshot, red splashes covering the shards. There was a scramble of feet as people in the station either hit the decks or came running towards the office.

A junior officer, reckless and young, burst in, his baton raised.

Nell lowered her arms. Her head drooped. 'He shot himself,' she said quietly, and then pointed. 'Look, in his hand.'

The officer looked over and saw the gun resting in Glen Ross's lap, the end sticky with blood. He stood up straight. 'Oh, shit,' was all he said.

Mike turned to Tony. 'You got your story.'

FIFTY-THREE

We'd hoped to sneak into town, but it didn't quite work out that way.

We were just hitting the fringes of Turners Fold, the fields breaking up into stone boxes, when I saw a police car, tucked away behind a petrol station. I glanced over at Laura. I could tell by her face that she'd seen it too.

I looked ahead and realised that I had a hundred yards to decide what to do. The last I'd heard, I was wanted for murder.

I looked around. The car was small inside, not many places to hide. I looked up. The patrol car was getting nearer. I put my hand against the window, trying to block out the view of my face. I looked over at Laura, who was staring straight ahead, her jaw set firm.

'Why don't you just put a sign on the car,' she said.

'What's he doing?' I whispered. 'Is he looking?'

'Just coming up to it,' she said, 'and there's no need to whisper. He can't hear you.'

I watched Laura trying not to look suspicious, but her head was rigid, her eyes fixed in front of her. Then she glanced in her rear-view mirror. 'He's pulling out,' she hissed.

'What, following us?'

'Seems that way.'

'Shit!' I dropped my hand and tried to think what to do, tried to work out the best way to go. I looked up at Laura. 'Take your next right.'

Laura glanced over. 'We've got a police car behind us. We're going down there just until he turns on his blues.'

'Okay, I understand, but I need to get away from town.'

Laura looked in her mirror. 'He's getting nearer.'

'Shit, okay, just turn off, nice and slow, no indications. Once you've turned off, get onto one of the back tracks.'

'Okay, okay,' she mumbled, and then the car swung to the right. 'He's still behind us,' she said, her voice getting higher. Her eyes flicked to her mirror. 'He's catching up.'

'Floor it,' I bellowed.

Laura looked at me, her eyebrows flicked upwards. 'A pursuit? Are you fucking crazy?'

Then she saw my look of determination. She had doubts for a moment, but then she shook her head and put her foot down hard.

I was pushed back against the seat, and then I heard the wail of a police siren behind us. I was thrown to my right as Laura took a bend.

'Where now?' she shouted.

I tried to work out where we were. Memories were flooding back, and I tried to reconcile them with the images rushing past the windscreen, the whistle of the tyres on the tarmac getting louder as Laura tried to pull away.

'Keep going down here. There'll be a turning to your left. I'll shout out when to turn. You'll go over an old canal bridge.'

The police siren was getting louder. Maybe just a few yards behind us.

'Get across the bridge,' I continued. 'There's a space to pull in just after it. Pull over so that I can jump out of the door. By the time he rolls across the bridge, I'll be under it.'

The car rocked as she swung it into the middle of the road, and then the traction got loose as Laura took another bend. I was jolted around as the car straightened.

'What do I do when you've jumped out?' asked Laura, shouting. 'Watch my career float down the fucking canal?'

'I'm sorry,' I said softly, 'but if I get hauled in now, it's all over.' I took a deep breath. 'Let him catch you up and keep him busy.'

She braked hard into a bend, and then the rear wheels slewed as she accelerated out of it.

'Jack, are you sure? What do I tell them?'

I thought for a moment, and then said, 'Answer every question honestly.' I smiled. 'Except about me.'

'And what are you going to do?'

'I can't tell you,' I said, 'and then you can't give it away.'

She started to slow down. The police car was just behind, the siren getting loud in the car.

'Don't mess me around, Jack. I need to know.'

'Okay, okay, just keep going.'

She accelerated again.

'I'm going to wait for Liza Radley,' I said. 'And I'm taking your phone. Tell Tony that I'll call him when I get set.'

Laura didn't say anything. I put my hand on her knee. She looked at me, shook her head and smiled. 'I must have gone as crazy as you.'

'It's the country air.'

Laura laughed, but then I shouted, 'We're getting near the bridge, just there on the left.'

I was thrown forward as she stamped on the brake, the car skidding in the road, and then she swung it hard into a turn, the scream of tarmac replaced by the rattle of a grit road. I gripped the door handle as the car swung violently and then jumped and bounced. The siren got quieter as he overshot the turning so Laura pulled away fast. Her hands were shaking on the wheel as we bounced out of potholes, and then the car took a lurch upwards as she shot over the bridge. I could hear the police car get back on track, and then we skidded to a halt as we got to the other side, the grit spewing out from under the tyres.

I didn't look. I just threw the car door open and rolled onto the floor, my shoulder kicking up dust as I landed. I reached behind and slammed the door shut. I hurled myself down the bank, wincing as my back hit tree stumps and rocks, before I landed with a thud on a brick towpath.

I heard the police car slam to a stop, gravel kicking

up, siren screaming, so I scrambled to get under the bridge. I listened.

A car door opened and I heard slow footsteps. Then a voice. 'In a rush, miss?'

I listened out as the policeman took Laura's details and got on the radio. He talked about traffic offences for a while, and then his radio burst into life. He checked the message again, and then said, 'Laura McGanity, I'm going to have to take you with me.' There was silence again, and then, 'Have you seen Jack Garrett today?'

I didn't hear the response, but I heard Laura's door open and the policeman talk into his radio again. It was time to move on.

FIFTY-FOUR

Laura looked around as the police car arrived back in town. The policeman hadn't said much on the way in. He'd talked into the radio mostly, let everyone know that she was on her way. Laura just didn't know what to expect. She was meddling, not even on the case.

Turners Fold seemed darker as it came back into view, more threatening. The last leg into the town square was done at a crawl. As she made her way round, Laura saw the media build-up. She wondered whether word was getting out, whether Tony's meeting with Glen Ross had made David Watts a news headline.

The cameras didn't pay her any attention and the car swung around the back of the police station without anyone stopping to look. They parked in the yard, and when she looked up she saw two people in suits walking across to meet her, male and female.

The car door opened and Laura got out. She stayed by the car, let the two suits come to her. As they got closer, it was the woman who spoke.

'Hello, I'm Nell Cornwell, and this is Mike Gray.

We're from New Scotland Yard.' Nell was smiling. Mike seemed pensive and withdrawn.

Laura held out her hand. 'Hello, I'm Detective Constable McGanity.'

'Yes, we know,' replied Nell.

That made Laura pause, and then she asked, 'Am I under arrest?'

Nell looked at Mike, and then back at Laura. 'No, not yet, but if you walk away, you just might be.'

Laura made as if to consider her position, but then said, 'Looks like I'm helping then.'

Nell smiled and stood aside to let Laura walk into the station.

After leaving Laura, I walked for around twenty minutes, along the canal on a slippy brick towpath. The buildings that backed onto it were solid blocks of stone, all the windows looking towards the road on the other side. A barge passed me, green and red, gypsy paintwork. The canal would take me right into town, but I wasn't going that far. I remembered a long-forgotten track that ran around the town, which would take me around the school and then drop me off right by Victoria Park.

The walk was short and dusty, an old bramble track. Once I got near to Victoria Park, I looked around. No one there yet. No police. No Liza Radley. No one at all. There were football fields running away from the park, with the nearest cover a few hundred yards away, so no one could be hiding down there with a decent view.

I was by an old stone church. I looked over the wall.

All I could see were gravestones, like bad teeth, grey and uneven.

I ran across to the park, waiting for either a shot or a shout. I got neither. I dived into the bushes, large buddleias, butterflies resting on the flowers, laurel bushes just alongside those.

I could see the aviary, about forty yards away. It was just a brick block, nothing more. But as I looked, I saw the remnants of crime scene tape fluttering against the corners. It was like a kick to the stomach, maybe even where my dad had been when he had seen David Watts running ten years earlier. I could hear the tape crackling in the wind like it was snapping at my heels.

I looked at the floor. This was going to be worse than I'd thought. I would have to sit and wait for something to happen.

Liza avoided Turners Fold. The events at the house told her she had little time left. She expected the town to be busy with police. As she drove around it, cutting along the dusty back roads, she could sense no difference.

Despite this, she felt nervous, excited. It was getting near the end, she could feel it. She drove for a few miles more before she found the track that led down to the high school. It had only been a few days since she had been there, but everything had moved on so much since then. It had always felt like it had haunted her, but now it felt different, like she was coming to reclaim it.

She could see the park ahead, the trees tall and strong, dark green against the grey slate of the town.

Her eyes flicked around, looking for movement. It looked quiet, empty and desolate, dark and moody, despite the blue sky. She didn't think the police would be waiting, David Watts was too much of a coward to call them, but still she didn't expect to find it so empty and quiet. It just looked like what it was: a small park on the edge of a small Lancashire town.

She looked again. She couldn't see David Watts. She smiled to herself. She had time to get set, she'd spent the last ten miles working out what she was going to do. She had to get Emma down there.

She went back to her car and reversed hard before swinging it round to head away from the high school. She had driven down to remind herself of the layout. It was just how she remembered it. Now she had to go and wait for him. But he couldn't see her first. She had worked out where she was going to be.

She put her foot down and sped along the track, leaving a cloud of dust behind.

FIFTY-FIVE

Laura was taken into a room at the police station, away from the front window and the growing clamour outside. She was following Nell, with Mike behind her, and when she went into the room she saw Tony leaning against the wall.

He was quiet, seemed subdued. When he looked up, he was expressionless.

Laura walked over. 'It's good to see you, Tony,' she whispered in his ear.

He shook his head. 'Glen Ross is dead,' he said.

Laura's eyes went wide with shock. 'What happened?'

Tony looked towards Nell and saw her nod. He looked back towards Laura and said simply, 'I played the recording.'

'What, and it killed him? The shock? Heart attack?'

Tony shook his head. 'I wish it was that simple.' He sighed. 'He blew his brains out, Laura.'

Laura was silent again for a few moments. She was tinkering with her conscience, but there was nothing there. She tugged at her lip. 'If he'd been less of a coward ten years ago, maybe things would have been different.'

Tony sighed. 'I saw a man die this morning. Go easy.'

Laura rubbed her eyes. She was tired. 'Last night, I was chased by a madman,' she said. 'He tried to kill Jack, maybe me as well. I have a few awkward questions to answer now, because I went along with Jack when I should have brought him in, and I was almost killed by Liza Radley. All of this because Glen Ross did nothing about a dead girl ten years ago. I'm feeling pretty strung out right now, so no, I don't feel like going easy. I just wish he'd hung around to answer some questions.'

Tony said nothing.

'Don't you feel the same, Tony?'

He looked up at Laura. Then he gave a thin smile. 'Maybe I do, in my own way. I just wish he hadn't done it in front of me.'

Laura said nothing, but she understood.

Then they both looked over as Nell coughed.

'Sorry to split you two up, but we need to talk.'

Tony and Laura exchanged glances, and then they both grimaced. They each hoped their stories came out right.

David Watts was hurtling into town, bouncing out of dips in the road, his eyes shining with anger, his mouth set fixed and firm. He kept on checking his rear-view mirror, sure he was being followed, checking out colours and makes, seeing if they were keeping up.

He jumped when his phone rang. He looked down at the passenger seat. The phone was flashing green, ringing out. He snapped out a hand and put it to his ear.

'Yeah?'

'Here she is, David.'

'I'm on my way to kill you,' he snarled.

'Good. I'm waiting for you.'

Then the earpiece went silent. He was about to throw the phone down when a voice came on that he recognised.

'David, David, help me.'

It was Emma. His breaths sank to nothing, his mind slowed down. He had thought it was just a bluff.

'Emma?'

'David, please help me. Just do as she says. Please.' She was crying now.

'Don't worry, Emma, I'll be there.' He felt a new urgency. 'You're coming home.'

Then he jumped when he heard a noise, like someone being hit, and the metallic voice returned.

'You know where to go, David. I'm waiting. You go there and you get Emma back.'

He started to shout, his hand gripping the wheel tight, too tight, when he noticed the call had ended.

He threw the phone back on the passenger seat and put his foot down harder. He could see Turners Fold getting bigger, the dots on the landscape turning into houses, the grey pinpricks into lines of chimneys.

This was going to end only one way.

FIFTY-SIX

Laura was sitting down, cradling a coffee Mike had brought in. He was leaning against the wall with his arms folded. He didn't like acting as waiter.

Laura had told Nell all about the trip to Liza's house. Then she'd told her all about the visit during the night from the American. Laura couldn't see, but Nell had transcripts of the 999 calls by people woken up by the shooting. It all matched.

Then Nell asked more about the American.

Laura stared into her coffee and shook her head. 'I don't know who he was.'

Nell moved her head in query. 'Was?'

Laura looked up. 'He's dead. He got on the wrong side of Liza Radley.'

Nell looked surprised, her head cocked like a hawk. 'Are you sure he's dead?'

Laura laughed. 'If he's not, that was some trick, because his head ended up a few feet from his body, and the last time I saw him, he was covered in flames.'

Nell raised her eyebrows. 'Where's Jack?'

461

Laura took a drink of coffee, tried to think about her answer. She smiled when she remembered what had been said in the car.

'I don't know,' she replied. It was an honest reply.

'Don't mess us around,' Mike barked, but Nell held up her hand to quieten him.

'Where was he the last time you saw him?' she asked.

'Where I was picked up,' she said.

Nell looked at Mike and raised her eyebrows. Mike shrugged.

'He thinks he's wanted for Rose Wood's murder,' Laura added. 'He just wanted to be out of town.'

Nell blinked. 'Okay,' she said. 'We'll get the maps out.'

I was starting to lose concentration, tiredness creeping up on me, when I was jolted awake by movement.

I sat upright, my mind switched on again. It was a man. He was on the other side of the road, just emerging into view along the field that ran away from Victoria Park. It was a familiar walk. A tall man, well-built, I could see that, even from a distance. I smiled to myself. I recognised him straight away. It was David Watts. Every sports fan in the country knew that walk. And he was heading towards Victoria Park. My hunch had been right.

But then it struck me how right my father had been. Same man from the same distance. Unmistakable.

But as I looked around, I realised I only had one part of the puzzle. Where was Liza Radley?

David Watts stopped in front of Victoria Park.

He had stocked up on coke, just enough to get

through, so his eyes were wild, his hand darting to his nose, twitchy, arrogant. He looked around, saw the trees, shadows, as his childhood rushed at him. The place looked deserted. It always did. But as he stared, the park filled up with noise, teenage dreams. He rubbed his eyes. It was too bright. Memories came in flashes, noises of the pack, his friends, secret cigarettes, stolen kisses.

He shook his head, tried to clear it out. There was no one there.

But he knew the answer was there. The whole of the last three days would melt away when he came out of the park. He would go back to London, maybe take some time off, but he would be back. He had to believe that.

He stepped forward, his steps nervous and slow, crossing the road, a thin grey strip, until he reached Victoria Park. When his foot touched the grass, he felt a tingle like a current as the blades crushed under his feet. He smiled. He started a slow walk, his feet pressing the grass gently, like he thought it might break. The memories came back so he began to spin as he walked, the park turning fast, his feet skidding on the grass. He laughed, the sound loud in the silence, bouncing around the park so that it came back on him and made him shut his eyes. He thought he saw something for a moment, a flicker, a movement on the edge of his vision, but there was nothing there. There was nobody there. Just trees, seats, grass. It was the same old Victoria Park.

He carried on spinning, laughing, the view blurring

now, his head turning. Then he stopped. He felt a jab to his head, a flash of light. He looked up and saw it. The aviary. A broken brick cube. He gasped as he felt another stabbing pain, like the scrape of glass. His hands shot to his head. He tried to look again. He thought he saw moving shadows, blurred struggles.

He stepped back quickly. His forehead was damp now, his hands trembling. The sunlight was piercing, making him cover his eyes again. He could still see trees and grass, but he thought he could see into the shadows as well, people hiding, watching. Where was she? His nerves were cocked, waiting for the sniper's gunshot.

He stepped forward and began to walk across the grass, turning round, backwards now, his hand shielding his eyes from the light. His mouth was dry, wrung out by nerves. He felt isolated, exposed. It wasn't supposed to be like this. He was coming for her. He began to curse, spitting venom. He stopped and stuck his chest out, arched his back to shout.

'Where are you?'

The noise echoed around the park, no one there to hear him. When the sound ebbed away, he stopped. The grass was about to turn into tarmac. He waited for a reply. There was nothing. He put his head back and laughed, manic and loud, driven by drugs and panic.

'Where the fuck are you?' he shouted again, and began to spin on the spot, the shout dying, the world screaming past in greens and blues and whites, a blur of daylight.

He stopped and jumped back when he heard the shot, a loud crack smashing the silence. He heard the soft smack of something slamming into the grass near his feet. He looked around, sank to his knees, couldn't place where it came from. There were too many hiding places and he was exposed. 'You crazy bitch,' he hissed, his eyes flicking around the park. He couldn't see her.

Then his phone rang.

He stopped in disbelief. The ring tone was deafening. He jabbed his hand into his pocket, his palms damp, and pulled it out. The screen told him everything. It was her. He looked around again, let the ring tone bounce around. He swallowed and then pressed to answer.

Her voice filled his head, seemed to fill the air around him, that metallic deadness.

'Get to where you left her.'

His hand gripped the phone, his knuckles white, his teeth clenched.

'Fuck you,' he replied in a snarl.

'Get there now,' her voice continued, sharp now, *'or I'll take the top of your head off. You've got ten seconds to move.'*

He screamed 'fuck you' into the phone and then pulled his arm back to throw it away. He heard it break against the aviary. As it clattered to the floor, he stood there, his arms by his side, breathing heavily, his eyes dark and brooding.

His breathing slowed down and he put his face in his hands. He felt the heat from his skin burn up his fingers, felt fresh tears cool them down again.

He went to his knees and sank backwards, his hands on his hips, and looked up to the sky. All he could see was blue, flecked with white and dotted by wheeling birds, the colours bright and full of summer. It seemed to rush along, as if he could feel the earth turn. He looked at the floor, tried to snap away the nausea. He could see his knees in the grass.

He put his head up again and hauled himself to his feet. He had no choice. He wasn't on his own.

His steps were heavy, dragging along the grass. He looked down all the way, watched every step, saw the blades wrap around the front of his shoes as he went, watched as he saw the green of the grass change to the black of the tarmac. Every step was soft and quiet, the only sound he could hear.

The grass turned to dust again and he realised he was there, by the aviary. He stopped at first, not wanting to do all he was asked, but then he remembered how many people had died, how willing she was to kill people. He stepped forward and felt himself rise onto the raised concrete. He closed his eyes, clamped them shut, felt tears break through again. His fists were clenched, his nails cutting into his hands.

He thought he heard something so he snapped his eyes open and looked down. He gasped. He could see black hair spread over the floor, thrashing around, sweeping the dust. His hands clasped his ears, blocking the sound. He could hear something. It was a cry, an echo, someone screaming, filling his head. He shut his eyes again, the screams making him gasp, but they were still there. He sank to his knees and put his head down, rocking, trying to shake off the noise. His fingernails dug into his skin, pulled down his head, drew blood, made deep scratches. Sticky wetness crept around his fingertips so he opened his eyes again. The black hair was still there, thrashing around, but there was no face, no form. He could feel her fingernails in his face, scratching at him, gasping, kicking. His fingers scraped down his face.

He closed his eyes again and all he could hear was her struggle. She was crying out, screaming, sobbing, trying to get out a last breath. He was breathing hard, inside her, pressing hard with his hands, pushing her head back onto the ground, feeling her fight, driving him on.

He gasped and then shouted out, his eyes flicking open. She was still.

He looked down. There was no one there. His face was wet with perspiration, with tears, with blood from fresh scratches. He shuffled round on his knees. It was silent again. He was on his own.

Then he spun round as he saw movement across the park. There was someone walking towards him, the figure blurred through his tears. As the person got closer, David recognised her. He gasped as he saw her and tears flicked onto his cheeks. It was Emma. She was coming towards him, her head down, looking scared, wary.

His eyes travelled the fields, trying to see where Emma had come from, but he couldn't see anyone else there.

He put his head down and covered his eyes. He shook

his head, but when he opened them again, she was still there, nearly at him, her eyes wild with relief.

He smiled.

'Emma, you're okay.' He sank back onto his knees. 'Thank God, thank God.'

He put his head down and let the tears fall. He was waiting for her to sink to the floor with him. He was waiting to feel her arms around him, holding him, her head in his neck, warm, safe.

It didn't come. He lifted up his head to open his eyes. As he looked, he saw she was unharmed, but there was something not right. It was the look in her eyes, measured and cold.

And then he looked closer. He saw that she had a gun in her hand. And as he looked, his eyes trying to work out what was going on, he saw that she was pointing a rifle. And she was aiming it right at him.

FIFTY-SEVEN

Nell and Mike had a map open in front of them. A couple of local officers were helping them.

Laura was picked up well outside of town, on some old farm track.

Nell turned to Tony.

'Who does Jack know out there?'

Tony walked over to the map. He looked around on the paper, but couldn't see anything. It was just an old track.

'I don't know. I'm sorry.'

Nell stood up straight, pushing the map to one side, and looked over at Laura. 'C'mon, Jack must have said something.'

Laura shook her head. 'He just said he needed to be at that spot.'

Nell sighed. This was getting frustrating.

'Why so much about Jack?' asked Tony. 'It should be Liza Radley you want.'

Nell nodded. 'Yes, I know. But Jack seems to have

done okay with hunches, so I was hoping to ride one more and get lucky.'

'There is one thing,' Laura said quietly.

Everyone turned to look.

'What is it?' asked Nell.

'He's got my phone.' She shrugged. 'I could just give him a call.'

David Watts squinted into the sun. Emma's blonde hair was translucent against the light, like a halo. He grimaced and shook his head, trying to clear the image. It wasn't right.

'Emma?'

She smiled. 'Good to see you, David.'

'What the fuck are you doing? You all right?'

'Oh, I'm just fine.'

David started to stand.

'Get the fuck back down!' Her gun was pushed into his face, her voice a bark.

He looked up again, confusion in his eyes. 'What's going on?'

'Nice of you to come. I knew you would.'

'But I came to get you.' His voice was quiet, but his mind was flicking through events, trying to work it out.

'Bullshit, David. You came to get Liza.'

He looked around. 'So where is she?'

She grinned. 'You're looking at her, you arsehole.' When his jaw dropped, his eyes looking away as his mind did the computing, she added, 'You can drop the Emma now.' When he looked up, she said, 'And you can call me Liza.'

His mouth dropped open, no sound coming out. She began to smile, but it was filled with hatred.

'It can't be you,' he began to say, and then shook his head. 'You were in New York. It can't be you.'

She laughed, eyes wild. 'I don't even work for a fucking airline, David.'

'But I drove you to the airport. I could hear it when you called me.'

'Ever heard of tape machines? Half an hour with a microphone in my hand got me that. And every time you took me there, I got the train back into town as soon as you left.' She paused to watch him take it all in. 'Do you know what was the best thing about being a stewardess?'

He didn't anwer. He just watched her, his head cocked, a confused look in his eyes.

'It took me away from you every few days,' she said. Her voice was quiet now.

He squatted back onto his heels, bewildered, and then he began to laugh, manic and loud, as tears streamed down his face. 'It was you, all this time? Fucking you?' He put his head back and his eyes filled with sky. 'Oh, Jesus Christ.'

She burned up with contempt. Her hand squeezed the trigger, the barrel shaking, and she took a few steps back as if to walk away, but then walked quickly towards him, her anger rising, her steps long and fast, and lashed out with her foot, catching him under his chin.

He fell backwards, scattered dirt, and blood speckled his bottom lip. He put his hand to his mouth to dab it clean. He pulled it away and saw it was streaked red.

'You bitch,' he spluttered.

She put the rifle back into his face. He sank back in recoil, his feet scrabbling, pulling himself along the concrete.

She pushed the barrel into his chest, forcing him down. 'Where did it go, David? The shouting? The bravado?' She smirked now, a shift of power. 'How do you like it, David? Lying back on the ground, scared and dirty?'

He lay back flat, tried to shrink away from the gun, his arms above his head.

'Nothing to say, David?'

He looked up into the shadow, too dark to make out her eyes. He shook his head slowly. 'Not a fucking thing,' he whispered.

She jabbed his chest with the barrel, making him wince.

'Say it!' she shouted. 'Say that you killed her.'

He rubbed his chest and scowled. 'Not ever,' he said, and shook his head.

She took a deep breath, and then another, her face reddening as she stood over him. 'Look at yourself, David. Coked up and sitting back, looking scared.' She shook her head, wiped her eyes. 'What do you think about when you're on your own?'

He said nothing.

'Does it get dark in there, David?' she asked, and tapped the side of her head.

He said nothing for a while, just watched the wave and twitch of the gun. Then the sun disappeared behind a small cloud for a moment and he got a shot of her

472

eyes. Behind the brashness in the voice, he saw flickers of doubt, fear and self-loathing. He thought he saw tears. He grinned. 'I think back on Annie,' he said, mocking, and raised his eyebrows. 'Boy, did she go some when she got juiced up.'

She let out a scream and hit him in the mouth with the gun, a sharp jab. She felt it bang on his teeth, and her eyes flashed wet with tears of anger. It knocked his head back, flicked more blood onto his lips. He gritted his teeth in pain, covered his mouth with his hand. A tooth was broken. She jammed the gun against his neck, making him cry out, her finger tight on the trigger. Her eyes were wide open, sinews up on her neck and arms, struggling to contain herself. She wanted to shoot, but she hadn't finished yet.

He looked up in shock and pain, confusion and fear, panting, sweat prickling his top lip. She snarled when she saw it, and then relaxed the pressure, so that the gun was just resting lightly on his neck, brushing the hairs, damp with perspiration.

She started to make small circles on his neck with the cold steel, a doodle on the skin, a tease. Then she slowly tracked the barrel up his neck and over his chin, just touching lightly, almost sensual, smiling, until it touched his lips.

'Open your mouth, David.' She said it in a whisper, almost seductive. She pushed gently against his teeth.

He tried to move his head away, thrashed it from side to side, his lips pursed, but she just pressed harder.

'C'mon, David, open your mouth.' She grinned and winked a cold eye at him. 'You know you want to.'

473

He blinked, tears in his eyes now, blood and sweat mixing around the tips of the barrels.

She raised her eyebrows. 'C'mon,' she whispered.

He sank his head back onto the ground and closed his eyes. A tear ran down the side of his face and disappeared into the dust. His chest heaved, and then he opened his eyes and looked up at the sky. He opened his mouth, parted his teeth. The gun slid in slowly, brushing his lips, until it rested on his tongue, cold and sharp.

'Feel nice, David.'

He didn't move.

'Still nothing to say, David?'

He didn't reply. Just stared upwards, tears tracking down the side of his face. She could sense him saying goodbye.

Her finger tightened on the trigger, giving the barrel a jab, making him gag. He wouldn't look at her.

'David? It's your last chance for salvation.'

Still nothing.

'I want to hear it.'

He looked at her. His eyes were red, his cheeks dark and grubby. He nodded slowly, his mouth puckering around the gun.

She raised her eyebrows.

He nodded some more, a low wail coming from him.

She pulled on the gun, taking it out of his mouth. He rolled to one side, put his hand to his mouth.

'Make it good,' she said, standing straight, the gun still pointed towards him.

He spat out the taste of the metal for a few seconds,

and then turned back to her. 'You tell me something first.'

She didn't reply.

'You sought me out, right?'

Again, no response.

'So why didn't you just kill me?' he asked. 'Why not stick a knife in my chest in the night?'

She snarled at that. 'What, and be some stalker, a crazy girlfriend?' She jabbed the gun at him. 'I did that, David. I got close to you so I could kill you. But then I sat there at night, looked down at you, peaceful, contented. I didn't want it that way. What would you learn from that? What would anyone learn from that? No, David, I don't want to kill you. I want to destroy you. I want everyone to know what you did.' She shrugged. 'So I thought of this.' She kicked out at him again, a push on the shoulder. 'So get talking.'

'But we made love? We were special.'

The gun pushed harder into his chest. 'You were nothing special, David. I saw it in your eyes that first time, like I should be grateful for the time you spent. Christ, all I had to do was make the noises.'

'And that's how you got Henri Dumas to Soho? He thought he was meeting my girlfriend, sleeping with you behind my back.'

She smiled, and then jabbed him again. 'Yeah, same as you. I fucked him like I fucked you, and he came to meet me to protect himself, to keep me away from the media.'

'And Nixon?'

She nodded.

He looked up at her, felt cheated, used. Then, as he watched her, saw the tears coming down her face, he thought that he ought to tell her, just to see how it ended.

'I was young,' was how he started.

She kicked at him, hitting him in the ribs. 'Louder. I want to hear this. I've waited long enough.'

He rolled over onto his back. His chest was heaving, his face a mix of dirt, sweat, and blood. He wiped his mouth with the back of his hand.

'I said I was young.' His voice was still quiet. 'Too young to know what I was doing.'

She leant forward and pressed the gun into his chest again. 'No excuse,' she snarled.

He put his hands up. 'I know, I don't have an excuse.' His breathing slowed down. 'All I have is a mistake. One mistake, and it's caused all of this.'

'Is that all it was to you? A mistake?' Her voice got higher. 'A fucking mistake?'

He nodded, his lips trembling again. 'I was drunk,' he continued. 'We'd been to the party and I was walking Annie home.'

'What else?'

He shook his head. 'I don't know,' he said, sounding desperate.

'You don't know?' She was shrieking.

He nodded, fast and eager. 'I thought she wanted me,' he continued, and then he collapsed backwards. 'When she didn't, things just got out of hand.'

'Out of hand? Out of fucking hand? Getting fresh is out of hand. Maybe wrestling is out of hand. But raping Annie? Killing Annie? Just "out of hand"?'

He sighed and shook his head. 'What more can I say?'

She jabbed him with the gun again, right at the top of his arm. 'You can say you're fucking sorry, that's what.'

He nodded slowly, his hands out. 'Okay, I'm sorry.'

'Sorry for what?'

'I'm sorry for what happened to Annie.' He exhaled loudly. 'I didn't mean for it to happen.'

'Sorry for killing her?'

He nodded. A tear ran down his cheek, collecting dust on the way.

'Say it.'

He took a deep breath and closed his eyes. 'I'm sorry for killing Annie.'

He lay still, tears streaming down his face. His head was filled with images, racing past. His parents, London, the crowd at an England game. He could hear his mother talking, the crowd cheering, could feel his team patting his back. All his life, the whole of his world, it was all there, racing through his head, one last run through at a small park in Turners Fold, Lancashire.

He lay there, his eyes clamped shut, chest heaving, waiting for the shot. What would it feel like?

Then he realised that Liza was quiet. There was no shot, no talk, no movement. He opened his eyes, and saw Liza looking down, the gun shaking, tears in her eyes. He heaved a breath and then said quietly, 'You don't have to do it.'

She blinked away some tears and set her jaw firm. She nodded. 'Oh yes, I do.' Her voice cracked as she spoke.

He shook his head. 'No, you don't.' He cocked his head to one side, watching her uncertainty. He felt some of his fear draw back, saw some weakness in her. 'Isn't it as good as you thought it would be?'

Liza looked at him. 'What do you mean?'

He raised his eyebrows. 'This. Maybe it's not what you want.'

She looked at him, fresh tears streaming down her cheeks. She gulped and then shook her head. 'No, maybe not.' Then she took a deep breath and put her head back. 'Maybe I just haven't got what I wanted yet.'

'Which is?'

'I want you ruined.'

'Ruined?'

'You got it. Ruined, just like you ruined me. Just like you ruined my family.'

David put his head down.

She pointed the gun back at David. 'You killed my parents as good as if you had stood over them with a gun. No, I'll change that. I saw how you getting away got to them. Made my father into a shadow; he hated himself, knew what he had allowed to happen. My mother saw it and hated herself for not making it different.' She leant forward and jammed the barrel into his chest, making him cough and cry out with pain. 'You did that. You changed everything for this town, just so you could go off and make big money. What about the ones you left behind?'

She stood up straight. David rolled onto his side and rubbed his chest. He gritted his teeth in pain.

'I thought this was about Annie,' he hissed at her.

Liza wiped a tear from her eye. 'It's always been about Annie,' she said, and started to sob. 'Every waking moment, every time I looked at my mum and dad, every minute I saw how they hated themselves, all of that, all of the time, it was always about Annie.' She screeched. 'You killed my parents, you killed my town, you killed my childhood. Always Annie. Always.'

He didn't say anything. He just watched her, the arm holding the gun starting to waver, relax, lose its focus.

'And about you,' she continued, her voice coming in chokes and sobs. 'Every time I turn on the television, open a magazine, there you are, smiling, laughing, winning. Always fucking winning. You get what you want. So it was always about you. About what you did to Annie. And to them.'

'And it was never about you?' David asked, quiet and careful.

She began to scream, the noise echoing round the park. David's hands shot to his ears, the gun waving around in front of him. She paused for a breath. Then she heard something. A phone. The ring of a phone. There was someone there.

She turned away.

I jumped, startled. Laura's phone. It was in my pocket. The ring tone was loud, filling the space around me.

I scrabbled about in my pocket. I looked up and saw that they had heard me.

I got the phone out of my pocket. The noise got louder. I could see Liza looking around.

I clicked to answer. 'Yes?' I said in a whisper.

Laura's voice sounded loud.

'Jack. Where are you?'

I could tell by the noise in the background that she was with the police.

'I'm looking out over Victoria Park.'

'Anything doing?'

'Everything is doing,' I answered. 'Liza Radley is here. And David Watts. You need to get some people down here now.'

Laura was silent for a moment. I sensed her shock, so I carried on.

'And if you can get a camera, you've got a million-dollar shot when you pull in by the park.'

'What are you going to do?' she asked. She sounded worried.

I watched Liza for a moment, looking unsure. Then something occurred to me.

'Turn off your phone. You'll get the next five minutes on the voicemail.'

I heard her shout my name as I took the phone from my ear, but when I pressed callback a few seconds later I went straight to the pre-recorded tones of the message service. I hung the phone off the waistband of my trousers and started to climb out from the darkness and into the sunlight.

Laura looked around the room. Nell and Mike were watching her expectantly.

She held Tony's phone in the air.

'Leave this switched off.'

Nell put her hands on her hips. 'But where is he?'

Laura grinned. 'Where else? Victoria Park.' She looked over at Tony. 'With Liza Radley and David Watts.'

Tony raised his eyebrows. This was turning into one hell of a story.

Nell began to smile. She looked over at Mike. 'Convinced yet?'

'Let's go,' he said. He made as if to go out of the room, but then he stopped when he saw Laura get up to follow him.

'You stay here, detective. You're off the investigation.'

Laura shook her head. 'I helped solve this. I'll get a book deal, maybe magazines. At the moment, it was solved by a reporter and an off-duty cop, while the rest of you ran around the country not knowing where to look. Take me with you, and maybe I'll talk up your help.'

Mike looked over at Nell, whose expression gave little away.

'You left London on a routine enquiry,' Laura continued. 'You'll go back a hero if I go with you. Your careers will orbit. Leave me here, and I'll say you just got lucky, or maybe worse.'

Nell began to smile as well, and as Laura walked past her, triumphant, Nell nodded and winked.

Tony stayed where he was. He passed his camera to Laura.

Nell raised her eyebrows. 'You not coming?'

He shook his head. 'Let them have their day,' he said. 'I've had mine. I only went along for the ride.'

Nell considered him for a moment, and then walked out of the room.

*

Liza looked around the park, to the fence curving around the slope, and into the trees, the bushes. As she looked over, the gun swung away, pointing the way she was looking.

David's eyes went keen, his body tensed.

Liza continued to gaze about her, unsure if she had heard it right. Someone was there, watching, listening.

David moved fast, athlete's speed, grabbing at the gun, his hands clasped around the barrel, his arms firm and strong.

Liza felt the tug and looked down, her eyes wide in panic, sensing the danger. She tried to get her finger around the trigger to fire it, but his grip was too strong. David yanked hard at the gun, throwing himself backwards. She flew towards him, falling forward, the gun still in her hand. He kicked up with his legs and caught her square in the chest. She winced and then felt her feet lift off the ground as he carried on backwards, throwing her over his shoulder, using the gun as a lever. She landed in a dust cloud, an untidy sprawl, and as she landed she lost her grip on the gun, her last grab desperate and tearful.

David sprang to his feet. He had the gun in his hand, pointing right at her. He was smiling now. He stood over her and looked down. She scrabbled backwards, off the concrete and onto the tarmac surround. He walked after her, the gun pointed down at her.

'Keep crawling, little girl, because when I catch you, I'm going to blow your fucking head off.'

Liza stopped and flopped backwards. She was breathing heavily.

'Looks like I win,' he said, his voice low and menacing. Then he spread his arms out, cocky and taunting. 'Did you really think it would be any other way?'

He then leant forward and put the gun against her head, pressed the steel into her skin, making a cold red ring.

Liza closed her eyes and pressed into the gun. Tears were streaming down her face. He snarled, grimaced, began to squeeze on the trigger.

Then he heard something. He turned round. There was someone walking across the park towards him.

FIFTY-EIGHT

I began to walk towards them.

I could see them, David Watts standing over her, the gun in his hand, set against the backdrop of the fields leading away from Turners Fold. There was no one around, and I was walking towards them, every step taking me nearer to somewhere that maybe I ought not to be. My hands were shaking, but I kept on going forward, my eyes fixed on David Watts, reminding myself of why I was there, reminding myself of what had happened the last time my father came down to the park.

The walk seemed to take forever. The grass was thick, the soil dry, and it seemed to drag at my feet, making my steps slow and heavy. I could see his surprise. As I stepped onto the concrete base of the aviary, just yards away, he looked down at the gun. As I got closer, he began to smile.

'Glad you got here,' he said. 'This woman was going to kill me.'

I stopped right in front of him. 'Bullshit.'

He was taken aback, too surprised to say anything.

'That's right, you got it.'

He looked down at Liza, who looked confused. 'She's the woman who has been shooting footballers,' he said.

I looked down at Liza and then back at David. 'Yes, I know.'

'Then why are you looking at me like that? I'm not the bad guy.'

I shook my head. 'Depends on where you look, because where I'm looking right now, you started all of this.'

He opened his mouth to speak, and then closed it again.

I stared into his eyes. 'You heard me, you bastard.'

Again, he opened his mouth, but still nothing came out.

I looked at his face, and for a moment it was hard to believe that it was David Watts. The face I was used to seeing was the confident king of the England team, dependable football star. He endorsed soft drinks, spoke up for charities, London's favourite adopted son. The person in front of me looked haunted. His face was filthy, streaked with dirt and sweat, his smile a grimace of broken teeth and blood, his top lip swollen and painful. His skin looked drawn and pale, as if he hadn't slept in days. But it was his eyes that I noticed. Gone was the easy smile, the glint for the cameras. His eyes looked dark and red, flitting around like he was fuelled, angry and wired.

'My name is Jack Garrett.' I watched for a reaction. There was nothing. Just arrogance. I raised my eyebrows. 'Sound familiar?'

485

David shook his head slowly. Then I saw something in his eyes, as if the name had started to turn some wheels.

'Garrett?'

I nodded, my mouth set in a thin line.

His jaw moved from side to side, the barrel of the gun starting to dip as I became his focus.

'My dad was a policeman,' I said, my face calm, my insides burning.

David Watts went pale. 'Was?' he asked eventually. I could tell he knew the answer.

I nodded again, slowly, trying to make sure he got the link in his own time. 'Died this week.' I looked towards Liza, who was starting to look interested. 'Died right back there, in front of the aviary, where you've just been. Right where they found Annie.'

David's hand started to shake, the gun waving at thin air. He was staring slack-jawed. He looked back to Liza, who had started to move backwards on the floor, away from him.

He turned to me as if he was about to say something, but I held my hand up to stop him. 'Don't waste your regrets on me,' I said. 'I'm not interested.'

I began to walk around him, away from Liza, so that he could only look at one of us at any time. He twisted his body to track me, tried to stop himself from turning away from Liza, but I kept on circling until he had no choice. I stopped when I was right opposite her, with David in between.

His eyes flashed to her, then back to me. The gun was pointing at the floor.

I looked at Liza. I didn't hate her. I pitied her for the life she had led and the choices she felt she'd had to make to get even. I saw something flicker back, maybe a smile, but then she went straight-faced again when David turned to his side and pointed the gun back at her, his head turning on a pivot to keep us both in his sight.

I looked to Liza. 'Did you know he'd sent someone after you?'

Liza stared back at me, unsure what to think. Then I saw recognition kick in.

'You were at the house.'

I nodded, and then looked at him. He looked uncomfortable, as if he thought we were acting together.

I thought I could hear cars getting closer, tyres bouncing along, the rush of an engine.

'Did you know that same guy killed Rose Wood last night?'

Liza looked confused.

'Rose Wood, Colin's mother. He killed her last night, once she had given him your address.'

Liza's eyes flashed back to David Watts, wild and angry. His breathing was getting fast, his face red.

I looked at David now, my own anger getting hard to contain.

'And he chased me out of my own house,' I continued, 'tried to kill me as I got away down the road.'

David's arm began to move, the gun twisting round to face me.

'And he killed my father,' I said, my eyes burning into his. 'And for that, I'll hound you for the rest of your life.'

I stepped closer. David began to lift the gun up at me. My stomach crawled with fear, but I contained it, beat it back. Behind David, I saw Liza scrabble to her feet. I kept my stare, dared David to keep going. I didn't keep a watch on what Liza was doing. The last I saw, she had her hands behind her back.

Nell's car screamed towards Victoria Park, no sirens. She felt tremors of excitement, sensing that something special was about to unveil itself as they got further along.

The trees came into view first, and the grass slowly spread as they got nearer. Laura gasped as she saw them. David Watts had a gun, and he was pointing it right at Jack's head. Then she saw Liza and her hand went to her mouth.

'Oh shit,' she heard Mike say, as the view was obscured for a second by the mist of dust. She pulled out her camera and pointed it. She began to reel off shots, zooming in. Then when she knew she had enough, she set it to record moving pictures. Laura zoomed in on David Watts. As soon as she heard a shot, she was going to capture the next ten seconds. This was evidence, strong and clear.

Mike and Nell jumped out of the car and ran round to Liza's blind side. They opened the rear doors and hissed at Laura to get out. She looked back at the scene on the field, and then grimaced before sliding out.

Once on the path, crouched behind the car, she retrained her camera on David Watts. She was ready again.

*

'I didn't ask him to do those things.'

David Watts was trying to swallow, his mouth dry. He looked round as the cars came into view. Two of them. One a marked patrol car, the other one a black Mondeo. I glanced over. I thought I could see Laura looking through the glass. I tried to hide my relief.

David looked back again. He licked his lips, nervous. He had an audience now.

I shook my head. 'Bullshit, David. He wasn't doing it for free.' I smiled, but there was no warmth.

'He's dead now.'

It was Liza. I looked over. She had her hands in her jacket pockets.

She nodded. 'That's right. Died this morning. He was going to kill me.'

I shook my head and tutted. 'You're in a lot of trouble, Mr Watts. That's a conspiracy.'

The gun carried on towards me. I flinched but held my ground.

'Who'll believe that crazy bitch?'

I looked him right in the eye. 'I do. I was there.' I shrugged. 'So it's not just her. And there are the calls you made to Glen Ross.' I began to smile again. 'Oh yes, do you think people don't remember that? David Watts, football hotshot on the phone, wanting to speak to Glen Ross? It almost went into their diaries.'

David was getting angry. I could see the gun waving as he squeezed hard, fighting an impulse to fire. His face was screwed up, his eyes dark.

'The guy you sent was at the station,' I continued. 'Did you know that? He was seen. People overheard him, you know, the little people who you think don't matter. Your name came up.'

The gun got closer.

'Do you think Glen Ross will help you out this time?' He blinked.

'Do you think I hadn't worked it out? The pay-off?' I snarled at him. 'How low can you go, David? As far as your money will take you?'

Still he said nothing, so I took a step closer to him.

'How did you do it, David?' I continued, mocking him, looking past the dark barrel of the gun, now inches from my face. I thought I could see my death in its shadows. 'How could you kill someone and just walk away?'

'I didn't kill anyone.'

I looked over at Liza. 'I heard you confess.'

He laughed, dark and bitter. 'That won't stand up in court. She had a gun in my face.'

'What about "*Rath Dé Ort EW*", scratched onto the back of your chain?'

He almost dropped his gun.

I nodded at him. 'That's right, Eugene David Watts. A little gold chain left at the scenes of all the football shootings. Just like you left in Annie's hand.'

'I still had that chain after Annie died.'

I nodded. 'Yes, I know. Glen Ross gave it back to you.' I cocked my head. 'Why did he do that?'

I watched a tear drop out of his eye, his chin tremble. He shook it away, tried to make himself strong.

'How much do you want?' he said.

'Is that all you have to offer?' I stepped closer until

I felt the gun barrel against my neck. 'I want what she wants. I want you ruined.'

He shook his head, and then grinned, dark and red. 'Money. That's what this is all about. That's all it's ever about. Name your price.'

I said nothing.

'C'mon, prick, how much? Ross took his cut.' He flicked his head towards Liza. 'Everyone took a cut.'

I saw a tear run down Liza's face, saw her hand scrabble in her jacket pocket.

David was snarling now. He pushed the gun into my neck, knocking me back, making me cough. I could hear shouting behind me, scrambled footsteps as people got behind their cars.

'You bought them?'

He nodded. 'Oh yes, I fucking bought them all right. Just wrote them a cheque like I was at Tesco's,' and then he laughed. 'Annie's daddy snapped it up like a lottery win. I could see it in his eyes. New car, new house.' He jabbed me in the neck again. 'I paid my dues for Annie.'

'But you couldn't buy my father.' I looked at Liza. 'Or her father.'

He flinched at that.

I saw Liza looking at me. She hadn't realised who I was, or how we were connected. She knew now.

'They'd seen you on the night,' I continued. 'My dad. Her dad. And they'd seen Annie, lying dead just there, blue, gold chain swinging in her hand.' I shook my head. 'You couldn't buy him, so you had him killed. One less person in your way.'

His eyes started to get angry. I saw him flash a quick

look to the cars parked not far away. I thought I could hear muffled warnings for him to put his gun down. I ignored them. My world was that spot near the aviary, a universe spinning in orbit around David Watts, Liza and me.

'Remember Colin Wood? He's the man in prison for what you did. Ten years of his life. What's that worth to you? A month's wage?' I could have hit him, but I said instead, 'I found out who his lawyer was. He's going to get Colin's DNA tested against the evidence from the scene.' I stared at him. 'It will match, won't it?'

I gripped the barrel of the gun, jabbed it into my chest. 'Or maybe Glen swapped the bags? Maybe when he lifted him for being drunk, Glen Ross just put some DNA swabs from you in his bag, just so that it would catch up with him later?'

David Watts pushed the gun into me, his jaw set, his eyes on fire, wanting to shoot.

'I've got friends out there,' I said. 'She's got a camera. If the police don't get this on film, she will.' I smiled down the barrel. 'You'll make the six o'clock headlines, whatever happens. It's like catching OJ with the knife in his hand.' I looked round the gun and at Liza. 'She knows she's caught, I can sense it in her. And she wants to tell the story. Whatever happens, the story is going to be told. Shooting me will nail it shut for you.' I smiled again. 'So go on, shoot me.'

He strengthened his grip on the gun.

I spread my arms out, put my head back. 'Go on, David. Squeeze the trigger.'

I saw the barrel lift, saw it move forward until I felt

it pressing into my forehead. It was cold and hard, packed tight with menace.

I saw a rush of film, like my life on fast-forward. My mother, laughing, loving. My dad, strong. School, work, home, Laura. It rushed through, and I felt the wind, like the memories were pushing me around, jostling me. I could feel my father, dead under my feet.

There was shouting in the distance, hollering, screams to put down the gun. I thought I could hear Laura shouting my name. Or was it my father? The anger seeping out of David Watts smothered me. He was trapped, losing control, everything crumbling in front of him. He was about winning. No more. I could smell it on him: the defeat, the shame. The metal of the gun dug deeper. I could feel the tension in his arm as he pushed and pressed and fought his desire to pull the trigger.

It came after a pause, like time had slowed down. I heard a scream, movement, saw a flash of colour from the corner of my eye. The gun just came off my forehead for a moment and I felt the breeze blow back onto my skin. Then there was a shot.

The smell of gunpowder assaulted me and I felt a sprinkle of blood on my cheek, warm, thick. There was a noise, a gasp, a crumpled fall, and the cold metal fell away from my head.

It was like the release of a pressure valve, a flood of light. I refocused and Liza was standing in front of me, a handgun clasped in her hand. She was staring wide-eyed, shaking. I looked down at the floor. I could hear shouts behind me. David Watts lay on his side, blood on his cheek, running from a star-shaped wound burnt into his temple. Then I saw the spread of blood from underneath his head, his life seeping out onto the grass.

I looked at Liza. She looked at me, then down at her handgun. I looked down at David. I nodded at her, understanding. He was sinking, his life becoming part of the soil. I knelt down. I looked into his eyes. They were still open, but glassy and dead. But I thought I saw something in them. Confusion, doubt, despair, knowledge he had lost but didn't know how.

I stood up again. I looked at Liza, who was staring back at me, the gun still in her hand. Her mouth was open, as if she no longer knew what to do now it was over.

'He's dead.'

She looked over to the people by the field. The police were still shouting, warning her to put down the gun. Tears started to run down her face and her mouth began to crease as her sobs came again.

I held my hand out to her. She looked like she was about to drop the gun, her hand shaking. She glanced at me and shook her head. I knew then what was going to happen.

I screamed, 'No!'

She flashed the gun to her head and jammed it into her temple. Her finger squeezed the trigger. She looked at me, her eyes wet and wild.

'Don't do it, Liza.'

Her finger wavered.

'Tell the story,' I said, quieter now, pleading. 'Tell everyone what he did.' I pointed down at David's body.

'Think about Annie one last time. Think what she would have wanted. Think about what your mum and dad would have wanted, deep down, if they could go back and do it again.' I shook my head. 'You die and he's just one more victim.' I held my hand out. 'You live, and you can tell everyone what he did to you.'

She shook her head. Her finger was tense on the trigger, her teeth gritted, waiting for the shot.

'It's not just about Annie,' I continued, taking a step closer, my eyes only on her, the shouts from the side-lines now fading away. 'People need to know what he did.' I shook my head. 'He mustn't die a hero, Liza.'

I was right by her. I reached out my hand. Her hand began to waver, the gun moved away from her head. Then she seemed to break and the gun dropped to her waist. I looked at her. I reached out with my hand and placed it over the gun. I could feel her grip on it, soft and warm. I clasped her hand and felt my fingers touch the coolness of the gun.

'Let me have it,' I whispered.

She hung her head and began to nod. Tears were streaming down her cheeks. I took hold of the gun and felt her fingers release it. I let it tumble onto the grass. I held her hand again. She hung her head and began to sob, her shoulders shaking, her head pressing into her chest.

I put my arms around her and drew her close. She turned to me and put her head on my shoulder. Then her arms went around me and I felt her cries. I started to hear running behind me, pounding on the grass. I knew they were coming to get her. I put one hand behind her head and stroked her hair, whispered small words of comfort. She squeezed me and sobbed, said she was sorry. I told her there was no need.

We stayed like that as I heard the police surround us. I opened my eyes and saw a woman in a smart grey suit. And behind her I saw Laura. There were tears. I could see them. And I had some too, warming my cheeks, mixing with Liza's hair as she squeezed me hard.

I looked up at the sky as I felt Liza taken away from me. I heard the metallic snap of handcuffs. I heard the police trying to speak to me but I didn't listen. I turned and walked away instead, slowly across the park, not wanting to see any more of what they would do to her. I heard footsteps behind me and I felt Laura wrap her arm around my waist.

We didn't say anything. There was nothing to say. We just walked past the police cars, and headed away from Victoria Park.

FIFTY-NINE

The Triumph Stag was running well. It would certainly get me as far as London.

It was four weeks after the shooting of David Watts and I was back at my father's house, clearing it out. The press frenzy had died down, put on hold until Liza Radley's trial. I'd given my exclusive to the *Star* in the days afterwards and then gone back to work. If anything, it had been my way of saying thank you. They had promised me the syndication rights if I wrote them the story, but I hadn't done it well. So I settled for an interview instead, my head too messed up to write clearly.

My father's funeral had been tough. Full police honours, a death in service. It had made me weep and it had made me angry, but it had also made me proud. His job had cost him his life, but he had tried to do the right thing in the end. That made me happy.

I didn't stay long afterwards. I said my farewells at the house, away from the huddle of seldom-seen relatives, and returned to the graveyard for my own private goodbye. I just stood and looked at the dirt, the hole freshly filled, and I felt lost, empty.

Laura had been at the funeral, more for me than my father. She's like that, I know that now. I'd seen her once as just a police officer, a source, someone to flirt with, but then I realised after my father's death that I had loved her for a long time, in my own way. I guess I just hadn't known that she loved me back.

Colin Wood was out of prison. At least one good thing had come from all this. He wasn't cleared yet, but he had been granted bail until the formal appeal hearing. I had been to see him, but he didn't look happy. He was a lot thinner than in the photographs on his mother's fireplace, now gaunt and grey, and there was a haunted look in his eyes I couldn't hope to make better, but at least he was free. He'll stay in Turners Fold, but only because he has nowhere else to go.

As I looked around my old house, I knew I wasn't taking many things with me. I wanted the memory of my father, the things that mattered to him. So I was taking a large box of photographs, a collection of Johnny Cash albums, and my father's 1973 Triumph Stag, gleaming in Calypso Red.

I looked up when I heard a noise by the door. It was Laura. I was at the boot of the car, loading it with boxes. Not that there was any room. The rest would have to go into her car.

'I've found some more photographs,' she said, her fingers flicking through a box.

I went towards her. 'We'll take them, sort them out later.' I could see she had smudges of dirt on her nose from going through old cupboards. I wiped them away, and when she looked up at me, I felt my spirits lift.

She picked one out, and I could see a picture of me in shorts, with pale skinny legs. 'You were cute,' she said.

I leant forward and kissed her, and for a few moments I was lost. When we separated, I saw her eyes glistening, her mouth creased into a smile. I put my arms around her and pulled her into me.

'You feel warm, Jack Garrett,' she said.

I agreed. I felt very warm. Blazing hot.

'Where do we go from here,' she asked, almost in a murmur.

I thought about that, and all I knew was that it would be with Laura. I felt less eager to get back to London. I tried not to think about the days I had missed with my father, but I knew that I'd moved to London to escape. Now he was gone, I wondered whether I still had the same urge.

Laura must have sensed my thoughts, because she said, 'I like it up here.'

I pushed her away from me, still holding on to her shoulders. 'You do?'

She nodded. 'I haven't run through long grass for years,' she said. 'And round here I get to see sheep and cows and real trees.' She pulled me back to her again. 'Bobby would like it.'

'What are you saying?'

She shook her head. 'I don't know,' and then she laughed. 'It must be the clean air. It won't let me think straight.'

But as I pulled her closer, I knew she was right. I was done with the city, done with all the noise and the rushing and the fumes. I needed to take some time out, to try to decide what I wanted to do with my life. And where I wanted to do it.

I knew one thing, though: Laura was the person I wanted to do it with. And as I felt Laura's arms close around me, I realised that it wouldn't matter where we were.

'What about Bobby?' I said. 'He won't see his father as much. That's not a good thing.'

'We'll work something out. Maybe he'll get to be a proper dad, one who spends proper time with him, instead of just trips to the zoo.'

'What about your job?'

She shrugged. 'I'll think about that. I can apply to move up here.' Then she gave me a hug, quick and playful. 'And you like the idea, I can tell.'

She was right. I did like the idea. Perhaps it was time to leave London for a while, take some time out in the north. I fancied the quiet life now.

Read on for an extract from Neil White's novel,
Lost Souls, out now.

Chapter One

The old man turned away and closed his eyes, clamped his hands over his ears, but the images were still there, searing, sickening. He tried to shut them out, screwed up his eyes and started to pace. It was no good. He ended up where he started each time, next to her.

She was tied to a chair, her arms behind her back, her wrists strapped tightly to the thin spindles. Blood covered her face and painted her shirt in splatter patterns. He looked at his hands. They were sticky with her blood.

He closed his eyes again, but the sounds were harder to shut out. Wherever he paced, whenever he couldn't see her, the noises were still there, like echoes, constant reminders.

He stopped to take some deep breaths. The woman he wanted to remember was the one he had known in life. She had been fun, vibrant, a face full of smiles. That was the image he wanted to keep, not the one in this room, her face a grotesque mask, nothing left of the person he'd known.

He couldn't shake the image away. He had seen her

face in life; and now he had seen it in death. And it was worse than that, because he had seen her die, her eyes wide open, in pain, in fear, the knife getting closer. She had known what lay ahead of her.

He started to walk around the room faster, tears running down his face. He clenched and unclenched his fingers, looked up and then covered his ears as he walked, as he tried to stifle the sounds that once again crashed through his head. He had heard her last word, forced out through clenched teeth. It had come out as a guttural moan, but he had known what it was. It was *no*. She had tried to say *no*.

He took a deep breath and stopped pacing. He turned to look at her. She was still the same. He put his head back and sobbed, and then he sank to his knees.

He stayed like that, rocking slightly as he sniffed back the last of his tears.

After a few minutes he stood up and slowly walked over to the chair. He put his hand on the woman's cheek and gently stroked it, her skin soft under his fingers. But she felt cold. He leaned forward and kissed her on the top of her head.

'I'm sorry, so very sorry,' he whispered. 'I tried to warn you. I really tried.'

The old man stepped away and looked down at his feet. He could feel the tears trickle down his cheeks, his skin parchment-thin, and as he touched them the blood washed away from his fingertips. He muttered a few words to himself, a private prayer, before reaching for the telephone.

'Police please.'

He waited to be put through, and when he heard the voice at the other end of the line, he calmly said, 'My name is Eric Randle, and I want to report a murder.'

Chapter Two

North or south, murders are the same.

DC Laura McGanity blew into her frozen hands and, just for a moment, dreamt of London. Two weeks earlier it had been her home, but already that seemed like a lifetime ago. She had only moved to Lancashire, a mere two hundred miles from the capital, but it felt like a foreign country as the frigid air blew in from the hills that surrounded the town. She paced along the yellow crime-scene tape and it snapped loudly as it blew in the early-morning wind. She shivered and wrapped her scarf tighter round herself.

It wasn't just the weather that felt alien. It was the quietness. She was standing by an open-plan lawn in a neat suburban cul-de-sac, with the hills of the West Pennine Moors as a backdrop, painted silver as the rising sun caught the dew-coated grass, just the snap of the crime-scene tape to break her concentration. She missed the London lights, the buzz, even the noise. In comparison, Blackley was like a constant hush.

Laura had been brought up in the south and trained by the Met, but love had brought her north. She had arrived in a small town, concrete and graffiti replaced by moorland grasses and dry-stone walls. She knew she couldn't afford a mistake. Her transfer north had been a risk, and she didn't want to destroy her new career so soon. She had seen the looks in the eyes of the other officers in the station. Wariness. Suspicion. She was the girl from the big city, come to tell them their jobs.

She had to be alert now, because there was no time for distraction. With any murder the first twenty-four hours were the most important. After that, evidence on the killer could be lost. Fingernails got scrubbed, hair got cut, cars got burnt out.

She looked up just as Pete Dawson, the other detective at the scene, approached her. He was holding two steaming mugs of coffee.

'You look like you need one of these,' he said.

It seemed to Laura like he barked the words at her, the staccato speech patterns all new, the vowel sounds short and blunt. The London rhythm she was used to had more swagger, more bounce.

She smiled her thanks, and as she wrapped her hands around the mug she asked, 'Where did you get them?'

He nodded over towards a house on the other side of the road, where Laura could just make out fingers on the edge of the net curtain, the light inside switched off so no one could tell that anyone was watching. 'She's been twitching those for half an hour now. I think she's hoping for an update if she gives us drinks.'

'Did you tell her anything?'

Pete shook his head. 'I'm holding out for a fry-up. But be careful. These old mill girls can lip-read.' When

Laura looked at him, confused, he added, 'So they could still talk over the noise of the machines.'

Laura smiled. She liked Pete. He was one of those necessary cops. Precise minds are great – those who can dissect complex frauds or see leads in cases that look like dead-ends – but sometimes you just need someone to kick down a door, or find a quick way to prise information out of someone. Laura reckoned Pete knew many quick ways. He looked one wrong word from hurting someone, all crew-cut, scowl and scruffy denims. He was normally with the drugs squad, more used to throwing dealers against walls than loitering around murder scenes.

She took a sip of the coffee and sighed. It was hot and strong, and she raised it in thanks to the parted curtains on the other side of the street.

'You look like you expected more,' Dawson said, nodding towards the crime-scene tape. 'Not used to the quiet life yet?'

A week before, Laura might have thought he was having a dig, but she knew him better now. Pete's smile softened his words and his eyes changed. They became brighter, warmer, and she sensed mischief in them.

But he was right, Laura *had* expected more activity, the usual commotion of lawns being combed by uniformed officers, or a squad of detectives knocking on doors. Today there was none of that. The body had been taken away, but the first two cops on the scene were still there, an ashen-faced probationer and a police officer not far off retirement. Scenes of Crime officers were inside, their white paper suits visible through the

6

front window, but out in the street Laura felt like she was on sentry duty.

'It doesn't seem like the quiet life,' she replied. 'I moved north for a better life, and I get this,' she nodded towards the house, 'and in the middle of the abductions. It seems pretty dangerous around here.'

Pete shrugged. 'It's not always like this. Once we catch the bastard who has been taking those kids all summer, we'll get more people to work cases like this.'

Laura looked back towards the house. 'And are we any nearer to catching him?'

'Every time there's another one, we're waiting for the mistake, the breakthrough.' He shook his head. 'He hasn't made one yet.'

The abductions had been the big story in Blackley over the summer. The first one only rippled the nationals – everyone thought it was a runaway – but the next one confirmed a pattern and the media all came to town.

Children had been going missing all summer, snatched in the street. They disappeared for a week, sometimes longer. When they were found, they seemed unharmed, but there were things the eyes couldn't see.

There had been seven of them so far, all boys: latch-key kids, early teens, cocky and street-sure. But that was a mask, protection from what they missed at home: love, security, attention. They came back with the mask slipped, and they seemed confused, frightened, days lost with no idea about where they'd been or what had happened to them. They'd thought they owned the streets, but now they realised how vulnerable they were, and that the world could be much crueller than they'd imagined.

They were found stumbling around, confused, lost, like they had just woken up. They were clothed, with no marks or injuries. They had to be examined intimately, just to check for a sexual motive, but there'd been nothing so far. They were sent home, back to the arms of their parents. The boys were all hugged a lot closer after that.

The eighth child was out there now, Connor Crabtree, with whoever was taking Blackley's children. He had last been seen cadging cigarettes in a small car park behind a corner shop, accosting strangers as they went to buy milk or something. That had been six days ago, and no one had seen or heard of him since. The press were on standby, waiting for the inevitable return, something to report; the nation was gripped by the story. The press had even given the kidnapper a name: the Summer Snatcher.

Laura didn't like the name – it sounded corny, no imagination – but she knew that it helped to keep the story in the news. It was more than just a story in Blackley, though. Everyone knew there would be more. Most parents had stopped their children going out, and the streets seemed quieter once it went dark. But the children being taken were the ones of parents who hadn't listened, whose lives were too difficult to make room for their children.

There weren't many clues. There were fibres on the boys, just tiny strands of cloth, from a blanket or something similar, but until they got the source they couldn't get the match. The first two children had dust on their clothes when they were found, small specks of concrete and traces of asbestos, but nothing specific. The police in Blackley were following leads, just to be visible, but everyone knew they were waiting for the return of Connor Crabtree, hoping it would bring fresh evidence.

Laura shuddered as she thought about her own son, Bobby. Four years old, in a strange town and a long way from his real father. She blinked, felt her eyes itch, took a deep breath. It wasn't meant to have turned out like this, but Bobby's father had decided a long time ago that Laura wasn't going to be the last woman he slept with. He'd left, and Laura had struggled on her own for a while, but when she had fallen in love again she was able to give Bobby a family life once more. But it was hard. She needed to be with Bobby in the mornings. She missed seeing his sleepy face, and she wanted to know that he needed her.

'What's your theory about the abductions?' Laura asked.

Pete considered for a moment, his face thoughtful, his hands jammed into his pockets. 'I don't know,' he said. 'Could be a woman. You know, the kids are looked after and then given up again, some nurturing instinct satisfied.' He smiled. 'Not that they'd ever ask me anyway.'

'Why not?'

'I've spoken my mind too often.'

'What do you think about this?' she asked, nodding towards the murder scene.

He exhaled. 'I don't know. Some nutcase is the obvious guess, but there is one thing.'

'Go on.'

'The victim knew the killer. There was no break-in,

9

no sign of a struggle anywhere else in the house. No one reported it until the old guy made the call.'

Laura knew there was some sense in what Pete said. This was no domestic or a burglary gone wrong. It was a sadistic execution. A young woman, Jess Goldie, small and frail, barely twenty-five years old, had been strapped to a chair and strangled with a cord. There were no signs of a fight, no evidence of sexual assault. There was just a chair in the middle of the room, a dining-room chair with strong wooden legs, and she was strapped into it, her wrists tightly bound with thin nylon rope.

But that wasn't what had struck Laura when she first went into the house. It was something else, the sight that had caused the young probationary officer to spend the next hour sitting outside, gulping lungfuls of fresh air in between dry-heaving.

Whoever had killed this young woman had ripped out her tongue and gouged out her eyes.

Laura had methodically examined the scene. She was at work, a detective, so the shock stayed away, her mind too busy to process emotion. It would come to her later, she knew that, maybe when she was in bed or taking a bath, alone and vulnerable.

There was nothing to suggest a struggle, no defensive wounds to the hands, no ripped clothing. But then Laura spotted the marks ringed around the woman's neck, as if the cord had been pulled many times over. It hadn't been a quick kill. It had been dragged out, made to last.

She turned to Pete. 'What did you make of the old boy who called it in?'

Pete stroked his cheeks thoughtfully. 'Eric Randle? Hard to say. He didn't look the sort, if there is such a thing, and the only blood on him looked like contact blood. No splashes or spray. But it's all too neat for me.'

Laura was about to ask something else when she heard a car drive into the cul-de-sac. It pulled up in front of the house, and she watched as a small man in a sharp suit climbed out.

'Oh great,' Pete muttered. 'Now it's all going to turn to shit. Egan's here.'

'Egan?'

'DI Egan,' said Pete, his voice low and quiet. 'Dermot Egan. We call him Dermot Ego. You'll soon find out why.'

As she watched the figure walk towards the house, Laura sensed that he was right.

Chapter Three

Sam Nixon parked his car and looked out of the windscreen. He used to like sunrise – it made even Blackley look pretty – but the view had lost its charm years ago.

Sam's office was in the middle of a line of Victorian bay fronts, with stone pillars in each doorway and gold-leaf letters on the windows, legacies of Blackley's cotton-producing heyday. The town used to rumble with the sounds of clogs and mills, and the mill-owners' money would end up in the pockets of the lawyers and accountants who spread themselves along this street. Blackley's life as a Lancashire cotton town had ended a couple of decades earlier, but it was marked by its past like an old soldier by his tattoos.

Sam could see the canal that flowed past the end of the street. The towpath was overgrown with long Pennine grasses, and ripples in the water twinkled like starbursts as they caught the early-morning sun. The old wharf buildings were still there, three-storey stone blocks with large wooden canopies painted robin's-egg blue that hung over the water, but they were converted into offices now. The sounds of a new day filled the car, the whistles of the morning birds as they swooped from roof to roof, the rustle of leaves and litter as they blew along the towpath. It was heritage Lancashire, lost industry repackaged as character.

But it was the only bright spot. The factories and mill buildings further along the canal were empty, stripped of their pipes and cables by thieves who traded them in for scrap, left to rot with broken windows and paint-splattered walls. Those that were bulldozed away were replaced by housing estates and retail parks.

Blackley was in a valley. A viaduct carried the railway between the hills, high millstone arches that cast shadows and echoed with the sound of the trains that rumbled towards the coast. Redbrick terraced streets ran up the hills around the town centre, steep and tight, the lines broken only by the domes and minarets of the local mosques, the luscious greens and coppers bright dots of colour in a drab Victorian grid.

Beyond those, Sam could see a cluster of tower blocks that overlooked the town centre, bruises of the sixties, dingy and grey, where the lifts reeked of piss and worse, and the landings were scattered with syringes. They had views to the edges of town, but everything looked bleak and wet from up there, whatever the weather.

Sam closed his eyes and sighed. He was a criminal lawyer in Blackley's largest firm, Parsons & Co. As soon as he hit the office his day would be taken up by dead-beats, drunks, junkies and lowlifes, a daily trudge through the town's debris. Criminal law was budget law, the most work for the least reward, so he had to put in long hours to keep the firm afloat. He started early and

13

finished late, his day spent fighting hopeless causes in hostile courts, and most evenings wrecked by call-outs to the police station.

He used to enjoy it, the dirt, the grime. A legal service. A social service. Sometimes both, with a touch of court theatre, just the right phrase or the right question, maybe just a look, could mean guilty or not guilty, jail or no jail.

But then the job had worn him down. He had two children he hardly saw, and he couldn't remember the last time he had hugged his wife.

And he was sleeping badly. He was staying up too late, and when he did finally fall asleep he woke up scared, bad dreams making the day start too soon. They were always the same: he was running through door-ways, dark, endless, one after another, someone crying far away. Then he would be falling. He woke the same way each time: a jolt in bed and then bolt upright, drenched in sweat, his heart beating fast.

He opened his eyes and sighed. He rubbed his cheeks, tried to wake himself up. He couldn't put it off any longer: he had to start the day.

His head was down as he walked towards his office and fumbled for the key. He had to put his briefcase down to search his pockets, and that's when he saw him.

On the other side of the street was a man, stooped, old and shabbily dressed, his clothes hanging loose from his body. His hands were clutched to his sides as if he were stood to attention, and his eyes were fixed in a stare, unblinking, unwavering.

Sam felt uneasy. The courtroom usually protected

him, shrouded in respect and court rules, but defence lawyers pissed people off. Victims, witnesses, sometimes just the moral majority. He felt himself grow nervous, checked his pocket for his phone, ready to call the police if a knife appeared. But the old man just stared at Sam, his face expressionless.

Sam eventually found his key. He took one last look into the street. The old man hadn't moved. He was still watching him.

Sam made a mental note of the time and turned to go inside.

Neil White • Dead Silent

Twenty years ago, Claude Gilbert murdered his wife, buried her alive and then killed himself – so everyone believes. But as Gilbert disappeared without a trace on the night of the murder, the mystery has remained unsolved. Until now . . .

When Lancashire crime beat reporter Jack Garrett is contacted by omeone alleging that Gilbert is alive, he eagerly leaps on the chance to solve the decades-old enigma.

But as Jack sets off on Gilbert's trail, he quickly finds that the truth is stranger than the headlines. Jack and girlfriend PC Laura McGanity quickly realize that they are now pawns in a twisted game, and the rules are about to get nasty . . .

A heart-stopping novel from one of the rising stars of British crime fiction, guaranteed to captivate fans of Peter James and Mark Billingham.

AVON

£6.99
ISBN 978-1-84756-128-2

Neil White • Cold Kill

When Jane Roberts is found dead in a woodland area, Detective Sergeant Laura McGanity is the first on the scene. The body bears a chilling similarity to a woman – Deborah Corley – murdered three weeks earlier. Both have been stripped, strangled and defiled.

When reporter Jack Garrett starts digging for dirt on the notorious Whitcroft estate, he finds himself face-to-face with Jane's father and local gangland boss Don, who won't stop until justice is done. It seems that the two murdered women were linked in more ways than one, and a dirty secret is about to surface that some would prefer to stay buried.

As the killer circles once more, Jack and Laura must stop him before he strikes again. But his sights are set on his next victim and he's watching Laura's every move . . .

A taut and terrifying novel from one of the rising stars of British crime fiction, for fans of Peter James and Stuart Macbride.

A V O N

£6.99
ISBN 978-1-84756-129-9

Killer Reads.com

The one-stop shop for the best in crime and thriller fiction

Be the first to get your hands on the **latest releases, exclusive interviews** and **sneak previews** from your favourite authors.

Browse the site and sign up to the newsletter for our pick of the **hottest** articles as well as a chance to **win** our monthly competition!

Writing so good it's criminal